Soult

For Mark & Rosie,

Don't worry, you're not in it!

Iain

Iain McCafferty

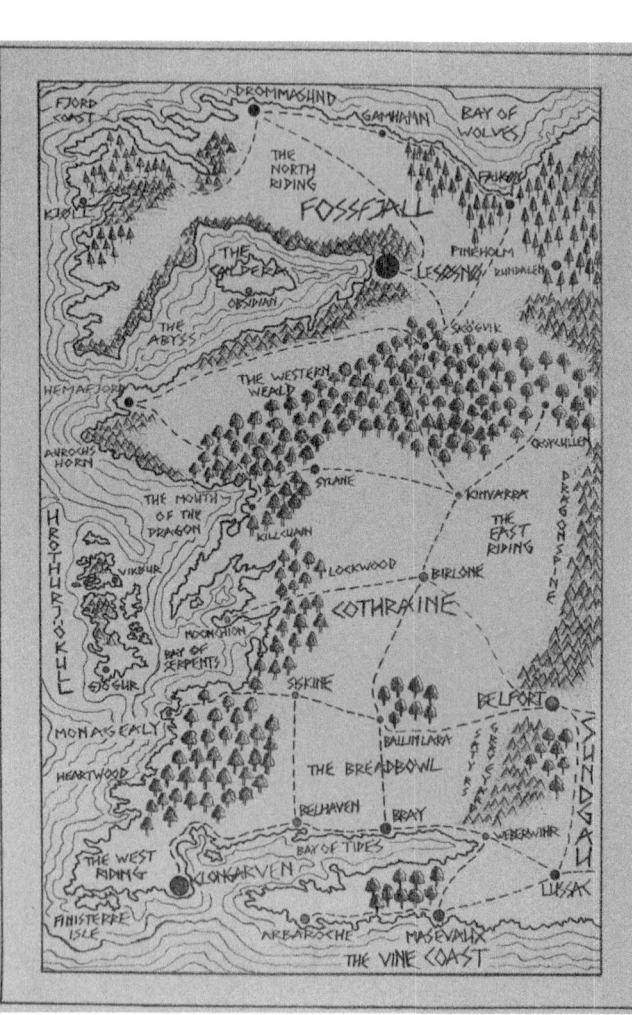

Prologue – The Master Diviner

If I was unable to find shelter within the next hour, I was certain that I would freeze to death. I blinked as a bitterly cold wind whipped across the road, wafting sheets of falling ice crystals in frigid, rippling waves that stung my eyes. Snow massed in drifts against the neatly clipped yew hedges marking the boundary between the public right of way and the private farmland beyond. I braced myself against the gale, trapping my staff between my side and upper arm beneath my armpit and leaning on it with my weight as I resettled the hood of my robe, trying to shield my eyes from the swarm of frozen needles buffeting my face. I could feel the ice already encrusting my beard and my forehead was numb, a dull portent of the headache to come. The blizzard had descended quickly from grey, cloudy skies as I cleared the ridge that divided the Western Weald from the North Riding, halfway between the city of Lesøsnø and frontier town of Skøgvik. As soon as I had cleared the forest the temperature had dropped rapidly, as the moist air rushing over the mountains surrounding the great fjord of the Abyss met the static, frigid air enveloping the wide open farmlands of the North Riding. Just a couple of leagues north from the protective microclimate of the Weald, snow had started to fall, first in glittering curtains of soft flakes and later as a raging torrent of sharp, icy needles as the vapour-laden air from the fjord cooled rapidly above the frigid prairies. Returning to the shelter of the Weald was not an option. I was already behind schedule to arrive at Lesøsnø in time for my convocation with the diviners at the Guild of the Art. Backtracking now would guarantee that I would be at least one day late for my appointment, a grievous breach of etiquette and protocol for a mage visiting a foreign Wizards' Guild. I regretted not hiring a horse and carriage at the border post near Skøgvik, but the instructions from my Arch Mage had been clear: travel frugally and with humility, so as not to attract unwanted attention. I estimated that it was at least a further ten leagues to the next way station and inn on the road where I had originally intended to spend the night. In normal conditions ten leagues represented a walk in excess of three hours. With snow starting to drift across the lumpy cobbles of the road, making the surface treacherously slippery, in this blizzard I would be lucky to walk another two leagues before nightfall, even though it was barely past midmorning. With no option other than to press onwards, I grasped my staff firmly with both hands, using it as a lever to drag myself forwards. I staggered into the freezing headwind, searching the horizon for a place where I might find shelter from the relentless torrents of snow. I trudged further along the stone highway, my robe becoming increasingly heavy under the burden of ice crystals clinging to the thick wool. I was beginning to feel the chill of the wind in my bones when a momentary lull in the snowfall allowed me to glimpse a small farmhouse just over quarter of a league from the road. The windows flickered with the glow of a fire and a dark grey column of smoke was being swirled up through the air by the wind. My heart raced in hope at the thought of sanctuary from the chill storm, and despite the numbness of my limbs, I scaled the drift of snow that spanned between the kerb and boundary hedge, my boots sinking knee deep into the snow before the flakes compacted into a firm enough surface to stand on. Using my staff for support, I clambered over the top of the hedge, falling onto my back as the yew branches buckled under my weight. A hard column of frozen wheat stubble poked into my side, tearing the seam of my robe beneath my right arm. I cursed vilely as I stood, stretching my aching back and feeling the skin torn by the rough stubble begin to seep blood. Cold air invaded the gap between the front and rear panels of my robe, chilling me further. The numbness spurred me on to reach the warmth of the modest farmhouse. The wooden frame encased thick walls of granite blocks, and the thatched roof looked to have been reinforced with fresh, golden straw in the weeks before winter. I rapped the oak door with the base of my staff three times, shivering under the eaves, which only gave me partial shelter from the snowfall and the wind. I was about to knock on the door again, afraid that the howling of the wind had drowned out my summons, when I heard the metallic click of the latch being unfastened. The door opened tentatively, revealing only a crystalline blue eye and a flash of pale golden blonde hair.

"Who's there?" The woman's question was tinged with fear and suspicion. She spoke nagyjik, the common trade tongue of the Western Triad. She had the soft Fossfjall accent typical of the region, with rounder, more melodic vowel sounds than my cothraini-nagyjik and none of the clipped, hard consonants heard in the Sundgau.

"A traveller from Clongarvan, bound for Lesøsnø. I fear I will freeze if I spend any longer in this blizzard. Please m'lady, may I enter?"

The door creaked open wider and I saw the look of shock on the young woman's face when she saw the piteous state I was in, encrusted in snow, with sodden, torn robes and scuffed walking boots. Only the support of my staff was keeping me upright. The wolfhound figurehead carved into the wood at the stave head psychically echoed my discomfort, shivering and trembling in the gale. She beckoned me inside, holding the door open just wide enough for me to enter without letting too much precious heat escape. "By the Earth Mother, you'll catch your death!"

"Thank you, m'lady!" I sighed in relief, resting my staff against the doorframe. I pulled back the hood of my robe and wiped the icicles from my eyebrows and beard before shucking my travelling pack off my shoulders and laying it on the doormat. Sheepishly I noted the cascade of snowflakes falling from my robes and making puddles on the slate floor. "Sorry, I am making quite the mess."

"Look at the state of you! You must be frozen to the bone. Come, let's seat you by the fire. Quietly, mind. I don't want to wake the baby. I've only just gotten her to sleep, with that gale blowing outside." She said, shepherding me across the living room to the blazing hearth. My skin prickled with the heat, colour and sensation returning to my blue fingers. The full extent of my perception began returning with the warmth and I was able to properly appraise my saviour for the first time. I estimated that she was in her mid-twenties, tall and slender, with a full figure and straight, shoulder length hair. She sat me down in the armchair closest to the fire before taking her own seat next to her baby's crib. She carefully adjusted the child's blanket, tucking it in around the slumbering baby with a feather-light touch. "What's a wizard doing out on the road this close to midwinter?"

"I am due to give a lecture on the prophecies of the Seer Nevanthi at the Tower of the Aether in Lesøsnø next week, m'lady. Thanks to you, I might actually arrive there on time and with all my fingers and toes." I observed wryly, wiggling my fingers to restore the circulation of blood.

"Well, m'lord, I dare say you're wishing this Nevanthi of yours had predicted that blizzard." She replied, raising a pale eyebrow. Her smile was simultaneously mocking and amused. It was really quite lovely. "We should get you out of those boots before you get foot rot, and pass me your robe. You can't go anywhere with that tear letting in the weather."

"I fear I do not have a spare robe." I said, pulling off my boots and socks to let them dry next to the fire. The leather of my boots would need re-waxing to weather-proof them again before I dared venturing back out into the snow.

"No need to be coy, m'lord." The woman laughed, delving into a woven willow basket beside the crib to retrieve a darning needle, some thread and a blanket I could use to maintain my modesty. She tossed the blanket to me, so that I could slip off my robe without fear of embarrassment. I passed her the torn garment and she gave the ripped seam a brief inspection before starting the repairs.

"Thank you. Might I ask your name, m'lady? It would be good to know whose mercy I should thank in my prayers tonight. My name is Eoghan and I cannot overstate how grateful I am to have made your acquaintance. My blood would be freezing by now, had you not answered the door."

"My name's Sigrid. And you're welcome." She didn't look up from her work, stitching the gash in the fabric closed with swift, precise movements of her hands. The silver needle reflected the flickering orange flames in the cast iron heath. As I watched her sew I noticed that there were no rings on her long, slender fingers. "Even unexpected company is welcome as winter draws in, provided it's not bandits."

"Do they give you much trouble this far from the city? Surely the brigand gangs will have all returned to town by now for the winter?"

Sigrid kept her head bowed, her voice cracking. "They don't trouble us any more, not after the last raid."

"Why, what happened?" I sat upright and gave her my full attention, sensing the bleak lilac misery in her psychic aura. Strong emotions in others are frequently manifested as colours, smells or tastes, depending upon how highly attuned you are to the psychic plane. It was a bizarre form of synaesthesia that resulted from studying the Art, but frequently an informative one.

"My husband was harvesting the wheat two months ago when he was cut down by a gang of four bandits. When I heard him scream I opened the door to the house to see what was going on. That's when they knocked me to the ground and rushed inside to steal my jewellery and our savings." Sigrid explained, weeping softly. "I couldn't do anything to stop them – the shock had sent me into labour. When they took the wedding band off my finger, I thought they were going to slit my throat, but the eldest thief convinced the youngsters to leave me be. My daughter came into the world as my husband left it."

"Sigrid, I am so sorry. You have my condolences." I said uselessly, wanting to reach out to comfort her.

The young widow sniffed and wiped away the tears from beneath her eyes. She stood abruptly and crossed the room to the dressing table, where she retrieved a large glass carafe of akvavit and two clay goblets. She filled the cups with viscous yellow spirit and handed one to me before retaking her seat. "Here. This will put some warmth back into your bones. I distil it myself from potatoes, rye and dill seed."

"What was his name, your husband?" I asked, taking a sip of the scented, ferociously alcoholic liquor. The akvavit burned my throat and immediately I felt heat flush back into my skin.

"Kjetil. He had such a feel for the land. The farm won't survive without him. I can't raise a child, tend the crops and feed the livestock. And thanks to the bandits, I don't have any money to hire hands for next season."

"What will you do?"

"I've no idea." Sigrid replied, bowing her head again and keeping her hands busy with the needle. She had almost finished re-stitching the burst seam of my robe. Her needlework was so precise that a casual observer would never have been able to tell that the material had been torn. "Sometimes I wish that the bandits had murdered me too."

"You must not say such things, Sigrid. Life is blessed in the eyes of the Empress – she gifted you a daughter." I reproached her gently as Sigrid emptied her goblet with a single long swallow. I saw the despair in her pale blue eyes as she poured more of the clear amber spirit into her cup. "I would like to help you, for your sake and for hers. After all, it is no exaggeration to say that I owe you my life for your charity and shelter this day."

Sigrid's temper flared as she took another gulp of akvavit. "Perhaps you could conjure a chest of gold and pearls, or convince the crops to grow over winter?" she snapped, hurling her goblet into the fire in frustration as her emotions boiled over. The hearth briefly flared blue as the flames ignited the alcohol that had still been in the clay cup. I flinched, not from the noise but the acidity that bubbled through her aura. The shattering of the ceramic woke the child, who wailed in fear at the sudden noise. Sigrid immediately stood and plucked her daughter from the crib. "Daeva shit! Hold her while I finish with your robe." I stirred in discomfort as Sigrid brought her baby over to me, wrapped tightly in swaddling clothes and soft woollen blankets. I stuttered feebly in protest as Sigrid placed the distressed bundle into my arms. "I- I am not sure I am child-friendly."

The young widow gave out a short, bitter laugh. "Hah! The mighty mage humbled by a baby. Rock her gently. Calm her."

I felt Sigrid's eyes watching me closely as I cradled her child in unnaturally stiff arms. The baby quietened herself as she looked up into my face, gurgling, confused by my unfamiliar appearance and seemingly transfixed by the ragged whiskers of my beard. I noticed that she had inherited her mother's luminous eyes. "Your daughter is really quite beautiful. What is her name?"

"She doesn't have one yet. After Kjetil died, I couldn't face choosing." Sigrid said, biting the thread to detach the needle from my newly repaired robe. Sigrid hung the robe over a wooden mannequin stood next to the fire to prevent the wool from shrinking as it dried. "There. Good as new.

Sorry I shouted at you. It's not your fault I'm going to lose the farm."

"No apology necessary, I assure you." I said, maintaining eye contact with the fascinated baby, who cooed in delight as I pulled faces and smiled at her.

"You're a natural, Eoghan. She never stops crying so quickly for me. You're sure you don't have a wife and child tucked away in your ivory tower?" Sigrid asked, her angst subdued for the moment as she watched me coddle her daughter.

"Oh no, while the Guild does not forbid such things, the study of the Art rarely leaves room for family life." I replied, with a hint of resignation.

"That sounds very lonely."

"It is not as bad as it sounds. We are magicians, not one of the Penitent's celibate monks." I explained as I rocked Sigrid's daughter back and forth in my arms in a slow rhythm, helping the unnamed child drift back to sleep. "The Arch Mage Karryghan is rumoured to have several mistresses in Clongarvan. Only he and the Empress know how many children he has sired."

"You have a lover, then?" Sigrid asked as she took her daughter from my arms and laid her back down in the crib, soundly asleep once more.

"No. I used to, many years ago. But once I was appointed to the rank of Master Diviner, my research occupied all my time. She understood well enough. She is a Master Illusionist."

"You don't miss having a woman?"

"Honestly? Not really." I said, rather taken aback by the directness of the question.

"I do. I miss having a man." Sigrid said, the longing plainly spoken in her words and written in the anguish twisting her pretty features. Before I could say another word she kissed me on the mouth, her hands pulling the blanket away from my armchair. Moments later we were making love in her bed until Sigrid had sated her desire to be held and touched.

"Well that was unexpected, yet wonderful." I told Sigrid, looking deep into her eyes. After the bitter chill of the blizzard, the sensation of Sigrid's hot, smooth skin pressed against me was heavenly. She had kept her legs tightly wrapped around my hips and her hands gripped my shoulders, her arms hooked beneath mine.

"Thank you, Eoghan. I needed that. You must stay the night, of course." Sigrid glanced over to the barometer mounted on the teak panelled wall of her bedroom. The brass needle had not budged from the bottom of the dial and the wind rattling the windows indicated that the snowstorm was still raging outside. "It won't stop snowing until morning. I don't suppose I could persuade you to stay longer?"

"Sorry, but it is impossible. If I do not reach Lesøsnø before Dark Rider's Day next week the consequences will not be pleasant."

Sigrid's face fell with disappointment, but she smiled bravely when I caressed her cheek. She kissed me on the lips, her aura sour with resignation. "I'll never see you again, will I?"

"Shall we find out?" I suggested, returning her smile. I eased myself gently from her embrace and retrieved a leather box studded with silver runes from my backpack. "Common wisdom is that the future is unknowable. But that is not true for a diviner."

"What?" Sigrid sat up on the bed, wrapping herself in one of the thick, woollen bed sheets.

I retook my place beside her on the mattress, unlocking and opening the box by tapping three of the runes embedded into the leather and I retrieved the purple satin pouch contained within it. Inside the pouch were four dozen vividly oil-painted cards, each one as large as my hand and as thick as a silver shilling. I spread the cards out on the mattress to show Sigrid the intricately detailed scenes on each one and the script identifying the card's suit, number and the keyword describing the card's primary elucidation. "The Tarot of the Planes."

"They're beautiful. How does it work?"

"The seeker holds the cards and thinks of a question. Then the deck provides the answer. The diviner is just there to translate." I explained, stacking the cards into a single pile and placing them in front of Sigrid.

"You don't shuffle the cards?" Sigrid asked, her fingers trembling, as if afraid to touch the deck.

"No. Holding them is enough, but you need to think very precisely about the nature of your question. If your

thoughts are not specific enough, the answer may be ambiguous." I gestured for her to pick up the cards.
"What should I ask?"
"Anything you like." I smiled as Sigrid closed her eyes and held the deck between her palms.
"I have a question."
"Put down the deck and turn over the first card." I instructed. The painting showed a buxom, redheaded lady of the night servicing a client, who held her against the stone wall of a dank city street by her bare breasts, a pile of gold coins glinting in the puddles underneath her bare feet.
"What does it say?" Sigrid asked, unable to read the ancient nagyjik script that identified the card, her cheeks flushed at the explicit imagery of the illustration.
I suppressed the urge to laugh. The card was the 3 of Sins, the minor arcana card representing lust. "That the answer to your question is yes."
"And what was my question?" Sigrid frowned sceptically.
"Whether we would make love again tonight." I saw from Sigrid's mortified expression that I had correctly divined her query.
"Eoghan, I-" Sigrid began with a stutter before I interrupted her with a kiss on her lips to reassure her that I was neither angry nor shocked.
"You can ask the Tarot anything, mundane or profound. The deck always knows." I returned the card to the top of the pile, picture side down and encouraged her to pick up the cards again. "See that we haven't changed the order of the cards. Pick a new question."
Sigrid was still and silent, spending a moment in pensive thought before picking up the Tarot deck again and closing her eyes to concentrate. "I have another question."
"Good. Hold your thoughts for a little longer and when you are ready, reveal the top card."
Sigrid flipped the top card exactly as she had done before and she snatched back her hand as if it had been burned. "It's different. How did that happen?"
At first I didn't reply. Sigrid had revealed the card correctly, but something was very wrong. That the card had changed from the 3 of Sins was not a surprise – I had expected that. The card had changed its face to The Aether, the zeroth major arcana card representing the beginning and the end

of everything – the very structure that bound the planes of the cosmos together. This in itself was not shocking. It was the fact that the card had presented itself reversed, with the image inverted. I picked up the card and inspected the orientation of the image relative to the decorative recurring pattern painted on the rear of the card. The card was definitely reversed. "This is not possible."
"Eoghan, what's wrong?"
"The Aether, reversed. The Tarot of the Planes does not permit major arcana cards to be reversed, ever." I explained, the card trembling in my fingers. "What was the question you asked?"
"I wanted to know my daughter's name."
"Sigrid, this is important." I placed the card on the mattress and interlaced my fingers with hers to stop my hands from shaking. "What were the exact words you had in your mind when you questioned the Tarot?"
"Eoghan, you're starting to scare me. What's wrong?" the young widow asked, recoiling from the deck as if it were a wild animal.
"I have read the Tarot for over thirty years. I have completed thousands of séances. Not once have I ever seen a major arcana card present itself reversed. The Tarot is a living thing of the psychic plane. It *sees*. And it *knows*." I held Sigrid by her shoulders, looking deep into her wide eyes so that I could try to emphasize the importance of what had just happened. "It gives us messages from the watchers on the psychic plane and it cannot be mistaken. I must know the precise phrase of what you asked, word for word."
"What I asked was 'Who is my daughter?' – did I do something wrong?" Sigrid asked, almost petrified with fear.
"No, no... Not at all," I reassured her, embracing her until she stopped trembling. "Close your eyes and concentrate now. Think that exact thought again, make it clear in your mind and then turn over the next card."
Sigrid did as she was instructed, revealing the next card on the top of the deck. It was the 3 of Virtues, Family. I placed it to the left of the reversed Aether card. "Good. Again."
Sigrid repeated the procedure, turning over the 8 of Virtues, Desire. Like the first card of the divination, it was also reversed. I set the card to the right of the spread and

gently caressed Sigrid's cheek to reassure and encourage her to complete the spread of cards. "The final card now." Sigrid's aquamarine eyes flew open in terror as I took in a sharp intake of breath. "What happened, Eoghan? What did I do?"

The fourth card completing the spread was another major arcana card, The Astral Plane, and like the other major arcana card in the reading, it too was reversed. I turned the card over in my hand several times to confirm that the impossible had happened not just once, but twice. I placed the final card below the other three on the mattress and covered my mouth with my palm as I tried to fathom the meaning of the spread of cards. One reversed major arcana card in a divination was unprecedented. Two was literally inexplicable. I repositioned myself on the bed, wrapping my arms around Sigrid, drawing her warmth and softness to my chest, as much to reassure me as her. I kissed her neck as Sigrid melted into my arms, her insistent fingers encircling my wrists, drawing my hands up from her waist to her chest. "You did exactly what you needed to do, my sweet. So did the Tarot."

"Then why do you sound terrified?"

"I have no idea what it means. I must meditate upon the interpretation of the spread."

"Do you want to be alone while you think upon it?"

"No." I held Sigrid tighter. "I need to have you close."

"For the divination?"

"No. For me." I said, kissing her with a passion I'd not felt in years. We made love again, as the Tarot had predicted, before falling asleep in each other's arms.

I dreamt of the cards Sigrid had picked for her unnamed daughter, the images and symbols skittering in and out of my mind's eye as my subconscious tried to unpick the meaning in the reversed Aether and Astral Plane cards. I heard Sigrid's question echo around the dreamscape again and again. *Who is my daughter?*

Ethereal clouds of brightly coloured dust and gas swirled chaotically around the planes, suffusing the universe in the energy required for life. A gorgeous, raven-haired maiden wearing nothing but crown of laurel leaves materialised out of the maelstrom. She stared through me as if I were not there with her incandescent green eyes and asked "Who am I? Everyone and no-one."

She unfurled a parchment scroll and I was drawn into the painting upon it depicting the reception party of a newlywed couple. The bride was youthful and blonde, clad in a sheer, figure-hugging gown of white lace. She danced barefoot with her groom, surrounded by their large, extended family as a band of garishly-clad troubadours provided the music. As the celebrations continued on deep into the night, I took my leave of the party and strolled into the orchard, plucking a ripe, pink apple from one of the trees as I felt drawn towards an ancient oak tree in the corner of the field, where a white, wooden stake fence separated the orchard from the forest beyond. As I approached the colossal tree, I saw the bride aggressively coupling with one of the farmhands on a rich purple rug spread beneath the boughs of the oak. Beyond them, lurking in the shadows was a lithe redhead wearing a green silk dress, who was observing the farmhand's discomfort with a sly, knowing smile. As the bride approached her climax, she gripped the boy's chin with one hand, forcing him to look at her as she rolled her hips and bit his right earlobe, drawing blood. "You knew from the beginning that you would always be mine."

The scene dissolved as she gave a high-pitched shriek of ecstatic release and I found myself standing outside a giant silver castle surrounded by endless fields of golden grass so tall it passed my waist. An armoured deva with broad, angelic wings of white feathers that spanned twelve feet from tip to tip strode purposefully towards me. I blinked and found that the maiden from The Aether stood next to me. She raised her left hand and clicked her fingers. Suddenly the castle was consumed with infernal flames, the silver walls charred and rent asunder. A giant, reptilian daeva with scaly, carmine skin and demonic horns charged towards me, screeching a terrifying battle cry. Before I could scream, the maiden clicked her fingers again, restoring the astral plane to its former glory. She turned to me with a smile. "Which future will come to pass, Eoghan? No-one knows but me."

She clicked her fingers a second time. The demonic warrior charged me again, thick crimson ichors dripping from the tanar'ri's clawed hands as the defiled ground shook with violent tremors, the walls of the angelic citadel beginning to collapse in the distance. The maiden's fingers snapped again, restoring order to the heavens. She transfixed me with a piercing stare. "Only I can choose."

She disappeared with a final click of her fingers, transporting me once again to the ruined astral plane. The daeva was now within arm's reach and it lashed out at my throat with talons as large and sharp as daggers. Before the blow landed I jerked awake, yelling in horror, covered from head to toe with cold sweat.

Sigrid shushed me quietly, kissing me on the lips and wrapping her arms around my shoulders to lower me back down to the bed. "It's just a nightmare. Hush, now."

I lost myself in the tenderness of her touch, her gentle caresses both calming and arousing me. I frowned as I stroked her beautiful face. "Not a nightmare – a vision."

"Whatever it was, it can wait until morning." Sigrid tightened her arms around my waist, resting her cheek on my neck as her soft fingertips stroked my chest and back. "Sleep now."

"Sigrid, I know who your daughter is." I said with regret, turning around in her embrace.

"You do? Tell me." Sigrid said, with equal parts trepidation and excitement.

"Forgive me, Sigrid. I cannot. No-one else can ever know."

"Even me?"

"Some knowledge is power. This knowledge is a death sentence." I said, glad that Sigrid had not yet named her daughter, as it meant her birth had not been recorded in the Litany.

"I don't understand."

"The Tarot is a living thing, remember? Once it has revealed a truth to one querent, that truth can be rediscovered via scrying to others. Seekers not just from the material plane, but the astral & the infernal planes as well." I picked up the reversed card of The Aether from where it still lay on the bed. "The Aether represents the eternal matter and energy that supports the planes. Your daughter has The Aether as her patron deity, but reversed. Do you see?"

"No, you're not making sense, Eoghan. Can't you just speak plain?"

"It could mean your death and your daughter's. If I tell you, it could be the doom of us all." I warned Sigrid, holding her tightly to my chest with both hands. We had only spent a few hours together, but already I knew that Sigrid and her daughter would become more precious to me than anything I had coveted in my career as a mage, even the title of Grand Master or Arch Mage.

"She's my blood, Eoghan. I want to know everything."

"So be it." I said, realising that this was the most important moment of my life. Once I shared my knowledge of her daughter's fate with Sigrid there would be no going back. Our destinies would be linked and I would never be able to return to my place among the Guild of the Art. I kissed Sigrid on the mouth to bolster my courage, took a deep breath, and told her.

1 - Keri

I was enjoying an aimless stroll east along the Coast Road between the town of Bray and the Satyr's Graveyard near the border between Cothraine and Sundgau, basking in the late summer heat reflecting from the granite cobbles, when the Mage Hunter blocked my path. His silver-gilt armoured plate shone brightly in the intense, blue-white midday sun. Full plate has always struck me as a poor choice of attire for fighting magic users. We don't carry swords and metal armour yields almost no protection against any form of offensive spell, whilst also being needlessly expensive and heavy. His two-handed greatsword with the five foot long blade however, that I understood. But the armour just seemed like overcompensation. I hefted my staff in versatile, two-handed grip, my fingers wrapped around the metal shaft in opposite directions, and I sighed with an air of weary exasperation.
"Back down, hunter. You know not whom you threaten."
Normally I would prefer not to speak using the cumbersome grammar used at court by the gentry to emphasize the quality of their learning and breeding, but the downside of being one of the kingdom's most wanted criminals is that it demands a certain degree of theatricality; especially if you're a notoriously capricious and unstable Wild Mage.
"Brave words, witch!" The hunter snorted, his apprehension hidden behind a mask of polished steel and faked machismo. He need not have bothered, as I could practically taste the citrus fear in his psychic aura; the familiar acrid stench oozing from every chink in his armour. "I know who you are, Keri of Moonchion. I've dealt with renegades more powerful than you!"
"The fact you still breathe is proof enough that you have not." I replied dismissively. I am known by a myriad of names and am renowned across a great swathe of the Western Triad for many abilities, but the forbearance to suffer fools is not one of them. I had not set foot in my birthplace of Moonchion since this mercenary had been nothing more than a remote possibility in his grandfather's

childhood dreams. It seemed inevitable that I would have to give this cocksure warrior a lesson in the meaning of the true power that came from knowing more about your enemy than they knew about you. "I know who you are, too: An imbecile, who does not wish to live to see dusk fall tonight."

"Ha! Many have tried, witch. All have failed." The Mage Hunter stepped closer, raising his greatsword with a flourish over his head into a striking stance. "Enough talk. Hand over your staff or fight. I don't care which."

"Fool! You poor, dead fool..." I said with regret and shook my head sadly, crouching into a coiled, defensive posture, standing side-on to the armoured figure, my feet set a yard apart, one behind the other. I held my staff horizontally across my body, the twisted and charred tip pointed at the centre of the Mage Hunter's chest. The warrior charged the remaining five yards between us, raising his greatsword to unleash a blow that he hoped would cleave my body in two from my neck to the waist. I remained still until the end of the greatsword started its descent from the apex of its swing.

A mage's power can be channelled and amplified through their staff, and I am particularly proud of mine. That is not unusual thing for a wizard, as their staff frequently presents a manifestation of their personality and capabilities as a psychically animated figurehead or effigy, usually in the form of an animal spirit the wizard identifies with. Appropriately for a Wild Mage, my stave has no such figurehead, only a tangled mass of metal strands that ripple like a field of maize in the breeze. On first inspection it might appear that my staff is made from painted and lacquered wood, but in fact is made from blue aetherium. Aetherium is not a metal of this world. You will only find its ore within the meteorite fragments that fall to the surface of Dachaigh from the Beyond. It is far lighter, yet stronger and tougher than even the folded steel used by the artisan oriental blacksmiths in Kyotka to make their famous curved longswords. Aetherium's rarity and durability makes it highly prized by warriors and magic-users alike. As the Mage Hunter began to swing their sword I infused wild aetheric energy into my staff, creating a mirror field able to repel matter between the blackened, curved shards at its tip. The greatsword's blade shattered from the reflected force of the hunter's blow as I caught it on the end of my staff, using the warrior's own strength to destroy his weapon. I pirouetted aside on my tiptoes, helping the unbalanced Mage Hunter to the floor by whipping around the other end of my staff to strike him in the middle of the back, the tempered steel of his breastplate echoing with a dull ring. I transferred some of the energy from my staff into his armour, leaving a shimmering violet echo of the blow on the metal where I had struck the back of his cuirass.

"You're going to have to do better than that, witch." The Mage Hunter laughed with contempt, as he regained his feet and drew the bastard sword from the scabbard at his left hip.

I let him come to me, again waiting motionless until he committed to his strike. The hunter was strong, precise and his sword-form was eminently competent, but his height and bulk were better suited to combat against barbarians and savages, rather than nimble, elusive wizards. I toyed with him, waiting for the seed of my spell to germinate, dancing around his cumbersome, lumbering strikes, effortlessly parrying his blows using the longer reach of my staff. As his frustration grew, so did the effects of my spell. The purple glow spread until it enveloped the inept warrior's entire breastplate and finally the awareness that something was amiss dawned on the Mage Hunter. He stepped back, lowered his sword and looked down as the coruscant gleaming rippled down the steel plates covering his arms and legs.

"What the-?" was all he managed to say before I took advantage of his lapse of concentration. I rushed forward and disarmed him with a quick sweep of my staff, spinning on the spot to knock him onto his back with a sharp, bottom-handed jab to the centre of his breastplate. With the final trigger for my spell now sprung, the Mage Hunter began to scream in surprise and then pain as the cobbled surface of the road beneath his body transformed into a mat of almost infinitely-fine spikes that extruded up through the armour covering his hands and feet and wrapping around his wrists and ankles before spearing back into the ground, pinning him to the earth, helpless. I struck the ground hard with the base of my staff, chanting a demonic incantation. The fire enchantment I had imbued into the blue aetherium seared a summoning circle of flaming runes around the warrior's prostrate form. The Mage Hunter bellowed in torment as the steel of his armour collapsed around him, as if being crushed by a giant invisible hand. The twisted plates jerked under the ethereal pressure, fracturing bones and squeezing flesh into an ever-smaller cube, which took on a glassy, amethyst hue.

"Better luck in your next life, fool." I consoled the trapped soul inside the spirit crystal, before I smashed it underfoot, the life essence within the crystal exploding into a wall of smoke that clung to the burning runes flickering on the surface of the road.

I am Keri of Moonchion: the Wild Mage; the Felbinder; the Spiritravager; demon-fucker; heretic and Soulthief. I am known as all of these things and many more. But no-one calls me *witch* and lives.

Instead of dissipating with the wind, the smoke condensed into a seething column that swirled like a dust devil in the deserts of Nagyjik. A moment later the cloud of smoke appeared to crouch and then stand, reforming into a muscular, strikingly-handsome tanar'ri daeva with a horned crown, angular visage and glistening, carmine-coloured skin, standing just shy of seven feet tall. The incubus recognised me immediately, grinning in wicked delight to show a broad array of razor-sharp, needle-thin, pristine white teeth. "Keri, my sweetling... You called."

"I did." I returned his smile hungrily, scooping my robe off over my head and dropping it to the ground before I stepped into the circle of flame that bound him to my will and desire. Night had fallen by the time I had reluctantly dismissed my deliciously attentive daeva, banishing it back to the Second Circle of the Hells to report back to our dread mistress, the Succubus. Buoyed and re-energised by the taste and ardour of its passion, the daeva's infernal seed burned in my belly, negating any need I might have had for food and sleep. I sat on the rotten stump of a fallen vine tree, gazing up through the gap in the canopy to the ocean of stars twinkling in the blackness of the Beyond. Suddenly feeling restless, I picked up my staff and began walking through the colossal vineyard that stretched for over a hundred leagues down the coast of the Bay of Tides. I had been wandering aimlessly along the Coast Road between the city of Bray and the West Riding for several months, enjoying the summer weather and availing myself of the ripe crimson and black grapes growing on the vines. Ever since my expulsion from the Guild of the Art in Clongarvan for practicing Wild Magic, I had lived on the road for almost two centuries and had travelled across the entire known world of Dachaigh.

I had sailed west across the Bay of Serpents to the volcanic islands of the Hrothurjökull archipelago to witness the Masked Rite of Spring, where the most virile men competed to marry the most fertile maidens in the shameless anonymity of a sex rite as volatile as the seismic eruptions that shook the islands almost every day. I had walked east to traverse the Rift across the Dragonspine Mountains so that I could taste the finest wines grown in the world on the Vine Coast at Lussac, before sailing further on past the wild jungle islands of the Reach. I had gathered rubies and emeralds the size of apples washed up on the tropical beaches of the appropriately-named Jewels, and I had been feted as a flame-haired, porcelain-skinned goddess by the polite, olive-skinned men of Kyotka. But it was in the abandoned cities studding the vast desert of the Desolation between Novyroya and Sundgau where I had discovered my talent for felbinding. Ever since joining the Arcane Circle as a young girl, I had been fascinated by the myths recounting the annihilation of the Nagyjik civilisation, which had been precipitated by arrogant wizards summoning demonic daevae they ultimately could not control. I kept my interest in demonology secret from my masters at the Tower of the Aether, since the study of demon lore was punishable by death. Once I had been excommunicated from the Guild of the Art however, there was nothing to stop me from exploring the ruined palaces and temples that had been consumed by the sandy wastelands. I had spent years among the crumbling, white marble towers, studying the runes and rituals from ancient tomes and tattered scrolls, teaching myself the language of the daevae. I scoured the desolate sands for months at a time, collecting scraps of aetherium from fallen meteorites to make a new staff capable of storing sufficient energy to summon and bind a daeva. I knew, of course, that the magic of binding demons was unspeakably perilous. The tiniest of errors would cost you your very soul. So I was determined not to repeat the mistakes of Nagyjik's mages. They had been too ambitious. They had wanted to bind demons to their will and use them to destroy their enemies. My desire was rather more prosaic. I simply wanted immortality. My mastery of Wild Magic enabled me to resist the physical corruption caused by the presence of demons or their immortal servants, the daevae, but I had understood the need to be cautious with my first few dozen summoning rituals and bindings. Daevae are powerful and deceitful creatures even when properly bound and rendered subservient. If I was going to be damned to the hells, it would be through my choice, not stupidity or carelessness. Over time I gradually became able to bind daevae from the Second Circle of Hell, the Demesne of Lust, to my will. Recognising that daevae from the First Circle, the Demesne of Murder, were too dangerous to summon, I devoted myself to the dread mistress of the Second Circle and Queen of the Daevae, the Succubus. It had been petrifying, that first time I had been inseminated by a tanar'ri, knowing that I would be burned alive from the inside out if I had made even the slightest mistake in the binding. But I quickly became enamoured with the power and control the demon seed gave me over my body and my magical abilities, so began to steal the souls required to power the summoning rituals ever more frequently. I was always careful to select victims whose absence would not be quickly noticed and my magical capabilities extended ever further with the increasing confidence that I could safely master daevae from the Second Circle. I was even visited and blessed by the Succubus herself, who commanded me to abandon the Nagyjik ruins and return to Fossfjall and Cothraine via the Sundgau. Occasionally she spoke to me across the planes with a voice sweeter than ice wine mixed with honey, giving me edicts and tasks. I had obeyed her whims for nine score years and five, becoming one of her most-favoured servants on the material plane and her most powerful mortal minion on the world of Dachaigh. It was inevitable that I would eventually take a misstep and she would claim me, but so long as I was careful, I hoped to evade the doom of her seductive embrace for at least another century.

Wordless voices on the aetheric wind whispered in the back of my skull, impelling me towards a small copse of elm trees at the top of a hill, which divided two immense rows of vines. I recognised from the narrow shape of the hill that it was a barrow tomb, which explained why the vineyard's owner had left the copse undisturbed. There was no sense in letting the essence of the dead sour the taste of the wine. As I grew closer and began to mount the side of the barrow, I noticed that a ring of standing granite stones had fallen, having once stood between the tree trunks. The stones were ancient, but their collapse was not. Intrigued, I stepped closer and saw something extraordinary. The breaks in the stones were fresh – I could still see chunks the size of pebbles scattered around the base of each henge stone – but that was not what had attracted my attention. I turned around twice when I stopped in the middle of the circle, scarcely believing my eyes. The fallen stones had not been toppled by natural forces. I knew this because the pattern they formed on the ground was a demonic rune. It simply read *seven*.
"Seven?" I asked aloud, leaning on my staff. "Seven what?" I did not expect an answer, of course, so I jolted in surprise when a much-missed, sensually feminine voice spoke to me across the planes.

Go north, and you will find your answer, my servant.

"Yes, dread mistress." I replied, being rewarded with a thrilling tingle of utter pleasure electrifying my entire body. Aroused, my thoughts churned, wondering whether I could solve the riddle with only the scant information I had been given. I visualised a map of Cothraine in my head. I was only a few days walk from its southern coast, near the port city of Bray. North of me were only the unremarkable towns of Ballinlara and Siskine. Sharp, stabbing pinpricks of delicious pain along my spine told me that I would find no answers there. My mind's eye drifted to Skøgvik at the border between Cothraine and Fossfjall. The prickles of pain intensified and I had to hold tightly onto my staff to remain standing.

Further north, then. I pictured the capital city of Fossfjall, Lesøsnø, and I gasped in relief as the pain abruptly disappeared. This was where I needed to go. I frowned, my physical eyes still closed as I recalled my memories of the city and its view over the Abyss and Caldera – the remains of a giant volcanic explosion that had opened up the once landlocked grassland plain to the ocean a million years ago. I felt the demon seed warm my belly when I pictured the Great Library of the Seven Scholars overlooking the waterfront, a giant marble and granite temple to knowledge that reputedly held copies of every book and scroll ever scribed. I opened my eyes and studied the rune on the ground again. I laughed in delight when it saw that I had initially misread it. "Not seven, *seventh!*" I exclaimed. "The seventh prophecy of Nevanthi!"

The reward my mistress gave me for my insight was so intense it had me shivering in ecstasy.

Well done, my servant. The time has come. Go. Do your research. Find the Nexus and bring it to me.

"I am yours to command, dread mistress." I replied, once I had regained control of my breath. It was nearly five hundred leagues to Lesøsnø and I had no horse, but I was undaunted by the scale of my task. I gazed up to find the star that would guide me north towards the border with Fossfjall. The Succubus's minions would see to it that I would not require nourishment or rest on my journey. I started to walk and licked my smiling lips, relishing the prospect.

2 - Ailidh

My father's fingers gripped my bicep like he was holding the handle of his favourite smithing hammer as he shook me awake from a dreamless sleep. It took a few seconds before the haze lifted from my mind and the look of panic on my father's usually calm, kind face immediately set my heart racing with fear. I blinked twice, still not entirely aware of what was happening.
"Get up!" Father whispered, looking back over his shoulder towards the door, which he had left ajar in his haste to rouse me from sleep. "We don't have much time."
"What's wrong, father?" I asked as he handed me my favourite dress and a bulging leather pouch of clinking silver and gold coins. I slipped the heavy woollen dress over my head without hesitation, perplexed to be woken so abruptly in the middle of the night. The moonlight was bright enough to cast shadows of the ash and pine trees outside my window across the wooden floor of my bedroom.
"You need to get out. They've found me, at last." Father said, his voice wavering with apprehension.
"Who? Who's found you? I don't understand." I said, slipping my feet over the side of the bed to the floor. I glimpsed the flickering from a score of yellow and orange torches across the courtyard from near the road through the leaded frame my bedroom's window. Several faint twangs of bowstrings were swiftly followed by the dull thuds of arrows striking the wooden shingles covering the workshop roof.
Father pulled me up painfully onto my bare feet, tugging me hard by the wrist. "They're setting fire to the house! Go, now!"
I had never seen my father in such a state of abject terror, and his fear was infectious. Without thinking, I rushed to the door, just as it was kicked open viciously from the other side. Wrenched off its hinges, the bulk of the door flew straight towards me and I hardly had time to raise my hands to protect my face before the wooden panel knocked

me off my feet, sending me sprawling to the oak boards of the floor, momentarily stunned.

"There he is. Do not let him speak." spoke a deep bass voice, heavy with masculine authority. I shook my head to regain my senses as two pairs of soldiers wearing cheap, boiled leather jerkins and red cloaks embroidered with gold livery ran through the shattered doorway, the first pair immobilising my father by seizing both of his arms. A third soldier prepared a cloth gag, while the final soldier grabbed my hair, pulling my head back roughly. Standing beneath the doorframe was an armoured giant – easily the ugliest and most fearsome man I had ever seen. The bald, hulking brute stood nearly seven feet tall and his cold grey eyes showed no remorse or empathy. The linen tabard over his solid steel chest plate bore the teal and scarlet checkers of the king's colours.

"What about the girl, m'lord?" the soldier yanking my hair asked, making me cry out in surprise and pain as he pulled backwards again hard, keeping both of my ankles trapped to the floor beneath his boot. I grabbed him around the wrist with both hands, trying to ease the pressure on the back of my neck.

"Leave her be!" Father's yell was muffled as the soldier standing behind him started to tighten the gag around his mouth and neck. "Don't touch her!"

The huge knight transfixed my father's wide, frightened eyes with a frigid, pitiless stare that made my blood run cold. "While my men would no doubt love to make you watch while they buggered her senseless, I am in a hurry." The huge armoured fiend dismissed the footmen with a casual wave of his gauntlet. "Take him away."

The weight on my ankles and neck suddenly vanished, releasing the tension in my arched back muscles like an uncoiling spring, catapulting me forward onto the floor. I just managed to stop my forehead from striking the floorboards, my arms flailing desperately to help me regain my balance. Propping myself up on my knees, I straightened my spine and looked up in terror at the soldier towering above me. "What're you going to do? Rape me? Kill me?"

The giant sniffed derisively, a tiny hint of a leer creeping across his gaunt, battle-scarred face. He crouched to take my jaw in his hand, turning my head to inspect my face.

"Girl, you are too skinny to be worth the effort, and blondes are not to my taste." He did not flinch when he brushed the hair away from my face with the metal-clad fingertips of his free hand. "Especially not damaged goods like you... If you are lucky, the smoke will kill you before the flames do."
"W-what?" I stammered, horrified. I tried to turn and pull away from him when he released his grip on my jaw, but I was too slow. I didn't see the blow he struck to the back of my skull with the knuckles of his armoured fist, but I felt it briefly as an agonising explosion of pain before everything went silently black.

I woke later, retching and coughing, to an overwhelming sensory cacophony of blazing light and heat, deafening sound, hellish smells, and agonies that were both throbbing dully and stinging with sharp, almost lightning-like stabs every time I took a breath. Fire crackled and spat all around me as it hungered insatiably for more fuel to consume. Cruel, flickering shadows leapt around my devastated bedroom while the beams supporting the roof and floorboards groaned and strained under the assault of the relentless flames. Still disoriented by the pounding headache that mired my thoughts and half-blinded by the thick, rancid, charred smoke filling the room and my lungs, it took me a few moments to realise that I was on fire. Burning embers from ruined shingles had fallen from the roof onto my back and neck, withering away my hair and igniting the wool of my dress. Long, brittle chunks of scorched hair broke off beneath my fingertips as I frantically used my hands to smother the cinders searing my neck and head, batting the glowing fragments of charred wood away onto the floor. With my hair successfully extinguished, I became aware of over a dozen places across my back where the red-hot ashes falling from the ceiling had set my dress alight. The thickness and density of wool had protected me slightly, as the tight weave of the spun thread had proved somewhat resistant to the heat of the fire. I had obviously lain unconscious for some time however, as the material was starting to smoulder in places and I could feel the tiny conflagrations singeing patches of flesh all across my back and legs. I spat out a gob of sooty phlegm that had erupted from the back of my throat as I continued to cough uncontrollably.

Able to breathe slightly more freely, I rolled onto my back to starve the tiny infernos consuming my dress of air. I retched and coughed again, tasting carbon and the metallic tang of copper in my mouth. The swirling smoke made it difficult to see, but I quickly surveyed the ruins of my bedroom. My bed and wardrobe were both ablaze, and I could see stars through the holes burnt in the roof, where damaged shingles and rafters had burned away and fallen, scattering ash and glowing fragments of wood across the varnished oak floorboards. One of the beams in the roof that had collapsed was blocking the door with both its bulk and flames, which licked voraciously at the doorframe. The heat in the room was so intense that I was sure my skin would blister, so I kept my body pressed flat and face-down to the floor, where I knew that the air would be cleanest and coolest. I was no stranger to fire. Under my father's guidance, I had almost completed my apprenticeship as a blacksmith. I knew I could not afford to panic if I wanted to live. The flames in my room and the first floor landing were too well established for me to even think about trying to escape through the building, and in any case, the fallen beam from the roof that blocked the door ruled out that possibility. I only really had one option. If I wanted to make it out of the house alive, I would have to leave via my bedroom window. Unfortunately, there were two large problems. Firstly, opening the window would feed extra air to the fire in my bedroom, which would be like using the bellows on a forge, intensifying the heat and volume of the blaze. Secondly, it was a height of twelve feet from my window to the safety of the gravel courtyard below. I could already see flames from the ground floor flaring past the checkerboard of window panes. It would be impossible to climb down, even if the stone facade of the house had not been coated with a sheer screed of pebbles and lime. I would have to jump. It was certain that I would suffer cuts from the glass as I leapt through the leaded framework of small window plates, but I was more concerned by the height of the subsequent fall. At best, there was a good chance that I would break bones when I landed in the courtyard. At worst, I could break my neck, but at least that would be a quick death, and infinitely more preferable to being burned alive. With a growing intuition that time was running out, I took one last deep breath from the fresher air in the inch or so above the floor. The floorboard beneath me creaked and sagged frighteningly as I stood. I raised my hands and forearms to provide some protection for my face when I smashed through the glass. I closed my eyes and started to run for the window. I had barely made it three steps when floor of my bedroom collapsed. Catastrophically weakened by the gnawing fires below, the beams supporting the floorboards slipped out of the recessed sockets in the stone wall at the front of the house, twisting and snapping under the weight of the floorboards, which split apart like a chasm opened by an earthquake. I fell into a fiery vision worthy of the Fifth Circle of Hell itself. I didn't even have time to scream when I saw that fate had me plummeting towards the workshop's anvil. I tried to turn my body in mid-air to avoid the impact. The roaring of the flames billowing out of the sabotaged forge was briefly drowned out by a sickening crack and the echo from my high-pitched shriek of anguish as my right thigh bone snapped and splintered when I struck the saddle of the anvil directly from above. The pain from my leg utterly overwhelmed the burning sensations seething on my back and legs. I would have passed out, had it not been for another shock of pain as I tumbled like a ragdoll from the top of the anvil the remaining few feet down to the cobbled floor of the workshop. The smithy was in total disarray, having been ransacked and torched by my father's kidnappers. The floor was littered with flaming debris; the shafts of pikes, spears and farming tools lay scattered among the remains of fallen roof shingles, fractured floorboards and smoking rafters that formed a flaming obstacle course between me and the door from the workshop to the courtyard beyond. For the first time since I had awoken in my burning bedroom, I genuinely felt despair and the crippling fear that I was going to die. The smoke irritated my eyes, throat and lungs and I cried as I choked on the searing, soot-laden air. My smashed leg felt as if a daeva had torn it off at the hip. Trying to move it was so agonising that it made me feel dizzy and light-headed. Each breath was an anguished whimper of pain and my vision was starting to blur. Desolate tears rolled down my cheeks from my raw, gritty eyes and I cursed the Lady of Luck for her fickleness. Why could she have not waited another few seconds before deciding that the floor needed to collapse? The broad, double-width doors to the workshop were not even a dozen yards from where I was slumped against the anvil, but they might as well have been a hundred leagues away. They were closed and likely barred from the outside by the soldiers that had trashed my home. It was unlikely that would be able to crawl that far, weaving my way around the burning wreckage scattered over the floor, blocking a direct path. It was even less likely that I would be able to stand to try to unlatch the door's lock, should I manage to get that far without being overcome by the heat and the smoke. I was gradually being starved of fresh air by the fire and I could feel my reserves of will and energy slowly draining away. I was tempted to just close my eyes and wait for the smoke to clog my lungs, but the sharp clack of a falling stone sounding from over my shoulder drew my attention. The sundered forge was spewing flames against the stone wall and the side of the house. Weakened by the heat, the mortar holding the sandstone bricks together had crumbled, causing part of the wall to collapse. Fed by the air seeping through the gap in the wall, the flames spewing from the broken forge licked higher, reaching up to the charred remains of the roof. More of the sandstone blocks tumbled loose from the edges of the crack allowing me to see into the garden and the forest beyond. The blue-white glow of Rionnag was starting to brighten the sky behind the trees. Dawn was coming.

I spluttered and gagged on the hot smoky air, frantic for breath, sticky liquid bubbling in the back of my throat. I gazed skywards through the gap in the wall and wept as I rolled away from the anvil, flopping onto my belly. I raised my head, looking directly at the first rays of sunlight creeping over the horizon. I was just five yards from the break in the wall. Fiery ash fell onto my back like crimson snow, smoking on the thick blue wool. In desperation, I reached out with my hands, my fingernails finding purchase in the narrow gaps between the granite slabs of the workshop floor, and I pulled myself slowly, inexorably, towards my only hope of escape, my broken leg an excruciating, useless dead weight slowing my progress. The heat was terrible. My palms burned on the stone floor as I passed the forge. I was tormented by falling embers from the destroyed roof, which burned more holes in the remains of my hair, blistering the back of my head and neck. I dared not stop to shake the burning fragments of wood loose, even as the wool of my dress began to burn more insistently. I screamed in defiance, my agony spurring me on as I started to mount the pile of rubble at the base of the crack in the wall. The horrid taint of seared flesh filled my nose and unable to bear any more pain, I grabbed the hem of my dress and ripped the smouldering material completely off my battered and burned body, tossing the ruined garment back into the workshop with a yell of fury. I dragged myself over the crest of the mound of ragged, ochre-coloured bricks, the abrasive sandstone leaving raw scratches on my bare skin. I wheezed in exhaustion, fluid gurgling sickeningly in my lungs as I panted for breath. At least here in the breach in the wall the air was noticeably fresher and cooler than the smoke-filled air inside the house. I stopped crawling and raised my torso to gulp down a lungful of clean air, and without any warning at all, my left arm went limp. It took a second for me to register the pain and find the cause. A brick had fallen from the top of the wall and struck my shoulder, barely missing my head and knocking my collarbone out from its joint at the base of my neck. I stared in mute disbelief at the stone as it tumbled away from the top of the stone pile towards the garden. I wept and cried out in frustration, again cursing the Lady for giving me such bad luck, just when it had seemed that I might reach the safety of the garden. I could hardly breathe, my body was covered in weeping burns and I had lost the use of an arm and a leg. My sobs turned hysterically to laughter. I had tried so hard to live, only to have fate snatch salvation away from me at the last moment.

Capricious bitch, I thought, lying my cheek down against one of the warm stone bricks. I would have given up, had a chance breeze not carried a smell to my nose that I had always associated with my father's love. For my tenth birthday, I had insisted that he plant a lawn of chamomile grass in the garden, so that we would always have a supply of the herb to make our favourite bedtime tisane. The heat from the fire had stimulated the chamomile leaves to release their fragrant oils. The familiar aroma was like a tonic, reinvigorating my desire to survive. I breathed it deep into my heat and smoke-ravaged lungs, tasting hope on the air. I raised my chin, seeing the lush green carpet of grass just a dozen feet away. Every inch travelled came at a cost of new scratches and bruises on my chest and belly, the rough stones grazing away layers of skin as I used my one remaining good arm and my unbroken leg to slither agonisingly down the rugged pile of shattered sandstone bricks. Eventually, I felt the cool, soothing tickle of the chamomile grass on my palm, and I smiled, continuing to drag myself onward, only stopping when I could feel the lawn's soft caress envelop my chest, belly and the soles of both my feet. This time the tears wetting my cheeks were ones of relief. The king's men had kidnapped my father, turned my home into a fiery hell hole and left me for dead, but somehow, I had escaped. I was burned and broken, but alive. I rolled agonisingly onto my back, to let the damp grass cool the heat of my burns. The constellations were starting to disappear from the night sky as dawn steadily broke and every time I blinked, the sky appeared to get brighter. I felt my consciousness ebb and flow like the rise and fall of the tides, making it impossible for me to judge how long I had lain on the grass. I closed my eyes again, this time keeping them closed. Dimly, I was aware of every cut, scratch, scrape, burn and broken bone in my body and I could feel the rasping struggle in my chest as my lungs tried to get enough air. I wondered casually if my struggle to escape my burning home had been worth the cost. Yes, I was alive, but for how long? I couldn't walk, I could barely breathe and without treatment my burns would likely become infected within a day. I didn't want to die, but it seemed unlikely that fate would smile upon me now. I let out a short, bitter laugh. The only thing you could reliably depend upon where the Lady of Luck was concerned was her bewildering inconsistency. Perhaps I had already died, but just hadn't realised it yet? I opened my eyes, to reassure myself that I still lived. When I saw a hooded, shadowy figure dressed entirely in black standing before me on the lawn, I moaned in horror.

"The Dark Rider." I gasped, unable to move. The black leather hood completely masked his face and he was broad, muscular and stood over six feet tall. Despite all my cynicism about the gods, for once I was certain that this was the Angel of Death himself. Tears of regret trickled

from my eyes across my cheeks. I whispered one final, resigned protest. "But I'm not ready…"
The black figure stepped forward as my eyes closed, the darkness claiming and consuming me once again.

3 - Cathal

The scratching at the bedroom door was insistent, persistent and all too familiar. The night was still black and quiet, so I reached underneath the bed, groping blindly for one of my boots. Once my hand found something solid, I aimed instinctively in the direction of the noise that had woken me and hurled the boot with furious strength. Soft leather boomed on hard wood, silencing the incessant scratching, as I heard a satisfying scrabbling of terrified keratin claws upon clay tiles. Smiling inwardly, I tried to go back to sleep. My respite was short-lived, however. The scratching resumed only a few moments later, this time accompanied by a plaintive yowling of distress. For a few seconds I seriously considered the merits of throwing my other boot at the door. While it might bring me a brief spell of peace, it was unlikely to completely discourage further annoying scraping from the other side of the door, and other than my second boot, there was nothing else within arm's reach that would have the desired effect and yet still survive being thrown at the door. I admitted defeat with a low growl under my breath, swung my feet out of the warm bed and placed them reluctantly on the cold terracotta tile floor.
"You better have a good reason for waking me in the middle of the night, trouble." I chastised the mewling ball of fur, which was seated innocently, swishing her long tail with an air of impatience and reproach over the floor behind the door. Stripes of silver fur rippled in the murk of the unlit corridor as the cat stretched its back and retreated towards the lounge. I walked behind the silver tabby closely, curious to know what the cat wanted. Large, crystal blue eyes transfixed me as the cat turned its head, making sure I was still following her, before nudging open the door to the lounge with the brow of her head and disappearing inside. I used the back of my hand to push the door open further so that I could enter, still gathering my alertness and wits as I scanned the floor for the cat. The logs in the fireplace had burnt to ash hours ago, leaving the room cold and dark. A quick scan of the bear and wolf pelt rugs placed on the

floor around the room yielded no sign of my nocturnal tormentor. The gentle tap of claws on glass told me that it would be no use looking further around the floor. Her long, striped tail twitched and swayed again to attract my attention over to the window, reinforced by a terse, annoyed yelp.

"If you want out, your flap is on the kitchen door." I testily reminded the cat. Sapphire cocked her head dismissively, yowled in disgust and looked back out of the window, pawing again at the pane for emphasis. I joined her at the window, scratching her behind the ear before looking up to see what had attracted the cat's attention and motivated it sufficiently to wake me. My eyes widened slightly as I saw a column of smoke illuminated by the moonlight on the south-western horizon. A telltale flickering of yellow illuminated the dusky wisps from below, indicating that the fire was still burning. "Daeva shit!"

Without hesitation, I turned and ran back to my bedroom, opening the recessed double doors on the wall beside my bed. Inside was a wardrobe and armoury. Even in the dark, it only took me a moment to dress and arm myself. I settled my sword belt on my hip and slung a quiver of twenty broad-tipped arrows across my back before shrouding them with a durable lambskin cloak dyed as black as midnight. Stopping only to pick up my longbow in the anteroom between the dining room and the lounge, I secured the front door and headed south-west in the direction of the fire at a brisk jog. It was difficult to precisely estimate how far away the column of smoke was on the horizon, so I compromised my pace to give me the best balance between haste and endurance. I had been jogging for nearly two hours when I began to smell the smoke. Recognising the stench of sulphur on the air, I picked up my pace, using the hellish scent on the wind to lead me closer to the source of the smoke. The smell of sulphur could only mean that the fire was deliberate and likely beyond control, judging from the tower of smoke still rising above the trees into the night sky. An accidental forest fire would have been bad enough, but a man-made fire increased the likelihood that lives were in danger. I only slowed my approach when I began to see flames dancing beyond the edge of the trees. I nocked an arrow on my bow and drew up the hood of my cloak, kneeling behind a large oak, as dark and still as a wraith. I waited in the shadows, watching and listening for signs of movement, with all of my senses primed and alert for the slightest sign of danger. Minutes passed. Stars winked out of the brightening sky as dawn approached and my silent vigil slowly concluded. The only sights and sounds of motion came from the death throes of the fire. I was relieved to see that the fire had mostly burned itself out and that there was enough of a gap between the house and the trees to prevent the fire from spreading to the forest. With the threat of a forest wildfire seemingly remote, I could concentrate on whether anyone required aid. Belatedly, I recognised the gutted remains of the building. It was the workshop of the blacksmith who had supplied me with the tools I had needed to build my cabin in the temperate, southern reaches of the Pineholm forest after the purge, four years ago. Only a few charred beams of the double-pitched roof frame and upper floor remained. The sandstone brick wall of the workshop itself had collapsed in several places, showing that debris still burned in the ashen remains of the ruined house. I re-slung my bow under my cloak and stepped away from the tree line towards the gravel courtyard. My attention was drawn to the channels and bumps that had been left behind by an uncommonly heavy horse-drawn carriage, plus hoof-marks from two dozen cavalry stallions. I studied the tracks closely, noting the flange on the outside of the foot that was characteristic of the royal blacksmith at Clongarvan. I knelt by one of the grooves carved into the gravel by the wheels of the carriage, measuring the depth of the ruts with my fingers. The driver of the carriage had clearly left the courtyard with almost panicked urgency, carving yawning chasms in the loose stone deeper than the length of my hand. I estimated the kind of weight needed to create such grooves and concluded that there were only two possibilities. Carriages this heavy were reserved for royalty or criminals. Intrigued by the mystery, I decided to conduct a proper search of the surroundings of the house. The ruins of the building were still burning and too dangerous to enter, so I began to walk around the partially collapsed walls, keeping my head down as I hunted for clues as to what had precipitated the fire. A faint, uneven wheezing caught my attention as I turned the corner of the building. On the lawn behind the house lay the body of a young woman. She was as naked as a newborn babe, her breathing was badly laboured and her milky, pale skin was covered in cuts, abrasions and raw, blistered burns. Her blonde hair had mostly shrivelled away in the intense heat of the fire and her body was blackened with soot. I began to lengthen my stride to cross the lawn and lend her aid when she gave a sudden, anguished moan and stopped me with a stare as her eyelids snapped open.

"The Dark Rider." She breathed, almost inaudible. Superstition held that those about to die saw a vision of the Angel of Death before he escorted the lost soul to the fugue plane for Eternal Judgment. A look of disappointment crossed the girl's burned features. "But I'm not ready…" Before I could reassure her that I had not come to send her immortal soul to the afterlife, her head lolled loosely back on her shoulders, falling back onto the fragrant lawn as she lapsed into unconsciousness or worse. I hurried to her side, placing my fingertips against her neck, feeling for a pulse at the artery beneath her jaw. Her heartbeat was strong, but irregular. The next few hours would determine whether she survived. She was showing the early signs of going into shock, and it was critical that she received medical help sooner rather than later. Even though I doubted she should hear it, I whispered a vow to her. "Fear not, young maiden. I shall see to it that your time is not yet done."

A quick triage revealed that some of her burns appeared to be serious and covered her arms, legs and back, but I was more worried about the unnatural angles her left arm and right leg had assumed when she had laid down on the lawn. A blow to the shoulder had dislocated her front left clavicle and her right thigh bone had suffered a horrific double break. The arm I could put into a sling to prevent further damage to her arm and shoulder, but the leg would be more problematic. I could not risk moving her without first splinting the leg, otherwise loose fragments of bone could shift in her thigh to tear muscles and blood vessels, potentially putting her life in danger. I drew my longsword and returned to the edge of the forest, selecting two sturdy boughs near the base of a mature ash tree, hacking them away from the trunk and trimming them to the right length for the splints, before shaving away the excess barks and twigs away from the wood to leave the splints straight and smooth. The young woman did not wake when I reset the breaks in her thigh bone, even though I knew from my own experience that the process must have been agonising. This apparent mercy was a bad sign – it meant that her shock was getting worse. I would have to work quickly to get her back to my cabin and treat her wounds. I removed the string from my bow and used my sword to cut it into lengths, so that I could tie the splints to her leg at the ankle, above and below the knee and at the top of her thigh, thus ensuring that the reset bone remained straight and true while I took the injured girl back to my cabin. Satisfied that the splints were sufficiently secure, I sacrificed one of the cloth arms from my ghillie shirt to restrain her arm in a tight sling across her chest. There was no time to give thought to the considerations of modesty or propriety. While her life hung in the balance, gallantry and politeness could be damned. I held her rib cage beneath the breasts as I lifted her gently, laying her over my shoulder at the waist, settling her bare legs against my chest and holding her securely with an arm wrapped behind her knees. Her free arm dangled down the middle of my back and I stopped her belly from sliding on the smooth leather of the cloak covering my shoulder by placing a firm hand on her hip. I oriented myself with a quick skyward glance at the rising sun, retracing my steps back to my cabin, as fast as my burden would allow.

Sapphire greeted me by unhelpfully getting under my feet and almost tripping me up as I opened the front door, squealing when I accidentally trod on her tail. "Kitten, make yourself useful and get out of the way!"
The silver tabby sulked and skulked her way moodily into the lounge as I carried the burned girl to the kitchen, setting her down onto her table on her back. She was still utterly insensate, showing no signs of awakening. Though her pulse was still relatively strong, her breathing had deteriorated to a barely audible wheeze. I lit the kitchen's three oil lanterns to give me better light to work with and took off my cloak, hanging it over the back of a chair before washing my hands in the sink. I had just finished soaping my hands when the sound of her breathing stopped. I immediately dropped the bar of soap and rushed back to

her side, placing my ear to her ribcage, listening intently. The burned girl was still breathing, just barely. A faint liquid bubbling sound told me that fluid was building up in her lungs. I used both hands to vigorously massage her ribs, making them flex under my applied pressure. I stopped every few seconds to pinch her nose shut, placed my mouth firmly over her heat-cracked lips and blew hard, trying to force fresh air into her lungs past the build up of mucus. I scarcely cared whether I cracked or bruised her ribs as I continued to try and expel the liquid from her lungs. After several minutes of massage that would no doubt leave painful bruises, I heard an accusatory mewling from behind me.

"Relax, kitten. This is not what it looks like." I reassured the overly judgmental cat, between breaths. "If I cannot clear the fluid from her lungs, she will drown."

It was another ten minutes and a hundred breaths before her lungs finally responded to my coaxing and she began to cough reflexively, still unconscious. I wiped the vile-smelling sputum away from her face with a clean dishcloth as it erupted out of her mouth, the sticky mucus black with soot. I waited until she stopped coughing before listening to her lungs again, this time satisfied that she was now breathing clearly and without distress. I could hear no signs of crackling or bubbling of fluid as her ribs flexed. With the immediate threat to her life averted for now, I concentrated on dealing with her remaining injuries. I had two further tasks: one large and one small. I decided that it would be best to re-seat her collarbone back into the joint before trying to salve her burns, since I did not want to risk doing further damage to the her arm or shoulder when I would have to turn her over to treat the burns on her back. Ensuring that her burns did not become infected when I dressed them would likely take the rest of the morning, so it was important that she did not wake up midway through the process. It would be akin to torture, cleaning and disinfecting the blistered skin and burnt flesh. The shock to the nervous system alone had been known to kill patients with a low tolerance to pain, and her burns covered most of the back of her body. I retrieved a vial of black seeds from the herb cabinet, measuring out two heaped spoons into the granite mortar bowl next to the sink, grinding them with the pestle into a fine powder. I warmed some water in a pan over the iron hob of my stove, sprinkling in the ground opium seeds to form a sedative infusion. Once the opium water had sufficiently brewed, I poured half a pint of the mixture into a glass and lifted the back of the unconscious girl's head, placing the rim of the glass to her seared lips. She drank the mixture mechanically as I fed it to her slowly. Eventually she emptied the glass, never regaining consciousness. I waited a few minutes for the drug to take effect and again placed my fingers to the underside of her jaw on the left side of her neck. I was relieved when I felt that her heartbeat was now slow and steady. The first test of whether I had given her a high enough a dose of the painkilling concoction was when I placed my knee on the table behind her head to keep it still and used my hands to reset the wishbone-like arm of her clavicle back into its socket at the base of her neck, with a loud, wet, sickening pop. She didn't even flinch. I exhaled with relieved satisfaction and prepared a large bowl of heavily salted, boiled water and a tall pile of soft cotton pads and strips of muslin cloth dressings. I disinfected a large muslin cloth to clean the woman's burns and blisters before I bound her wounds. As I anticipated, it took several hours to salve and cover her burns. Sapphire kept me company, occasionally voicing an encouraging yelp of support and approval for my thoroughness as I drained the larger blisters of fluid and wrapped them in cooling, sterile pads of raw cotton I had soaked in saline. I worked slowly and methodically, starting from the top of her head and working my way down to the burns on her feet. For the first time since discovering her lying on the lawn several hours ago, I had the chance to pay greater attention to her as a woman, rather than a person in dire need of first aid. The burns to her head, face and neck were mainly superficial, with her hair bearing the major brunt of the damage, shrivelling away to almost nothing on her neck and the back of her head, while leaving a dishevelled fringe and parting around her face. A ragged blonde curtain fell over the right hand side of her face and neck, partially hiding a long, livid pink scar from a much older, healed burn that disfigured her from just beneath her hairline, across her right eye socket and down her cheek and neck to her collarbone. The leathery tissue stood out starkly like a fork of lightning against her naturally smooth, pale skin. The lobe of her right ear was half melted away from the same burn and I could see that it had even left its mark in a defensive wound along the underside of her right forearm. Clearly, the young woman was no stranger to fire and its perils. The strange burn had given her skin a disturbing, reptilian texture, hinting at a magical or even demonic origin. The thought unsettled me greatly, but I did not have the luxury of time to worry about it. The fresh burns to her arms, back and legs were deeper and more serious than those on her head and some would likely leave scars. A handful of the bigger burns on her back were already starting to weep with yellow, repugnant-smelling pus. I took my time cleaning them delicately, taking care to preserve as much skin as I could, placing soothing pads over the burns and binding them delicately in sterile muslin bandages. As I bound an irregularly-shaped burn on her left arm, I noticed that her hands were aged beyond her years, the skin hardened by working with the intense heat of a smelter and forge. Her arms and legs were long and lean compared to her slim, short torso. The ligaments of her fingers were slender and strong, showing that she was obviously accustomed to hard physical labour. She was just in the first flush of womanhood, barely more than a girl, though she had been generously blessed by the Empress with a fine, classical figure of broad hips curving in sensuously to a slender waist and out again to the pointed globes of her firm, heavy chest. Were it not for her burns and the disturbing nature of her disfigurement, I would have found her comely in the extreme. I put the thought out of my mind, instead deducing from her physique, scars and the location of where I had found her that she must have been related to the blacksmith in some way, or worked for him as his apprentice. It had been two years since I had seen or had dealings with him, and he had never mentioned having a family during the brief time we had spent together, discussing my commission of his services. In a certain light there appeared to be a semblance between the two of them, though not enough for me to be completely sure that they were blood related. Such doubts were irrelevant to her injuries though, so I concentrated on cleansing and binding her burns. Perhaps the subject would come up when she awakened and I could satisfy my curiosity then. It was mid-morning by the time I was satisfied that her wounds were properly cleaned, bound and unlikely to become infected. As well as tending to her burns, I had also cleaned and covered the worst of the abrasions she had suffered on her legs, belly and chest. I fetched a simple white linen smock from my wardrobe for her to wear as a temporary nightshirt, sitting her upright in one of the chairs at the kitchen table as I slipped the garment over her head and eased it down her torso, being careful not to dislodge any of the bandages I had spent so many hours placing on her battered and scorched body. I prepared another draft of opium water to keep her sedated. It could be anything up to a dozen days before the pain from the burns that had penetrated beyond the outer layers of her skin would subside and become manageable by will alone, and I saw no sense in making her endure such excruciating agony. With the painkilling and anaesthetic drug successfully administered, I carried the injured blacksmith's apprentice to my bedroom, settling her down delicately on the mattress and laying two woollen coverlets over her torso to keep her temperature stable. I would need to check and change her bandages at least once per day, keeping her under sedation until her burns showed signs of healing. I hoped that her youth would help her recuperate quickly, as I did not want her to suffer any of the negative side effects of opium treatment. The effects of withdrawal from using the drug for too long or giving her too much were potentially worse in the longer term than not using it at all. Sapphire jumped onto the mattress as I rubbed my eyes, walking up the bed to the woman's head, purring reassuringly, as if proud of my efforts.

"Away with you, trouble, it would not do if your fleas gave her a pox now!" I said, shooing her off the bed and back down to the floor. Grievously affronted by my insult about the standard of her personal grooming, Sapphire hissed and swiped at my leg with her claws extended. I scooped her off the floor, attacking her belly with my fingertips.

"Come. Let us retire to the lounge and leave her in peace. I need sleep."

Sapphire writhed in protest in my arms, like a salmon on the end of a fishing line, until I tickled her under the chin, kissing the top of her head affectionately. By the time we took our place on the divan in the lounge, I had been forgiven.

4 - Ailidh

I woke up choking on the urge to scream. I remembered having a nightmare of five daevae pouring molten iron over my back and legs while they held me down by the shoulders, wrists and ankles. With my thoughts still clouded by the crippling weight of terror, dull pain and a numbing fog that rivalled that of a hangover induced by a pint of rye vodka, I was surprised to find that instead of lying in a pool of red-hot iron on a bed of bare obsidian rock, my cheek was pressed into a soft down pillow and I was resting upon a firm, linen mattress, thickly stuffed with fresh straw. I opened my eyes and looked up, appreciating the workmanship of the dovetailed oak planks that knitted together to form the wall panels and the ceiling. The banality of the room's decor calmed my fear and I felt my heart rate slow as my anxiety subsided. I tested my limbs to see if I could move, only to be rewarded with a sharp stab of pain that cut through the ethereal, remote discomfort I could feel on the fringes of my senses. My left arm and shoulder were so stiff that I could barely move them, and when I tried to shift the weight of my right leg I was rewarded with a stab of agony so acute that it made my eyes water. I swallowed a gasp and screwed my eyes shut, waiting for the pain to subside. When I concentrated, I could feel the precise location of every burn on my back, arms and legs. The pain rippling from them was subdued by a vaguely euphoric mist around my consciousness, making each burn seem distant and almost detached from my body. When my head cleared enough for me to recall the circumstances in which I had received my many injuries, I was gripped by a blind panic. I opened my eyes again, properly seeing the room I was in for the first time. With what looked like home-made terracotta tiles and a wolf-skin on the floor, hand-carved oak panels and an oil-painted portrait in a gilt frame on the walls, it certainly didn't look like a prison, but after what had happened to my father, I was unwilling to make assumptions. I made to turn over onto my back and sit up. Having not learned the

lesson from the last time I had tried to move, this time the signal of protest from my right leg had me shrieking.
"Careful, my lady," warned a rich, bass voice from the other side of the room. "You have much healing to do yet."
I turned by head on the pillow. The voice's owner sat a respectful distance from the bed, an adult tabby cat with immaculate silver and black fur and the most extraordinary, radiant crystal blue eyes seated on his lap. The man languorously stroked the cat's shoulders and back, watching me with bright, attentive, tawny-coloured eyes. He was tall and powerfully built, but his handsome face exuded an openness, calmness and grace that instantly attracted me to him. My pulse started to race once more, but not from alarm. I was glad that my disfigured right cheek and mutated eye was hidden, pressed deep into the pillow. *Always show your best face* my father had told me repeatedly, after my accident. I had wandered too close to my father's forge as a toddler and been lucky to survive a backdraft of arcane fire that melted away my right ear and badly scarred my right arm, cheek and neck.
"Who are you?" I asked, finding my voice. "What am I doing here?"
"My name is Cathal, Baron Ranger of Cothraine's Order of Sylvan." He replied, bowing his dark, close-cropped head respectfully as he introduced himself.
"A green cloak?" I asked, astounded. Rangers were widely respected throughout the Triad as agents of the Earth Mother, defenders and custodians of the wilderness.
"Indeed. It will be many years yet before the Dark Rider comes to claim you, I hope." Cathal said, smiling thinly as he recalled the circumstances in which I had greeted him on the chamomile lawn of my father's smithy.
"Thanks to you, my lord."
He stopped stroking the cat briefly to wave away my formality. "Please, just Cathal will do. The Order in Cothraine was scattered and destroyed during the purge. These days I am a baron in name only. In practice, I am an outlaw – a fugitive."
"Then I'm grateful that at least some outlaws are honourable. How did you come to be in my garden so late at night?"

"Not entirely by chance. Though for that, you may thank Sapphire here. She saw the smoke from the fire and woke me up." The silver tabby stretched her neck as Cathal stroked her chin and throat in long, indolent strokes with strong, dextrous fingers. The way the cat responded to his touch provoked a pang of jealously that I could not recall him treating my wounds.

"I'm doubly grateful, then. Though I'm curious why a self-confessed fugitive would go out of their way to investigate a fire."

"I am still a ranger by nature, my lady. An uncontrolled fire could threaten the entire forest. When I realised the fire had been set deliberately, my duty was to preserve life and prevent the fire from spreading."

"How bad were my injuries? I felt as if I were dying when you found me on the lawn."

"They were quite severe. You did well to get out of the house at all." Cathal said, his eyes regarding me with a mix of sympathy and admiration. "It will be several weeks before the worst of your burns are completely healed. Even longer for your leg to mend. How did you come to break it, my lady?"

"I've been called many things, but never 'my lady'. My name is Ailidh." I corrected him, a hint of sourness in my tone. Following my disfigurement, I had found it difficult to make friends with other people in my village, as my scars made me a target for bullying and ridicule. As a result, I had rarely left the sanctuary of my father's workshop, even after I had come of age.

"As you wish, Ailidh, but that does not answer my question."

"I fell through the workshop's ceiling onto the anvil."

"Little wonder the break was so bad." Cathal said, grimacing.

"How long will it be before I can walk?"

"Now that you are awake and most of your burns are healed, I can make a cast for your leg. But it will be at least another five weeks before you can walk without crutches."

"That's too long. I need to go back home before the trail goes cold."

"What trail?"

"The one leading to my father, of course," I said, lifting myself up onto my left elbow. The stiffness in my shoulder made me wince. "Some of the king's men kidnapped him last night when they set fire to the house."

"I suspected as much." Cathal replied, frowning. "Ailidh, even if there ever was such a trail, it will have long gone cold by now."

"What d'you mean?" I asked, turning my head to study him with both eyes. I saw him fail to entirely repress a flinch of revulsion from the sight of my scarred cheek and my scarlet eye. I smoothed what was left of my hair across the right hand side of my face self-consciously. I only wanted him to see my best face. "The attack was just last night."

Cathal shook his head sadly. "Ailidh, your father was abducted eleven days ago."

"How-?" I didn't have chance to finish my question before the ranger explained.

"I had to give you opium water, for the pain. Otherwise the shock from your burns could have killed you outright."

"You drugged me?" I asked, outraged. Now the feeling of diffuse euphoria made sense to me. Cathal nodded, silent and contrite. "You drugged me!"

"I sedated you. There was no choice. It would have been worse than torture to keep you awake."

"I suppose you had no choice to paw at my body while I was unconscious, either?"

"No, there I did have a choice. Clean and treat your wounds, or let your burns become infected and have you die from a taint in your blood." Cathal replied, in a cold tone that betrayed his indignation.

I took a moment to swallow my rage and pride. What right did I have to be so angry with the man who had saved my life? "Cathal, I'm sorry. I'm in your debt and forever will be. But why wake me so soon? You should've kept me under until I was fully healed. It would've been better that way."

"Again, I had little choice. Opium water is habit-forming if used in high doses for too long. The withdrawal would be worse than the pain."

"Then you can't drug me again?"

"Not in amounts that would sedate you, no. But I can use it to help you manage your pain."

I laid my head back down on the pillow, relieved. "Then there's nothing else to do but wait until I can walk again."

"Indeed. Nothing, but attend to your burns, cast your leg and keep each other company." Cathal said, sounding pleased by the idea. "Life as an exile often lacks good conversation."

"No doubt." I replied, my heart pounding when I saw him smile. Suddenly flustered and lost for words, I pondered what topic to bring up next, when my stomach growled so loudly that it startled the cat from Cathal's lap. I blanched, mortified. I was only partially consoled by the fact that the ranger had the tact not to laugh.

"My apologies, Ailidh. You must be ravenous. You have not eaten in over a week." Cathal stood and moved fluidly to the door, his footsteps utterly silent on the terracotta tile floor. "I find that good conversation is aided immeasurably by good food and good wine. I shall return shortly."

There was a soft impact on the mattress next to my right shoulder. I turned my head on the pillow and came face to face with Cathal's silver tabby. Her glorious blue eyes bored through me, as if staring into my soul. I brushed my hair behind the remains of my right ear, challenging the cat to accept the face her master could not. Unlike Cathal, the cat didn't shrink from the sight of my scar and blood-red eye, sitting down so close to me that I could feel the rhythm of her purring on my face. I returned her stare, undaunted by the cat's unnatural intensity. The cat wore a hand-stitched black leather collar, adorned with the largest cut jewel I had ever seen – a sapphire bigger than my thumbnail. It matched the colour and clarity of her eyes perfectly. I reached up to caress the gemstone, only for the cat to avoid my touch, leaning back and meowing a polite warning.

"Sorry." I lowered my hand, tickling the toes of her front paws to reinforce my apology. "You must know that your name tag is worth more than my father made in the last two seasons. I can't blame you for being possessive, Sapphire."

The cat responded by purring, nuzzling my scarred cheek with her whiskers and licking the tip of my nose. Delighted by her acceptance, I scratched the cat gently between the shoulder blades at the base of her neck, making Sapphire arch her back sensually as I tickled the cat along the length of her spine.

"I see you have made a new friend." Cathal said, amused, seemingly having reappeared in the room from nowhere.

"Are you talking to me or the cat?" I asked, enjoying the sensation of Sapphire's luxurious fur under my fingertips.
"Both of you," Cathal chuckled. "Sapphire does not usually take to strangers."
I turned my head back to face the fugitive ranger. He set down a large, steaming brown earthenware bowl on the nightstand next to the bed, a silver-handled spoon resting on the rim. Cathal offered me his left hand. "Let me help you turn over."
I reached back with my right hand and returned his strong grip as our palms touched. I felt his other hand rest on my hip and he pulled me over onto my back, seemingly without effort. He set my broken leg down on the mattress considerately, without any quick movements. He then helped me sit up, placing pillows behind me to support my back, before he handed me the spoon and passed me the bowl.
"What's this?" I asked, sniffing the steam rising from the bowl doubtfully. I needn't have worried. The scent of the stew immediately had me salivating.
"Boar, braised with root vegetables and wine."
"It's delicious." I said, between spoonfuls.
"You sound surprised." Cathal's tone was ironic.
"Forgive me, Cathal, but in my experience, men that can cook are as rare as hens with teeth."
Cathal laughed; a pleasant, deep booming of amusement that pealed like the ringing of a church bell. "This is true. Fortunately, my mother taught me the basics when I was very young. The rest I learned with the rangers."
"Is that her?" I asked, pointing my spoon at the portrait of an elegant, olive-skinned brunette with azure eyes that was hanging on the wall opposite the door.
"No. That is my younger sister, Gormlaith."
"Forgive me for saying so, but the family resemblance is slight."
"Half-sister, technically: same father, but a different mother." Cathal replied, tactfully ignoring the crudeness of my observation. "In these parts, they would call my father a wench farmer."
"Like father, like son?" I asked with a raised eyebrow, hoping to provoke him into more laughter.

"Oh, no!" Cathal smiled, closing his eyes as his rich chuckle of mirth echoed around the room. "Outlaws cannot afford to risk such a dangerous hobby."

"But you can afford silver spoons and wine?"

"I may be an exile and outlaw, Ailidh, but that is no reason to live in poverty like one of the Penitent's monks." Cathal replied in a tone of mild reproach. "My resources are somewhat limited, but not enough to warrant foregoing the niceties of life."

"Tell me of your mother." I asked, deciding to change the subject. "She was obviously a good cook. What else?"

"Why so curious?" Cathal's eyes narrowed in suspicion.

"I never knew my mother. She died during the birth. Father raised me alone."

"My condolences, Ailidh. Do you know anything about her?"

"Nothing. Father refused to speak about her, but he must have loved her. He never remarried."

"Curious. My father delighted in talking about the women he loved, often in much too lurid detail... But you asked about my mother. She was a barmaid from Bray, until father married her. According to father, she looked like an angel, cooked like a deva, had the temper of a pit fiend and made love like a succubus. A redhead, naturally."

"Naturally." I said, snickering along with him in amusement.

"Though even when she was angry, she was always full of love. She knew about father's roving eye and infidelities. She raised Gormlaith as if she were her own."

"She sounds extraordinary. Where is your mother now?"

"With father, in an unmarked, shallow grave outside our home town of Monagealy. They died during the outbreak of oriental flu during the winter of '76."

"How old were you?" I asked, aghast. "I wasn't even born then."

"Six years old. Gormlaith was only four. We lived on the streets for over a year before we were taken in by a ranger who took pity upon us when he found us while resting between patrols in the wild."

"To lose both your parents so young... that's terrible."

"In the end, we were lucky. Most orphans die young or are taken in by criminals. I apprenticed with the rangers, but it was found that Gormlaith was more suited to the Wizards'

Guild. She was always much brighter than I was, even when we were children."

"Your sister is a witch?"

"She would not appreciate being called as such, but yes. She is a student of the Art, a chronomancer. Her particular talent is in divining and truth-telling."

"Are you still in contact with her?"

"We saw each other whenever our duties allowed it, but after the purge it became impossible to send messages to each other. I do not know whether she still lives or not."

"Don't you want to find her?" I asked, setting aside my empty bowl on the nightstand. The boar stew was so tasty I had practically inhaled it. "I'd have to know, one way or the other. That's why I need to go after my father. I must know where the king's men took him, and why."

"I cannot simply march into the Tower of the Aether demanding to see her. I would be dead before I saw the walls of the capital. If Gormlaith is alive, I hope in time she will come to me." Cathal said, gazing pensively out of the bedroom's window. "Though I fear that will not be an option for your father. I do not understand why the king would order your father to be taken. Did he have any enemies? Or dealings with the black market?"

"Hardly. How does a blacksmith living on the edge of a tiny village on the edge of the northern forest, a hundred leagues from the nearest city have enemies?" I scoffed. "He could barely make a living selling spades to farmers and spears to the local militias."

"He mentioned nothing to you? No dissatisfied customers or disputed contracts?"

"No, he never allowed me to get involved with the customers directly. I helped him work the forge and smelter, and crafted the odd sword or plough blade for clients, but I didn't get involved in negotiations."

"Perhaps we could find a clue in the workshop?"

"We?"

"I will help you find your father, Ailidh. I have little else to do, and the mystery intrigues me. Odd occurrences such as this, the kidnap of someone so apparently inconsequential, carried out at the behest of the king, should be investigated."

"Thank you, Cathal. Perhaps there might still be something that might help at the house. There's a safe underneath the floor of the workshop."

"A safe? It will probably have been looted by now."

"They'd have to find it first. It's well hidden and it's not the one he used for the business. Father said that it would only open for him or me and that it if something ever happened to him I would need what's inside."

"Your father sounds rather cryptic for a blacksmith."

"You have no idea." I replied ruefully. My stomach rumbled again, only partially satisfied. "You don't happen to have more of that stew, d'you?"

"Certainly," Cathal stood, taking the empty bowl. "Give me a minute."

This time Cathal returned with a wooden tray, laden with two bowls of stew, a plate of wholemeal bread, a crystal carafe of ruby-coloured wine and two silver goblets. Cathal set the tray down on the nightstand, handed me my refilled bowl and poured us a goblet of wine each, before pulling his chair closer to the bed, so that we could both easily reach the plate of bread on the tray. Cathal tore the end off one of the small loaves and handed it to me. I dipped the chunk of bread into the bowl, letting the crust soak up some of the rich, dark sauce of the stew. The bread fell apart in my mouth, adding overtones of yeast and nuts to the luscious, meaty liquor.

"Did you make the bread as well? It's heavenly."

"Thank you, Ailidh. I buy the flour and yeast from the mill outside Croycullen."

"Why some lucky duchess hasn't got you safely stashed away under lock and key, I'll never know." I said, hiding my baleful right eye behind by seared fringe, hoping not to sound too brazen.

Cathal chuckled again, a lovely bass rumble. "Rangers do not wed, Ailidh. It is forbidden by the Order. A life roaming the wilds is not compatible with the obligations of marriage."

"So you'd have me believe that you've lived a solitary life, like some kind of celibate deva? Given what you've told me about your father, I don't think so." I said, my teasing hitting its mark immediately.

"I have known and enjoyed the companionship of women." Cathal said, sounding rather defensive. He avoided my gaze as he took a sip of wine.

"Anyone special?" I asked, wondering how honest his reply would be.

"You are far too inquisitive for a blacksmith's apprentice." Cathal sighed, setting aside his bowl, even though it was still almost half full. "Yes. There was."

"Who was she?" I couldn't help myself from asking, even though the way Cathal spoke in the past tense implied there would be no happy ending to the story. "A ranger?"

Cathal nodded. "Aoibheann. We trained together. Rules and edicts can be used to govern over the mind, but they cannot govern the heart."

"What was she like?"

"Lean and tenacious, like a wolf. Agile as an acrobat. And as stubborn as an enraged bull."

"A redhead?" I guessed.

"Naturally." Cathal replied, this time without a smile. He looked away, out of the window as he drained his goblet and refilled it with wine from the carafe. "We spent many years in the wild together."

"What happened to her?"

"She was killed during the purge." In the months following Maeryn's regicide of Connell and the royal family, the country had been gripped by months of chaos, as the new regime dismantled the old order and eliminated people and organisations loyal to the royal family, replacing them with mercenary toadies willing to sacrifice honour and principle for personal advancement.

"Oh, Cathal, I'm so sorry. I shouldn't have asked." I looked down at my lap, silently cursing my selfish nosiness.

"Do not apologise. It is good to speak of her and honour her memory." Cathal said, looking out of the window and into the trees as he remembered his fallen lover. "We had been on patrol in the East Riding, following up reports of attacks on merchants by a pack of vampiric wolves. We were ambushed on the road into Birlone by a dozen of Maeryn's grey cloaks. Aoibheann and I fought them off, but she was mortally wounded by three arrows. I held her in my arms as she died."

"That's horrible." I said, tears wetting my cheeks. I wanted to reach over and hug him, but I could not move due to the pain from my broken leg.

"Yet it was only one of the many tragedies to occur during Maeryn's rise to power." Cathal sighed, taking another long sip of wine. "He has much to answer for, our so-called king."

"He is a cruel and evil man. I dread to think what that tyrant will do once he has my father." I said, shivering with apprehension. "I've heard dark tales of what occurs within the royal dungeons. I must rescue him. Petition the king for his freedom. Father is a lawful man. He pays his due of taxes and has committed no crimes. Why would the king's men kidnap him?"

"I have no idea. But do not forget, they left you for dead and razed his property. Whatever transgression or slight the king accuses your father of, it is serious."

"Then the sooner we can go after him, the better." I declared, mopping up the last dregs of sauce around the bowl with another crust of bread. I set aside the earthenware bowl on the tray and replaced it in my hands with the silver goblet of wine Cathal had poured for me. I was not used to drinking wine, but the salt in the meaty broth had left me thirsty. The ruby liquid was bursting with the scent of sour cherries, the vanilla tang of oak and the sweetness of redcurrants, with a good kick of alcohol lingering on the tongue and in the back of my throat as I swallowed. I gave a wordless murmur of satisfaction as my pain receded a little further towards the back of my mind.

"All in good time, first you must rest and heal. I will make the cast for your leg as soon as your burns no longer require treatment. Then we can get you mobile on crutches."

"When'll that be?"

"A few days, perhaps. I will have a better idea when I change your bandages tomorrow."

"And then we can search my house for clues and see what's in the safe?"

"Patience, Ailidh. You have suffered a great trauma. It would be wise to build up your strength first. It is over eight leagues from here to your father's workshop; a long enough journey on foot, never mind crutches. It will be at least a week before I will consider taking you on such a trip, especially bearing in mind that we must do the return trip in one day."

"Couldn't we just stay at the village inn?"

"Maeryn no doubt assumes you are dead, but he is no fool. He will have left spies and informants behind. If we are to safely pursue your father's kidnappers, it is best we do not give him evidence that you still live. It will be safer for your father as well."

"What d'you mean?"

"Whatever scheme or plot Maeryn has in mind for your father, we cannot risk you becoming a pawn or bargaining chip in it." Cathal replied ominously.

5 - Fiacre

"Who pissed in the king's wine this morning?" I muttered to myself as I heard rapid, uneven footsteps echoing along the blue slate flagstones on floor of the corridor leading to my personal quarters in the Field Army Headquarters. I knew it was the king not only from the gait and cadence of his footsteps, but he announced his presence with his detestably thin, reedy voice.

"Duke Fiacre! Where are you, you worthless, dumb brute?" Moments later the door to my office crashed open, striking the wall. King Maeryn stood in the stone portal, fuming. His golden half-plate armour glistened in the sunlight streaming over my shoulder, the silver and purple filigree on the breastplate looked as out of place as the gilt crown disguising his thinning brown hair. His stance was lopsided, thanks to a childhood injury that had stunted the growth of his right leg. His demeanour was intended to intimidate and threaten, but as I rose from my chair, the king had to look up to me, blinking and squinting as I cast a shadow over his eyes, the top of his head several inches below the level of my chin. I was well over a full foot taller, a great deal broader and nearly a decade and a half older than the king, so there was little chance of him cowing me into submission. If truth be told, I thought the king would struggle to intimidate a child.

"Good morning, your grace." I recalled what I was told by one of my first trainers in the Field Army - *We honour the rank, not the man* - remembered my manners and addressed him with the deference his position was due. I had no love for the king, despite his patronage. He had appointed me to the position of Field Duke and Lord Commander of Cothraine's land army in the immediate wake of the rebellion, after I had ordered my legions to fight for his faction during the insurrection. I had not chosen his side out of any sense of idealism or loyalty, but because I had been astute enough to correctly gauge the direction of the winds of change and ally myself with who I thought would be victorious. I had not been impressed by some of Maeryn's subsequent edicts, but having made my bed, I was forced to lie in it.

"I told you to report directly to me as soon as you got back from Croycullen!" Maeryn raged, his demeanour that of a moody child.

"Your grace, my men are still returning to barracks. We only arrived in the city an hour ago." I replied in a neutral tone, not having any desire to indulge or placate the king's poor temper.

"Save your excuses. Was the raid on Croycullen was a success, at least?"

"Yes, my liege. We found the blacksmith identified by Arch Mage Karryghan and took him into custody. As you ordered, we left no witnesses."

"Very good, Fiacre. Where is he now?"

"Field Lord Nuall's prison carriage should be arriving at the Stockade in the next half hour, sire. Then the Arch Mage can do as he likes with him."

"Any losses?"

"Two footmen only, your grace. They went missing while standing overnight guard in the Lockwood." I had hoped to gloss over this detail, but it would have been unwise to lie about the disappearance of the men.

"Deserters?"

"Unlikely, sire. They were both serfs in good standing. It's more likely they were taken by beasts or bandits during the night."

"You are certain they are dead?"

"Yes, your grace. The region is known for being infested with spider nests and worse. There were signs of a struggle at their guard post. I thought it imprudent to risk more men investigating."

"Perhaps there is a brain inside that thick skull of yours after all." Maeryn snarled. "Grant their widows a small annual stipend and tell them that they died in training accidents."

"By your command, my liege." I nodded and took a sheet of blank paper from the pile of fresh sheaves on my desk and a goose quill from my desk to make a note.

"Keep your men on their toes, Field Duke. I will have other tasks for you in the coming months."

"Yes, your grace." I retook my seat as the king turned on his heel and stormed out as abruptly as he had entered, hobbling away on his uneven legs. One of the king's Royal Guards remained behind as the rest of Maeryn's entourage followed in his wake. He entered as I retrieved a map of Cothraine from the drawer of my desk and spread it out on leather-bound surface before me.

"Good morning, my lord Fiacre. Did you enjoy your sojourn into the country?"

"Not overmuch, my Duke Aiden." I told the Lord Commander of the Royal Guard, my voice sour as I marked the location of where the two footmen had gone missing on the map. It was useful to know when planning the site of overnight camps if dangerous beasts might be in the area. "The borderlands are cold and desolate, even at this time of year."

"Much like the women there, or so I am told." Aiden said, seating himself uninvited in the chair opposite mine on the other side of the desk.

"I would not know." I bit my tongue, neglecting to tell him that my wife and I were from the north of the country, as I knew that Aiden was aware of the parlous state of my marriage and did not want to provide him with more gossip. The Duke Companion was the principle rumour-monger in the palace, so I was always careful not to overshare information with him. He was also a devotee of the Goddess and a serial womaniser. I did not share Aiden's profligate and casual attitude to carnal liaisons with women, hence why I had not been tempted in the least to violate the blacksmith's daughter in the wake of his abduction. I did not permit my troops to rape, as I considered it a sign of poor discipline in a fighting force. Besides, neither my wife nor my mistress would appreciate it if I had returned home with a genital pox from some common northern wench. "What puts the king in such a foul mood this morning?"

"Queen Reilynn has refused to meet him in the King's Tower again. The handmaidens tell me that they have never slept in the same room, let alone the same bed, despite four years of marriage. No wonder he wants to bugger the some poor bastard from the border. Even now, he cannot get the queen to sup from the mouth of his wineskin." Aiden's amusement was plain as he smoothed the golden hem of his purple cloak.

"You should not speak in such a manner about your king, Duke Companion Aiden." I frowned, again more out of self-preservation than any sense of loyalty. The walls had ears. It was dangerous to openly slander the king's reputation.
"You worry too much, your grace." Duke Companion Aiden said, waving a hand at me dismissively. I bristled irritably when he raised a knee to rest one of his armoured boots on the edge of my desk. I would not have permitted it from a man of lesser rank and I was grateful that at least his boots were clean. "Any other king would simply take a mistress or bed an eager horde of whores. Gods know there are enough of them on any street corner in Clongarvan after dusk... but no. Maeryn keeps himself *pure* for her. His balls must be bluer than a pirakian tanzanite by now. The man is a fool."
"Reilynn is the last link to Connell's royal line. Maeryn needs her if his rule is to have any legitimacy in law."
"Then it is a shame that he had the rest of her family purged. Regicide and the mass murder of your entire family is hardly an aphrodisiac. Little wonder that Reilynn finds his company so repulsive." Duke Aiden scoffed. "If Maeryn had not somehow won the backing of the Arch Mage Karryghan and the Wizard's Guild, his little rebellion would have been snuffed out like a candle in a winter storm."
"And you would still be digging shit holes behind the grey cloaks' prison house." I reminded him. We had both done well out of Maeryn's regicide and insurrection, but there was royal blood on our hands.
"True enough. Though I swear Maeryn doesn't entertain a thought in his head unless the Schemer has it first. The Arch Mage converses with the king almost daily."
"Karryghan? He is older than my grandmother, but his very presence chills my blood. I fear little in this world, but I am not certain he is truly human." I had more reason than most to be wary of the Arch Mage, as my mistress Dervla was one of his grand-nieces. Karryghan had introduced us at a royal function prior to the coup and I had been instantly smitten with her. I had not known until after I had taken her as a lover that Dervla had not yet come of age. The Arch Mage had then played on my fear of the affair being revealed to blackmail me into supporting Maeryn's coup. Karryghan had expertly created and manipulated the situation to his advantage, giving me an uncomfortably

personal insight as to why he known somewhat less than affectionately as The Schemer of Siskine.

"Brighe would still make a coward of him, I fancy." Duke Companion Aiden chuckled, only half joking. He had once found himself the unfortunate recipient of one of my wife's pitiless tongue-lashings. "But you are right, my friend. Evil radiates from him like heat from an oil burner."

"What do they talk about?" I asked, eager for information about the true motives behind why the king had ordered my elite regiment away from the capital for two months to the northern border with Fossfjall. If the king was unwilling to tell me, at least I could rely on Aiden to keep me informed. The Lord Commander of the Royal Guard was not yet thirty years old and his boyish good looks and athletic physique were matched by his prodigious libido and ambition. Aiden's choice of the Goddess as a patron deity was unusual for a fighting man, but his devotion was sincere enough that his patron had blessed him with an almost supernatural appeal to the fairer sex. He used his position, not to mention his popularity with the queen's handmaidens and the other women of the palace's serving staff, to keep up to date with the gossip surrounding the king and his dealings.

"No-one knows." Aiden shrugged, the pauldrons of his golden-gilt full plate armour clanking.

"Someone must know. Seduce more of the serving wenches until you find the right one." While I did not approve of the duke's thoughtless promiscuity, I was reluctantly forced to admit that the information he gleaned from it was useful at times.

"If only it were that simple." The Royal Guardian replied, laughing. "Karryghan hardly ever speaks with the king in person. The Arch Mage prefers to manifest by apparition remotely from the privacy of his tower and permits no-one else in their meetings. Whether conversing in person or via simulacrum, the Schemer is canny enough to use his magic to sound-proof the king's Privy Chamber and prevent my little mice from overhearing any juicy details."

"Well, if you ever do learn of anything, let me know at once." I used the tone of my voice to ensure that the lord commander of the purple cloaks understood my request was also a dismissal.

"Regardless of how many wenches are required your grace," said Duke Aiden as he stood, smiling. "I had better return to the palace before I am missed."
"Farewell, Duke Companion."
"And to you, my lord Fiacre." The young duke bowed deferentially as he stood. He turned on his heel at the nadir of his bow and left with the enthusiasm and speed of youth, the hem of his heavy purple and gold velvet cloak flapping dramatically in his wake.

I looked back down at the map, tapping my quill thoughtfully against the rim of the ink pot recessed into the corner of the desk, wondering which village or town I would be ordered to next. Recent months had seen disturbing reports coming back to the capital from our ambassador in Fossfjall that Crown Prince Sjur was stepping up the pressure on his mother, the Dowager Queen Vigdis, to declare outright war on Cothraine. The peace treaty that had been signed in the wake of a decade-long trade dispute between the two nations, regarding tariffs on the import of wheat and wine, had stipulated that the Crown Prince would wed Reilynn when she came of age. Maeryn had broken the terms of the treaty by deposing Connell and marrying Reilynn before her betrothal to Sjur had been completed. Diplomatic relations between the kingdoms had been steadily deteriorating ever since. I wished that I had better information coming from the Fossfjall Royal Court, but the black cloaks, Cothraine's secret service of spies, had gone to ground and disappeared following Connell's regicide. No-one other than Connell himself knew how many black cloaks operated throughout the Western Triad and he had taken that knowledge to the grave. I did not like the idea of a rogue force of spies operating inside Cothraine without oversight, but in the four years since the coup I had not found a knife at my throat in the middle of the night, so I tried not to worry about factions beyond my control. I had more than enough concerns within the sphere of my own power and dominion. To quell any hints of unrest, it had been necessary to redeploy some of my troops from the capital to reinforce garrisons at the border, as skirmishers from Fossfjall had been conducting regular incursions across the frontier. It had not been their intention to cause any damage, but only to test the strength of our defences and the speed of our response to raiding parties transgressing over the border. In response I had increased the frequency and strength of our border patrols. So far, the encounters between our patrols and the skirmishing bands had been cordial, with both sides unwilling to initiate hostilities, but as the celestial conjunction approached with the winter solstice, I was increasingly fearful that one of the hitherto playful encounters of brinkmanship between scout troops would turn into a bloodbath, precipitating open warfare on a grand scale. The alignment of the planes during a conjunction frequently sparked chaos and disorder, as daevae and aberrations from other planes crossed over to the material plane for whatever passed for a monster's idea of fun. It was not unknown for the resulting carnage caused by these extra-planar raids to be misinterpreted and spark wars between nations. With diplomatic relations between Fossfjall and Cothraine currently being strained at best, I was particularly concerned about the state of security on our northern border. I knew that despite having a large advantage in numbers over Fossfjall's Field Army, Cothraine was still potentially vulnerable, as most of our experienced commanders had been fatally retired during Maeryn's coup and the subsequent purge. It was regrettable that they had not shared my insight into the events leading up to the coup and had chosen to remain loyal to Connell, resulting in their liquidation by the regiments under my command. My promotion to Field Duke had come to me practically by default, having been the highest ranking officer to support Maeryn's coup. The majority of my Field Barons were inexperienced and newly promoted Lords or Knights who had been elevated not because of their ability, but their willingness to swear fealty to the new king, Maeryn. The majority of these officers were untested in battle and I did not fancy their chances against the more experienced generals leading the Fossfjall army. I had a total of thirty-two thousand men at my command. Twelve thousand I kept in reserve in the capital at Clongarvan. Eight thousand were based at the Birlone garrison to secure the Rift at our eastern border with Sundgau and there were token garrisons at Bray and Moonchion of two thousand men each to assist the city guard. In response to the increasing number of raids across the border by companies of Fossfjall cavalry, I had reallocated two thousand men from Clongarvan to reinforce my two northern fortresses that guarded the two main access roads crossing our northern border. The Pineholm garrison, north of Croycullen, now numbered four thousand men, and I had a further six thousand soldiers based at Sylane and Kinvarra guarding the border on the west coast road between Clongarvan and Lesøsnø. I hoped that the extra battalions I'd assigned to the northern frontier would provide a sufficiently obvious deterrent to discourage further groups of skirmishers from making jaunts across the border to test our defences, but I was concerned that it was only a matter of time before one of the encounters between my troops and the Fossfjall scout cavalry sparked a major diplomatic incident. Spirits frequently became heated in the run up to an alignment of the planes, and the conjunction due to occur at the coming winter solstice was particularly ill-omened. As fate would have it, the solstice this winter coincided exactly with the largest and most perfect alignment of the celestial planes for several thousand years. The last of these conjunctions had resulted in the destruction of the Nagyjik Empire, the forerunner of the Western Triad of Fossfjall, Cothraine and Sundgau. Nagyjik had once been the cultural heart of the world of Dachaigh, but the hubris of its rulers had precipitated its catastrophic downfall at the hands of demons, which had taken advantage of the thinning of the boundaries between the planes during the conjunction to flood onto the material plane and overwhelm the cities of the Nagyjik Empire, leaving only a vast, parched desert and ruins in their wake. Even the most level-headed of men were known to make poor decisions during times such as these, when the heavens themselves appeared to abandon reason, and Maeryn could hardly be described as a man of good judgment. While I found it unlikely that the king's intemperance would cause a disaster as dramatic of the disintegration of the Nagyjik Empire, I was still wary of Karryghan's ultimate motives. Why he would throw his support behind the purge of a widely loved and respected royal family in favour of the largely unknown son of a disgraced baronet remained a mystery that no-one had divined an answer to, despite a full four years having passed since the coup and purge. Even though I had participated in the coup for purely selfish reasons and had little respect for the new king, I did love my country. Whatever happened in the coming months in the lead up to the solstice, I prayed to my patron deity, the Warrior, in the hope that I would still have a country left to protect after the conjunction.

6 – Karryghan

It was a rare day that called for me to conduct business outside of the Tower of the Aether. This day would prove to be doubly rare, in that I had two appointments to attend to beyond the tower in the wider city of Clongarvan. Neither was likely to be pleasant, but both were vital. My first port of call was the Stockade, the most secure gaol in the Western Triad, which formerly had been run by the black cloaks, Cothraine's Royal Secret Service of spies and assassins. The black cloaks had gone underground and apparently self-immolated following the regicide of King Connell, just as I had anticipated, allowing me to install my own cadre of interrogators in the clandestine facility. Dozens of my enemies, both great and small, had found themselves unwilling and permanent guests in the city's least welcoming dungeon in the four years since the coup. I rarely visited the Stockade in person, but today was a truly special case. My second appointment beyond the tower was with King Maeryn himself, the man I had elevated to the throne to further my own agenda. The outcome of the interrogation I was about to supervise in my first appointment would determine the nature of the second. Normally I would not stoop to dealing with a fool as lowly as Maeryn in person. I generally preferred to use a simulacrum or apparition to speak with him remotely, but I was well aware of Maeryn's mental laxity and his overbearing fondness of the fermented grape, which meant that genuinely important tasks had to be assigned in person. It was a mild inconvenience, but ultimately an essential one. I would not have chosen Maeryn to be the beneficiary of the coup deposing Connell had he been a more capable or conscientious individual. His weakness of character, his lack of insight and paucity of conviction made him tiresome to deal with, but Maeryn's overweening neediness left him exceedingly vulnerable to manipulation, which was exactly the quality I wanted in my proxy for the throne. Unwilling to attract too much attention on the short journey across the city, I had left the Tower of the Aether via a hidden portal and dispensed with my formal robes of office and usual escort of eight Masters, one from each of the licensed schools of the Art. While it was unlikely that anyone would recognise me as I walked through the trade quarter to the Stockade, I had not held onto my position as Arch Mage for over four decades by being careless. Any would-be assassin foolish enough to get too close to my walking stick would quickly and fatally dispel the glamour charm that disguised its actual form and unleash a force-shield shockwave capable of throwing a knight in full plate armour thirty yards. I kept up a brisk pace, my confident and purposeful demeanour alone being sufficient to deter the idle curiosity of the throng of shoppers and stall-keepers in the hive of markets that cluttered the square around the Guildhall. The Stockade was a nondescript, unimpressive building, as you would expect from a former stronghold of the secret service. From the street it appeared to be a single-floored, oak-framed town house with plain wattle & daub walls and a dull grey slate shingle roof, easily mistaken perhaps for the domicile of a modestly successful tailor or iron merchant. Beneath street level however, it contained an extensive stone dungeon, specifically engineered to contain the most dangerous enemies of the state. The gaol had no less than three score cells, each one designed to host a single prisoner in solitary confinement and complete sensory deprivation. Half a dozen of the chambers were lined with aetherium cages, which had been enchanted to prevent the casting of arcane spells. The prisoner I was coming to see was being held in one of these, though I would not visit him there. I would not permit myself to enter an environment where I was unable to access my aetheric affinity and mastery of the Art, not even temporarily. I rapped the wyvern head carving at the apex of my walking stick three times in the centre of the door to signal to the guards inside the Stockade that I had arrived. There was a muffled scraping of half a dozen heavy aetherium bolts being withdrawn as the door was unlatched. The door opened silently on well-greased hinges and I was greeted reverentially by the ranking grey cloak officer in charge of the small detachment of City Guards that secured the anteroom to the dungeon.

"Welcome, your Excellency. Lady Laoise is expecting you in the main interrogation chamber. She is just making the prisoner comfortable as we speak." The Baron Constable reported, with a hint of irony at the last.

"No doubt, my Lord Kester. I trust the blacksmith arrived to you unharmed?"

"Yes, your Excellency. He was a little worse for wear from the road, but nothing more serious than dehydration and a bruised arse." Baron Kester said, as he signalled to his men to re-secure the front door. The grey cloak officer turned and courteously pointed me in the direction of the interrogation chamber with an open palm. "This way please, your Excellency."

"I daresay a tender posterior will be the least of our blacksmith's troubles before the day is out." I said with a resigned sigh. Personally I found the notion of violence and physical torture distasteful, but recognised that the threat of bodily harm could be a profound motivator for people untrained in resisting such techniques. "Lady Laoise's enthusiasm for her craft occasionally gets the better of her."

Baron Kester, wisely, kept his own counsel on what he thought about Laoise's level of dedication to her chosen profession. Likewise, I did not volunteer to further my own opinion, as it was a subject she was legendarily, one might say infamously, touchy about. I noticed the air temperature dip by half a dozen degrees as Kester escorted me down two dozen flights of steps into the belly of the dungeon. The mottled salt-and-pepper amphibolite stone was flecked with tiny crystals of red garnet that caught the flickering light of the gas lamps studding the walls attractively, belying the grim purpose of the Stockade's construction. The choice of stone used for the dungeon's construction was no accident. The amphibolite had not been selected for its aesthetic qualities, but because it was extremely strong and hard-wearing, plus the tiny garnet crystals studded throughout the rock absorbed spells more readily than the stone. When the Stockade had been constructed during the First Succession War with Sundgau two hundred years ago, the Arch Mage of the time had inculcated the dungeon walls with aetheric charms that were capable of restraining or killing any prisoner attempting an escape via either physical or magical means. The centuries-old energies still made my senses tingle with apprehension whenever I had to visit this place, giving me all the greater reason to conduct my business swiftly.

Lady Laoise waited for us patiently in serene silence before the steel-reinforced oak door sealing the main interrogation chamber. To the untrained eye, Cothraine's chief torturer did not appear to be a threatening figure at first glance. Laoise was a petite, ashen blonde woman in her mid-thirties, slight of build and plain in looks. But at second glance, the air about her would unnerve the bravest of knights in Cothraine's Field Army. Her constantly-moving, dextrous fingers were long and thin, with short unpainted nails. Her lips were equally thin and humourless, but it was her powder blue eyes that were most unsettling. There was no life or joy in or behind them at all, as if they had been blown from glass. Laoise was arguably the most prolific killer in the Western Triad, albeit one on the Crown's payroll. She was the only black cloak of King Connell's Secret Service who had not deserted her duties after Maeryn's coup. When you learned the nature of the abuse she had suffered for years as a young child, it was easy to understand why she had remained in her post, but only an imbecile would discuss such matters openly, lest they end up on the receiving end of Laoise's dedication.

"Your Excellency Karryghan, I have prepared the prisoner in accordance with your strict guidance," said Lady Laoise, her voice as flat as a windless lake.

"Thank you, Shadow Count Laoise." I briefly bowed my head in gratitude, mindful of protocol. Officer ranks in the public services of Cothraine were not distinguished by gender or sex, unlike an honorific. "Your attentiveness to detail is noted and appreciated once again, my Lady."

The torturer did not smile, simply half-turning her head towards the closed door behind her. "Shall we begin the interrogation, your Excellency?"

Baron Kester interjected before I could respond. "With your permission, your grace, I should return to my post."

"By all means, Baron Constable, you may go." I said inclining my head, dismissing the grey cloak with the barest hint of gratitude. I turned back to the diminutive interrogator. "After you, my lady Laoise."

As I passed the threshold of the torture chamber, I was pleased to note that my instructions had indeed been followed precisely to the letter. The stone floor and walls had been thoroughly scrubbed and disinfected with surgical spirit and at least one bundle of incense had been burned to cleanse the atmosphere of the stench of previous interrogations. The gruesome paraphernalia of Laoise's trade were laid out on benches and shelves lining the stone walls. Pincers, tongs, knives, saws and pokers of every size and shape imaginable were arranged meticulously in cabinets and each one was freshly polished and sharpened. Vices to crush fingers, toes and limbs were also hung on the stone walls. A freshly lit fire in a brazier crackled and popped at the far end of the room, occupying the corner opposite an iron maiden, its case open wide, ready to embrace its next victim. A rack, centrifugal breaking wheel, iron chair and torture table formed the corners of a square in the chamber, each device facing inward towards each other, so that multiple prisoners could see each other suffering during a group interrogation. At the centre of the square, a recessed steel grate covered a pipe that would allow blood and viscera be washed away after the conclusion of a torture session. Seated in the torture chair was the man I had come to see, the blacksmith Maeryn's men had kidnapped at my order in Croycullen.

The wiry, grey-haired man had been stripped nude before being manacled to the chair with aetherium chains around his wrists, ankles and waist. He had not been gagged or blindfolded, to let his sense of dread build and fester. Letting him anticipate the horrors to come would hopefully make him more receptive to persuasion before there was a need for any bodily mutilation. His skin was beaded with a slick sheen of nervous sweat, despite the chill air in the torture chamber, and his brown eyes looked furtively around the room. As Baron Kester had reported, he was physically unharmed, save for a few bruises and lesions from the journey from Croycullen to Clongarvan. Laoise made a show of deliberating languidly over which implement of torture she would first use upon his flesh, picking up each instrument in turn and caressing it with an obscene tenderness; A poker first or a pincer? The thumbscrew, or a scalpel? Maybe a bone saw, or perhaps an iron spider? She took her time, pondering so many

difficult decisions. When I stepped into the blacksmith's field of view, I saw the tension in his body abruptly vanish.
"I was wondering whether you would come." said the blacksmith.
"Eoghan of Ballinlara. I can barely believe my eyes." I replied, shaking my head slowly in disbelief. "A Master Diviner, masquerading as a blacksmith in a northern hinterland of the kingdom... how does such an oddity come to pass?"
"I'm sure you'd like to know, Schemer." Eoghan replied, the contempt evident in his voice.
I fixed Eoghan with a stare of withering contempt and siphoned the aetheric energy from the glamour charm disguising my mage staff back into the wood, revealing the true form of the enchanted stave that had been granted into the custody of the Arch Mage of Cothraine ever since the formation of the Western Triad. I slammed the heel of the staff into the amphibolite stone floor, sending an echo reverberating around the chamber. The carved ebony wyvern figurehead at the top of the staff above the fore-grip sprang to life, opening its jaws to flash its myriad poison-laden teeth at the captive diviner, hissing fearfully.
"Remember your manners, Master Eoghan. Lest I have Lady Laoise feed you your heart. One does not desert your duties and obligations for a score of years without consequence. You know that your life is already forfeit. All that remains now is determining how much pain you will suffer before you tell me the information I need."
"Ask your questions, Arch Mage." Eoghan said, raising his bearded chin defiantly, even as the sweat on his creased forehead began to roll into his eyes. "You may ask, but I can't guarantee that I'll answer."
"Oh, you will - one way or the other." I glanced over at Lady Laoise, who had finally selected a set of narrow pincers and was heating their razor-sharp metal jaws in the yellow flames guttering from the top of the wood-fired brazier.
"But I would rather avoid the need for any unpleasant physical coercion."
"You mean torture. You can speak plain, Arch Mage." Eoghan rolled his eyes, his bravado in the face of certain doom holding fast.
"Would you prefer a prolonged, excruciating ordeal that would test the endurance of a deva, or might you rather

speak the information I seek and be rewarded with a swift, merciful death? I hope that is a rhetorical question, for your sake." I looked down at Eoghan, feeling only pity for the man who, two decades beforehand, had not only been a personal friend, but also an exemplary diplomat and a highly-valued member of the Wizards' Guild. "I do not wish for you to suffer unduly."

"Your concern is touching, Karryghan. But we both know that the only one you truly care about is yourself."

"Eoghan, your words wound me." I said, placing my palm over my heart in feigned distress. "But let us start from the beginning. One score years ago you were to lecture on the Art of Divination in Fossfjall to inaugurate your assignment to serve as Cothraine's attaché to the Guild of the Art in Lesøsnø. You could have sat as a Grand Master on the Council by now. Instead, you never arrived. Why?"

"I do not owe you any explanation or answer, Karryghan. Know this, instead: there's nothing that you can threaten me with. No duress or torture you that or your lackeys can envisage that'll compel me to answer your questions." Eoghan said without fear. "Everything I say will be a lie."

I sighed, quietly disappointed. "If you must tell me lies, at least do me the honour of not making them banal. I should give you credit, Eoghan. You forsook magic and lived as a commoner for two decades. Again, I must ask why?"

"I was seduced by a young maiden and fell in love."

"Do not insult my intelligence, Eoghan. If you continue to do so, Lady Laoise will hurt you most grievously." I snapped back, looking over my shoulder at the torturer for emphasis. The tips of the pincers she was heating in the brazier were almost white-hot. "Surely you must know that the epoch of the Seventh Prophecy of Nevanthi is upon us. To earn your title as a Master Diviner, you studied the texts just as thoroughly as I have. Tell me what really happened to waylay you on the road to Lesøsnø."

I picked up on a subtle, involuntary twitch in his cheek when I mentioned the prophecy, but still Eoghan bristled with defiance. "Ah, I see. You fear the judgment of the Dark Rider as much as you fear old age and death. You want the Nexus."

"If the prophecy is true, the aetheric nexus is manifest on the material plane here on Dachaigh for the first time in one hundred dozen millennia." I said, stepping closer to the captive diviner. "The Nexus grants the one who wields it almost unimaginable power. The ability to walk the planes from the Silver Citadel at one end to the Fel Pits at the other, or travel between the myriad islands of matter scattered across the material planes. I will have it. And you will help me."

"Help you, Schemer? Perhaps you're already senile, if you think thus." Eoghan scoffed.

"You had a revelation all those years ago linked to the manifestation of the Nexus. A secret you carry with you still. It is the only reason that explains your self-imposed exile. No maiden's beauty could ever compete with the wonders and rewards of the Art. Still, I wonder - the girl at your workshop, was she an apprentice, a lover or a daughter to you?" I asked, detecting a peppery flicker of anguish from Eoghan's psychic aura as I mentioned her. Intrigued, I attempted to probe deeper for the details of his attachment to her, but his mental defences were resolute and impenetrable.

"An irrelevance." Eoghan replied, his voice flat, revealing nothing.

"It matters not. Her bones will have burned to ash by now." I sensed a violet flash of regret seep through the psychic barriers erected around the renegade diviner's thoughts. The soldiers had been ordered to eliminate any witnesses. I silently reproached myself for not considering that I could have leveraged any personal attachments Eoghan had formed during his time in hiding. "You discovered something relating to the Nexus, something so profound that it impelled you to abandon everything that you once held dear. I am certain of it. You will either tell me what it was, or you will tell Lady Laoise. One of these options is far less agonising. The choice is yours, Eoghan."

"Do your worst, Schemer." Eoghan spat.

I glanced over to Laoise and gave her an almost imperceptible nod. She flexed the pincers in her left hand, opening and closing them with a rhythmic tap. Laoise let Eoghan get a good look at the glowing serrated jaws of her pincers, letting Eoghan contemplate where she would place them upon his body. The torturer the lifted the end of his manhood with an utterly obscene tenderness with her free hand before the pincers descended and bit through flesh with a sharp, metallic *snick*. Eoghan's scream was long, loud and terrible, but the smell of seared flesh was worse. Laoise picked up the severed testicle with the pincers and let it ignite between the glowing blades, holding open Eoghan's eyelids with the fingers of her free hand so that he was forced to watch it shrivel and char.

Laoise's face showed no signs of emotion, but her alto voice drawled threateningly in Eoghan's ear. "This is just foreplay, wizard. If you think this is pain, just wait."

The distress in my voice was genuine when I spoke next. I detested the need for violence, but I would let nothing stop me from possessing the Nexus, not even the agony of an old friend. "You can make this end without suffering further. Just tell me what you found. A clue to where the Nexus is located? Or something more?"

"Hells take you, Karryghan." Eoghan fixed me with his stare, grimacing bravely. This time Laoise didn't wait for my approval and worked the jaws of her pincers again, taking Eoghan's other testicle. She let the incandescent steel linger at the base of his manhood, searing skin and flesh to cauterise the wound so it would not become infected. Eoghan's shriek of anguish was even louder and longer than the first.

"Scream all you like, wizard." Laoise said with sadistic relish, whispering into his ear. "The chamber walls are baffled to block all sound. No-one outside can hear and come to your rescue."

"Do not resist further, Eoghan." I said as Laoise replaced the pincers on the heating stand next to the brazier and began collecting a dozen aetherium needles, each one as long as my forearm, from one of the cabinets lining the stone walls. "It will be a waste of your life. Tell me what you know about the Nexus. Do you know what it is? Where it is?"

"I've had twenty years to prepare for this, Schemer. My soul is ready for death. Is yours?" Eoghan asked, steeling himself for the next torture. His breathing became shallower as Laoise approached his chair once more, playing with one of the giant needles, spinning it around the fingers of her left hand. Eoghan bellowed in agony once more as the needle penetrated his flesh, spearing through his manhood clearly from one side to the other. When the helpless wizard appeared to master his suffering Laoise repeated the process with a second needle. Eoghan's shrill cries made me close my eyes and turn away, the taste of bile in my throat. I could hear the aetherium chains securing Eoghan to the chair jangle as his limbs quaked in torment and pain. It was several minutes before Eoghan ceased trembling and screaming. The torture chamber echoed to the sound of his rapid, ragged breathing and Laiose's satisfied chuckle of amusement.

"Do you know the wonderful thing about pain, wizard?" she asked, her thin, bloodless lips almost nuzzling Eoghan's earlobe. "Just when you think it can't get any worse, you find that there's always more."

Eoghan's next scream could only be described as inhuman, as Laoise studded his manhood with four more needles in quick succession.

"Stop." I ordered Laoise and she stepped back from Eoghan obediently, with half a dozen needles still held in the palm of her left hand. I winced in sympathy at the tears streaming down the wizard's cheeks. "I wish this were not necessary, old friend. But if you continue to make poor choices..."

"You always said I was a slow learner." Eoghan said, his voice cracking with agonised amusement. The captive Master Diviner twitched against his restraints, each one of his exhalations a short, hysterical bark of unhinged laughter.

"Then you leave me no other option. I am afraid that I must leave you to get better acquainted with my Lady Laoise." I turned to the torturer. "Do what you must, but you may not kill him. Send for me when he is more talkative."

"I will, your Excellency. Wizards can be difficult to break. It may be a few days." Laoise said.

"I leave the matter in your capable hands, Shadow Count. I will await your message with much anticipation." I managed to close the door to the torture chamber behind me before Eoghan's anguished screams recommenced.

I retraced my steps back to the Tower of the Aether, entering Cothraine's stronghold of the Wizards' Guild via the same hidden portal I had used earlier that morning. As I rode the paternoster up from the basement to my private chambers at the apex of the tower, I tried to quell any thoughts regarding whatever horrors Laoise was now visiting upon Eoghan. He had chosen his path, just as I had mine. There was no time for regret or doubt, as time was the one resource I had in limited supply. Even though I had the constitution of a man more than three decades younger, I was reaching the midpoint of my ninth decade of life and even though my mastery of the arcane arts was stronger than ever, I was aware that I was perilously close to the end of my time on the material plane. The manifestation of an aetheric nexus on the world of Dachaigh at this point, when my power was sufficient to master it and my life force was only just beginning to ebb away, was a welcome coincidence. A Nexus only came into being every ten millennia on the material plane, and as I had intimated during my conversation with Eoghan, it rarely appeared on Dachaigh. It was tantalising to have the key to my eternal salvation so close, but I knew I would not be the only one searching for the Nexus. Other forces, both angelic and demonic, were also certainly scouring all of creation for signs of its presence. Fortunately, I had a head start, thanks to the prophecies of the seer Nevanthi, a high priestess of the fallen kingdom of Nagyjik. I had divined that her seventh prophecy detailed the circumstances that were now upon us, and her predictions were renowned for their accuracy. I had already precipitated the insurrection Nevanthi had anticipated, which had deposed King Connell and installed Maeryn as my proxy on the throne. Maeryn's marriage to Reilynn had stoked unrest with Cothraine's relationship with Fossfjall, as the continuity of the peace treaty between the two nations was dependent upon a marriage of alliance between Reilynn and Sjur, the Crown Prince of Fossfjall. Tensions were already simmering at the border, which suited my purposes as they provided me with an excuse to prompt Maeryn to send more troops to the northern regions of the kingdom – not to secure the frontier, but to search for the Nexus.

I stepped off the paternoster into my chambers and was greeted warmly by my adjutant. "Your Excellency, I was not expecting you back quite so soon. Was your business at the Stockade successful?"
"Not yet, Dervla, but it is only a matter of time." I said, placing my staff upon its bespoke stand of red aetherium next to my alchemy workbench. "Please bring my formal robes. I have a meeting later with the king."

"At once, your Excellency. Would you care for refreshments as well?" the teenaged apprentice asked.

"Just a goblet of water Dervla, thank you." It was far too early in the day for wine and I avoided drinking tea because oils in the leaves upset my stomach. I crossed the chamber over to one of my many bookcases, retrieving the leather-bound grimoire containing the prophecies of Nevanthi. I placed the journal on my writing desk next to the pewter goblet of chilled water my personal assistant had prepared for me. I stood silently next to my chair as Dervla redressed me, exchanging the plain commoner's shirt and trousers for my magnificently embellished raiment of office. The heavy purple velvet robe was stitched with thread inlaid with real gold, and the sigil of the Arch Mage was embroidered upon the chest panel, encrusted with cut diamonds, sapphires and rubies. Dervla settled the padded pauldrons on top of my shoulders and ensured that the high collar was correctly centred on my neck. She left the hood down, smoothing the tip to let it settle between my shoulder blades. I dismissed the apprentice as I took my seat at the desk. "That will be all for now."

Dervla bowed respectfully and returned to the privacy of her room to continue her studies. My eyes followed her out with an appreciative smile. The girl was the Guild's the outstanding apprentice in the Invocation school of the Art. At just the age of nineteen, she was already able to cast fireballs and frost-cones, and was a formidable elemental duellist. Dervla was the youngest daughter of my favourite niece and had shown an uncommon fascination with the Art almost as soon as she had left the womb. I had gladly sponsored her admission to the Guild of the Art and I expected her to be promoted to the rank of Master Wizard before she turned the age of one-score-and-five, as she was on the already cusp of being ready to take the Trials that would see her graduate from the rank of apprentice to Wizard. Dervla was also one of the few women still able to arouse and satisfy my few remaining embers of carnal desire. Her predilection for older men had made it easy for me to convince her to take Fiacre as a lover, so that I could blackmail him into siding with Maeryn in the coup. Most importantly of all however, Dervla was also wise enough to know when to leave me alone and not hover expectantly behind my shoulder like an intrusive serving wench at an inner city tavern. She would go far with my patronage. I opened the tome on my desk to the page I had bookmarked with the tail feather from a golden eagle. The chronicle detailing Nevanthi's seventh prophecy was shorter than most of her predictive accounts but still ran to some four dozen pages. I had scoured the text hundreds of times over the last three decades, searching for insight into the location of where the Nexus would condense from the aetheric plane and what form it would take. All I knew for certain was that the Nexus had entered the material plane in Fossfjall. This was why I needed Maeryn to provoke a conflict with the northernmost kingdom of the Western Triad, so that the agents I had embedded in the Field Army could cross the border and retrieve the Nexus for me. Of course, I needed to know exactly where to find it first. I re-read the dozen pages of script detailing the appearance of the Nexus on Dachaigh. Using the oblique clues Nevanthi had included in her account of astronomical phenomena at the time of the manifestation of the aetheric nexus, I had been able to cross-reference her predictions with the latest data provided to me by the Astromancer Royal and calculate the exact date the Nexus had arrived in Fossfjall. It was surely no accident that the date coincided with the time when Eoghan had left Clongarvan and been due to take up his position as Cothraine's emissary to the Guild of the Art in Lesøsnø. The timing of Eoghan's disappearance was far too convenient to be mere coincidence, though I thought it unlikely that he had found the Nexus itself. It seemed more probable that he had discovered a clue to its location or form. If my suspicion was correct, it was reasonable to deduce that he had hidden this evidence in the blacksmith's hovel he had been hiding in for the best part of two decades. I needed a contingency plan in case Lady Laoise was unable persuade Eoghan to cooperate. I gulped down a mouthful of water from the goblet on my desk before standing. I collected my staff and stepped onto the descending chain of the paternoster, riding it down to the main reception chamber at the ground level of the tower. I sent one of the apprentice candidates waiting there to call for my carriage to be brought around to the courtyard at the front of the tower. As befitting my status as Arch Mage of Cothraine and Royal Consul, my official transport was more than capable of carrying a dozen people in the most opulent of comforts, while still being thickly armoured enough to withstand fire from anti-cavalry ballistae. The carriage was so heavy that it required ten horses to pull it at a reasonable speed, though even this was symbolic: each horse represented one of the ten gods of the Angelic Pantheon. Even though it was only a little over a league from the Tower of the Aether to the King's Tower in the Royal Palace's grounds, protocol demanded that I made the journey by carriage, rather than using one of the many portals maintained by the Wizards' Guild throughout the city. The trip may have been brief, but the solitude and calm was a blessed contrast to my earlier walk through the streets near the Stockade. I was able to gather my thoughts as the carriage rocked gently on its steel wishbone spring suspension, the motion as comforting as lying in a babe's crib as it swayed to and fro at the behest of a mother's touch. I was grateful for the opportunity to centre myself and simply be alone for a time, as my duties and responsibilities rarely gave me much time to enjoy the comforts of solitude.

My impending appointment with king was a singularly contrary case in point. Usually I preferred to converse with the king via a scrying apparition, as I found him intensely aggravating in the flesh. He was far too psychologically insecure to tolerate in person for long. The neediness of Maeryn's psychic presence was in stark contrast to the pompous bluster that he used to conceal his deep-seated inadequacy and fear of not being loved. Intellectually and emotionally Maeryn was as stunted as a brooding adolescent nursing the grudge of a perceived slight or injustice – precisely why I had chosen him to be the public face of the coup that had deposed Connell. Though manipulating him into doing my bidding and passing it off as his idea was child's play, it was a tedious game at best. It would not be difficult for me to persuade Maeryn to send a scouting party back to Croycullen to properly search Eoghan's hideout for the information I required, but having to redeploy the very same troops that had only this morning returned to barracks necessitated a personal audience. Maeryn could not be afforded the possibility to delay or ignore my request. I stroked the gemstones embedded in the aetherium circlet wrapped around my bald skull absentmindedly with my fingertips as the carriage drove along the avenue of white marble gravel chips that ran down the centre of the palace grounds, from the gatehouse in the citadel's defensive wall to the twin towers bracing the central keep. The jewel-like displays of summer-blooming flowers in the immaculately maintained parterre signalled that I was about to reach my destination. The carriage's wheels skidded to a jolting stop in the courtyard before the pale, limestone brick royal palace. I summoned my staff into the palm of my right hand with a click of my left thumb and middle finger. The gesture also unlocked the carriage door as my driver reined in the horses and stilled them with a single spoken word. A wave of my hand pushed open the door with a small impulse of force. I descended the steps onto the avenue and experienced a momentary bout of vertigo as I looked up at the towers either side of me. On my right was the Queen's Tower and the King's Tower was on my left. As their names suggested, they were the private refuges of the reigning couple of the nation. The King's Tower was taller, more robust and more obviously built with defences to repel an assault than the more elegant and ornately decorated Queen's Tower, but a keen eye could easily identify the fortifications embedded within the stonework of the smaller structure that would extract a fearful toll of casualties should anyone be foolish enough to try and seize the palace by force. I blinked to allow my eyes to readjust to the intense blue-white sunlight reflecting from the surface of the courtyard as I heard the rhythmic crunches of heavy boots on the gravel approaching from the portal to the King's Tower.

"Welcome, your Excellency. The king is expecting you." Duke Companion Aiden said, greeting me with a respectful bow that belied the seething fear and disgust in his psychic aura. Far from being offended, I was delighted to know that my presence still inspired the proper amount of reverence my position and abilities demanded. The young bodyguard gestured with his gauntlet towards the King's Tower. "This way, please."

I followed the purple-cloaked knight in silence and half a dozen steps in his wake, just to unman him further as he led me up the spiral staircase to the king's Privy Council Chamber. I made no attempt to make polite conversation. It would not do for the young duke to think we were peers

in any way. His promotion to Duke Companion was entirely due to the man's profound lack of moral fortitude. The ease with which he had accepted Maeryn's order to personally slay Queen Reilynn's younger siblings was evidence enough of that. Not that I could take the moral high ground in this regard, given that I had been the one to persuade Maeryn of the necessity to execute the entire royal family (barring Maeryn's beloved Reilynn, of course), but at least my motives had a higher purpose than personal advancement at court. My ambitions were far grander than ruling a single mortal nation. Duke Aiden announced me to the king, who sat slumped in his seat at the privy council table like a sulking child whose favourite toy had just been taken away. Maeryn nursed a crystal goblet half-full with red wine idly, already drunk before midday. I dismissed the Royal Companion without even making eye contact, the tone of my voice leaving no room for argument. "Leave us."
"As you wish, your Excellency." Aiden retreated out of the room, closing the heavy oak door behind him with an overly-loud thud, as if to signal his displeasure at having been deemed a surplus party to the meeting.
Aiden's reputation as a gossipmonger preceded him. I knew he would remain standing just outside the door, with an ear practically resting against the wood, such was his desire to learn of events above his station. A silent tap of my staff on the purple slate tiles on the floor conjured a shimmering, vibration-damping bubble that swelled to fill the room in a heartbeat. No sound could pass through the ethereal membrane, ensuring that no-one would overhear the details of the discussion I was about to have with the king. Maeryn swirled the wine around the bowl of his glass, watching the full-bodied liquid leave skeins and droplets behind that clang to the surface of the crystal as the wine rolled around the inside of the goblet. I did not inquire as to the cause of Maeryn's sullen mood. The king's mercurial whims held no fascination for me and I was certain that he would volunteer the information soon enough. I cut straight to the chase, having no inclination to salve the king's insecurities. Maeryn wore the crown only with my unspoken permission and I did not hesitate to remind him of it when necessary. "Maeryn, pay careful attention to what I am about to say. The details are of critical importance. I require

you to send a troop of men back to Croycullen to search the remains of Eoghan's workshop. A staffel of no more than three score men and horses will suffice, but they must all be experienced trackers. And they must leave before sunset. Speed is of the essence."

"Send men to Croycullen? Have they not just returned?" Maeryn drawled, paying more attention to the intoxicating fluid in his glass than my words. "Did you forget something the first time around?"

My temper flared and a violent flick of my finger projected a wave of force that ripped the goblet from Maeryn's loosely curled fingers, splattering wine into his eyes and dashing the crystal to smithereens against the frame of Maeryn's newly installed portrait, which had been mounted on the oak panelling above the fireplace. Maeryn staggered to his feet in shock, wiping away the alcohol that was stinging his eyes. I spoke loudly and sharply to communicate a sufficient amount of disappointment and displeasure in Maeryn's ability to carry out my edicts. "Had you paid proper attention to my instructions the first time, you would have thought it prudent to have your soldiers conduct a proper survey of Eoghan's domicile before razing it to the ground."

The so-called king raised his hands in supplication, his high, weak voice queepling in reply as meekly as a newly-hatched duckling desperate for the warmth and security of its mother. "No, please stop!"

"Do not question my orders again Maeryn, lest I show you the true nature of power." I warned him, contempt dripping from my every word. "You rule the palace only because I permit it."

"Sorry, your eminence, I will do as you command." Maeryn's cheeks were stained with wine, the only colour on a pale face drained of blood by his fear. "Much preys on my mind lately. Reilynn still shows me no respect and I am told that there are rumours in the city that question my ability to sire an heir."

"Such pathetic mewling is not becoming of a king." I scoffed with a loud snort of derision. "Monarchs do not ask for respect. They command it, as demanded by their divine right. If you wish to truly make Reilynn your queen, put your child in her belly."

"But she will not permit me to stay the night in her chambers." Maeryn said, crestfallen.

"Maeryn. You recall why the coup was necessary, I hope? Once we find the Nexus, the mortal concerns of kingdoms and heirs will be trivialities as far beneath us as the rivalries between neighbouring ant colonies on the royal parterre. If you cannot impose your will here upon a mere woman, then you shall not be of any worth to me on the astral planes."

"Then what is your recommendation regarding Reilynn, your Excellency?" Maeryn asked, his watery eyes opened wide in the anticipation of my wisdom and guidance.

"Find your backbone and use it prise open her thighs, if you truly want her." I told him, with a dismissive wave of my hand. I made my way to the council chamber's exit with long, purposeful strides to emphasize my physical supremacy over the hobbled king. "This talk bores me. I have more important matters to attend to than your lovelorn cock. Ensure that your scouts are on their way to Croycullen before nightfall, Maeryn. If I need to remind you of your duties again tomorrow, you will not have a prick with which to sting Reilynn."

7 - Cathal

It was midway through the fifth week of her recovery when I deemed that Ailidh was ready to make the trip through the forest back to her ruined home in Croycullen. Her burns had healed much faster than I had anticipated. I wondered whether this was due to the disfigurement she had received in the past and if it had better trained her body to heal burn damage. It seemed a plausible theory, but I did not dare broach the subject with Ailidh. At first, she had been reticent about being dependent upon me for the daily checks and replacement of her bandages, but the placement of the wounds and the catastrophic break in her leg did not leave her any choice in the matter. As the days passed and we talked to get to know each other better, I gradually sensed that she was less coy about letting me clean and nurse her. Indeed, by the time she had healed enough for me to set her broken leg in a cast, two days into the third week of her convalescence, it was I who had to conceal my discomfort and embarrassment. Ailidh had perched herself on the edge of the bed, her right leg fully extended, with her foot propped up on a stool. The splints held her lean, toned limb perfectly straight, allowing me to check whether the orientation of both breaks in her thigh bone had properly realigned and that the bone had started to reform without an offset between the fractures. I had been concerned that I might not have properly straightened the breaks in her upper leg during the hasty resetting of the fractures I had been forced to carry out on the smithy lawn, but it appeared that the Lady had smiled upon me. As far as I could tell, Ailidh's shattered femur had begun to reform as perfectly as I could have hoped. Given enough time to heal, the bone would be stronger than if it had never been broken in the first place.

Ailidh had pulled the hem of her smock up past her hips, bunching the thin cotton just above her waist, so that I had free access to the whole length of her leg as I worked to apply the cast. She held herself still, her left foot firmly braced on the tile floor, her elbows supporting her torso as she partially reclined on the mattress, legs parted and her sex fully exposed. I tried to ignore the delicate shifts in the way Ailidh repositioned her hips as I slowly withdrew the splints, meticulously binding her right leg from hip to toes in strips of cotton soaked in liquid plaster clay. It took over an hour to apply the cast and Ailidh's girlish giggling did not help with my sense of unease.

"I'm sorry, Cathal. It's cold and it tickles." Ailidh explained, biting her lip and hiding her face behind her fringe.

At first I had tried to dismiss her coquettishness as a mere childish infatuation, but over the weeks I had begun to notice her start to display frequent, subtle signs of a more profound burgeoning attraction: flushed cheeks, dilation of her pupils and lingering glances that bordered on impropriety. While I enjoyed her company, I was not romantically attracted to her, so I was careful not to lead Ailidh on, ignoring her lapses into flirtatiousness and ensuring that she could not interpret any of my attentiveness to her inappropriately. Once the cast had cured and was sufficiently dry and rigid, Ailidh was back on her feet with enthusiastic relish, albeit with the aid of the pair of wooden crutches I had made for her. She wasted no time in exploring the rest of the cabin and my woodland enclosure. I was pleasantly surprised to learn that she knew how to read. That was something I would not have normally expected of a blacksmith's apprentice. She steadily devoured her way through the bookshelves in my library of second-hand books and scrolls I had scrounged during my exile, selecting texts indiscriminately from subjects as diverse as metallurgy, military tactics, genealogy, theology and the history of magic. We spent long evenings discussing her thoughts on the books she was reading over leisurely dinners and warming goblets of wine. Ailidh proved to be an engaging and opinionated companion, willing to discuss any topic from the best techniques for forging weapons to the evidence for the existence of the gods of the Pantheon. We disagreed quite often, especially about theology, but always in good humour. She talked with the broad, clipped vowels and accent of a northern commoner in marked contrast to the received pronunciation of the Clongarvan nobility I had been taught to adopt during my apprenticeship to the Sylvanian Order of Rangers, but it rapidly became clear to me that her mind and wit was as sharp as my longsword. It had only required two pointed debates for me to realise that despite her humble origins, Ailidh was capable of eviscerating the logic of my arguments as easily as a bear might disembowel a sheep. I was so used to my younger sister Gormlaith dismantling my intellectual reasoning that I felt no resentment at being bested by the apprentice blacksmith. If anything, it made me appreciate her company and intelligence all the more. Had it not been for the difference in our ages and the mysterious and repellent nature of her disfigurement, I might have considered Ailidh more seriously in the romantic sense. I noticed that she always chose to seat herself so that I only ever saw her face from the left profile, never from the right. She was careful to stay at my right shoulder whenever we walked together, self-consciously trying not to reveal the burned side of her face, even though I had not reciprocated any signs of her romantic interest in me. Now that it was re-growing, Ailidh had trimmed her hair to disguise where it had been frazzled away, giving her an exotic, asymmetric appearance. She parted her hair over her left eye, combing her fringe to the right, dropping a blonde curtain of hair over her inhuman right eye, along the ridge of her nose and the side of her mouth until it reached her collar bone, concealing her scarred cheek, neck and half-melted ear from view. On the left side of her face, her hair only reached down to her chin and Ailidh kept it tucked behind her ear. She had used a razor to blend the two different lengths together around the back of her head, keeping her hair short at the top of her neck. The effect was striking and suited her well, but I often found it unsettling when Ailidh let her gaze linger on me for too long, her crimson eye hidden sinisterly behind a golden shroud. Occasionally a gust of wind, or the slip of a misplaced crutch, would give me a glimpse of the disfigurement Ailidh went to such lengths to conceal. The sight of it always made me flinch. I shuddered to imagine the pain and terror that had caused such a horrible scar. I was reluctant to ask about the circumstances of its origin, unwilling to make her revisit or relive an obviously traumatic event.

After having spent over half a month in bed recovering from her burns, Ailidh was eager to get back onto her feet and push beyond the boundaries of my compound, her enthusiasm for exploration curtailed only by my warnings of the boar, wolves and other more dangerous creatures that inhabited the forest beyond. I resorted to keeping her distracted by tasking her to maintain my small forge and smelter. In just three days, Ailidh managed to refurbish the bellows and cast me a completely new set of metalworking tools. As she worked, Ailidh seemed oblivious to the heat, demonstrating that her experience in her father's ruined workshop had not given her a phobia of fire. I was equally impressed with the quality of her workmanship, which was superior to my own and easily on a par with that of her father. As her next project, Ailidh cast a pair of pig-iron crutches to replace the temporary wooden ones I had carved for her. She made the moulds from scratch, adding decorative ivy leaves and vine-like flourishes on the feet and handles. Ailidh dedicated nearly a week into making them, spending an entire afternoon attaching padded leather cushions to the top of each crutch with individually hammered brass rivets. The weight of the crutches helped Ailidh rebuild her strength and endurance as she followed me around my compound as I carried out the daily chores; weeding the allotments, restocking the wood store, digging over the compost heap and fetching eggs from the duck and chicken houses. It did not take long for our days to settle into a pleasant routine. Each morning I would wake Ailidh an hour after sunrise, check and change the bandages covering her burns before we shared a leisurely breakfast. Then we would busy ourselves maintaining my enclosure and checking the perimeter fence for signs of damage from the packs of wild boar that foraged in the woods around my cabin. When the daylight began to fail, we would retire back to kitchen where Ailidh would help me prepare dinner, finally sitting down for the remainder of the evening in the library room to read and make conversation. Every morning, Ailidh would ask the same question as I checked and changed the dressings on her burns, just after I had woken her. "Are we going to find out what father hid in the safe today?"

Today, a full three score and six days after I had brought her back to my cabin, I remained silent and I took my time before answering, loosening each bandage in turn, sponging each burn site delicately with warm, salty water and checking the wound for signs of infection. I heard Ailidh's breathing quicken and felt the almost imperceptible shift of her hips as I untied the bandages around her buttocks and left thigh. She shivered gently as I sponged the burns, thankful that they had almost completely healed. Only the two wounds between her shoulder blades on her upper back required bandaging again.

"Well?" Ailidh asked again, looking back over her left shoulder, as she lay belly down on the bed.

"I think today may be the day."

"Really?" Ailidh said, genuinely surprised and delighted. She turned over onto her back to sit up, apparently oblivious to the fact she was undressed.

My gaze was drawn by primitive instinct along the soft lines of her long, toned limbs to the curves of her breasts, waist, hips, and the fine tangle of fair hair framing her sex. Any feelings of arousal were quickly extinguished when the swaying of her hair allowed me to glimpse her scarred cheek and neck. I looked towards the wall, as if trying to preserve her modesty, when in fact I did not want her to realise how much her disfigurement still disturbed me.

"Yes," I replied, turning towards the door and coughing a polite, unspoken prompt to encourage Ailidh to cover herself with the bedsheet while I re-centred my thoughts. "Your burns have healed well enough to not be aggravated by walking, so there is little risk of infection. If you feel that you have the stamina to make the trip, we should go today while the weather still holds."

"Do we have time for breakfast first?" Ailidh asked hopefully. A quick glance over my shoulder was enough to confirm that she had made no effort to wrap herself in the bedsheet. I suppressed an unfamiliar resurgence of hot, carnal desire when I noticed that the hard buds cresting her breasts were flushed pink with excitement. I feigned a smile and looked away again, perturbed that she was so casual about leaving herself so wantonly exposed to my eyes. In the four years since Aoibheann's death, I had grieved for her and my desire to even so much as look at another woman had lain dormant. Now that the rough abrasions and scalds on her skin from the burning embers that had fallen on her during her flight from the ruined blacksmith's workshop had mostly healed and were starting to fade away, it was impossible not to notice that Ailidh's pale figure was capable of monopolising the attention of any man and inciting their desire.

"Of course," I replied, retreating quickly to the sanctuary of the kitchen to avoid the dissonant feelings of arousal and discomfort I felt in Ailidh's company. "We will both need to be properly-fuelled before making the journey."

After a large fried breakfast of duck eggs with boar belly rashers accompanied by buttered bread and beer, we set off on the most direct route to Ailidh's old home through the woods. Having anticipated a few days previously that our trip was imminent, I had made a quick expedition to procure her some new clothes. I could not simply loan her some of my own, given that her leg was still in its cast, so I had made a shopping expedition into the nearby village of Brogmor to visit the tailor and the leatherworker. The tailor provided me with a replacement dress of densely woven blue wool, a copy of the one Ailidh had described to me as being her favourite while arguing about the importance of fashion after our evening meal a ten-day ago. Naturally I had lost the debate, being unable to refute Ailidh's assertion that a woman needed dresses of different cuts and different colours to suit the sensibilities of events occurring at different times of the year and in various social situations. Not for the first time, I felt relieved to be free of such complex expectations, as men in Cothraine were rarely judged by the clothes they chose to wear. The double standard had infuriated my sister Gormlaith, which explained why she never chose to wear anything other than her wizard robes in public. From the leatherworker I had bought Ailidh a sturdy pair of knee-length walking boots and a fur-lined ox hide jacket, which she would need for the coming winter. Ailidh's cast meant that she was unable to wear both boots, so she had made a protective iron footplate for her cast, both to keep the plaster dry and provide extra grip underfoot from a series of short spikes around the edge of the sole.

As we made our way back to Croycullen, Ailidh set an impressive pace on her crutches, powered by her delight at being free to roam in the mid-morning sunlight. Ailidh had taken to navigating the rough terrain on her crutches like a duck paddling on water, using them to batter aside fallen branches and vault athletically over other obstacles in her path. The weather was cool but fine, with barely a cloud in the sky. The young blacksmith's apprentice was in a cheery mood, glad to be free of the confines of my cabin and enclosure. This early in the day it was unlikely that we would encounter any of the wild boars, wolves or other beasts that frequented the forest, but I had armed myself with my longsword and bow, regardless. We made excellent time, thanks to Ailidh's boundless energy and enthusiasm, reaching the razed workshop well before noon. We approached the wrecked building from the garden, pausing at the tree line. We listened and watched intently for signs of activity in and around the house for just shy of half an hour before breaking cover and crossing the overgrown chamomile lawn. The ruins were in an even worse state now than they had been when I had found Ailidh on the herbal grass. Only a few charred timbers from the first floor and roof remained standing and three of the workshop's stone walls had partially collapsed. Ailidh followed closely behind me as I conducted a cautious circuit around the house, checking the courtyard for any fresh disturbances in the gravel since I had last been to the ravaged workshop. The heavy ruts from the prison wagon that I had noticed on my last visit had been mostly weathered away and while it was possible to discern some new footsteps and hoof marks in the gravel that had been made after Eoghan's abduction, none of them had the characteristic sharp outline of a recent visitor. I estimated that no-one had come to the workshop in at least two weeks.

Ailidh pointed to a mound of collapsed stone blocks at the bottom of a large gap in the outer wall of the workshop, which had fallen due to fire damage from the sabotage of the forge weakening the integrity of the wall. "That's where I got out. The safe is probably under that pile of bricks. Father put it under the floor next to the forge."

"Let us hope that it is not buried too deeply. I would prefer not stay overlong. It would be unfortunate if I had to shed blood this day. Pray that no-one stumbles along to discover us here. We cannot risk word of your survival getting back to the king."

"The Lady owes me a bit of good fortune, Cathal." Ailidh said as she hopped up the ragged slope on her crutches into the devastated workshop. "But you're right. We shouldn't push our luck. This way, let's get to work."

The fire had absolutely gutted the house, but that had not stopped some of the more enterprising and less scrupulous locals from ransacking the remains. All the metal had been stripped from the forge and smelter. Even the brazier and anvil had been stolen. Warped plough blades and spearheads too badly damaged to be worth stealing littered the sooty stone floor. The charred oak floorboards of the kitchen and lounge had been ripped up to see if anything had been hidden underneath. Only the collapse of the staircase had prevented the looters from doing the same to the upper floor. I shook my head sadly. "Even an Arbaroche vulture has more decency than this."

"At least they couldn't get to the safe." Ailidh replied, moving a couple of the fallen bricks across the floor with the foot of one of her crutches. "Here. See this flagstone? It's under here."

"How do you know?" I asked, stepping back across the debris-strewn workshop floor to her side.

Ailidh smiled and tapped the four corners of the granite slab with the end of her crutch, pointing out where her name had been chiselled carefully into the stone, the letters just a quarter of an inch tall. "You just have to know what to look for."

I helped Ailidh clear away the other bricks obscuring the slab. It was unbroken and nestled in flush with the other flagstones around it, with no visible finger holds I could use to lift it. "Hmm. Is there any special way to lift it up?"

"I don't think so. You'll have to break it." Ailidh replied with a shrug.

"You might want to stand outside." I advised Ailidh as I retrieved my bow from where it was slung over my shoulder. Ailidh retreated back through the gap in the wall while I selected an arrow from my quiver with a fine, carbon steel head, nocking it securely to the bowstring before taking careful aim at the volcanic stone slab. My longbow had a draw weight of 180 pounds and the case-hardened, needle-like pointed tip of the arrow was easily capable of passing clean through a knight dressed in boiled leather armour at 100 paces. Breaking the flagstone would not be an issue. The problem was where the arrow might rebound after striking the slab. Standing at the top of the pile of

bricks, I directed the arrowhead precisely at the centre of the carved stone slab Ailidh had identified before letting fly with the arrow. As anticipated, the flagstone shattered under the impulse of the arrow's impact, fracturing from the dead centre of the slab in a spider-web pattern.
"Cathal, Look out!" Ailidh yelled as she took cover instinctively, shrinking towards the safety of the floor as the sound of metal striking stone echoed in our ears. The wooden shaft of my arrow splintered on impact as the wood and steel projectile ricocheted from the floor slab, shattering the tile into myriad stone fragments. The arrowhead and shards of wood from the fractured arrow shaft bounced wildly back up from the floor, the heavy steel arrowhead deflecting back from the stone wall at the far end of the workshop and embedding itself in one of the ceiling panels just a few feet above my head. The impact split the charred wood in two and I had to duck out of the way as the blackened planks came crashing down onto the stone floor. There was also a soft metallic clink, as a small bag of heat-cracked leather fell along with the broken boards. I pulled the blunted point of the arrowhead from one of the fallen ceiling panels and replaced it in my quiver. I left the wooden shaft of the smashed arrow and the goose-feather fletching where they had fallen, as they were cheap and easy to replace, whereas steel was expensive. Ailidh's eyes glinted in delight when as she retrieved the charred pouch from where it had fallen. "Hah! My purse! I told you the Lady owed me one."
She attached the purse by its semi-charred drawstring to the sash of her dress and joined me at my right side as I knelt to lift the fragmented granite pieces out of the stone floor. Having disposed of the larger debris, I swept away the remaining shards of stone and the dirt beneath it with my palm until my fingers felt the cold touch of metal. Ailidh handed me the blackened chunk of a warped plough blade to use as a trowel, so that that I could dig out the safe more easily. It only took a few minutes of work to be able to remove enough of the soil so that I could lift the deceptively heavy iron box up onto the workshop floor. A quick inspection of the safe's case revealed that a sealed, hinged lid was on one of the sides of the metal cube, but I could see no signs of a locking mechanism, and nor was there a

handle to assist in opening the box. I looked up at Ailidh, confused. "How do you open it?"

"I've got no idea." Ailidh shrugged, equally bemused. "Can we take it back to your cabin?"

"It would be better to open it here. I do not fancy carrying this lump of iron eight leagues."

Ailidh laughed. "But you carried me that far."

"Your weight is not quite so compact. It is not so much of a burden when you can spread the load." I explained. "You said that Eoghan told you that only he or you may open it?"

"Yes, but he never explained how." Ailidh said, settling down on the floor and laying down her crutches next to her cast. A strange look crossed her features as Ailidh regarded the safe. When she reached out to touch the lid, it unexpectedly jolted open on a spring mechanism, making both of us recoil in surprise.

"What did you do?" I asked, after taking a deep breath to try and calm my heart beat.

"I- I don't know." Ailidh replied, looking at me in wonder. Tentatively, she opened the lid of the safe fully and reached inside to retrieve the leather satchel inside. Ailidh opened the bag and emptied it, placing the contents on the floor before us. Inside there were just five objects. A heavy, scarlet cloth purse filled with gold sovereigns; a brown leather box embossed with tarnished silver runes; a small glass vial containing a dense, glistening liquid metal; a lump of obsidian glass larger than my palm, which was carved ornately into the shape of a nautilus shell; and finally a folded sheaf of vellum, addressed to Ailidh and bearing Eoghan's wax seal. The date written in black ink beneath the seal was just one week prior to the blacksmith's abduction. Ailidh turned to me. "He knew. Father knew they were going to come for him."

I replaced the contents of Eoghan's cache back into the satchel and gestured for Ailidh to sling the waist length strap over her neck and shoulder. I then assisted Ailidh to her feet. "We should go. It is not safe here."

Our return back to my cabin was, if anything, even quicker than the journey out to Eoghan's workshop. Firstly, because we wanted to avoid the possibility of being accidentally discovered by any of the king's agents that might be keeping an eye on the ruined building, and secondly, because Ailidh was desperate to discover the message that had been left for her by Eoghan in the safe. As soon as we were sat down at the kitchen table, Ailidh cracked open the wax seal and unfolded the large vellum sheet, shifting her weight on her stool in trepidation as she began to read what had been written by her father aloud for us both to hear.

My sweet Ailidh,

If you are reading this, I have failed to keep you safe until you're ready and it's likely that I'm dead.
My only desire has been to protect you from those that would bring you harm, but in order to do that, I'm sorry to say that I haven't been entirely as honest with you as I should've been. It pains me to admit that I'm not the man you think I am.
I have withheld many a truth from you, and now the time of reckoning is upon us. I will take the secret of your destiny to the grave if I can. Not to do so would place you in an even greater danger than the peril in which you currently find yourself. I leave all of my worldly possessions to you. I know that you'll use them wisely.
I make one final demand of you, my daughter. Even if suspect or know that I live, you must leave Cothraine immediately. You may find temporary refuge in Fossfjall, but for you to remain in Cothraine would mean your death, or worse. A dire epoch, as foretold by the seer Nevanthi, lies ahead of us all, where the dark intentions of Men and Demons alike could spell disaster for the very planes themselves. Knowledge will be your only defence in the time of strife to come, but you must uncover it for yourself. Visit the Great Library in Lesøsnø should you wish to learn more – I say too much as it is.
I regret that we never spoke properly of your mother. Fate brought me to her door during a winter storm worthy of the third circle of Hell. When we met, Sigrid was recently widowed and you had barely seen the light of your second moon. She was young, beautiful, kind and lonely. I loved her dearly and adopted you as my own blood. For a short time we made each other very happy. Sigrid died during the labour of our stillborn son, just weeks after we had celebrated your first birthday. I know that she must look down from the heavens upon you with pride. I wish I'd

been able to better prepare you for your role in the events to come, but you have a good soul. Stay true to yourself, trust your instincts, and the path to your destiny will be revealed.
Farewell, my fair, sweet Ailidh, I fear we shall not meet in this life again.

Eoghan of Ballinlara

"Cathal, I don't understand. If he knew when the king's men would come to take him and that we were in danger, why didn't he just have us leave months ago? And what does he mean by 'I'm not the man you think I am'?"
I took the letter from Ailidh's hand, scanning it quickly.
"Eoghan of Ballinlara – that is the moniker of a wizard. Your father is no common blacksmith, he is a Mage. And he left you some trinkets. What is that?" I asked, pointing at the obsidian glass nautilus shell.
"It's a Catalyst. Most proficient blacksmiths own one."
"What does it do?" I picked up the carved chunk of volcanic glass from the kitchen table, studying the glass shell intently. It was heavier than it looked.
"An Arcane Catalyst allows energy from the aether to be channelled into the fire of a forge. They're used to create the arcane fire needed for enchantments." Ailidh explained. "They're quite rare, and they need to be attuned to a person's aura so you can use it. A new one would cost perhaps as much as a hundred sovereigns. This one is attuned to my father and me, so it's not worth nearly that much now. It would take a couple of years for it to get accustomed to someone else."
"You make it sound like the Catalyst is alive." I said, raising an eyebrow sceptically.
"They are, in a way. I suppose it's like taming a wild animal. Without the guidance of the blacksmith, the Catalyst can't do anything with the aetheric energy inside it, but without the Catalyst, the blacksmith can't bring the aetheric energy out onto the material plane. It's symbiotic." Ailidh said, looking thoughtful. "But unless you've been taught how to use one, they're little more than a paperweight."
"What else do we have here?" I mused, as picked up the other items, inspecting them carefully. I held up a small, shimmering bottle to the light. "Is this quicksilver?"

"Yes, it's an enchantment reagent." Ailidh said as I sloshed the heavy, shiny liquid back and forth in the crystal phial. "It's poisonous, so be careful."

Chagrined, I placed the bottle back onto the kitchen table delicately. I devoted my attention instead to the embossed leather box. It did not appear to have a lock or an opening, but its weight indicated that it was neither empty nor a solid block of leather. I resisted the temptation to rattle the box and looked more closely at the runes. The silver markings were tarnished with grey oxide. The box clearly had not been used or cleaned for some time. I used my thumb to rub away some of the residue from the dulled metal and was surprised to see that I could actually read some of the runes. "Ah! I know what this is: a tarot box."

"Tarot? As in the cards?"

"Indeed. Your father, it seems, is a diviner." I turned the box over in my hands twice, searching for some kind of way to open it. "I have no idea how to open it, though. Not that it matters, since I cannot read the cards anyway."

"I didn't even know that Father owned them." Ailidh took the box from my hands to feel its weight and gave it an experimental shake. She shrugged in disappointment when it failed to make a noise.

I looked over the letter for a second time, quoting out loud again. "'You may find temporary refuge in Fossfjall' – might you have family there?"

"I doubt it. Father was the only family I ever knew. I'm more worried about this talk of a 'time of reckoning' and 'dire epochs'. It sounds like the ravings of a madman. And what's this poppycock about demons? I can't say I've ever met one." Ailidh scoffed.

"Pray that you never do. They do not venture onto the material plane often, but they are all too real." I said, with a shiver of fear. I had once seen the bloody aftermath of a daeva's attack on a remote holding in the West Riding. After eviscerating all the livestock, the farmer and his five children, the daeva had then raped the farmer's wife, its seed eating away the flesh of her belly like acid. The look of anguish on the face of her corpse was not a memory I cared to revisit. I was grateful for the distraction when Sapphire leapt onto the table next to my hand, angling for a scratch behind her ears. "Many seers and diviners have written about the Celestial Conflict. I am not entirely certain, but the name Nevanthi sounds familiar. Gormlaith spent many years studying prophecies during her apprenticeship as a chronomancer."

"It's a shame we can't just ask her." Ailidh said, her fingers competing with mine for the cat's approval. Content that she was being suitably pampered, the silver tabby laid down on her side and closed her eyes, purring with approval. "What d'you remember about it?"

"Not much, I am afraid. I never read any of the prophecies myself. But Gormlaith told me that the Angels and Demons have been squabbling over something called an aetheric nexus since the formation of the planes."

"Aetheric nexus?" Ailidh asked as Sapphire yelped, demanding further attention. Ailidh quieted her by stroking the cat beneath her chin.

"It supposedly has the power to form a portal between any two points within the aetheric plane, meaning that you could bypass the shadow and astral planes and go directly from the heavens to the hells. If it were ever to get into the possession of the Executioner the consequences do not bear thinking about."

"D'you suppose Father found it?"

"Not likely. If memory serves, the Nexus only forms once per ten thousand years, and can manifest itself anywhere in the material planes. It has not appeared on Dachaigh for hundreds of generations."

"I think I'd like to visit this Great Library. Would they have a copy of these prophecies there?"

"They have copies of *everything*: legend has it that all of the books ever published on Dachaigh may be found within its walls." I said. "If you are to leave Cothraine, as your father suggests, Lesøsnø is as good a place as any to go. Braden, the Lord Commander of my order, took refuge there after the purge. I could report your father's abduction to him in person. I daresay he would be strongly inclined to give you aid."

"You'd accompany me on the trip, then?" Ailidh asked hopefully.

"Of course, it is too dangerous for you to attempt the trip alone. But we cannot leave until your leg is fully healed. It is over four hundred leagues to Lesøsnø as the crow flies and nearer to six if we take the roads. You will not be able to make the journey on crutches, not now that the season turns to autumn. Besides, I need some time to make the necessary preparations for a trip of that length. After all, we will not be coming back."

8 - Ailidh

I smiled with a perverse pleasure when I threw my iron crutches into the smelter. Cathal had reluctantly agreed with me that I didn't need them anymore, now that I'd had a week to put some strength back into my leg after he had finally removed the cast. My leg had healed well, thanks to Cathal's expert resetting of the breaks in the bone and the rich, nutritious diet he'd fed me with since taking me into his care. My leg no longer ached in cold weather and a week of rigorous exercise followed by protein-packed meals had restored some of the atrophied muscle mass in my right thigh and calf. We were making our final preparations for the long trip to Lesøsnø, the capital city of Fossfjall, to meet up with Braden, Cathal's former mentor and the exiled Lord Commander of the Rangers. Cathal had advised me to reuse the iron in my crutches to make myself a weapon for self-defence. He had also requested that I use any excess metal to forge him a stiletto, to replace the one he had lost during the ambush that had killed Aoibheann during the purge. I decided to cast the stiletto first, since I had a limited amount of metal to work with, and given that I had no experience at all with using bladed weapons, I reasoned that Cathal's stiletto was far more likely to see use than whatever sword I decided to make for myself, so it ought to take precedence. I added a carefully-calculated amount of coke to the smelter, pumping the bellows at a steady rhythm at ensure that just the correct amount of carbon fused with the raw iron to transform it into a far tougher, more durable steel. Cathal watched me, fascinated by the precision of my work, as I poured the molten steel into the two moulds that would form the basis for his new weapon and mine. I moved over to the forge so that I could reheat the steel bars repeatedly over the course of several hours, folding and refolding the steel with my hammer, adding strength and durability into the rods of glowing metal. Once I was satisfied by the shape and feel of the two bars of tempered steel, I placed the longer rod for my own weapon into the brazier to maintain its pliability and focussed on the smaller bar I was going to use to create Cathal's stiletto. I looked over my shoulder towards the ranger and raised an eyebrow inquisitively. "Cathal, d'you have any paper?"

"Paper? Whatever for?" he replied, nonplussed.

I left the glowing steel bar on the top of my anvil as I retrieved my father's arcane catalyst from the pouch on the front of my leather apron and threw the enchanted chunk of carved obsidian into the heart of the forge's fire. I concentrated hard to feed aetheric energy into the heat spiralling inwards along the nautilus-shaped spiral, and the forge's flames immediately changed colour from a natural yellow-orange to an otherworldly blue-green. I fed more air into the forge and turned to face Cathal, smirking in delight at the idea of showing him my mastery of arcane enchantment. "How'd you like to never have to sharpen your knife?"

"The reagent for everlasting keenness is *paper*?" Cathal asked, gawping at me in disbelief.

"You've never had a paper cut? It's worse than losing an arm to a Kyotkan katana, or so I'm told." I said, only half-joking. I had cursed my father on several occasions for the injuries suffered to my fingers while filing invoices for his annual tax contributions to the Crown, but never for accidentally cutting myself on a newly-cast blade.

"Give me a moment." Cathal replied, disappearing briefly back inside his cabin. He returned a few minutes later with a thick, leather-bound tome from his library. "How much do you need?"

"Cathal, no! You can't!" I protested, horrified at the idea of burning a book. Father had taken great pains to instil an almost religious reverence for the printed word within me during my childhood.

"Ailidh, it is no sacrilege to commit these pages to the flame." Cathal said, showing me the ornately embossed leather cover, a sly smile in the corner of his mouth.

"Gonagall is the worst poet to ever to be committed to print. Gods know why I ever allowed it in my home in the first place."

"It's really that bad?" I asked, raising an eyebrow at him questioningly.

"You need proof?" Cathal smiled, flipping the huge book open to a random page. He began to read, loudly and theatrically.

The dark maiden sighed in delight,
As his weight pressed down
Her soft thighs parted without a fight

"Give me the fucking book." I interrupted him, my right hand outstretched and my fingers flexing, imploring him in an urgent and unequivocal demand. Cathal wheezed quietly in amusement, passing me the huge, weighty tome without question or further comment. I tore the offending page of terrible prose from the crimson leather binding and cast it into the arcane fire. As the blue-green flames leapt in enthusiastic delight, I plunged the short steel bar into the heart of the forge. I rolled the bar in the magical fire for several moments, waiting for the colour of the metal to change, which would tell me when the enchantment was fully infused into the steel. The steel bar glowed yellow from the heat, but it wasn't until I saw the metal shine ethereal chartreuse that I knew the enchantment had taken. I withdrew the bar immediately from the arcane fire, hammering it on the nearby anvil to reshape the rod into the diamond-like cross-section I wanted for Cathal's stiletto. The process was slow and methodical, as I reheated and reshaped the hot metal bar by fractions, my hammering eventually giving the knife a thin, fourteen inch long blade with a full tang extension into the slender, one-handed hilt, which I gave a spiked cross-guard, to both protect the user's hand and allow the weapon to be used to entrap and disable an attacker's weapon between the stiletto's blade and guard spurs. As the finished metalwork of the stiletto cooled, I pondered what to make with the remains of the steel I had smelted from my recycled crutches. I folded, reheated and refolded the metal a dozen times over the course of the afternoon, while I pondered what to make. I was grateful that Cathal was nearby to help guide the outcome of my thought process and ultimately help me make a decision.
"Have you fought with a sword before?" he asked.
"No, never."
"You will want a short, sturdy blade then."
"Why's that?"
"Shorter blades stay closer to your centre of gravity. They are harder to disarm and even quicker to strike than larger

swords. They can also be more versatile, depending upon your preference for stabbing or slashing blows."

"What d'you recommend, given the amount of steel we've got?"

"A sword with a single edge will be easiest for you to master. You said you are familiar with the Kyotka School of Metallurgy?" Cathal asked.

I nodded. "A wakizashi, then?"

"That would seem to be the most appropriate choice." he agreed.

The ranger remained silent by my side as he watched me work, enraptured by the intensity of my concentration. I refolded the longer metal bar twice more, each time adding extra coke to the fire to harden the steel that would form the tip and blade of the sword. The rhythm of my hammering was so regular that I almost entered into a trance while I shaped and refined every single iota along the iridescent cutting edge of the twenty-two inch blade into a glorious, almost infinitesimally-fine ridge of steel, which I blended gracefully into a robust quarter-inch thick flat bar at the rear, giving the sword its heft. I added a triangular groove to both sides of the blade near to the top of the fuller of the sword, from just behind the wedge-like tip all the way down the full length of the blade. This would prevent the build up of blood on the sword that could create enough suction to stop me freeing the blade from an enemy if I ran them through. Happy with the length and profile of the blade, I tore more pages from Cathal's sacrificial tome of horrible poetry and tossed them into the forge. I waited patiently for the arcane fire to turn the metal the correct shade of luminous green. Confident that the everlasting sharpness enchantment had imbued itself into the steel of my sword, I withdrew the glowing bar from the fire and plunged the nascent weapon into a trough of cold water, rapidly quenching the metal. As I'd planned, the thicker back edge of the wakizashi expanded less than the cutting edge as it cooled, giving my sword a viciously-pointed tip and a delicate, but lethally-curved cutting edge, making it equally deadly should I want to slash or stab at an enemy. I could see the layers in the steel give the temper line of the sword a beautifully undulating scallop shell-like appearance. It did not take long to cast the accessories that would turn the blade into a true sword. I used brass, alloyed with the last few remaining scraps of the steel to make the hand guard, blade collar and spacers, which would allow me to seamlessly attach the two-handed grip to the tang of the sword. Cathal helped me carve the wood for the grips of both my wakizashi and his stiletto, and I assembled the parts of my sword, using short, double-headed rivets to attach the two halves of the handgrip to the tang of the weapon. Cathal did the same for his stiletto and handed me a long strip of leather to cushion the grip. Once I was satisfied with the weight and feel of the grip, I secured the loose end of the leather underneath a spiked brass cap that I hammered on to cover the bottom of the hilt. I set down my tools and presented Cathal with my sword, the blade lying flat on my palms as I lifted the wakizashi at arms' length. The ranger slid his replacement stiletto into the empty studded leather scabbard at the right hip of his sword belt, and bowed respectfully as he lifted my weapon out of my hands. He took a few steps away from the forge into the yard to create space around himself, hefting the short sword in a two-handed grip. He whipped the tip of the blade through the air for several minutes in a practice form, almost too fast for me to see, testing the balance of the blade.

"Exquisite. I am almost tempted to keep it for myself, but I prefer a blade with a longer reach." Cathal said, turning to me with a respectful nod of his head, impressed by my workmanship. He flipped the grip of the blade around in his hand, pointing the sword's tip at the ground as he offered me the hilt. I took it from him uncertainly, trying to get a feel for the weight. "A sword as expertly-crafted as this deserves a name."

"No, definitely not." I laughed nervously. "Swords with names belong in fairy tales."

"Not true." Cathal replied, drawing his longsword. My mouth fell open when I saw the quality of the metalwork. "This is *Dìcheall*. It was given to me by my master when I completed my apprenticeship with the rangers."

I watched in wonder as Cathal danced on his tiptoes, alternating between a single and two-handed grip as the broad, straight and double-edged thirty-seven inch blade whistled through the air in a precise pattern of cuts and arcs. He stabbed the elegantly-curved tip of the sword vertically down into the ground less than a yard from my toes, letting me study the intricate, fine detail of the engraved runes decorating the sword's fuller, cross-guard and pommel.

"It's gorgeous." I gasped, hesitantly caressing the cord-bound hilt of soft black leather. I felt a jab of static when my fingertips touched the immaculately polished silver blade. I glanced up into Cathal's face, my eyes wide in surprise. "This is aetherium."

"Indeed. Green aetherium, to be precise."

"I can enchant this. Father left a phial of quicksilver for me in the safe." I told Cathal, excited. I'd only had the opportunity to work with aetherium a couple of times during my apprenticeship, because of its scarcity.

"What does that do?"

"Green aetherium is the best medium for ice damage enchants. Quicksilver is the only metal that's naturally a liquid. When infused to aetherium with arcane fire, it draws the heat out of anything it touches. Ice-enchanted aetherium is supposed to be the only metal that can pierce the hide of demons and daeva." I explained, laying my wakizashi down on the workbench next to the forge so that I could retrieve the bottle of quicksilver from the leather pouch I had liberated from my father's safe. The glass vessel of dense fluid was far heavier than it looked, and I held the small bottle of glistening liquid up for Cathal to see. "May I?"

"You would do this now?" Cathal asked with a doubtful frown. "It is almost nightfall as it is."

"Father left me the quicksilver for a reason, Cathal. I can't think of any better use for it than this."

The ranger considered my earnest plea with a resigned smile, seeing that I was unwilling to let the opportunity pass. "You have worked all day, but you are not even tired, are you? Very well, I would be honoured by this gift, Ailidh. I can only hope to prove myself worthy of it."

"Yes! Thank you, Cathal. You'll not regret it." Unable to contain myself, I leapt, whooping in joy, before turning to pump the bellows vigorously to reheat the forge, concentrating hard to bring the arcane fire back to up to the necessary intensity. When I saw the flames take on the correct hue of cyan and teal, I removed the cork stopper from the vial of quicksilver and threw the dense liquid metal into the flames. The forge erupted with violet and orange light. I thrust the blade of Cathal's longsword into the fire, turning the blade over constantly and watching the aetherium intently, waiting to see the tell-tale change in colour that would tell me when the enchantment had taken. I kept feeding the forge with air from the bellows, maintaining a constant temperature as the arcane fire worked, my patience and concentration never wavering while I watched the violet and cyan glow gradually spread from the sword's tip to hilt. As soon as the entire blade glowed from the enchantment, I plunged the longsword into the quenching trough, laughing in shocked delight when the water instantly froze into a block of ice at the enchanted metal's frigid touch.

"Well done, Ailidh." Cathal took my shoulders into his hands, congratulating me with a brief, heartfelt squeeze of affection. I looked over my shoulder at him and felt my heart melt under the warmth of his smile. "You have truly earned your dinner tonight. Seven hours at the smelter and forge, without a single break. Surely your sword can only have one name: *Caranachd*."

It was the ancient cothraini word meaning *endurance*. When I looked at the wakizashi lying on the workbench, I was struck by how appropriate the name seemed, considering the suffering I had gone through in the weeks leading up to its forging and enchantment. As I extinguished the forge, Cathal brought me a suitably large goblet of wine from the kitchen. I smiled, pondering the notion that perhaps swords with names didn't just belong in fairy tales after all.

9 - Aiden

As soon as she opened the door, Sìne ushered me swiftly into her bedchamber. It was long after midnight and the Royal Palace had been locked down until dawn. She kissed me long and hard on the lips as her small, deft hands busied themselves unfastening the straps on my armour. "What does my favourite little mouse have to tell me that could not wait until morning?" My hands were also occupied, but with carefully extracting the pair of long, lethally sharp aetherium hairpins restraining her waist-length, raven-black curls. It was actually true that Sìne was my favourite informant amongst the girls in the palace. She was also the eldest and longest-serving of the queen's dozen handmaidens. Her virtue was as loose as her lips and, rather sweetly, she jealously resented my dalliances with the other servant girls of the palace that I had seduced into my network of informants within the palace. I found the teenaged handmaiden lovely, though perhaps not beautiful in the truly classical sense, as her features were a little too flat and her dark eyes were fractionally too far apart, but her smile was full, her ears were delicate and her nose was as pretty as her petite figure was firm and slender. I also suspected she was hopelessly in love with me, which was almost as useful to me as her position as Queen Reilynn's most trusted companion and bodyguard. "Something very special, your grace, though it'll cost you." Sìne placed my golden, lion-crested breastplate quietly against the door and knelt to remove my boots, sword belt and thigh guards. It was not long before she achieved her goal and claimed her reward. Her mouth enveloped me, the only time her lips were not loose. Her hot, prehensile tongue and urgent, grasping fingertips left me gasping and she made appreciative, wordless and wanton sounds of pleasure as she finished me, tasting my seed in her mouth. "You had the roast duck tonight, and not too much wine. Good. It'd be a shame if you couldn't meet my price." "How is it that you always know?" It amazed me that she was never wrong about my choice of evening meal.

"A lady never tells, your grace." Sìne said cryptically, licking her full, scarlet lips with relish and giving me a predatory look of pure, erotic hunger that had me hard again in seconds. She led me to her narrow, single bed, peeling the sheer, bronze satin nightshirt away from her body like the skin from an orange, revealing the fair, fleshy temptations beneath.

"Fortunately, you are no lady, my little mouse. How much might that secret cost me?"

"More than you could afford." Sìne pulled me down over her as she lay back on the velvet bedsheet. My hands found her gorgeously pointed breasts and I squeezed her swollen nipples hard between forefinger and thumb as I mounted her. She granted me just a tantalising moment to let me feel her wetness and passion before easing herself off me and lying on her belly. "I've told you before, my lord. You can only have my slit after you marry me. Remember what happened to Aoife."

"Temptress!" I hissed like a wary adder, pretending to be annoyed. In truth, I understood her reasoning. The queen would not tolerate one of her handmaidens carrying a bastard. Just a month ago, the queen had dismissed Aoife, an orphaned servant girl working in the palace kitchens, for becoming pregnant by one of the chefs. I took Sìne's angular, sharp hips in my hands, lifting her upward, raising her onto her knees. Sìne turned her head back around over her shoulder. The look in her brown eyes was incendiary as she reached back to spread herself for me, her lustrous, raven-black tresses sliding off her back and falling down over her shoulders. She expelled a low moan under her breath, as I narrowed the gap between her hips and mine. I wrapped my arms around her slim form, my left hand holding her up to my chest by one of her small, apple-firm breasts, the fingertips of my right hand urgently exploring the slick cleft she had just denied me between her taut, wiry thighs.

"Oh, my love…" Sìne whispered, groaning softly, closing her eyes. She grasped the bed covers, twisting the fabric between her fingers when her slim buttocks pressed against my pelvis, her legs quaking gently.

"What did the queen say?" I breathed into her ear, licking and nibbling the tender pink lobe in the manner I knew inflamed her.

"Make me come thrice and I'll tell you." Sìne gasped with her eyes still tightly shut, already in rapture.

"This had better be good." I said as she began to move her hips sensuously in long, leisurely circles, sliding herself along the full length of my manhood to provoke the maximum amount of stimulation for both of us. Sìne's extortions for her information were always pleasurable ones, to the point that I feared her affections for me were far nobler than I really wanted them to be. The other servant girls of the palace were more mercenary: they always demanded gold, for both their information and their company.

After Sìne had extracted her price from me, we lay together on her bed, catching our breath and keeping warm beneath my purple and gold cloak. Sìne held my arms in a tight embrace around her and I kept her pulled close to my chest, enjoying the softness and warmth of her body against mine, feeling sated and drowsy. I was almost asleep when I remembered the original purpose of my visit.

"So, my little mouse," I stroked Sìne's smooth, silky skin lovingly, teasing and pinching her taut, pink nipples between my sore thumb and fingertips, to ensure that she remained awake. The teeth marks where Sìne had bitten me to silence her cries while I had caressed her sweet face at the height of her passion were still red. She always sucked my thumb to prevent waking any of the other handmaidens in the neighbouring bedchambers, but for me it meant that her pleasure was frequently a painful, but always worthwhile exercise. "What mysterious squeaks do you have for me?"

"The king tried again to work his way into the good graces of the queen again today." Sìne wriggled back against me, her voice soft and her speech drowsy and languid. "Reilynn wasn't impressed with what Maeryn had to say."

"I knew this much already, little mouse." I spanked one of her sleek buttocks lightly in jest, feigning disappointment. "I escort the king practically everywhere he goes. I demand a refund."

"I promised you something special, your grace." Sìne turned her head to kiss my lips. "It will not disappoint. Maeryn spoke to Reilynn about his plans with the Arch Mage."

"What?!" I sat up in surprise, fully awake again in an instant. My cloak tumbled away, falling off the bed, causing Sìne to shiver and press her body more firmly to mine, seeking warmth. "He spoke of what plans?"

"The Arch Mage has a grand ambition for himself and the king hopes to be swept along with him on the hem of his robe." Sìne retrieved my cloak from the floor and wrapped it around us again.

"Tell me everything." I demanded, turning her by the shoulders to face me.

"I will, my love. But you may not believe it." Sìne cautioned, correctly as it turned out. After she had finished her account, I rubbed and pinched my face to make sure I was not dreaming.

"You heard this from the king's mouth yourself?"

"Yes, my lord."

"And how did the queen react to this... plan?"

"She called him mad and a fantasist and threw him out of the tower." Sìne giggled.

"I must inform Field Duke Fiacre at once." I made to get out of the bed, but Sìne snaked a surprisingly strong arm around my shoulders to prevent me from moving.

"Aiden, it's late. Stay here tonight." Sìne tempted me with her offer, smiling seductively in the candlelight as she caressed my chest with soft, hungry hands, her lovely dark eyes glittering with intent as she imitated a coquettish, aristocratic accent. "Have I not done well, your grace? Do I not deserve a bonus?"

"Sìne, I may marry you yet." I said, returning her smile. The message for Fiacre would have to wait until dawn.

I left Sìne's chamber shortly before dawn, sated, thrilled and exhausted. As I kissed her farewell there was a genuine pang of sorrow in my heart that the continued deterioration in relations between the royal couple meant that I would not be seeing her later that day during the course of our duties. I resolved to find a pretext that would give me an excuse to call upon her again that evening, but first I needed to speak with the Field Duke before attending to the king. There was nary a cloud in the sky to greet me when I exited the Queen's Tower. The white roses on the parterre sparkled ultraviolet in the pre-dawn gloom, bringing a smile to my face. The weather would be warm and the skies would be clear today. It was a perfect morning for a walk to gather my thoughts. Rather than take one of the guarded alleyways that linked the royal palace grounds to the fortified compound that held the Army Headquarters, I took the long way instead, following the drive through the parterre to the gatehouse that separated the palace grounds from the city. I turned east towards the Bazaar and the trade district, walking along the freshly swept pavement. To my left was the reservoir and city waterworks that held the majority of Clongarvan's supply of fresh water, as well as several colonies of raucous gulls, ducks and terns, whose constant calling frequently kept me awake during the night when I slept in my quarters at the palace garrison. I turned right at the crossroads that hosted the city's most infamous drinking house, The Crimson Cutlass Inn, which was appropriately named, given that it neighboured The Warrior's Guild. The inn was notorious for the bawdiness and violence of its clientele. During my service in the City Guard, I learned very quickly that it was often better to let incidents run through their natural course, rather than try to intervene whenever patrols were called to quell a disturbance of the peace at the inn. A pair of young, brown-haired whores stood arm in arm, tired and bored, at the mouth of the alley between the two timber-framed buildings. The girls were barely in their teens and were desperately trying to turn a final trick before the sunlight hounded them back into the shadows. The taller one tried to entice me with a flash of her breasts and propositioned me loudly and crudely from across the street. "Wanna cum on my titties, m'lord?"

The second girl licked her painted lips provocatively as I passed in front of the inn. "Two copper pennies 'n I'll suck you dry, han'some."

Without even breaking stride, I strode by the nightwalkers as if they were invisible and ignored their increasingly depraved catcalls offering me their services. I offered up a silent prayer that the Goddess might grant the whores some protection and good fortune. All too often had I heard serving girls at the palace share the gruesome tales of murders that befell the unfortunate souls selling their bodies on the streets of the capital. The streetwalkers quickly lost interest when it became apparent that they had failed to persuade me to open my coin purse. The shorter woman spat a glob of phlegm onto the stone cobbles in disappointment and withdrew into the darkness of the alley with her companion.

The soldier manning the portcullis to the Field Army's city compound seemed less alert than the two prostitutes had been, as it took several moments for him to recognise the insignia on my breastplate and the royal coat of arms embroidered onto my cloak. The dozy serf apologised as he started to crank open the gate. "Beg yer pardon, m'lord." While it would not have been unjustified for me to castigate the soldier for his lack of focus, I let the lapse of attention pass uncommented, as I remembered the tedium of guard duty from my time as a teenaged serf in the grey cloaks all too well. As soon as the portcullis had been raised high enough to allow me to pass without stooping, I entered the stone-walled compound, making directly for the Field Duke's citadel, walking between the rows of barracks housing the lowest-ranked soldiers. A glance through the arrow slots in the citadel walls as I ascended the limestone staircase to the apex of the keep afforded me a spectacular view over the Bay of Tides, even though the blazing blue disk of Rionnag had barely poked above the horizon. The water shimmered and rippled in the early morning sunlight, and I paused to appreciate its beauty. Fiacre was a noted early riser and was no doubt already in his office, but with Sìne already having belayed my urgency to inform Fiacre of what she had told me about the Arch Mage and Maeryn, another moment or two of delay would scarcely matter. I wondered idly what the view of the sunrise would look like from the Royal Promenade, the private beach that was overlooked by the sea fort guarding the Royal Palace. It was the place where I had first seduced Sìne a couple of months after she had come of age, the fine white sand on the beach glittering like tiny diamonds in her obsidian black hair. A twinge of longing gripped my heart as my thoughts returned to the young handmaiden again. I swallowed my feelings quickly, trying to rationalise the sensation as nothing more than a lustful memory. I shook off my sense of unease, returning my thoughts to the business at hand and ascending the final flight of stairs quickly.

I knocked on the heavy oak doorframe of Fiacre's office to announce myself. The Field Duke raised his bald head in surprise. "Duke Companion, what brings you here are such an ungodly hour? I thought you would still be tucked up in bed with one of your talkative wenches."

"We need to talk. Well, I need to talk. You need only listen, to begin with." I replied, as I closed and locking the door behind me.

"What ails you this morning, Aiden?" Fiacre set down his quill and gestured for me to sit.

"I know what the king talks about with the Arch Mage." I said as I eased myself down onto the padded leather cushion of the armchair opposite Fiacre's desk with care, spreading my cloak to cover the frame. The Field Duke would not appreciate it if my armour scratched the varnish on the wood.

"Your network of mice finally overheard one of their conversations?" Fiacre asked, placing his quill back in to the ink pot on his desk. His interest was now firmly piqued and I was certain that I had his full attention.

"Not directly, no. The Schemer is still far too clever and paranoid for that. Maeryn let it slip during one of his arguments with Reilynn." I explained. "Maeryn was trying to persuade Reilynn of his love for her again and why he was a worthy husband. He told her that Karryghan personally chose him to be the beneficiary of the coup and that it was the Arch Mage who had planned it all."

"Yes, well we both suspected as much. What else?"

"The Arch Mage needed Connell out of the way so that he can use Cothraine's army to hunt for something called the Nexus. Karryghan believes it is somewhere north of the border with Fossfjall."

Fiacre bristled with undisguised irritation. "The Arch Mage already thinks we are little more than errand boys at his personal command. Did you know that on the very same day we brought back that rogue wizard masquerading as a blacksmith near the border, the king demanded that the wreckage of the smithy in Croycullen needed to be thoroughly searched for any arcane objects? Two scout troops of cavalry barely had time to feed and water their horses before being sent back through the Belhaven gate. I swear, Aiden, the conjunction drives men to insanity. What even is this Nexus supposed to be? What does it do?"

"It supposedly acts as a key to the astral plane. The Schemer does not lack for vision and ambition. He intends to use the Nexus to depose the Mystic."

"By the Warrior's sweaty ball sack!" Fiacre cursed, with a dramatic roll of his eyes. "Madness, I say."

"Indeed." I gave Fiacre a brusque nod of agreement. "Maeryn, of course, intends to cling to the Schemer's robes throughout like a child hanging onto their mother's skirts. Perhaps he thinks a trip to the astral plane will unhobble his leg and put enough iron into his rod to finally bed Reilynn."

"I take it the queen was not impressed."

"Hardly," I snorted. "She summarily banned him from the Queen's Tower. The magical claptrap worries me less than the idea of sending troops into Fossfjall to search for this Nexus. I fear Karryghan will stop at nothing to get his opportunity to take a tilt at the Mystic, even if it means starting a war."

"It would not require much in the way of provocation, either. Crown Prince Sjur is already seething at Maeryn for marrying his betrothed and breaking off the unification treaty. Border skirmishes have more than doubled in the last year alone." Fiacre said and drew my attention to over a dozen annotations that the Field Duke had made to the map of the border regions laid out on his desk. Each addition marked the location and date of a raiding party crossing the frontier between Cothraine and Fossfjall. "A full scale conflict would be a disaster for Cothraine. The purge badly weakened the officer corps. I have Barons appointed to command legions who do not have enough experience to effectively lead a company or regiment."

"Please let me know what your scouts turn up in Croycullen, your grace." I requested, slowly rising to my feet. "If I learn anything else about Karryghan's designs, you will be the first to know."

"Thank you, Duke Companion." Fiacre likewise stood, offering a meaty hand that dwarfed my own, despite the fact I was wearing a full-plate gauntlet. We shook hands amicably and Fiacre nodded his appreciation.

"I have to get back to the palace before the king wakes. I will send word if I learn anything about the location of this Nexus. We should endeavour to prevent any large-scale incursions across the border. I do not fancy ending up on the front line myself if Sjur retaliates."

"Agreed, my friend," Fiacre's scarred face betrayed his own concern. "It will end in slaughter if anything larger than a staffel crosses the frontier. I will not commit troops into Fossfjall unless I know exactly where this Nexus may be found."

"That is reassuring to know, your grace. Farewell for now." I said with a profound sense of relief. I gave Fiacre a respectful half-bow before unlocking the office door and returning to the King's Tower.

10 – Karryghan

I was accompanied by a heavy feeling of regret and disappointment when I returned to the Stockade. The previous morning I had received a characteristically terse letter from Lady Laoise informing me that despite her best efforts over some seventeen days, she had failed to break Eoghan. The renegade chronomancer had refused to give up any information of note regarding the Nexus, and Laoise had no more tortures available to her that she could employ without posing a clear and immediate danger to his life. I had therefore no option other than to take personal charge of Eoghan's interrogation and use all the methods at my disposal to coerce the information I needed from him. It was imperative that I take possession of the Nexus before the winter solstice in order to give me enough time to prepare the planewalking ritual that would transport me to the astral plane during the astronomical conjunction that coincided with the apoapsis of Dachaigh in its orbit around Rionnag. My divinations had revealed that the probability of me being able to assume the portfolio of the Mystic were highest on this most auspicious of cosmic coincidences. But everything depended upon finding and possessing the Nexus. I would have Eoghan's secrets, even if I had to bathe my hands wrist-deep in his blood.

Laoise greeted me at the entrance to the dungeon, her aura humbled and contrite. "Your Excellency, permit me to offer my deepest apologies. I've failed you."

"There is no shame in acknowledging when your talents have reached their limit, my dear Lady Laoise." I told her with genuine empathy. "I am certain that you have done everything within your power. Life would be so much easier if success was always guaranteed."

Laoise held her tongue, but nodded her acceptance of my kind words. They would have been accompanied by a friendly, reassuring touch to the arm or shoulder had I gifted them to anyone else, but being all too aware of the grisly details of the molestation Laoise had suffered as a child, I stayed my hand. Laoise would not tolerate even the slightest of touches from a man, even if their intentions were to offer comfort. My informants told me that Laoise only took young girls as lovers and that her proclivities were sadistic in the extreme. I shuddered to think of what state she had left Eoghan in before abandoning her efforts at extracting information from him. Laoise unlocked the heavily reinforced aetherium door to Eoghan's torture cell and lit one of the oil lamps mounted on the stone wall, revealing the pitiful shell of a man that had once been one of the preeminent diviners on the continent. Leather tourniquets were bound tightly around his elbows and knees, doubling as restraints that held Eoghan motionless on the metal frame that substituted for a chair. Almost every square inch of his skin bore the mark of some kind of mutilation or injury. Eoghan's cheeks had been slashed with a razor and his face was still covered by ichors that had leaked out from a burst eyeball. His genitals had been bifurcated and flayed of their skin. The room stank of urine, which leaked from a puncture wound in his lower abdomen that had punctured his bladder. The wound had been cauterised with a red-hot poker to prevent infection, leaving pale burn scars surrounding the hole. Eoghan's fingers and toes had been stripped of their flesh, leaving pale white bone exposed to the air. The soles of his feet were currently resting on orange plates of searing iron as they slowly roasted the flesh to charred cinders. I swallowed bile and resisted the overwhelming urge to vomit. Eoghan saw the look on my face with his one remaining eye and chuckled hysterically with amusement.

"Come to say goodbye?" Eoghan's voice taunted me, even though it was a weak, quavering shadow its former richness and tenor.

"In a manner of speaking," I replied with grudging respect. A lesser man would have succumbed from the shock and blood loss days ago. "Your endurance for pain is remarkable Eoghan, but sadly my patience wears thin."

"Your time on the material plane draws to a close, you mean." Eoghan coughed rather than laughed.

"I have longer than you do." I warned him, stepping closer to his torture chair, vermillion flames billowing from the eyes of the wyvern's head at the top of my staff. "Much longer."

"If you're hoping to appeal to any sense of kinship we once shared during my apprenticeship, I fear you will be sorely disappointed." Eoghan's eye regarded me with pity, as if our situations were somehow reversed. "I haven't always lived a blameless life, but the Dark Rider will judge me fairly when I ascend to the fugue plane. The balance of my life leaves behind a greater legacy of good than of evil. Can you truthfully claim the same, Karryghan?"

"I cannot." I admitted with a resigned shrug. I had not returned to the Stockade for philosophical discussion. Eoghan would either reveal his secret to me in person, or I would end his life before the sun had the chance to set. "But once I possess the Nexus, such concerns will be far beneath me."

"Such arrogance! It beggars belief that you can still pass your skull beneath the frame of a door." Eoghan scoffed. My temper flared hotter than the desert wastelands of a Nagyjik summer and I momentarily lost control, my fury transmuting the fingers of my left hand into a broad, razor sharp blade the length of my forearm. A backhanded swipe across Eoghan's chest severed his right arm above the elbow and left a deep slash exposing his sternum. His scream was long and loud, an extended cry of agony that made even Lady Laoise wince. I placed the head of my staff under Eoghan's chin, the jaws of the wyvern eager to bite out his throat. I summoned all the power I dared into my staff's enchantment charm, the wyvern's teeth glowing celadon blue as they nipped at the jowl of loose flesh hanging beneath Eoghan's jaw. "You will tell me all that you know about the Nexus. And you *WILL* tell me now."

Blood pooled on the stone beneath Eoghan's chair, gushing profusely from the stump of his arm, yet the captive diviner giggled with feverish, demented pleasure as his life ebbed away. "For all your power Arch Mage, I still have one thing that will always grant me the strength defeat you."

"I care nothing for your self-righteous musings. Speak to me of the Nexus and I will grant you the mercy of a swift death."

"Unlike you, I have no fear of the Beyond. You ask what I found to that was important enough to abandon the Art. Something you will never know or understand, Karryghan: love."

I plunged my talon-like fingers deep between Eoghan's ribs, twisting hard to tear through one of his lungs. I snarled in anger as Eoghan coughed blood. "You dare to lie to me, even now?"

Eoghan coughed blood as he laughed deliriously in my face. "It's sad. You can't see the truth, even when it rests beneath your nose."

I stabbed him again, puncturing a kidney. Eoghan gasped for breath between pale, bloodless lips. "The Nexus will be mine, with or without your help. You know this. And you will be feeding worms by nightfall."

"I know that your schemes have failed you, Karryghan. In time you will be forced to accept this reality. Rest assured that I will be looking down upon you from the heavens when the time comes."

I hissed a wordless command to the wyvern head of my staff and its jaws snapped shut, crushing Eoghan's windpipe. I struck his torso half a dozen times with my transformed hand, the pointed blade tearing through his chest, shredding internal organs with each punch. I tore at Eoghan's mind like a starved wolf ripping at the flank of a maimed stag to break down his mental defences and plunder the knowledge I wanted from his memory. An agonised smile twisted Eoghan's lips as I found that I could not breach the walls he had erected around his mind. Eoghan tantalised me with the image of a lovely woman with golden hair holding a baby girl to her bare breast before blocking my second sight with a wall of blackness. I lashed out a final time with my steel-tipped fingers. My strike tore his heart in two and I stared Eoghan down until all life and light faded from his eye and his psychic aura faded, evaporating to oblivion. I reformed my knife hand back to normal, lamenting at the reappearance of age spots and wrinkles on the skin between my wrist and fingertips. This time it was Laoise's turn to offer words of condolence at my failure to extract the information I desired from the prisoner.

"In all my years as an interrogator, I've never met a prisoner quite so obdurate, your Excellency."

Feeling embarrassed for losing control of my emotions and failing to elicit any useful information from Eoghan, I turned on my heel and rushed for the stairs leading back up to street level. "Please dispose of the carcass as you see fit, Lady Laoise. I have urgent business back at the Tower I must deal with."

"Of course, your grace, it'll be done at once." Laoise didn't even follow me with her eyes out of the cell, knowing better than to attempt to mollify me with superfluous chatter.

I walked back across the city in a daze, forgetting to bypass the crowds using a portal, feeling relieved when I reached the familiar sanctuary of the Tower of the Aether. When I stepped off the paternoster into my apartment at the apex of the tower, Dervla greeted me with a smile and a goblet of wine. Within seconds she sensed the discomfort in my aura and frowned with concern, placing the lead crystal glass on my desk. "You seem upset, Master. What is wrong?"

"An old friend of mine died today." I answered truthfully, after deciding that it would probably be for the best if I omitted the minor detail that I had murdered him myself.

"How awful! My condolences, master." Dervla said, touching my cheek in consolation. Her fingers were soft and warm, and I could smell the sweet vanilla residue from the cream she used to moisturise her hands after conjuring fireballs and frost cones. "Were you very close?"

"Not recently. But by rights he could have lived another score of years or more." I replied, distracted by thoughts of my final exchange of words with Eoghan and my need to find the Nexus. "He ought to have outlived me. Such a tragedy to be taken before your time, but enough of this morose and maudlin talk – I must get changed and attend to matters of state."

"Yes, master." Dervla looked into my eyes with an air of total understanding, able to comprehend both my desire to keep busy and to make the most of the time I had left. "Let me help you into your robes."

Dervla knelt on the floor before me and unfastened the buttons at the waist of my trousers. My right hand found the smooth skin at the nape of her long, slender neck and my worries vanished for a brief moment as my universe collapsed into the space enveloped by her eager mouth and tongue. A hushed gasp escaped from my lips. *Yes,* I thought, *this girl will go very far indeed.*

11 - Ailidh

We'd been walking for nearly two weeks when we finally reached the Mistvale. The forest had a slightly different character from Pineholm, where I had lived before Father had moved us to Croycullen. Mistvale was stocked with fewer firs and evergreens and more temperate oaks, birch, yew and ash trees. Cathal was helping me learn how to recognise the different types of tree by the form of their canopies, the colour and texture of their bark and the shape of their leaves, so that I could to gather suitable wood each night to make a camp fire. Cathal had also taught me to how to use stones to construct a fire pit big enough to ward off the beasts of the forest. His knowledge of the forests was encyclopaedic, thanks to his years with the Order of Sylvan. I could have written a book on bushcraft with everything he had told me. Unfortunately, one thing he had been unable to teach me was how to stay warm while walking in the rain. Cathal drove us on hard, despite the inclement weather, now that my leg was completely healed and back to full strength. Now that we had cleared the Pineholm, we covered upwards of fifteen leagues a day, following the West Road that ran down to the border with Fossfjall. It would still be over a week until we reached the frontier at Skøgvik, but Cathal was anxious to push on as quickly as we could, to minimise the risk of getting overtaken by troops patrolling northwards out from the garrison at Birlone. Our luck had held so far in terms of encountering other travellers on the road, but lately the weather had been miserable. I wrapped my cloak around Sapphire's woven willow cage to give the poor creature some respite from the raindrops being whipped along by the gusting wind. The cat's long, thick fur was matted and sodden, and she wailed constantly in distress, unable to even sit properly on the furs lining the bottom of the cage to groom herself, as the cage swayed back and forth in my hand as we walked. I sympathised entirely with the cat, being in need of a good grooming myself. I had not washed or changed my clothes in five days, and the smell emanating from beneath the armpits of my crimson blouse was not an alluring one. The linen was saturated with sweat and rain, despite my best efforts to keep it dry under my cloak. My only consolation was that Cathal was faring no better.

"When'll this rain ever stop? It's been three days now." I lamented, shaking off the droplets clinging to the black leather of the cloak Cathal had given me. Sapphire yelped as her cage was battered sideways by a vicious gust of wind, almost tipping the cat off her feet.

"Cheer up, Ailidh." Cathal's reply was sunny, even if the weather was not. "Night will fall soon. Then we can make camp."

"Cathal, we've been walking since dawn." I complained, yet still managed to trudge one foot in front of another, trying to match his relentless pace. "I'm cold, wet and hungry. Can't we get off the road now? The light'll be gone in a few minutes."

I shrank beneath his hard, unforgiving gaze as he stopped, turning to gauge my ability to carry on. Mercifully, he seemed to remember that I was not an experienced, wilderness-hardened ranger, but a soft, weary, young woman nearing the end of her tether for the day. His stern countenance melted with compassion as he took in my pitiful state, and he led us off the road into the trees, until we found a suitable camp site, far enough away from the compressed gravel path to not be directly observed by anyone walking it. The limb of the sun had already touched the horizon when Cathal found us a small clearing in the middle of a patch of yew trees to set up our tents for the night. I used the curved tip of my wakizashi's blade to scrape away the grass, stones and moss in the centre of the tiny glade, forming a broad but shallow fire pit in the dirt, which I circled with rocks to create a barrier between the pit and the surrounding foliage. By the time I had finished, Cathal had pitched both of our tents and gathered a sufficient amount of fallen wood to create a fire large enough to cook on and keep us warm and safe for the night. Cathal had me hold open my cloak to shield him from the wind and the rain while he invested some of the precious, bone-dry tinder from the box in his pack to ignite the fire. The firewood was green and wet, so it took almost twenty minutes to get it to catch a spark, the wood billowing thick grey clouds of soot when it eventually did light. I coughed and spluttered as the smoke rose into my face, waiting until Cathal gave me his permission to stand back, only when he was certain that the fire would not go out. When the colour of the flames turned from a dull red to an iridescent yellow, Cathal finally nodded his assent for me to stop acting as a wind break and sit down next to him to help him cook our meal for the night.

"This wolf meat should keep us going for another couple of days." Cathal said as he opened his pack to retrieve a small haunch of meat wrapped carefully in muslin. Yesterday a desperate, lone wolf had shambled across our path on the East Road. I had not even known it had been stalking us until Cathal had unslung his bow, drawn a single broad-headed arrow from the quiver at his side and let fly into the scrawny wolf's throat. I had watched with fascination as he used his stiletto to gut and skin the unlucky beast, taking its pelt and the choicest cuts of meat from its carcass. Cathal sliced several thin strips of flesh from the haunch and tossed them into a smoking pan resting on a makeshift trivet on top of the fire. The wolf meat immediately began to curl and crackle and Cathal used the tip of his stiletto to move the meat around the pan, preventing it from burning. Wolf, as I had discovered over our last few meals, was not good eating. The meat was lean and stringy, requiring far too much chewing to be worth the uninspiring taste. I desperately hoped that the next creature Cathal would hunt on our journey would be a fat, succulent chicken, though the odds of that seemed slim. Failing that, a wild boar would do nicely. Boar stewed in red wine had been a favourite of my father's. Not that we had any wine, but my mouth watered when I thought about eating boar. At least Cathal had assured me that the wolf meat was packed with protein, which would keep my muscles strong for the journey that still lay ahead of us. As I chewed thoughtfully on a mouthful of bland wolf, trying not to let the thin fibres of seared muscle get stuck between my teeth, I turned to Cathal, who was likewise trying ineffectually to make headway with the tough meat.

"Cathal, I'd like you to teach me how to hunt like you do." I pronounced, setting down my enamelled iron plate, unable to stomach any more of the sinew-heavy meat.

The ranger stopped chewing, swallowed, and met my eyes, surprised but intrigued. "Really?"

"I learnt how to use a bow when I was young, but I never practised as much as I wanted to."

"Why?" Cathal asked, with his dark eyebrows raised questioningly.

I shrugged. "Apparently it's not ladylike. Father made me give it up when I turned thirteen. He was afraid it would put off potential husbands. Not that there were any of those in Croycullen."

"Hmm." Cathal left his plate by the fire and stood, looking closely at the trees nearby. I watched intently as he selected a long straight bough at the bottom of a yew tree and withdrew his longsword to hack it free, chopping through the wood next to the trunk. Cathal sheathed his longsword and swapped it for his thin stiletto, sitting back down next to the camp fire and working rapidly, peeling away the bark and exposing the dense, hard grain beneath.

"What're you doing?" I asked, watching closely, intrigued by his speed and precision in the way he shaved away at the wood, long, thin skeins of wood fibre falling off the bough to rest between his legs. Every so often, Cathal tossed the wastage onto the fire, the sap-rich, paper-thin wood popping and cracking away in the intensity of the flames.

"Making you a shortbow." Cathal replied, concentrating hard, visualising the form of it in his head and making it real with his hands. It took more than an hour before the four foot long bough became recognisable as a weapon. Cathal held each end of the bough over the fire for several minutes, driving out the moisture and letting the wood warm enough for him to bend a recurve at each end of the bow's shaft, to generate extra power from its short draw. He used the stiletto to trim one of his spare bowstrings to the correct length and then cut deep notches at either end of the piece of wood, using his strength to string the bow, bending it into shape. He carved a handle into the centre of the wooden arc, lining it with a strip of leather to make if more comfortable to use. Finally, after nearly three hours of intense labour, Cathal sealed the grain of the wood with a waterproof wax from a tin dug out from the dark recesses of his pack. Pleased with his handiwork, Cathal presented me with my bow. "There. Not bad for a rush job. It will suffice until we reach Lesøsnø, in any event."

I took it from him uncertainly, turning it over in my hands. I hadn't touched a bow in seven years. I felt strangely honoured to have had one made specifically for me. Cathal tugged me to my feet and plucked a thin, steel-tipped arrow from his quiver. He gave me the arrow, pointing to an old oak tree standing proudly out of place among the yews, which was barely visible in the light from the fire, even though it was no more than fifteen yards away.

"Try and hit that tree over there." Cathal said, watching my technique carefully as I nocked the arrow on the bowstring instinctively. The bow creaked as I drew back the string, my fingers and arms straining against the tension in the wood. I kept pulling until the silky goose feathers of the arrow's flight touched my cheek. I looked down the shaft of the arrow with my left eye closed, taking aim carefully, biting my tongue in concentration. Unable to hold onto the string any longer, I let go with my right hand, the arrow hissing through the air as the string emitted a resonant twang.

"Warrior's cock!" I cursed as the tip of the arrow skimmed off the thick bark of the oak, leaving only a graze on the trunk as the arrow ricocheted away into the moss. Cathal's rich, deep laughter did not lessen my disappointment at the miss. Annoyed, I glared at him, but he simply handed me another arrow from his quiver, standing close behind me.

"Try again. This time, keep both eyes open. Focus on the tip of the arrow."

I frowned but followed his advice as I restrung the bow. My fingers trembled on the string and my biceps strained as I started to take aim for a second time. A loud, critical tut echoed in my ear.

"Stop." Cathal commanded. I felt his presence at my back and he overlaid his hands on mine as I struggled to maintain the tension in the string and wood. He pointed the bow back down towards my feet, easing off the draw of the string, without letting go of the arrow. "You must not fight the bow. Relax. All the strength you need is already in the wood. All you should do is guide it. Like this."

I let him move my hands, enjoying warmth and decisiveness of his touch in the never-ending torrent of freezing rain. In a single smooth, swift motion, Cathal helped me raise the bow into a striking posture, simultaneously aiming at the target and pulling back the string to its full extension. As soon as the string pressed my right cheek, Cathal prized my fingertips free and the arrow flew straight and true, embedding itself in the centre of the tree trunk, five feet above the forest floor.

"Do you see?" I turned my head and saw that Cathal smiled at me, his eyes glittering with amusement at how easy he had made it appear.

I nodded reluctantly, not wanting him to let go of my hands. "Yes."

"Show me." Cathal gave me another arrow and stepped back, the master watching his student with an expert, critical eye. I kept the bow lowered as I nocked the arrow on the string, my eyes staring at where I wanted the arrow to land. Without even thinking about the mechanics of it, I replicated Cathal's demonstration perfectly, visualising his hands directing my own. This time the arrow arced gracefully through the air, and I watched its flight, almost in slow motion, until it came to rest less than an inch below Cathal's in the trunk of the oak tree. Cathal applauded before moving to recover his three arrows. "Well done! Tomorrow we can try with a moving target."

"Uh, moving?" I asked doubtfully, my fingers suddenly restless again on the bow's leather handle.

"Dinner rarely stands still." Cathal told me with a smile, looking back at me over his shoulder as he yanked the arrows from the oak tree.

I was almost ready to concede the point when something occurred to me. "It does in taverns."

Cathal laughed in surprise at the absurdity of my joke, appearing happier than I had seen him since we had left his cabin. It cheered my spirit to see the normally taciturn ranger laugh. As we retreated to the warmth of the camp fire and our tents, I wondered if he enjoyed my company as much as I did his. I was frustrated that I while thought I had made it clear that I desired him, he had been seemingly oblivious to my overtures, not even acknowledging them. That night I slept fitfully, dreaming of his weight on my belly and chest as I held his body against mine, with my arms and legs wrapped tightly around him as he passionately transformed me from a maiden into a woman.

The next morning I briefly entertained the notion of exiting from my tent nude just to see what Cathal's reaction would be, but quickly thought better of it, rooting through my pack to change my crimson blouse for the olive tunic. Its scent was marginally less revolting than that of a rotting ox carcass. I left the top three buttons unfastened, wanting to at least look attractive, even if I smelled worse than a slaughterhouse worker after a day-long shift. I tried to establish some kind of order over the disarray of my hair, running my fingers through the long tresses until the majority of the knots were untangled. Feeling ready to face the world again, I poked my head out of my tent and was pleased to see that it was no longer raining.

"What's this? Sun? At last!" I exclaimed in delight and relief.

"Indeed. I can finally bid you a good morning and be right." Cathal turned from the fire, tossing the contents of the frying pan as he greeted me. Cathal's smile was a tired one.

"That smells good. What're you making?" I asked, sitting next to him by the fire. It did not escape my notice that his gaze flickered uncertainly between my face and the cleavage exposed by my partially-fastened tunic. I felt flattered, but annoyed that he would not voice the nature of his true feelings for me.

"The last of our eggs, with your favourite: wolf." Cathal turned back to the pan, not wanting to let the meat burn. It was barely edible even when served rare and rested. "You will need the energy. The road gets no shorter while we sleep. It would be good if we could make the most of the good weather today. The rain has put us behind schedule."

I started to repack my tent while my breakfast finished cooking, taking apart the frame and folding the fabric carefully. I was almost finished when Cathal called me over and handed me a loaded, enamelled tin plate. Ravenous, I devoured the eggs first, opening them with my fork and letting the molten yolks coat the rashers of wolf meat to make the densely fibrous flesh more appetising. My culinary experiment was only a partial success.

"Did you sleep well?" Cathal asked to make small-talk as he shredded his own rashers of wolf meat into even thinner strips using two forks.

"Eventually." I stretched, rolling my aching shoulders. "That pack is killing me, though. My back hasn't stopped aching since we passed Kinvarra."

Cathal snorted without sympathy. "You think your pack is heavy? Try mine."

"Is it much further to Lesøsnø?"

"It depends on how the weather holds. The rain has not granted us any favours. Three weeks perhaps, if it rains heavily again; we are only just passing halfway on our journey."

"Another three weeks?" I groaned pitifully, my shoulders sagging as I set down the empty plate on my lap. "We've been walking that long already. You said it'd only take a month to get to the city."

"I cannot help it if you are slow." Cathal raised his eyebrows, playfully mocking my complaint with an utterly deadpan tone. Disgusted, I snatched up my plate and pitched it at his chest as hard as I could. Without even flinching, Cathal snatched the plate effortlessly out of the air and laid it beneath his, before wrapping them both in a cloth and replacing them in his pack. I was astounded by the swiftness of his reflexes. His courteous manners belied the fact that he was a seasoned ranger, with years' of experience walking the wild places of Cothraine. I swallowed nervously, wondering if he could do the same thing with arrows. "There is a tavern just shy of the border near Skøgvik, about two days' walk from here. We can stop there for a night. It will be a good place to have a proper rest and resupply."

"A tavern?" I tried not to let my response sound too enthusiastic. I didn't want Cathal to get the wrong impression about the depth of my experience with inns and the contents of their cellars.

"The Sundered Shield. It is quite infamous in these parts. It has a reputation that can generously be described as colourful, but the beds are clean, the food is hearty and the beer is strong."

"I've not heard of it." I said, closing my eyes as I pictured myself lying in a proper bed. "I'd kill for a proper mattress and a pint of ale right now."

"On your feet, then. We need to get moving." Cathal stood, smothering the camp fire with handfuls of moist dirt.

Twenty minutes later, Cathal and I had returned to the road. Not a single trace of our camp site remained in the small clearing. It was almost as if we'd never been there at all.

12 - Keri

I had kept human company so infrequently in the last decade that it took me a few moments to realise that the voices I could hear were coming from just beyond my sight in the material world and were not related to the guidance I received periodically from my demonic mistress across the aetheric planes. Since leaving the Bray vineyards at on the fringes of the town of Ballinlara, I had spent two months crossing The Breadbowl, before cutting across the heart of the Lockwood forest between Balnoch and Gallowgarry to join the East Road just two dozen leagues shy of the tiny hamlet of Skøgvik at the frontier between Cothraine and Fossfjall. The weather had turned unseasonably hot in comparison to the unremitting, torrential autumn rain that had marked the last few days. The new voices were discussing this bizarre turn of events. I identified them from their dialects as a young northern woman from a common background and a slightly older man with a refined, bass accent, which I placed as originating from the Cothraine capital of Clongarvan. I weaved my way through the trees towards them, homing in on the sound of their conversation. The woman was complaining about the midday heat, something I did not have to worry about, thanks to the chill aura I had emanating from my staff.
"Cathal stop, please. I can't take this heat anymore." I stretched out with my perception, hearing the slap of leather as her pack dropped on the road and the rustle of gravel as she slumped down next to it. She made muffled, slurping noises as she took long gulps of water from an almost empty canteen skin. "First the rain, now this sun. Can't the weather just make up its mind?"
"Such extremes are not normal in the beginning of autumn." There came another scrape of leather on stone as I sensed the man sit next to his companion on the road. I heard a cat yowl in frustration. Then there was the metallic snick of an iron latch on a wooden cage, followed by a languid, contented purring. "Come on out, kitten. You will need a drink, too."
"How much further do we need to walk today?"

"Another four leagues, if you want a proper bed tomorrow night. But we can rest for now. We should carry on once the temperature drops this afternoon. Come, Ailidh. Here, into the shade. We are too exposed here on the road." I heard the snapping of branches as they made their way into the underbrush, finding the cool shadows underneath a mature ash tree. The cadence of the woman's breathing told me that she was trying to nap, while the scratching of claws against a pebble told me that the cat was playing on the road, making the most of being free from the confines of its cage. I approached the tree line as I made to cross the road towards them, the heat haze rising from the surface of compacted gravel shimmering and disrupting my view, when the cat began to growl and hiss; a warning to its human companions. "Sapphire? What is it, kitten?"
"What's wrong?" I heard the woman ask, too weary to be frightened.
"Stay there. Keep out of sight." I heard the metallic scrape of a weapon being drawn from a leather-lined scabbard.
"What is it?" inquired the woman, in a barely audible whisper.
"There is a chill wind coming from the south."
I had been detected, then. The cat continued to hiss and spit in agitation, despite the man's attempts to calm it. I heard his apprehensive intake of breath as he noticed the glistening, icy light of my staff's aura shining out from behind the boughs and branches of the trees between us. I took note of his longsword – an enchanted masterwork from the Royal Armoury in Clongarvan, judging from the maker's mark on the crossguard - jet black leather armour and the gold-embroidered trim on his green cloak as I stepped plainly into his view, smiling a friendly greeting.
"Well met, friend."

They are no threat to you.

The silky voice of my mistress reassured me, but I kept a firm grip on my staff. The cat emitted a fearful hiss and arched its back. I ignored it for the moment, concentrating instead on the leather-clad warrior. He seemed more capable and self-assured than the Mage Hunter I had dealt with outside of Bray. He straightened up from his combat-ready stance, but his eyes lingered on my staff. I looked into his tawny-coloured eyes and addressed him soothingly. "Sheath your weapon, friend. If I meant you any harm, you would be dead already."

The cat went into a frenzy of hissing and spitting at my words, its body language defensive and hostile. I looked down at the creature, amused to have provoked such a reaction. Its manner tweaked a distant memory, but my mistress was silent and did not provide me with any further insight. I was surprised to be forcefully rebuffed when I attempted to touch its mind, and I took a step backwards in alarm. The man raised the tip of his sword, leaving us at an uncomfortable stand-off. I looked at the cat with fresh eyes, no longer amused.

"What do we have here? A changeling?" I turned to the man, meeting his eyes as I kept the tip of my staff between myself and the cat. "Do you know what accompanies you, friend? I should put it out of its misery."

The cat screeched in alarm and retreated behind its keeper, obviously understanding my threat as clearly as he did. The black-clad warrior likewise kept the tip of his sword raised, the razor-sharp point aimed at the base of my throat. "She is under my protection, friend. Might I ask your name?"

"Oh my, what courtesy!" Taken aback by his unexpected good manners, I lowered my staff. After a few seconds, he also lowered his weapon, the tension between us suddenly gone. "You may ask. Some call me witch, though they rarely live long enough to regret it. My peers call me Keri of Moonchion, and my friends call me Keri. Take your pick, but choose wisely."

"You are a mage of the Guild, then? This corona of yours, I have never seen magic like it."

"Alas, I am no longer a member of the Wizards' Guild. I was expelled for carrying out..." I smiled and raised an amused eyebrow while I paused to search for the right euphemism. *"Experiments..."*

"You mean Wild Magic." I was pleasantly surprised to see that the man was clearly no fool. He was intelligent enough to be scared, but also wise enough to keep his longsword pointed to the floor, despite his fear.

"Some call it that, but they are mostly inbred ignoramuses." I said with a snicker, glad to have taken back the initiative and position of superiority in our verbal exchange. "I prefer the term *primordial practice*."

There was movement from the trees and I saw the young woman for the first time. Our dislike of each other was immediate, undisguised and mutual. I despised her voluptuous curves and effortless femininity. She was a full head shorter than I, but her figure was broader and fuller than mine, and her manner oozed the casual sexuality and vitality of youth. She was barely more than a girl, and I thought that the favour granted upon her by the Empress seemed excessive. Then I noticed that she hid the right side of her face behind a lank curtain of filthy, golden blonde hair. When I caught a glimpse of the eye that had been mutated by exposure to arcane fire, I understood why. She stood by her guardian's side, as she tried to gauge what kind of threat I posed. "What's Wild Magic?"

"Dangerous. Unpredictable. Illegal." His words carried a hard edge of fear and I sensed the woman's thoughts as she looked between me and him. She feared me not for my ability with magic, but for my intrusion into their group. I could feel her desire for him, though the reason for it eluded me. I supposed he was handsome enough for a man, but he lacked the raw, dangerous aura of the semi-tamed tanar'ri daevae I consorted with. I sensed that she worried I would steal him away from her, and she fretted silently as he explained the reason for my expulsion from the Guild of the Art. "It was outlawed by the Wizards' Guild almost two centuries ago. Mages caught using Wild Magic are excommunicated from their society."

"Quite so, though I was expelled long before the practice of Wild Magic carried the death penalty. That was only imposed retrospectively." I chuckled, playing up to my role, turning my voice ice cold as I studied their expressions for signs of their intent. "I do hope you are intelligent enough to realise that it would not end well for you if you tried to claim my bounty."

After a moment of deadly silence, Cathal swallowed a mouthful of air with trepidation and sheathed his longsword. Even the cat remained quiet. Ailidh picked up the silver-furred feline and stroked its neck and back to keep it calm. I gave them my broadest, friendliest smile, pleased to have reached an accord. Seconds later I was given an edict by my dread mistress.

Walk with them.

"Excellent! I like you already. You know my name now, friends. Might I know yours?" I asked purely out of the pretence of politeness. I was simply trying to find an excuse to prolong our conversation. I had already overheard their names during my approach.
"I am Cathal. My companion is Ailidh."
"A pleasure." I bowed formally, reaching outward with my mind, deep into the recesses of his memory for an image that I could use to seed the deception that would allow me to join them on their journey. I had found it before I completed my bow. A let a flicker of recognition pass over my features. "Cathal... but of course! I could not place you at first. You are a ranger, are you not?"
"We have met before?" Cathal's reply betrayed his wariness and scepticism. He would not be easily fooled. I dug deeper for more detail.
"Not formally. It was many years ago in Clongarvan when I was passing through the city. I saw you in the courtyard of Sylvan's Dell being given a lesson in defensive swordplay by one of the master rangers." I lied, before pointing to his right forearm. "You carry that lesson with you still, yes?" The scar was hidden from view beneath the sleeve of his jerkin and bracer. Cathal touched his arm self-consciously, convinced that I could not have known about the childhood injury unless I had seen it happen. "My technique has improved much since then."
"Oh, of that I am certain." I said reassuringly, to help salve the embarrassment I had caused him in front of Ailidh.
"Still, a green cloak in plain view is a rare sight in these troubled times. Where are you headed?"
"To The Sundered Shield, an inn at the border in Skøgvik. And then onward to Lesøsnø."
"A happy coincidence! I am bound for Lesøsnø myself."
"May I ask why?" Cathal asked with an air of wariness, his suspicion not completely dispelled.
"Perhaps later, my dear ranger." I replied, evading the question. "We are headed in the same direction. Shall we journey together awhile?"
The screech of alarm emitted by the cat was so loud and unexpected that Ailidh dropped it, startled. I gave the feline

a deadly stare, again trying to read the cat's thoughts to get some clue as to its true nature. For a second time I was baffled by the resistance it was able to put up against my psychic probes. The creature was definitely no ordinary feline. Cathal and Ailidh exchanged a silent glance as the cat lay down on the road, submissive and silent again. Ailidh shrugged at Cathal and he nodded reluctantly. "Your company would be welcome, Keri."

"Wonderful!" I chose to acknowledge only the words, rather than the sentiment poorly hidden behind the ranger's courteous lie. "It is decided, then. I will keep us cool with my magic and the ranger shall keep us safe from any stray beasts of the forest. Come, there is much ground for us to cover. Let us talk more after nightfall."

I let Cathal and Ailidh gather their packs and put the cat back in its cage, before beckoning the ranger to lead the way along the road to the border. He set a brisk, consistent pace and despite the undulation of the terrain, before stopping for the night we had covered more than five leagues, over half of the remaining distance to the border. As the light faded, we left the road and found shelter out of sight from the road in the lee of a valley peppered with thick bracken and gorse bushes. We made camp on the shingle banks of a fast-running stream, shielded from the wind by a copse of ash trees surrounding the large, fresh-water pool that we had pitched our tents by. As Ailidh refilled her skin of water, Cathal built a fire pit and was trying to get the wood he had gathered to light, striking the thin, hard blade of his stiletto against a chipped, heavy piece of flint. The rain over the previous few days had soaked the wood, and even with Cathal's canny knowledge of bushcraft and supply of dry tinder, the green wood steadfastly refused to catch a spark.

"Come on, light, damn you!" Cathal took out his frustration on the flint, showers of hot yellow sparks cascading ineffectually onto the smouldering tinder, which seemed unable to generate sufficient heat to ignite the moist wood.

"Having trouble?" I asked sardonically, stood behind him with my staff in hand.

"The wood is too damp. It will not light."

"There is an easier way, you know." I admonished him, readying a fire spell. "Stand back."

The ranger had barely the time to scramble clear of the pit before I unleashed a thin tongue of fierce orange flame from the tip of my staff into the heart of the fire pit. The heat was so intense that the wood hissed and steamed, almost instantly igniting into a fireball that roiled up into the sky like the angry belch of a dragon. The flame was almost as hot as Cathal's temper, furious at having been frazzled at the fringes of the conflagration. "Keri! Be careful!"

"Ah, delightful." I sat cross-legged by the fire pit, utterly ignoring Cathal's admonishment. I turned to him and asked, "Now, what do you have to drink?"

"Water." Cathal's reply was deadpan and unimpressed, still angry with me for the singes on his brow he had suffered as I had lit the fire.

"Oh, that simply will not do." I said, with a roll of my eyes. My gaze found a large limestone boulder resting on the shingle at the edge of the stream. I aimed my staff at it, whispered the appropriate Word of Power and channelled energy to transform the boulder into the image I desired. The stone glowed white-hot in the darkening shadows of nightfall and I dropped my staff with a short shriek of pain as the spell partially backfired, the feedback manifesting itself as a blue arc of lightning, linking me for an instant with the rock.

"Keri, are you alright?" Cathal's concern was immediate and genuine. I was touched and flattered enough that it helped dispel the pain.

"I will be fine." I grimaced, flexing my affected arm for signs of damage. I was relieved to feel that everything was still in working order, but nonetheless channelled aetheric energy into the tissues to regenerate the damage done to the cells in the skin and bone of my right arm. "I will need to practice that one more often."

"Cathal, look!" Ailidh exclaimed, pointing to where I'd cast the spell. The boulder had vanished and had been transformed into a large crystal carafe of red wine and three large, pewter goblets. Ailidh turned to me, amazed. "How'd you do that?"

"A mere parlour trick of conjuration and transmutation." I said, fetching the carafe and goblets, setting them down by the fire and filling each pewter vessel nearly to the brim. I set down the carafe, which was still full, thanks to the enchantment I had imbued into the crystal. I raised my hand in a toast after giving a goblet each to Ailidh and Cathal. "To new friends and companionship."

I filled my mouth with the wine, sipping noisily to let air bubble through it, releasing complex flavours of cherry, oak, vanilla and blackcurrant. I closed my eyes to concentrate on savouring the taste of the wine, sighing softly with satisfaction as the alcohol warmed my throat.

"Mmm, that's delicious!" Ailidh took a sip and clutched her goblet in both hands just below her nose, breathing in the vapours. "What is it?"

"A '39 Baron Lussac. The best wine in the Western Triad. A hundred sovereigns a bottle, in most cities."

"A hundred sovereigns?" Ailidh exclaimed, appalled. "That's obscene. Father wouldn't earn that in three years!"

"The rarest vintages command the highest price. Just like the bounties on rangers and witches. Are we not just as rare, Cathal?"

Cathal looked uncomfortable at the comparison. "If you say so, Keri."

"These days the road north to Fossfjall is not well-travelled. What brings you to Lesøsnø?"

Cathal took a mouthful of wine, but failed to meet my eyes. "We are visiting friends in the city."

I laughed before addressing him with a chiding tone.

"Cathal my friend, if I had wanted half a truth, I would have asked half a question."

"Did the Guild teach you how to read minds?" Cathal snapped back at me, defensive and annoyed. "Why ask when you already know the answer?"

"I cannot read your thoughts." The lie came from my mouth as easily as the wine poured out from the narrow crystal throat of the carafe as I topped up our drinks. "But do not take me for a fool. One does not walk a road frequented by brigands and worse to visit friends, no matter how dear they are. No, you would have taken a passenger coach from Siskine or Birlone. People only walk these roads if they do not wish to be easily found. And I should know."

There was a long, awkward silence before Ailidh spoke. "You're right. That's not the whole truth. King Maeryn ordered my father kidnapped and home destroyed. I barely escaped and would be dead, had it not been for Cathal. There's nothing left for me in Cothraine now. Cathal's taking me to Fossfjall to find out more about why the king had my father taken."

"Maeryn..." I made no attempt to hide the contempt from my voice. "Maeryn is an imbecile and a lame impotent. He could not lay a cheap whore, even if he had the brains to know where to find one."

"His only talent is for treachery and murder. By marrying Reilynn he risks war with Fossfjall. Connell had promised her to the Crown Prince as penance for the trade dispute." Cathal's response echoed my disdain for the Usurper King. "I do not know how the abduction of Ailidh's father fits into this, but I will find out. For the good of Cothraine and the stability of the Western Triad, Maeryn must be removed from the throne."

The voice of my dread mistress whispered in the back of my mind.

Allies...

I tilted my head onto one side, considering potential outcomes, as a myriad of possibilities swarmed in my thoughts. I studied Cathal closely as he brooded in silence. I wondered where his hostility for the king originated from, but was so intrigued by this new information that I postponed the search through his mind for the answer. "I was not aware of this. I doubt these machinations are of his will alone. Maeryn is a weak, insecure toddler barely worthy of the honour of being called a tyrant. He is nothing more than a puppet."

"But if Maeryn is just a puppet, who is the master that pulls his strings?" Cathal inquired.

I snorted with derision, amazed that Cathal did not already know. "Who else? It can only be Arch Mage Karryghan and the Wizards' Guild."

"Why though?" Ailidh asked, bewildered. "What're they hoping to achieve from this chaos?"

I stroked my hair thoughtfully, guiding it like a copper snake over my right shoulder to drape over my chest. I picked up my goblet by the stem, swirling the wine around the bowl to aerate it before draining the vessel in a single gulp. I sighed in satisfaction as I savoured the hints of tannins and bramble in the aftertaste of the wine. "Now that, my fair Ailidh, is a good question. A very good question indeed..."

13 - Ailidh

Despite the soporific effect of half a dozen goblets of wine and an hour of tossing and turning on my bed roll, sleep would not come. The sudden appearance of Keri on the road had disturbed me greatly. I was wary of her on two counts: firstly, Cathal was fearful of her magical abilities. My own knowledge of magic was next to none, but Cathal knew a great deal more, thanks to his sister's affinity with the Art, and Keri's power worried him. Secondly, I disliked Keri's intrusion into our group just on general principle. I did not like the way she looked at me with her intense jade green eyes. Keri possessed a heartless, fierce splendour, the look of an experienced predator of men with sharp, chiselled features that could have been carved from marble by a master sculptor. Her long, lustrous copper-coloured hair, her sleek, willowy figure and flawless porcelain skin were enough to turn head of any man, or woman, for that matter. It was bad enough that my disfigurement left me unable to compete with her in terms of physical beauty, but I also worried about what other, more magical methods she might be able to employ to ensnare Cathal's affections. I waited until the crackling of the camp fire had almost died before poking my head out of the tent. Cathal sat by the glowing embers of the fire pit, half-asleep as he kept watch in a trance, listening out for the slightest rustles of motion, his hand tightly gripping his bow. He snapped awake as the entrance to my tent flapped, meeting my eyes in alarm. I put a finger to my lips, pointing silently at his tent, where Keri slept soundly, her staff close to hand. I crept on hands and knees over to Cathal, as quietly as I could, unable to take my eyes off Keri, fearful of waking her. Cathal waited by the fire pit for me to come to him, likewise unwilling to make any unnecessary noise.
"Can you not sleep?" Cathal whispered, when I was finally close enough for us to talk together with hushed voices.
"Not with her in the camp." I glanced between Cathal and Keri, wondering if she could hear our conversation in her sleep using her magic. "How dangerous is she?"

"Very. She must be extremely powerful indeed to have achieved a mastery of Wild Magic." Cathal's response was not encouraging. "Gormlaith once told me that the majority of the wizards that attempt spells from the school accidentally kill themselves. The unpredictable natures of the energies involved innately defy control."

"What d'you think we should do? Leave the camp now and run?"

Cathal shook his head. "No, I do not think that would be wise. Keri was certainly telling the truth about one thing. She would not have to wait until we were asleep in our beds if she intended us harm."

"What should we do, then?" I asked, sitting next to Cathal by the fire pit, close enough to feel the warmth of his breath on my face.

"Nothing for now. Wild Mages are said to be as capricious as the magic they wield. I will be watching her closely." Cathal's brow furrowed with concern.

"I know nothing of magic. I trust your judgment in this." I replied, seizing his hand and meeting his eyes.

"Not that we have much choice. We must try to make ourselves useful to her, if only for our own safety. I suspect we shall part company when she wills it, not before."

"I'll watch your back if you watch mine." I squeezed Cathal's fingers to demonstrate my solidarity with him and he smiled back, grateful for my vow of support.

"Thank you." My heart sang when I saw there was a glint of affection in his eyes as he stroked the back of my hand, urging me to return to my tent. "Go. Sleep. We have another long day's walk ahead of us in the morning."

Reluctantly, I retreated back to my tent. As I opened the canvas flap of the tent, a bright flash of light caught my attention. Cathal and I both looked skyward as the blue-white streak of a shooting star flashed from one horizon to the other. I saw Keri's slender fingers reflexively twitch on her staff, but she didn't wake. Cathal and I exchanged a brief glance before he gestured silently for me to get some rest. It would be a full day's walk before we reached our long-awaited goal at border town of Skøgvik. I only managed a couple of hours' sleep before dawn broke, but was relieved to see that my late night discussion with Cathal appeared to have escaped the attention of Keri. She conjured us a breakfast of a dozen fresh eggs, which

Cathal fried in a pan heated on the re-stoked fire. The weather had turned cold again, but at least the chilly northern breeze hadn't brought rain along with it. While the remaining distance to the border was not as far as we had walked in the previous day, Cathal still anticipated that we would not reach the inn before nightfall, as we would be unable to follow the road from now on. The risk of being discovered by a wandering patrol of the king's men was simply too great. Cathal led us off the road and into the woods as soon as he was satisfied that no trace of our camp remained. Here Keri proved to be a great help, using her magic to restore the shingle of the river bank to its original pristine state, filling in the fire pit and leaving no evidence of our stay behind. It was less than a half a dozen leagues to the border, so while the rough terrain off the road slowed our progress somewhat, we could have easily reached Skøgvik well before nightfall, had Cathal wished to force the pace. Wanting to avoid the attention of prying eyes and minimise the risk of being discovered by an army patrol as we entered the town, Cathal instead led us on at a cautious, modest rate, both to conserve our stamina and let night fall before we left the cover of the forest.

Our destination, The Sundered Shield, stood on the outskirts of Skøgvik, only a few hundred yards from the stone keep guarding the frontier between Cothraine and Fossfjall. The inn was a three storey oak-framed building with a green slate roof and a bleached wattle-and-daub facade cladding clay brick walls. We skirted the edge of the fields of the neighbouring farm, hidden from the view of the road by the tall hedges, approaching the tavern in silence. When the road was clear in both directions, we hurried the final few hundred yards down the road to the relative safety of the inn. Oil lamps glowed on the ends of ten foot tall poles, lining the final hundred yards of road to the tavern entrance. The stables next to the main building were full. Five carriages and more than two dozen horses were being tended to by a scruffy bunch of young teenage boys, their clothes worn and stained by the travails of mucking out the horse boxes and grooming the large, powerful animals. Cathal took me aside briefly as Keri yanked open the tavern's heavy oak front door.

"Watch yourself in here and stay close to me." Cathal warned me in a low voice. "The patrons can be lively."

I tapped the hilt of my wakizashi with my palm in acknowledgement and kept the sword's leather-bound grip within easy reach as we followed Keri inside, making our way to the bar. The tavern was almost full. Only a handful of tables were unoccupied, the others being surrounded by small clusters of travellers, merchants and mercenaries. The atmosphere was not unlike that of the tavern back in my home town of Croycullen - smoky and raucous - though here the customers were more numerous and a cold edge of threat hung in the air. Keri's mage staff drew openly hostile glances from several tables. Several of the mercenaries fidgeted with discomfort as she crossed the ale-stained wooden floor to attract the attention of the rumpled, middle-aged barkeep, who was taking orders from customers and barking them on to be fulfilled by his small army of serving staff. A score of serving wenches, similar to me in both age and physique, applied their ample charms around the tables, avoiding the pinches of overly familiar hands and pocketing tips as they served customers with huge stoneware pitchers filled ale, accompanied by equally generous flashes of their cleavages. A solitary sellsword sitting at a table for one next to the bar sneered wordlessly at Keri as she passed him. The aloof mage did not even seem to notice the scale mail clad warrior as she found a space at the bar and tried to attract the barkeep's attention with an enchanting gaze and smile. He turned to serve her almost immediately, despite the fact that other clients at the bar had been waiting to be served before we had even entered the tavern. I saw the landlord's acne-scarred cheek involuntarily twitch in recognition when he saw Keri's staff. The hairs on the back of my neck stiffened in alarm, my sixth sense tingling. I tried to look casual as I surveyed the salon bar for signs of danger. The lone mercenary stared at Keri, Cathal and me with a fearsome intensity, his right hand already gripping the hilt of the longsword at his left hip. His battle-scarred face was almost impossible to read. His left eye was milky white, clouded by an old injury, but his right eye caught the light of the flickering oil lamps, the pupil narrow and malevolent. Keri addressed the barkeep, still seemingly oblivious to the mercenary's malign attention.

"Do you have any rooms?" Keri asked the barkeep, raising her voice over the din of background conversations."

"Two." The barkeep's reply was curt to the point of rudeness. He would undoubtedly accept our custom and money, but beyond that, he clearly wanted as little to do with us possible, having recognised the potential implications of Keri's mage staff. Cathal had told me during the day's walk that wizards rarely strayed far from their respective guild towers. Commoners rarely crossed paths with mages and a wandering spellcaster was rarely considered to be a welcome visitor.

"How much?" Keri asked, as the barkeep retrieved two large iron keys from beneath the bar. The keys were attached to long, slim balsa wood plaques by thin brown leather strips, the room numbers painted in black onto the pale wood.

"Eight shillings." The barkeep looked at the three of us in turn. I tried and failed to suppress a gasp at the extortionate price. The barkeep frowned at me and added, "Each."

Keri simply chuckled and placed her palm on the bar. When she withdrew it, a single gold sovereign coin was left behind, enough to cover the cost of the rooms with four shillings to spare. Keri flicked the coin into the waiting palms of the landlord, who bit the edge of the coin to check its authenticity. He was surprised to find that he was able to leave a mark on the pure gold disc. He quickly pocketed the coin and pushed the two keys forward across the bar to Keri.

"Keep the change, of course. Have some food and ale sent up in an hour." Keri ordered, keeping one of the keys for herself and handing the other to me. The copper-haired wizard slid her arm around Cathal's waist, a flirtatious look in her eyes. "Only two beds and three to fill them. You can bunk with me."

"I don't think so." Even I was taken aback by the instinctive hostility that provoked my emphatic, contradictory response to Keri's proposal.

Startled, Keri glared at me before caressing Cathal's cheek and letting him go, with a short burst of laughter. "I jest, of course, my fair Ailidh."

"If you're looking for company, I'd lay with you tonight." The offer came from the lone, scarred sellsword that had been watching us so intently since we had entered the tavern, his voice a cold, emotionless drawl.

Keri dismissed the mercenary with a derisive snort. "I would rather rut with a pig."

"Some say that you already do, Keri of Moonchion." The mercenary glowered, wrapping his fingers more tightly around the hilt of his sword.

"Hah! No, I only fuck men or daevae. Unfortunately, you are neither."

"Witch!" The bounty hunter stood angrily, drawing his longsword with a flourish. "A renegade mage and a green cloak... Travelling together? I was tempted to just pass on word to the town garrison, but not after that. The king will reward me greatly, I think."

"No! I'll have no bloodshed in here!" The barkeep exclaimed in panicked tones, stepping backwards from the bar.

"What - what was it you called me?" Keri asked, her face a picture of innocence. "I am not sure I heard correctly."

"Witch!" The mercenary snarled, raising his longsword, ready to strike. The entire bar fell silent, having taken notice of the dispute. "Or d'you prefer *bitch*?"

As the sellsword stepped forward to attack Keri, Cathal made to draw his longsword, but before he had a chance to intervene, Keri snatched an empty glass from the bar and hurled it into the mercenary's face. I gasped in shock when, instead of breaking, the glass sank into the sellsword's forehead. He dropped his weapon and clutched at his face, not even able to scream as his form began to melt, shimmering and quivering until it reformed into that of a large cockerel. A nervous, slightly hysterical laugh came from an elderly female merchant sitting at a table towards the back of the tavern, which had otherwise fallen into stunned silence. Before anyone else could react, Keri stepped forward and grasped the bird in both hands, looking into its eyes for half a second before snapping its neck with a single, violent twist.

"These bounty hunters never learn." she muttered to herself, before tossing the dead bird onto the bar, addressing the stunned barkeep. "Goodman, have that plucked, roasted and sent up to my room."

A deathly silence hung over the tavern until Keri disappeared out of sight up the staircase to find her rented bedchamber, the clientele exchanging fearful glances and whispers. Cathal stepped alongside me and took my elbow into his hand, instructing the barkeep firmly, "See to it that we are not disturbed."

The barkeep swallowed in trepidation and nodded before pouring himself a large glass of a clear, caramel brown spirit, emptying it in a single gulp to calm his nerves. Cathal took the key from my hands, checked the number on the wooden fob and led me upstairs, anxious to find the security and privacy of our room. We did not speak until Cathal had closed and bolted the door.

"I don't believe what I've just seen."

"Now you understand just how dangerous Wild Magic is." Cathal slipped off his pack, unhooking Sapphire's cage from the left shoulder strap and placing it on the table between the double bed and the shoulder-high paper screen that partitioned off the third of the room furthest from the door.

"That - that wasn't magic. That was... I don't know what that was." I took off my own pack and placed it on the floor next to the bed, sitting down on the mattress, glad for the opportunity to take the weight off my feet. "And to think that she wanted you to lay with her tonight. What would've been left of you by morning?"

"I dread to think." Cathal turned to me, his face full of concern. "Do not think that I am ungrateful for what you did, but you should not vex her again. Next time she might not find it quite so amusing."

"I promised you I'd watch your back, and I will. I don't trust her."

"Neither do I."

"I wouldn't want to leave you alone with her."

Cathal avoided my gaze, uncomfortably aware of the implicit logic behind my statement. "I think she has had enough amusement for one day. We can relax for now." Cathal took a deep breath and sat wearily at the table, opening the door of Sapphire's cage. The cat mewed gratefully and stampeded straight for the comfort of the double bed, purring as she walked in a circle in the middle of the mattress, trying to find the perfect spot, paddling with her front paws at the bedcovers before lying down, grateful for the opportunity to be free of the confines of her cage.

"Do not think you are going to stay there all night, kitten." Cathal chided, wagging a disapproving finger at the cat.

"Leave her alone, Cathal." I reproached him, giving the cat a quick stroke before standing to investigate what was behind the partition screen. I peered over the translucent, shoulder-high wall and was delighted by what I saw - a fully-plumbed bathroom suite, including a sink, privy and, most importantly, a large, white, enamelled steel bath. I turned back to Cathal, a broad smile on my face. "A bath! I've been dreaming about having a bath for weeks!"
Cathal laughed. "Go ahead. You deserve one."
I turned the long, straight handle of the plain steel tap to run the water and stooped down to light the oil burners under each end of the bath, the orange flames leaving sooty marks on the blackened, exposed metal. As the bath filled and the water warmed, I opened my pack, searching for my nightgown. Cathal remained seated at the table, calmly honing the edge of his longsword with a wafer-thin sharpening stone. I retrieved a small package wrapped in waxed paper along with my now inexcusably grubby nightgown - it had not been washed since we had left Cathal's cabin. Inside the paper were the last few crumbs of the bar of soap I had insisted Cathal bring with us. He had considered it an unnecessary luxury, but I had been able to persuade him that if he expected me to wash in cold rivers and streams, I would need something to compensate for the lack of hot water. I placed the remains of the soap on the enamel dish next to the tap and draped my nightgown over the partition, dipping my fingertips into the rising water to check the temperature. The water was only lukewarm, barely above body temperature, so I opened the nozzles on the oil burners, letting the flames turn blue. I shut off the tap when the bath was three-quarters full and started to undress, folding my clothes over the top of the paper screen, next to my nightgown, as I waited for the water to reach a good temperature. I peered over the top of the screen, resting my arms on the top, my chin resting on my crossed wrists. "D'you think they have a laundry service?"
Cathal didn't even glance in my direction, still lazily scraping the whetstone along the edges of his sword. "Probably. I will ask when they come with our food."
"Would you? I'd kill for some clean clothes." I checked the water again and this time the temperature was perfect - just short of scalding. Steam rose from the bath as I

ducked down again, this time to turn off the burners. I eased myself into the bath, sighing as I immersed myself into the water, the heat reinvigorating my tight, tired muscles. I sank down into the bath, ducking completely beneath the surface, holding my breath for half a minute before resurfacing with a gasp. I sagged back against the hard tub, letting the energy from the water soak into my aching flesh. "Gods, that's good."

"It has been a hard journey. But now that we have reached the border, the terrain becomes less demanding. If the weather holds, we could reach Lesøsnø by the end of the month."

I took half of the remaining soap and lathered it in my hands, scrubbing the accumulated grime and sweat of three weeks of walking from my scalp and hair, the soap suds infusing the water with their lavender-scented perfume, coating my skin as I rubbed myself down with one of the cotton flannels that had been left for our use on the towel rail next to the bath. After over thirty days in the wilderness, it seemed bizarre that something as simple as a hot bath could feel like the height of civilisation. "I could stay in here all night."

"You would regret it in the morning." Cathal laughed. "I could do with a good wash, too."

"I wasn't going to mention it, but..." I teased, glad that the screen spared me the full force of the withering stare Cathal was no doubt aiming at me now. "Seriously though, the only thing I'd like more than a bath is to sleep in a proper bed. I never want to see another bed roll again."

"I have said that a few times myself, believe it or not."

"I'm not sure I do. You look more at home in the wilds than you ever did in your cabin." I said as I eased my legs over the rim of the bath, satisfied that had cleaned myself to a suitably civilised standard. I dried myself down with a clean towel from the rack next to the paper screen and retrieved my nightgown, recoiling slightly at the smell. I looked down at the filthy linen in my hands and considered whether I really wanted to wear it in this state. I tossed the nightgown into the hot water with disdain, working the fabric vigorously beneath the water between my hands, rubbing the worst stains with lather to disguise the infused scent of sweat with the fragrant floral oils from the soap. I pulled the soaking nightgown from the water and wrung the fabric as hard as I could in my hands, until no more drops of water fell from the damp fabric. Fortunately, the heat from the oil burners had left the room as warm as a summer's day. It would not take long for the fabric to dry and I would not risk a cold by putting the nightgown on now. The moist fabric clang to my skin, and I smoothed the creases out of the linen, the gown sticking tightly to the curves of my body. I suppressed a flush of pride when Cathal did a double-take as I stepped back into view from behind the screen. After the weeks of walking on and off the road, I was in the shape of my life; my figure lean and toned by the many hours and leagues of daily walking. I had lost half a dozen pounds since our journey had begun, and I felt as strong and fit as I ever had. Cathal did a poor job of pretending not to notice, but the moment was interrupted by a soft knock on the door.

"Who is it?" Cathal called out, standing to move to the door, his stiletto hidden from view, the hilt concealed in his palm and the blade pointed upwards behind his forearm, flat against his wrist.

The nervousness of the girl that replied was evident from the tremors in her voice. "I've brought your food, m'sir." Cathal flicked open the cover on the spyhole and peered through the door to confirm the identity of our visitor. Satisfied that all was in order, Cathal unbarred the door and let in the tavern barmaid. She was even younger than me, her long brown hair plaited into a single braid that fell midway down her back. The girl almost dropped the tray on her way to the table, looking wildly between Cathal and me, her sense of fear and panic only barely suppressed. The plates, glass goblets and pitcher rattled against the tray as her hands trembled. Cathal hid the blade of his stiletto inside his sleeve, his fingers and palm wrapped around the hilt, concealing it from the girl's view.

"Will there be anything else, m'sir?" the barmaid asked, anxious to leave, her fingers twitching against the short hem of her green cotton dress.

"Would it be possible to have some clothes washed?" Cathal asked, pointing to the trousers and blouse I had left hanging on the screen surrounding the bath.

"Not until morning I'm afraid, m'sir."

"Never mind. Thank you. You may go." Cathal gave her a reassuring smile, dismissing her with a silver shilling coin for her trouble, and the serving girl backed out of the room with a terrified, but grateful bow. He relocked the door as I made my way over to the table, drawn by the smell. It had been many hours since lunch and my stomach was beginning to make some very indelicate noises.

"I hope they didn't bring up chicken. I don't think I could stomach it right now." I told Cathal as I sat down and took up a serving spoon and fork, lifting the chunky cuts of meat and scraping aside some of the thick brown gravy to identify what had been brought up from the kitchen. Cathal sat in the chair next to me, pouring us both tall glasses of golden ale.

"What have we got?" asked Cathal, taking a long pull of ale from his glass and instantly topping it up.

"Beef, pork and lamb, roasted with potatoes and honeyed carrots. Nothing special, but better than wolf." I started loading our plates with generous stacks of meat, leaving only a little room for the vegetables. We had long since exhausted the supply of vegetables Cathal had packed, and over the course of our journey I found that I had developed a taste for unaccompanied meat, provided that it was well-cooked. To stop our meals from becoming too monotonous I had always taken pains to gather edible leaves and herbs on our journey, but I had not seen nor tasted a potato in over two weeks. The ones on the platter were a crispy golden brown and glistened with goose fat and salt crystals. The potatoes both looked and smelled divine, but I served myself sparingly. It would not be ladylike to gorge myself to the point of being sick.

"No herbs or seasoning on the roast. Disappointing." was Cathal's summary verdict. "The beer is excellent, though."

I picked up my glass and sipped the ale, getting sweet hints of caramel, citrus tones and a long bitter finish from the hops, accompanied by a strong hit of alcohol burning the back of my throat. "Oh my, where'd they get this? From the hold of a pirate ship?"

"Careful now. Drinking on an empty stomach is deadly." Cathal warned, spearing a quarter-inch thick slab of beef with his fork. "They buy it from Raghnall, an artisan brewer in Kinvarra."

"I can see why." I set down my glass and chomped down a slice of pork and a couple of potatoes, wanting a good layer of food in my stomach before I risked any more of the delicious, strong ale. "A couple of pints of that and I'll sleep like a log tonight."

"Make the most of it. We shall be camping again tomorrow night, only we will no longer be in Cothraine."

"What more can you tell me about Fossfjall and Lesøsnø? I've never been this far north. Father never spoke of the city, or how he met my mother. The subject was too painful for him, I think."

"Lesøsnø is the oldest city in the Western Triad. It was built by the Forefathers after the fall of Nagyjik, two score centuries ago."

"The Forefathers of Man, right? They were the ones who founded the Guild of the Art, yes?"

Cathal nodded and cut a roast potato in two with his fork, steam rising from the fluffy centre before dipping it in the gravy coating the meat on his plate. Then he popped both halves whole into his mouth and chewed thoughtfully for a moment before continuing. "Amongst other things. They also formally established the Churches of the Pantheon and built the Great Library of the Seven Scholars, one of the true wonders of the world. You could spend a lifetime in its halls and still only read a fraction of its collection."

"I can't wait to visit it in person, and not just because I can read the Nevanthi prophecies to find out why Father has been kidnapped. We didn't have that many books in Croycullen and most of the ones Father had did have were about metallurgy."

"Thrilling reading, I am sure." Cathal's voice was deadpan, though the look in his eyes was anything but.

"Only if you like to know how the amount of coke you use in a blast furnace affects the brittleness of iron."

"Valuable knowledge for an apprentice blacksmith, no doubt."

"No doubt." I agreed. "Is it true that the city is built on the edge of the Abyss?"

"Yes, The Great Library and the heart of the city both overlook the Caldera, the island at the heart of the Abyss. It is the oldest volcanic canyon in the world, and the largest, too."

"How big is it?"

"The Abyss is five leagues deep, almost three hundred leagues long from the Lesøsnø docks to the ocean at Hemafjord, and four score leagues wide, on average. The

island of Caldera itself is three score leagues long by thirty leagues across and is almost entirely made from black obsidian glass. The island is all that remains of the volcanic plug sealing the volcano after the eruption that blasted out the fjord. Pirates carved a town into the glass centuries ago. The port there is almost busy as Lesøsnø itself."
"That sounds amazing."
"It does have to be seen to be believed, though I do not recommend visiting the town of Obsidian itself. It is the world's foremost safe haven for privateers and cutthroats." Cathal pushed aside his plate and retreated behind the bath screen, relighting the oil burners and refilling the bath. "The eruption of the volcano that created the fjord must have shaken the world. It beggars belief that Nature can wreak destruction on such a scale. It is just as well that the volcano has shown no signs of activity in over a hundred thousand years."
I swallowed a final mouthful of roast potato before setting down my cutlery and moving to the double bed. I turned back to the table and refilled my glass with ale, taking it with me to rest it on the nightstand next to the bed. I pulled back the cover sheets, nudging Sapphire delicately away from the centre of the bed, sliding onto the firm mattress and enjoying the feel of the soft linen covers. I stroked the ears of the cat as she purred sleepily, lying insensate on the bed. "Lesøsnø has never been conquered, has it?"
"Many ambitious kings from Sundgau and Cothraine have laid siege to the city over the years." Cathal's voice sounded clearly from behind the screen, accompanied by the splashing of water as he bathed. "But every single one was defeated. The very nature of the place defies conquest. All of the approaches to the city by land or by water allow the defenders to rain down a tempest of arrows on any armies occupying the planes below. The city walls are too tall and too thick to breach with siege weaponry and the gates are easily defended. The wood of the city's buildings is magically warded and impervious to fire. And the troops that guard the city are among some of the best-trained in the world. They might only number ten thousand men, but they could repel an army that outnumbered them by a score to one with ease."
"This all sounds very idyllic: a picturesque city of high culture and literature that's invulnerable to attack from the

rest of the kingdoms. There must be something wrong with the place." I observed, settling down into a comfortable spot on the deep, soft mattress.

Cathal laughed as he stepped clear of the bath, satisfied that he had done all he could to free himself from the layers of accumulated sweat and grime that were a consequence of weeks on the road. As he put on his nightshirt, he replied in a tone of playful chastisement, looking at me over the top of the paper privacy screen. "Ailidh, you are far too young to be so cynical."

"Father always told me that if something sounds too good to be true, it is. Good's always balanced by bad in all things." I replied, as I idly stroked Sapphire's back fur. The cat's eyes were tightly closed and she was sleeping soundly. It would be impossible to remove her from the bed now without risking a major feline temper tantrum.

"This is true." Cathal dried his hair and sat back at the table, his face hidden by the towel. "It is difficult to find much fault with the city, though. The goods and services there are rather expensive and some find it overcrowded, but there is little crime, the residents are polite and friendly, and it has the finest theatres, artisans and restaurants in the Triad."

"I see." I was intrigued to know more, but too tired to press him for further details. I took a last gulp of ale and laid my head back on the pillow and was about to close my eyes when it occurred to me that Cathal showed no signs of getting ready to sleep, even though he must have been just as weary as me. "Aren't you sleeping? Surely you don't need to keep watch in here."

"I will sleep soon enough." Cathal drained another glass of the rich, strong ale and reached down under the table to retrieve the bed roll from his pack.

"You don't have to sleep on the floor. There's plenty of room for both of us."

"Thank you for the offer, but I am not certain that is such a good idea."

"Cathal..." I paused, plucking up my courage and wondering just how bold I should be. "I want you to sleep with me. To lay with me."

Cathal stammered incoherently for a second, shocked by my directness. "Ailidh, what you ask is not something you should do lightly."

"I know." I said, pulling my nightgown off over my head as I stood and moved across the room to stand next to Cathal at the table. The ranger stirred uncomfortably in his chair and crossed his legs, perturbed by my nakedness, even though I knew this was not the first time he had seen me without clothes. I ensnared his wrist in my fingers and placed his right hand on my left breast, so that he could feel how my heart raced. "I *want* you, Cathal. I want you to touch me, to love me as I love you."

My stomach churned as the silence lingered for several moments, Cathal unable or unwilling to find the words to voice an answer. I had hoped that the feel of my skin beneath his palm would free his repressed desire and inspire him into carrying me over to the bed, but as the time passed, I realised that my hope was just a fantasy. Finally, his reply came and he avoided meeting my eyes, embarrassed. "Ailidh, I am sorry, but I cannot."

"Why?" I demanded, my temper rising. I had laid my desires bare before him, only for him to seemingly reject them out of hand. "Are my legs too short, my hips too narrow, or are my tits too big, or too soft? You couldn't take your eyes off them earlier!"

"Ailidh, please." Cathal said, now intensely self-conscious and troubled with the way I pressed his fingers hard into my breast.

"Then what? Should I dye my hair red? Perhaps I should have let Keri take you after all." I released Cathal's wrist and he pulled back his hand reluctantly, looking away to his left-hand side, appearing distressed. Perhaps I should have stopped, to allow the ranger to explain himself, but his rejection had left me feeling hurt, angry and frustrated. I lifted my fringe away from the disfigured side of my face, exposing my half-melted ear, reptilian eye and the arcane fire burn that scarred my forehead, cheek and neck.

"Cathal, look at me. *Look* at me. It's this, isn't it? This is why you won't take me to bed."

I was crushed when he faced me down, tears of regret forming in the corner of his eyes. "I am sorry, Ailidh. In time you will come to know the difference between love, desire and lust. If I were to lay with you tonight, it would be to satisfy my lust, not my desire, and this is something I cannot do. Not with a woman I am proud to consider a friend."

"A friend, but not a lover." I said sourly, slipping back into my gown as I retreated to the bed to find refuge and solace on the mattress, beneath the crisp linen sheets.

"Ailidh, I have not taken a lover since Aoibheann died. She was the love of my life." Cathal sat back down, fortifying himself with a long draft of ale.

"And you are mine." I snapped in retort. It was the truth. I felt it in the way that my gut churned in the wake of his denial of my desire.

Cathal looked at me sadly and spoke in a condescending manner that made my blood seethe. "It may seem that way now, but you are young. It is difficult to tell the difference between love and lust at your age. That is why it is better to wait until you are sure before sharing your body. The pleasures of the flesh are compelling, but transitory – true love is eternal."

"I'm not so young that I don't know my own feelings." I scoffed, annoyed by his patronising, superior tone. "I love you, Cathal. Why won't you love me back?"

"If only it were that simple. Your figure would make the most beautiful courtesan from the Jewels envious, but love must come from a place deeper than that. I have grown to enjoy and value your friendship, but that is not the same thing as romantic desire. It was never my intention to hurt you. I apologise if I gave you a false impression of the nature of our relationship. I regret that I am not seeking the same kind of companionship as you." For once Cathal didn't flinch when he saw my scar, meeting my gaze evenly. "It is late. We can talk more about this tomorrow if you wish."

I didn't reply, unable to find any words to say. I drew the bedsheet tightly around me like armour, and laid my head down on the pillow, still watching the ranger's body language. Cathal checked the latch on the door a final time, retrieved a spare bedsheet from the linen closet and turned out the gas lamps before settling down on his padded cotton bed roll, his longsword and stiletto unsheathed and lying on the floor beside him in easy reach, in case we should be disturbed by an intruder during the night. There was a ripple of fabric as Cathal covered himself with the bedsheet.

"Goodnight, Ailidh. Sleep well."

"Goodnight, Cathal." I replied, exhausted, but also aroused, frustrated and dejected. Despite Cathal's blessing and the comfort of the bed, sleep eluded me.

14 - Aiden

King Maeryn mouthed inaudibly to himself as he gazed over the ramparts with glassy, unfocussed eyes. We stood on the fortified curtain wall surrounding the Royal Palace, looking north over the bustle of commoners and nobleman conducting their business on Dara's Square and the Guildhall market to the imposing spire of the Tower of the Aether. My cloak flapped like a slackened sail in the wind as I used my bulk to shield the king from the warm, wet southerly breeze whipping inland from the Bay of Tides. Maeryn teetered unsteadily on his one good leg, grabbing onto the corner of a merlon in the crenellations that ran along the length of the battlements for support. The Arch Mage had not spoken with the king for over a week, so Maeryn had taken to spending his afternoons standing on the balcony his chamber in the King's Tower or here on the wall above the gatehouse, simply staring at the silver spire on the other side of the city. As he pined for Karryghan's guidance, Maeryn waited with seemingly infinite patience on the castle walls, talking silently to himself until a signal of insight came from across the city. Whether the king believed that he was speaking with Karryghan or directly towards his patron deity I dared not ask. It was another erratic turn of behaviour from the king, whose temperament had never been a paragon of stability to begin with. Even though I was not party to the meetings between the Arch Mage and the king, it seemed clear that Karryghan held the king's will in the palm of his hand. I had no doubt that Sìne's account describing the last confrontation between Maeryn and the Queen was utterly faithful. Karryghan had been appointed Arch Mage at the unprecedentedly early age of thirty-six and had served in the office for nearly five decades. He was renowned for his political astuteness and ability to manipulate events through careful forward planning, earning him the backhanded epithet The Schemer of Siskine. There were more rumours surrounding the circumstances of Karryghan's ascension to Arch Mage than there were grains of sand on the beaches between Clongarvan and

Bray, but none of them were complimentary with regard to the character of the leader of Cothraine's Guild of the Art. Karryghan had helped Maeryn's predecessor, King Connell, resolve a trade dispute with Fossfjall and negotiate the unification treaty that had committed Connell's daughter Reilynn to marry the Crown Prince of Fossfjall, Sjur. It seemed inexplicable that he should have invested so much time and effort to guarantee the security of the kingdom, only to deliberately throw it away just a handful of years later by precipitating a coup and violating the terms of the treaty he had helped draft by having Reilynn marry Maeryn to shore up the usurper's claim to the throne. The story Sine had recounted to me of Maeryn's argument with the queen made sense when you factored in Karryghan's foresight with his reputation for ruthlessness and ambition. The Arch Mage was nearing the end of his time on the material plane. While no-one would have the temerity to imply that Karryghan's power was in decline, not even his arcane mastery was sufficient to defy the passage of time and the inevitable meeting with the Dark Rider that awaited us all. It was only too plausible that Karryghan would take advantage of the chaos that usually accompanied the astrological conjunction of the planes to achieve his aim of transcending to divinity and evading the Dark Rider's Judgment upon the moral righteousness of their conduct in life. A man like Karryghan would happily allow nations to burn if it served his goals. And Maeryn was vain enough and gullible enough to believe that he was instrumental to Karryghan's goal of utilising the Nexus to travel to the astral plane, making it all too easy for Karryghan to prey upon his insecurities and manipulate him. The king had already spent more than an hour staring at the Arch Mage's apartment at the apex of the Tower of the Aether and he had not stopped silently talking to himself the whole time. I kept myself amused by watching the crowds in the market around the Guildhall. It was a microcosm of the city and country as a whole. Commoners, artisans and nobles all rubbed shoulders as they bartered for goods and services. Even from quarter of a league away it was possible to make out some of the enthusiastic haggling around the stalls selling cured meats, dried fish and spices imported from the Reach. It was a welcome reminder that normality did still exist outside of the palace walls. Maeryn was oblivious to it however, as he closed his eyes and continued his mute vigil, his thin, bloodless lips constantly moving as he maintained his soundless commune. At least the wind from the coast had begun to wane as the sun had warmed the land over course of the morning. I was just beginning to wonder how long Maeryn would spend gazing at the wizards' tower like a disconsolate lover mooning out of a window for an absent sweetheart when I was disturbed by the scurry of rapid footsteps ascending the stairs of the gatehouse. The sound had me instinctively placing a hand on the hilt of my longsword, but my fingers relaxed their grip when I saw the flushed cheeks of one of the king's pageboys appear over the edge of the wallwalk at the mouth of the staircase. The boy had clearly run all the way from the King's Tower. I held up my hand to prevent the page from approaching too closely to the king, and he put his hands on his knees as he bent over to try and catch his breath.

"What is it, lad?" I put a hand on his shoulder to steady him. The boy was still gasping for air when he raised his head to answer me.

"His majesty asked to be told if Queen Reilynn left the palace." The page said, wheezing. Maeryn's head snapped around to look at the boy, his attention on the Tower of the Aether was finally broken by the mention of the queen's name. "She's collecting cut flowers on the parterre." Maeryn immediately made for the staircase with a look of thunderous fury on his face. I gestured to the nearest sentry. "Give the lad some refreshment and escort him back to the palace."

"Yes, your grace." The sentry replied, grinning craftily as I silently told him what kind of refreshment I had in mind, mouthing *beer* to the soldier with a wink. I had a suspicion that the pageboy would find his afternoon duties far more palatable after a goblet or two of ale, especially if the king's discourse with the queen on the parterre played out in the manner I was anticipating. I handed the boy over to the care of the soldier and hurried down the staircase in pursuit of my liege. It was not difficult to catch up the king's head start. The injury that he had received to his thigh as young apprentice ranger during a sword sparring session had stunted the growth of his right leg, leaving Maeryn with a lopsided gait. The effects from the training accident had been so serious that it resulted in Maeryn being discharged from his apprenticeship with the Order of Sylvan and left him so badly hobbled that he would never be physically able enough to serve in any of the branches of Cothraine's military services. To say that the experience had left Maeryn embittered would be a gross understatement, especially since the other trainee involved in the incident was not even reprimanded and went on to serve the rangers with distinction for many years, or so I had been told.

The parterre garden was bisected by the white gravel avenue that led from the gatehouse to the front of the royal palace and comprised of two regimented beds of cultivated flowers, each over a hundred yards long. The queen and half a dozen of her handmaidens trod lightly between the ranks of brightly coloured asters and dahlias, carefully selecting the boldest and most perfectly formed blooms for harvesting. Reilynn was demonstrating to a couple of the younger handmaidens how to identify the flowers with the strongest, straightest stems and exactly where to cut to stimulate the flower into growing replacement blooms. The elder handmaidens followed closely behind, placing the cut flowers carefully into wicker baskets, which hung from handles looped over their elbows. The queen ignored the approach of Maeryn until he rudely interrupted her in the middle of a sentence as she was indicating to her attentive handmaidens when to choose between single and globe forms for a cut flower arrangement.

"Reilynn. You have been avoiding me." Maeryn interjected brusquely.

"I have nothing to say to you, snake." Reilynn looked down her nose at the king as if she had been presented with a cow pat on a silver platter.

"You are my wife and queen. I demand that you accompany me to the King's Tower." Maeryn said, unperturbed by Reilynn's icy putdown.

"I will do no such thing. Be gone, wretch. Your very presence makes the flowers wilt, and I will not be deprived of what little beauty remains in this place." Reilynn made a dismissive gesture with her secateurs and made to turn her back to him.

Incensed, Maeryn reached out and grabbed the sleeve of the queen's dress. "Now wait a minu-"
Before he even had chance to finish his protest, three of the handmaidens had interposed themselves between Maeryn and the queen, each one with a foot-long aetherium hairpin clutched in their fists. Maeryn gasped in shock as the lethally sharp points hovered less than an inch from his throat. I took an involuntary step backwards when I saw the look of determination written on the faces of each of the handmaidens. One of the girls was just eleven years old, but her eyes glowed with the molten steel of a veteran assassin just before the kill. The temperature on the parterre seemed to drop a dozen degrees as the other handmaidens moved to flank me, their own weapons held rock steady in their hands. My heart fluttered in alarm when I noticed that the handmaiden taking up a position behind me was Sìne. There was no question of me intervening on behalf of the king. I knew with an absolute certainty that if she had to choose between me and the queen, Sìne would choose Reilynn. She would embed her hairpin deep into my throat before my sword even cleared its scabbard.
Reilynn tapped Maeryn's offending hand with the blade of her secateurs, hard enough to sting, but gently enough not to break the skin. "Off! Touch me again and you will regret it."
Maeryn let go of her arm and found himself being shepherded towards the palace along the avenue by the triad of handmaidens still holding their weapons at his neck. Two handmaidens remained with the queen on the parterre as Sìne ushered me along in the king's wake, her own hairpin held ready in her hand. The handmaidens broke formation when we were a few dozen yards away from the gateway to the King's Tower, stepping away from him but forming a barrier between him and the avenue that led back to the parterre. Maeryn snarled with impotent rage and hobbled as quickly as he could back to the safety of his chambers. I anticipated it would require several flagons of wine to dull the edge off his foul mood. After the other handmaidens began to make their way back to the parterre to continue their botany lesson, Sìne lingered

behind, just for a moment, to favour me with a wink to show me that she felt that there were no hard feelings between us. Butterflies churned in my stomach at the thought that she could have ended me in the blink of an eye, had the queen wished it. I visited her quarters in the Queen's Tower later that night and the lingering tension between us after the incident on the parterre was palpable as the handmaiden greeted me silently. I hardly had chance to close the door before Sine grabbed the pauldrons of my armour, hooked her leg behind my calf and wrestled me to the floor, her lips firmly pressed against mine. Our lovemaking was ferocious and lasted almost until dawn.

15 – Fiacre

It had been three weeks since Aiden had visited the city garrison to warn me about King Maeryn's aspirations of godhead and the Arch Mage's undermining of the monarch's grasp on reality. Rather than simply wait for the inevitable summons to the King's Tower ordering me to send men across the Fossfjall border to retrieve this so-called Nexus, instead I had used my time to comprehensively review the command structure of my troops across the kingdom. I had a limited pool of experienced officers following the purge, most of which I had been assigned to regiments securing the capital in the time following Maeryn's coup. I could depend upon the loyalty and discipline of these units, but my confidence in the troops occupying garrisons along Cothraine's northern and eastern borders was less certain. Their commanders were either young, inexperienced or unreliable, or sometimes the unwelcome combination of all three. I had gathered a dozen of my most senior and best-trusted commanders for a confidential meeting and shared Aiden's concerns with them. It spoke well of my Field Barons that hardly any of them seemed surprised in the least when I told them the Duke Companion and I had proof that Karryghan was undermining the rule of king and potentially the security of the kingdom along with it. We agreed that there was little threat to the security of Cothraine along the eastern border with Sundgau. The mountain ranges of the Dragonspine and the Satyr's Graveyard were all but impassable, save for the glacial valley of the Rift and the coastal path between Bray and Weberwihr. Both of these natural chokepoints were strongly garrisoned merely out of constitutional formality. The previous King of Sundgau had died prematurely in a hunting accident, falling from his horse and breaking his neck while pursuing deer in the forest south of the sundgauvian capital city, Belfort. The regent ruling in his stead was in his mid-sixties and was not belligerently disposed to anything save carafes of wine from the lush vineyards of Lussac and Riquewihr. He was content to let his waistline expand and his liver rot while the new, infant King of Sundgau spent the best part of the next decade and a half coming of age. So there was no question of hostilities arising along our eastern frontier, provided that the Sundgauvians were not directly incited. The northern border with Fossfjall, on the other hand, was of far more concern. The diplomatic services had already reported that Crown Prince Sjur was already openly advocating an assault against our border garrisons in retaliation for Maeryn breaking off the unification treaty that would have been secured by Sjur's marriage to Reilynn. My desire was to redeploy some of my Field Barons to take command of the frontier garrisons so that their current commanding officers could be embedded into the better-disciplined units nearer the capital. This would allow the greener officers to be retrained by more experienced personnel, strengthening the overall competency of my officer corps. I had anticipated some resistance to my plan, but instead the Field Barons practically fell over themselves to recommend their units to re-house captains from the frontier. In the end I had to negotiate postings for several of the Field Barons, horse-trading access to luxury goods in return for less challenging garrison assignments on the Fossfjall frontier. Competition for the command of the garrisons in the Western Weald was fierce, where the Field Barons anticipated the greatest potential opportunities for glory in battle with troops marching south from Lesøsnø. The backwater garrisons near Sylane on the coast adjoining the Bay of Silence and the Mouth of the Dragon were more challenging to fill, as were the frontier posts bordering Pineholm and the Dragonspine mountains at the eastern end of the North Riding. The troops here were perceived to be the dregs of the Cothraine Field Army, and for good reason. The postings were so quiet that any adolescent in a leather jerkin able to hold a polearm upright was deemed a competent enough soldier to secure the border. I had little patience nor talent for conducting training drills myself, but several of my Field Barons were delighted by the notion of whipping a garrison into shape (literally, in a couple of in cases) and moulding a lax group of ill-disciplined soldiers into a coherent fighting force. They still drove a hard bargain in terms of the perks they expected to derive personally from giving up cushier posts nearer the capital for the frontier, but since the costs would be borne from the coffers of the royal purse, I had no qualms about giving my Barons what they wanted, since I would be repaid handsomely by their efforts in just a few months. Not only would I have a better trained officer corps, but Cothraine's borders would be manned by better-disciplined, more effective troops as well. By the time King Maeryn sent a messenger to demand my attendance at a war council in the Royal Palace, all of my plans to redeploy my senior commanders and improve the standard of training in the Field Army were already underway. If I could delay any potential incursion north of the border into Fossfjall for another month, I felt that we would stand a better than even chance against any force Crown Prince Sjur would be able to muster against us. The longer I was able to prevent open conflict with the forces of Fossfjall improved our chances of victory in any kind of extended conflict. As the wheels of my horse-drawn carriage crunched the marble gravel of the avenue leading towards the palace, I closed my eyes and drew a deep breath, wondering why I had been summoned by Maeryn.

After my coach came to a halt, I was pleasantly surprised to be met at the foot of the King's Tower by Duke Companion Aiden, the king's principal bodyguard himself. We shook hands and bowed a formal greeting before Aiden wrapped an arm around my back to clasp one of the pauldrons of my armour, leading me away from both the tower and the carriage for a moment in silence. He smiled just before rediscovering his tongue. "My lord Fiacre, it is good to see you again. The day finds you well, I hope."
"That it does, my lord." I replied cautiously. While more of an acquaintance than a friend, Aiden nonetheless was a valued confidante. I knew that it was no coincidence that he had intercepted me before entering the palace – he had information he wished to share with me, preferably in private, before the number of prying ears got too numerous. "What news have you?"
When we were out of earshot from the footmen and squires attending to my carriage, Aiden explained why he had pulled me aside. "The Arch Mage is here. Be mindful of your true feelings and what you might wish him to know.

Once you are in the same room as him, you might as well be made from glass."

"Succubus's slit, that is all I needed." I swore under my breath. "Anything else?"

"Just that Maeryn is in a foul mood, though that seems to be the norm, these days. The king drinks so much lately that the palace cellars are starting to run dry." Aiden said, without his typical air of amused self-confidence. As the king's personal guardian Aiden bore the brunt of Maeryn's mercurial tempers for hours every single day, and it was clearly beginning to weigh down the Duke Companion's famously sunny disposition. "It is a good day when he has drunk himself into a stupor by noon. But today is not a good day."

"I will mind my manners, then." I replied, equally without humour. "Shall we get this over with?"

"Please." Aiden escorted me into the palace, where the king and the Arch Mage awaited us in Maeryn's Privy Chamber in the King's Tower. We bowed in deference to the king when we entered, before taking our seats at the council table. Aiden took his customary position at the left hand side of the king, while I was placed on the opposite side of the table to the king, to emphasize my place as the subordinate. Karryghan was seated immediately to Maeryn's right. His wyvern-headed staff stood behind his chair, seemingly without support, as if it were a sentinel standing guard on the citadel walls. I lost my composure for a second when I noticed that Karryghan had brought an aide to the meeting, my lover Dervla. It was a subtle reminder of my indebtedness to the Arch Mage and the power he had to change the course of my life both professionally and personally. Dervla said nothing, her petite hands folded neatly on the table before her as she sat subserviently to the Arch Mage's right, but we knew each other's moods so intimately that she didn't need to speak. Just one sultry glance along the length of the table had my pulse racing as she licked her lower lip suggestively. It was a clever move from Karryghan, to use my infatuation with Dervla to unnerve me and make it easier to manipulate my emotions and decisions. I steeled myself and attempted to pretend she wasn't there, so that I could focus on the business at hand. After all, war is a business that should be decided with a cold head and a cold heart. Passions get in the way of wise choices. Karryghan regarded me with a glacial stare and I allowed myself a tiny wry smile, conceding a grudging respect for how the Arch Mage had played his opening gambit.

"You wished to see me, your grace?" I said, directing my words to the king, but my eyes to Karryghan. Everyone in the room knew exactly who was really in charge, except for the king himself.

"You will recall, Field Duke, your recent journey to Croycullen." Maeryn said, more as a statement than a question.

"Yes, your grace, the business with the fake blacksmith. Did his interrogation yield information of value?" I asked, without really wanting to know the details. Given the amount of time that had elapsed since the abduction, I doubted that any flesh remained on his bones.

"Yes, valuable information indeed. Of incalculable value, perhaps." Maeryn said, his eyes glazing over.

Karryghan placed a cautionary palm on the back of the king's forearm. "The king's enthusiasm is understandable, but is perhaps premature at this point." The Arch Mage's tone was mild, but the level of disrespect in his choice of words was breathtaking. No-one else at the table would have dared to speak so dismissively. "Eoghan had in his possession, or otherwise knew the location of, an item of extreme interest to the Crown."

"Did he tell you were to find it, your grace?"

"Sadly not, Field Duke. At least not directly," Karryghan stroked his beard. "But I am certain it is north of the border. You *must* find it. Nothing is of greater importance."

"I will need more information than that, your grace. What am I to look for exactly?"

"Eoghan encountered it just prior to his disappearance. This much is certain. It was somewhere on the road to Lesøsnø, in a farmstead occupied by a blonde woman and her baby daughter. The girl would have come of age by now." Karryghan explained.

"Forgive me, your grace, but you have just described half of the steadings in the North Riding. And I still do not know what I am looking for."

"The exact form of the object is not known. But it is a magical device of unspeakable power – an aetheric nexus." Karryghan said, somewhat reluctantly. "It is suffice to say that you will recognise it when you see it. Even the most backward of your footmen could not fail to perceive its power. Eoghan must have gone to great lengths to conceal it. I have spent the last few weeks scrying for it, but it is hidden well enough to evade even my second sight. It has become necessary to conduct the search in person. Time is of the essence. It must be found before the winter solstice."

The imposition of the solstice as a deadline was intriguing, but it was beyond my place to inquire why such urgency was needed. I turned to face the king. He appeared to be in raptures at the Arch Mage's words – the prospect of an omnipotent magical artefact being dangled before his eyes.

"Your orders, my liege?"

"You lack the wit to deduce them for yourself?" Maeryn replied, aghast. "Take the army across the border at Skøgvik and conduct house-to-house searches for the Nexus. Raze every farm between the frontier and the gates of Lesøsnø if you have to."

"You wish the destruction of the kingdom, then?" I asked, with a resigned sigh.

"I beg your pardon?" Maeryn shouted, incensed.

"That would be the consequence of carrying out such a reckless order, your grace." I said, lifting my chin in defiance. "I will not do it."

Maeryn leapt to his feet. "I can have you executed and replaced by someone who will!"

"I assure you, my liege, not even the least experienced of my Field Barons would carry out such a request. The Fossfjall army would not fail to respond to such an invasion across the border, and they would annihilate us on the battlefield."

"We outnumber the Fossians three to one!"

"And it would still be a slaughter. The majority of our troops are not battle-hardened and would be no match for a well-drilled, disciplined force like the Fossfjall army. I am a general, your grace. Not an abattoir worker. Brute force will not find this Nexus, not without unleashing the full wrath of the Fossfjall army upon the gates of Clongarvan."

Karryghan addressed the king with a dismissive wave of his hand. "Sit down, Maeryn. The Field Duke is correct."

Maeryn bristled, his temper still boiling over. "Once we have the Nexus, such concerns will be beneath us!"

"Sit down." Karryghan thundered. The deadly look in his eyes did not brook disagreement, even from the monarch. Maeryn swallowed his ire and resumed his seat without another sound. "You have an alternative plan, Field Duke?"

"I assume Eoghan is no longer able to cooperate?" I asked the Arch Mage and the emotionless stare I received in reply told me with absolute certainty that he was dead. "Hmm, then we need some other way of gathering information of where to search. A small, nimble force could penetrate the border easily without provoking a counterattack. But they would have to know precisely where to look before crossing the frontier."

"It is possible such clues may remain in Eoghan's workshop." Karryghan mused, seeming to peer beyond the back wall of the chamber. His keen eyes refocused on me with an almost physically painful intensity. "Duke Fiacre, you will return to Croycullen and conduct a search of the area. If Eoghan stashed the Nexus in a hiding place, it surely will not be far from his smithy. And you may wish to inquire as to the fate of his daughter while you are at it."

"I will assemble a scouting troop immediately, your grace." I replied.

"You misunderstand, Duke." Karryghan's eyes glowed with malice. "You will attend to the matter personally, since the last band of scouts you sent failed miserably to report anything of importance. Besides, it would not be to our advantage to let word of the Nexus spread beyond this room further than is absolutely necessary. The secrecy of your mission is paramount, Field Duke, but I would not expect you to do this task alone, of course. You will be accompanied by Malvina of Ballinlara. She is the Grand Master of Divination in Cothraine – little escapes her powers of scrying and she was once a student of Eoghan. Such insight will no doubt prove invaluable when you reach Croycullen."

I did not need magical powers to sense Karryghan's satisfaction at having so deftly removed my troublesome presence from the capital while he schemed with the king in my absence. I could hardly refuse the request. Better to accept it implicitly than have the king demand it of me. I had averted the possibility of war for the time being, but I would be away from the city for weeks carrying out this fool's errand, all the while being under the scrutiny of one of Karryghan's Grand Masters. Dervla looked at me sympathetically when I wondered whether it would have been better just to let Maeryn have me executed.

16 - Cathal

I was relieved to be back in the forest after the awkwardness of our overnight stay at The Sundered Shield. The landlord was unambiguously delighted to see the back of us. He was so happy, in fact, that he provided us with a week's worth of water and field rations without an extra fee. In response, Keri gave him the chicken wishbone she had removed from the carcass of the mercenary that she had transformed in the bar. *Something to remember us by*, she had told him, accompanied by her sweetest, most innocent and profoundly insincere smile. I doubted that I would ever be welcome to set foot in the place again. While Keri had left the tavern in buoyant spirits, Ailidh was rather more reluctant to get back on the road and her morale had not improved noticeably in the two days since. We had barely spoken since I had turned down the proposition to lay with her. It was painful to see Ailidh in such a sullen mood, but I had no regrets. I hoped that she would come to appreciate that it would have been unwise to act solely upon our physical attraction alone. As much as I respected her abilities as a smith and enjoyed the stimulation of her company after so long alone in exile, I did not see her as she saw me, as a potential life partner. It was not just her disfigurement that made me wary. The difference in our ages and the pain I still felt from Aoibheann's loss discouraged me from opening my heart too much. Living alone and in isolation after the purge had made me suspicious of people and their motives. It was difficult enough to grasp the possibility of a true friendship again. The notion of an intimate companionship, even with someone I liked as much as Ailidh, was a step too far for me to contemplate. I hoped that once we reached the Fossfjall capital that the splendour of the City of Spires would act as a great distraction and take her mind off the infatuation she held for me. Once we had made use of the Great Library and its endless documentary resources, I was certain that we would discover enough information to renew our hunt for Ailidh's abducted father and uncover the reason behind his kidnap. Eager to reach Lesøsnø as quickly as possible, I stepped up the pace as I led us north to take advantage of the last of the autumn sunshine. The Western Weald was familiar territory for me, even on the northern side of the Cothraine-Fossfjall border. It was a temperate forest predominately stocked by elder, beech, rowan, willow, birch, yew and oak, which I had spent years ranging in tandem with Aoibheann during our service together in the Order of Sylvan. The fauna in these parts was relatively benign for the most part: foxes, deer, badgers, plus the occasional family of wild boars or a straggling pack of wolves looking to establish a territory after having been pushed out of richer hunting grounds to the north-east in Pineholm or the Hemafjord peninsula to the west. Since Maeryn's coup, the number of trade caravans travelling on the road between Birlone and Lesøsnø had collapsed, along with any need to maintain the roads. In just a couple of years, much of the road had become overgrown and uneven thanks to the prodigious amounts of rainfall saturating the region during the growing season. Red and fallow deer had reclaimed much of the forest neighbouring the road, taking advantage of the reduced traffic to feast on the saplings, bracken and heather growing in the absence of carriage wheels, hooves and boots trampling any fledging growth back down between the weathered limestone cobbles. As I led Ailidh and Keri through an avenue of young hawthorn, rowan and elder encroaching onto the overgrown cobbled pathway, gradually I realised that the usual ambient sounds of the forest were absent. The unnatural silence set my danger sense tingling. There was no birdsong, nor any of the background chattering that you would expect to hear from the multitude of insects and arboreal creatures that ought to be buzzing and scurrying around us. Even the rustling of the wind through the canopies of the trees was subdued. I knew from hard-earned experience in the wilds that this could only mean one thing: predators. Deer were not the only species that had taken advantage of the reduced human traffic along the roads to reclaim territory in the Weald.

With my senses instantly on high alert, I signalled the danger to my companions with a single sharp click of my fingers. I unslung my pack and placed it on the floor. I readied my longbow and nocked a broad-headed arrow on the string. Ailidh set down Sapphire's cage and her own pack next to mine and took a handful of arrows from my quiver for her own recurved shortbow, mounting an arrow onto the string but leaving the bow undrawn until a target presented itself.

"Cathal, what's wrong?" she asked in hushed tones, her wide, wary eyes scanning the forest around us.

I did not have time to reply before Keri hissed, "Quiet, girl! We are being hunted."

The sorcerer seemed just as attuned to the rhythm of the wilderness as I was. She gripped her staff in both hands, the tip glowing with aetheric energy as Keri swept a wide figure of eight pattern in the space before her, reaching out with her mystic awareness to feel for the presence of whatever threatened us. The skin on the back of my neck crawled with the sensation that we were being watched. The ferns and bracken of the undergrowth were still. With no visual sign of what stalked us I listened intently for clues that would help me identify and locate the predator. The unnatural silence itself told me what I needed to know. We were dealing with an ambush predator, which only meant one thing in the Western Weald: ettercaps. And wherever there were ettercaps you were also sure to find giant spiders that obeyed their commands like faithful hounds.

"Keep watch on the canopy." I warned my travelling companions, slinging my bow across my back and drawing my sword and stiletto from their scabbards at my waist. I gestured for Ailidh to do the same and trade her shortbow for her wakizashi. By the time our enemies revealed themselves, it would be too late to let fly with even a single properly aimed arrow. The preferred tactic of monstrous spiders when springing an ambush was to surprise their prey from above. "And be careful where you tread. This whole area must be webbed."

Ettercaps used the silken webs of their arachnid pets to locate, rather than entrap their prey. Their web sense gave them an extended awareness able to detect any vibration created within the area with such a degree of sensitivity that they were able to tell not just where creatures were in their traps, but also what they were as well.

"Stay close to me." I told Ailidh, my voice barely above a whisper. "Keri, can you sense anything?"

"Half a dozen spiders and a pair of ettercaps. They are all within two score yards of the road." The mage replied, aiming her staff at an ancient oak tree at least three centuries old, judging by the girth of its trunk. The lowest boughs of its crown stretched across the fractured, overgrown cobbles of the poorly maintained road surface. "I will deal with the spider-fuckers. You exterminate the vermin."

Keri directed us forward with a shake of her staff and I nodded my assent to her plan. I had fought by the side of mages before. Ailidh and I would act as bait to trigger the ambush, hoping that we could stay alive long enough for Keri to unleash her arcane firepower. As I took a careful step towards the oak, I gave Ailidh her instructions. "Keep two yards behind me and guard my back. The exoskeleton is weakest at the joints. Aim for their legs and keep your sword between you and their mouths. You do not want to get bitten."

My eyes flicked constantly between the floor and the canopies of the surrounding trees as we edged forward. There was still absolutely no sound beyond our footsteps and no sign of any movement in either the trees or the undergrowth. The spiders were eternally patient. I glanced down every time I placed my feet, ensuring that I was stepping between the silk filaments criss-crossing between the trees. They were only about as thick of my bowstring, but were immensely strong. The grid was suspended less than an inch above the floor and the tension in the silk was so high that even the slightest touch would set the whole web quivering, revealing our location to the waiting spiders. I edged forward at such a slow rate that I could have been outpaced by a leopard slug. There was still neither sight nor sound of the monsters that awaited us, even as I approached the fringes of the oak's canopy. I could hear Ailidh's breathing quicken as her anxiety mounted. I looked over my shoulder to give her a reassuring smile. "Steady now."

Ailidh's boot slipped on a moss-covered cobble as the words came out of my mouth, sliding the toe into one of the taut silk threads as she lost her balance for less than a second. Realising she had given away our position, she swore through gritted teeth. "Daeva shit!"

Instinctively I looked up to see two giant spiders with a leg span in excess of twice my height dropping from the boughs of the oak almost directly over my head. Ailidh screamed in terror, scrambling out of the way as I let the spiders fall almost within arm's reach. I sidestepped to get both spiders in front of me, so that I could dispatch them one at a time. A swipe of my longsword clipped off two of the left legs at the joint between the femur and patella, sending it sprawling to the floor. Before I could finish it off, the second spider jumped over the prone body of its companion, fangs and claws flashing towards my face. I dodged to the right, barely avoiding the downward snap of the spider's fangs, which would have delivered a fatal bite. I left my arm trailing out behind me, timing my blow to stab the lunging spider with my stiletto directly into the largest of its eyes on the left side of its head. The knife was torn from my grip as the momentum of the spider carried the blade deep into the arachnid's skull to pierce into the brain. I hit the ground, rolling back to my feet, hefting my longsword in a firm, two-handed grip as the spider thrashed its death throes, flipping onto its back. Before the first spider was able to adjust to the loss of two of its feet, I rushed through the gap between its two remaining left legs and its head, jumping onto the spider's thorax so that I could decapitate the spider with a heavy, double-handed slash. There was no time to admire my handiwork, as there were still two ettercaps and four spiders to be dealt with. Ailidh was facing off with a spider that had dropped out of the trees behind us. The tip of her wakizashi darted left and right, the steel cutting edge nipping at the spider's outstretched claws as the two adversaries tested each other's defences. The final trio of spiders were between me and Keri, but a quick glance around the tree line revealed no sign of the ettercaps. The trio of spiders scattered as Keri unleashed a jet of fire from the tip of her staff. I ran to support Ailidh and the spider she was fighting chittered in alarm at being outnumbered, calling out to its brood-mates. The spider closest to Keri erupted into flame, sending the other two scurrying back towards Ailidh and me. Ailidh feinted towards the right foreleg of the spider in front of us. As the spider shifted its feet in response, backing off and turning to its right, I was able to take a couple of steps forward and cleave my sword through the femurs of its two rear left hand legs, exposing the abdomen. The spider shrieked and Ailidh whipped her wakizashi through the metatarsus joint of its left foreleg. As the arachnid flailed in pain, I pushed it to the floor with my boot pressing down on its thorax. I thrust my sword down into the centre of its abdomen, stabbing it through the heart. The chitin of its exoskeleton crunched as I twisted the blade with both hands.

The two remaining spiders charged Ailidh, who retreated a few steps back as her courage wavered. I called across to her as I hurdled over the spider's twitching carcass to intercept the incoming monsters. "Get behind me."

A purple force bolt flashed by, just inches from my face. I snapped my head back and followed the glowing trail left behind the flight of the bolt. It struck one of the ettercaps hidden in the oak tree in the throat, blowing open the fatty jowls that hung beneath its spider-like head down to its chest. The aberration lost grip with its long two-clawed hands and feet on the broad bough it was clinging to, falling like a stone into the bracken. An agitated hiss reminded me that the final pair of spiders was almost within melee range. I sensed Ailidh standing behind my right shoulder with her sword raised. She mirrored my steps as I tried to manoeuvre into a position that would allow me to fight both arachnids without leaving either myself or Ailidh vulnerable to a flanking attack. The two remaining spiders appeared to be a mated pair. The female was huge; a good yard larger in both length and span than her mate and her abdomen was swollen with eggs. Her chelicerae and palps twitched as she raised both of her front-most forelegs in a threatening posture. The female watched us warily with its eight eyes, as if weighing up the risk of an attack versus the nutritional value of its prey. The smaller male bared its fangs and lunged at Ailidh, sensing her hesitancy and fear. I leapt to my right to interpose myself between the spider's attack and Ailidh, using the reach of my longsword to smash through the tibias of its two front right legs. The male reared up, shrieking and spreading its chelicerae, ready to bite. I lunged forward and swept my sword up in between the curved fangs, splitting the spider's head in two, bisecting the gap between its clusters of eyes.

"Cathal, look out!" Ailidh screamed as I finished my swing, bringing my sword back into a guard position. I hardly had the time to turn my head before the enraged female rushed me with a body slam, knocking me to the floor with her forelegs. The spider's momentum sent me tumbling and rolling over the ground, my sword flying free from my hand and clanging loudly as it bounced away over the cobbles. Dazed, I twisted onto my back to see fangs the size of daggers just inches away from my face. Ailidh screamed again in horror as the spider pinned me to the floor with her palps. "No!"

I grabbed the black bone-hard fangs by their roots, where they grew from the female's chelicerae and used all my strength to push them apart, grunting in effort as I attempted to straighten my arms. Venom dripped from the canals at the tips of the fangs, wetting the cobbles on either side of my head. I tried to squirm out from beneath the spider's palps, but there was just too much weight on my chest. The spider's mouthparts flexed as the arachnid tried to wrest her fangs out of my hands. Time seemed to slow down as the monster used its sheer bulk to press its fangs down towards my shoulders. I continued to grapple with the spider's chelicerae, even though I knew it was a futile battle as I had neither the strength nor the leverage to work myself free. Then time seemed to stop completely as my world literally turned upside down. A barrage of purple light illuminated the road beneath the spider's abdomen and I felt myself be thrown through the air. I lost my grip on the spider's fangs as I fell, tumbling head over heels twice into the undergrowth. I yelled in surprise rather than terror as my fall was cushioned by a waist-high patch of ferns.

Ailidh rushed over to my side as my head swam. I was feeling so dizzy that I could see stars swirling between the gaps in the forest canopy. "Cathal, are you hurt?"

I propped myself up on one knee to make sure the giant female spider was not about to leap onto my chest again. I need not have worried. The spider had been utterly dismembered by whatever spell Keri had blasted it with. The abdomen and thorax had been split in two and its eight legs littered the road, shattered into pieces strewn over an area some three score yards long. Ailidh helped me up onto my feet, my legs trembling as the adrenalin started to drain out of my bloodstream. I looked around to find Keri eviscerating the second ettercap with a luminous crimson blade emanating from the head of her staff, which she wielded as expertly as an elite anti-cavalry officer would use their polearm. She had discovered the second ettercap's hiding place in the oak and cut off the bough from the tree, no doubt to the surprise of the flabby aberration. Despite the length of their claws and potency of their venomous bite, ettercaps liked to rely on their arachnid pets to incapacitate their victims and this one had proved to be no match for the willowy spellcaster. "No, Ailidh, I'm fine. Just a bit bruised."

I gave myself a moment to let strength return to my leg muscles and walked over to Keri who was working as precisely as a surgeon with her oversized polearm blade to extract the ettercap's venom glands. "Keri, what did you hit that spider with?"

"A force bolt the size of a horse," she replied with a hint of amusement. "Under the circumstances, I thought it better not to risk doing things by halves."

"Thank you." I said, hoping that a suitable level of gratitude had been conveyed in my tone. Had it not been for Keri's intervention, I would be lying dead in the dirt.

"You may thank me properly later when we make camp." Keri's eyes glittered with mischief as she regarded me from head to toe with a predatory intent that I found more frightening than when I had lain beneath the fangs of the huge female spider. "Gather your weapons and pack, Cathal. We should be on the move once I have finished harvesting the glands from the spider-fuckers."

"What do you want them for?"

"They are highly sort after and very valuable to certain people. The glands can be milked to derive anaesthetics, anti-venom and they are a reagent for many spells."

"I suppose their poisons are quite in demand, too." I added dryly. Keri simply nodded without comment and returned to her work.

Retrieving my longsword and bow from where they had landed after my brief flight into the undergrowth was simple enough, but I was only able to recover less than half of the arrows that had scattered to the five winds after falling from my quiver. I was not overly concerned, as it would be easy to source replacements once we reached the city. The trade markets in Lesøsnø were the largest and most diverse in the Western Triad. Ailidh followed me as I walked back towards the oak, where the first two spiders had sprung their trap. I had a fit of common sense and nocked an arrow on my bowstring while I was still a good two score yards away from the spider I had stabbed through the eye with my stiletto. I took careful aim and shot the spider through the central eye on the right side of its head. The spider flipped back over onto its clawed feet with a high-pitched shriek, now almost completely blinded, blood weeping from both sides of its head. Ailidh swore in panic, instinctively taking a couple of steps back and she tripped over, catching the heel of her boot on one of the silken filaments that still webbed the area. As the spider located the sound and vibration of Ailidh's fall, it turned to charge us. The wounded arachnid barely made three steps before I lanced a hardened steel arrow with a narrow bodkin tip through the pale patch of chitin on the spider's abdomen. The arrow tore a hole right through the spider's heart, shattering the exoskeleton above the spinnerets on the rear of the abdomen as it crashed out of its body. The arachnid slumped to the floor, this time very dead indeed. I wrapped my fingers around Ailidh's forearm, helping her onto her feet.

"You knew it was faking?"

"No, but I thought it was worth investing a couple of arrows to find out. Giant spiders are patient and cunning. Better to know before getting too close." I said, approaching the corpse slowly, waiting for its death throes to stop before approaching the head. I did not want to risk getting too close to those scimitar-shaped fangs while the chelicerae twitched involuntarily. Even a chance bite due to reflex action would almost certainly deliver a fatal dose of venom. I reached my hand into the smashed eye socked to grab the handle of my stiletto, grimacing at the horrid slickness of the arachnid's still-warm blood as I pulled my knife free from where it was embedded in the optic nerve.

"Disgusting."

I wiped down the stiletto's blade and leather grip with a fern leaf, using a squirt of water from my canteen skin to wash away the remaining spider blood and to clean my fingers and palm as best as I could before placing the weapon safely back into its scabbard. I then led Ailidh back down the road to where we had left our travel packs. Sapphire called to us frantically from her cage as we approached.

"Did you enjoy the show?" I teased the cat, as I re-shouldered my pack and helped Ailidh don hers. Sapphire's curt yelps of reply told me that she definitely had not. Keri beckoned us towards her, already leading the way north towards the waiting city.

"I'll be glad to see the back of this forest." Ailidh said, with a shiver of fear. I put my arm around her shoulder in sympathy and nodded silently in agreement.

By nightfall we had put several leagues between us and the site of the ambush. The gentle chirrup of birdsong that accompanied the dusk was a reassuring sign that no predators were abroad and that we could stop safely for the night. Ailidh was now well-practised at assembling our modest camp and having pitched the tents, she was dozing next to a gently-popping fire as I dug through my pack to retrieve a frying pan and cooking utensils. Keri had already conjured one of her bottomless carafes of wine and was drinking deeply from a crystal goblet. She propped herself up against a large basalt stone opposite the tents, watching the leaping of the flames with an air of casual disinterest.

"You fight well, Cathal." Keri ventured to start up a conversation. "Not your first encounter with ettercaps, I presume?"

"Indeed not." I said, confirming her speculation with a nod. "I was called upon to clear several spider nests during my time as a ranger."

Keri poured me a goblet of wine and set it down next to the fire as I opened one of the ration packs we had acquired from the Sundered Shield and laid out its contents upon my frying pan for reheating. "I was impressed. Warriors able to master their fear when confronted by a brood of giant spiders and their ettercap masters are few and far between."

I shook the pan to prevent the cutlets of meat from sticking to the warming iron before replying. "The Order of Sylvan prepared us well."

"For *all* the perils of the wilds?" Keri asked pointedly, biting her lip as she swirled the crimson liquid in her glass.

I flipped the three steaks in the pan with a wooden spatula and the tip of my stiletto, pausing to let the implicit criticism in her question pass without comment. "As well as can be taught without direct experience, yes."

Keri's eyes sparkled in the firelight, noting that my temper could be provoked, but that it was not an easy target. "What is the most dangerous creature you have fought during your service to the Order?"

"Other men."

"How disappointing. Nothing exotic? No daevae? No dire wolves? Not even a vampiric snow bear or two?"

"No, no daevae, thankfully. Though I have seen the devastation they leave behind. But even they are predictable in their nature. You may expect a daeva to act evilly with consistency. The motivation of men is far more erratic and it is that which makes them more dangerous. Whatever is in a man's heart may not be reflected in their words." I said as I removed the cutlets from the pan and set them aside on a plate to rest, replacing them with a couple of handfuls of par-boiled potatoes and an extra knob of butter.

"You have wisdom of sorts, Cathal. Little wonder Ailidh craves to bear your children." Keri observed with a mocking tone.

"And you, Keri, have a tongue sharper than most swords." I chided her. "Ailidh's heart is far purer than yours or mine. You should not be so quick to stoop to ridicule. She fought bravely today. You underestimate her, and we both do her a disservice by speaking behind her back."

"Perhaps. Though she would make a poor match for you. I think you would find her wide-eyed pining tiresome in the end." Keri snickered between sips of wine.

"As tiresome as this conversation, no doubt," I retorted with a sigh, tossing the potatoes in the pan as their skins began to brown and caramelise. "I am not seeking the companionship of anyone. Ailidh and I are friends, no more."

"If you say so, Cathal…" Keri returned to her stone pew to refill her glass with wine. "We are more alike than you realise. Perhaps one day I will prove it to you."

I took the pan off the fire and met her eyes. There was a primitive fierceness in her gaze that chilled me to the bone.

The smile on her face was both cruel and enthralling in equal measure. "What do you mean?"

"Just that if you ever do seek companionship, you would do well to ask for a demonstration of the other uses I have for my tongue." Keri said, relishing in my discomfort. There was a loud yawn as Ailidh stirred from her nap and any opportunity I might have had to reply was lost.

17 - Aiden

I had become increasingly concerned about the king's sanity in the month following the night I had spent with Sìne where she had revealed Karryghan's ambitions and Maeryn's place within them. The Arch Mage had just left another private meeting with the king in the Great Hall of the palace's central keep and it had left Maeryn in an especially foul mood. Despite having been forbidden from entering Reilynn's chambers in the Royal Palace by the queen, the king summoned a pair of footmen from the garrison and had spent the last twenty minutes hammering at the door to the Queen's Tower, her private wing of the palace.

"Reilynn! Open the door!" Maeryn yelled, again and again, until finally there was the sound of the latch being lifted. Maeryn lowered his shoulder and barged the door open, knocking the handmaiden behind the door sprawling with a cry of shock. As Maeryn stormed past to confront the queen, I lowered my hand to help the prostrate girl up off the floor. I was glad that the king's back was turned, as Sìne blew me a silent kiss when I lifted her onto her feet and I could not contain my smile. I had not spent the night with her since the incident on the parterre and just the sight of her sped up my heartbeat. I resolved to pay a visit to her bedchamber tonight just for her company, regardless of any new information she might have.

"Why have you come here, serpent?" Queen Reilynn's total contempt for the king dripped from her voice. She was dressed in the finest royal purple silk: her dress and bodice were elaborately stitched with gold thread, as befitted her status. Reilynn was tall, regal and proud, her temperament and heritage making her worthy of the royal title bestowed upon her, in marked contrast to her husband and king.

"I wish for you to walk with me into the city." Maeryn said, stood only a few feet before Reilynn, drawing himself up to his full height. It was not an impressive or imposing sight, as he was several inches shorter than the queen.

"You would let me out of the palace?" Reilynn's russet eyebrows arched with suspicion. Maeryn had kept her locked up in the Royal Palace grounds since the insurrection and feared her flight from the capital so much that he had not given her access to the keep or marina. "There is something I wish to show you." Maeryn pointed her in the direction of the door, and Reilynn reluctantly walked towards it, wary yet anxious to leave the seclusion of the palace grounds for the first time in years. "Your handmaidens can wait here. You will not need them. We will not be gone long."

The two junior soldiers ushered Sìne and the other handmaidens away from the door with their polearms, though they were careful to not let the blades get too close to the young women. The handmaidens looked toward me for guidance, and I put my finger to my lips, signalling for them to remain quiet and do as they were told. I bristled at the heavy-handedness of Maeryn and his men, but remained silent, wary not to draw attention to myself, given Maeryn's volatile mood. Though had one the footmen genuinely threatened Sìne or one of Reilynn's other handmaidens, they would have been missing both hands before they had the chance to blink, consequences be damned.

"Where are you taking me?" Reilynn asked as we left the palace courtyard and entered its gardens, the king leading the way. With winter rapidly approaching, the usually immaculate gardens lay dormant, the herbaceous annuals and summer-flowering perennials withered and dour. Only a handful of autumn blooms provided a sporadic glimmer of colour on the parterre. The queen followed Maeryn deferentially at his side, followed in close attendance by the two young serfs. I watched over the whole group from the rear, my danger sense tingling in the pit of my stomach. My instincts told me that something terrible was about to occur, but I could not identify where the sensation was coming from. My eyes roved the surroundings continually, discomforted by the sense of agitation around our group, hunting for the slightest signs of threat.

"You shall see soon enough." Maeryn snapped in reply, turning abruptly across the parterre to the path leading to the Palace Garrison. Reilynn's footsteps faltered when she recognised the building, remembering all too well what was in its stony foundations. When she made to run, the two footmen dropped their weapons and seized her by the arms, forcing her to walk along with the king. I also knew what lay in the foundations of the garrison building and my belly began to turn to ice, my sense of foreboding growing by the moment.

"Unhand me!" Reilynn demanded of the footmen. "I will have your heads on spikes for this!"

"You are in no position to give orders, Reilynn." Maeryn's voice had a callous edge to it. Alarmed by the knowledge of where we were unquestionably headed, I kept my hand on hilt of my longsword.

Maeryn used his set of master keys to unlock a side entrance into the garrison reserved for the private use of the king, bypassing the guards at the front gate. The queen struggled and shouted in protest the entire way as we made our way into the cold bowels of the building, until finally the king unlocked a thick metal door with a large iron key and directed us inside. A single oil lantern lit the cold, dank stone chamber, its orange light casting fearful, knife-sharp shadows over the stone floor of the torture cell. The floor was stained with blood, crusted streams layering the mortar between the bricks, leading to a single drain in the centre of the dim chamber. The centre of the room was dominated by a torture rack and in the far corner opposite the door was an iron maiden, its metal doors open, revealing the sharp, blood-flecked spikes within. Maeryn directed the footmen to stand Reilynn next to the rack, which had been tilted upright, so that the soldiers could tie her wrists into place on the sturdy wooden frame with thick leather straps.

"Why have you brought me here, viper?" Queen Reilynn spat in fury, still attempting to free herself from the two footmen who restrained her. "Is this to be my new home?"

"This is to be your last chance, Reilynn. I have tried to be patient." Maeryn wrung his hands, pacing back and forth before her. "I have suffered the indignities of your words and deeds for the last four years. But my patience wears thin."

"So you bring me here? You hope to scare me into obedience and into your bed?"

"Four years we have been married. Four years I have waited for a kind word, or a kiss, a child and heir. Yet you spurn me still. I grow tired of waiting."

"I would rather die than bear your children, usurper." Reilynn sneered, her hatred for the king utterly complete. "And for three years I have suffered the rumours. It is not right when a king has no heirs. Do you know what the small-folk say?" Maeryn turned on Reilynn, his mood flipping from anguished to furious in the space of a single heartbeat. "They say that the king must be impotent to not have an heir after being married so long to one so beautiful! I should tell them the truth! I should shout it from the battlements of the palace! I should tell the peasants that you are too proud to open your legs!"

Queen Reilynn snorted and scoffed with unvarnished derision as the serfs finished securing her arms against the rack. "As if you would know what to do if I did!"

I winced as Maeryn slapped Reilynn hard across the face with the back of his right hand, his signet ring leaving a mark on her cheek and the unexpected blow stunning her into silence. The fingers of my sword hand flexed, gripping and releasing the leather-bound hilt of the longsword at my left hip in agonised indecision. The oath of protection I had sworn when I had been appointed as Lord Commander of the Royal Guard extended not just to the king, but also the queen. I almost drew my sword, but stayed my hand, knowing that I was outnumbered if I chose to intervene on the behalf of the queen. Immediately Maeryn looked remorseful and went back to pacing before her, wringing his hands in distress as Reilynn's form momentarily sagged, leaving her hanging limply from the frame at both wrists.

"See what you make me do?" Tears of distress welled in the corners of Maeryn's eyes, unable to look at his Queen. Reilynn gradually came back to her senses, her face flushed with crimson fury and she resumed her futile fight for freedom as Maeryn paced, talking more to himself than her. "I am sorry, my love. For your family. For not being a better husband. Everything."

"Save your apologies." Reilynn retorted, her own temper boiling over. "You were not sorry when you authored the death warrants for my kin. You had no regrets when the crown was placed on your balding, bastard head. I! I am sorry! I am sorry that I ever agreed to live and legitimise your rule!"

"But I did it all for you!" Maeryn protested, his eyes ablaze with passion. "Connell was an old fool! We have enemies at every border! The Guild... Arch Mage Karryghan, he told me we can still save Cothraine. A Nexus has formed. A singularity of the aether so powerful that the men who control it will become gods! Gods! And I will be one of them!"

"You have told me this madness before!" Reilynn yelled back to him, her voice tinged with fear at the depth and sincerity of his delusion, as if not recognising the creature before her as human, her arms twisting as she strained at her bonds. "You murdered my entire family for this? For the fantasy that you will be made a god?"

"It is no delusion!" Maeryn's temper flared again. "The Arch Mage has foreseen it!"

Queen Reilynn laughed bitterly, trying again ineffectually to break free from the restraints binding her to the rack. "The Schemer of Siskine foresees many things. He once told me I would have seven sons and seven daughters."

"You still can!" Maeryn's tone turned to a pleading one.

"Not with you." Reilynn icy gaze pierced Maeryn and he seemed to wither and deflate before her. "Never."

Closing his eyes in apparent regret and distress, the king drew the dagger from his belt and stepped forward with murderous purpose. The queen screamed, her eyes wide in mortal terror, trying to twist away from him as Maeryn grabbed Reilynn and ripped the bodice away from her dress with one hand, the laces tearing through the luminous purple fabric. He tossed it aside, raising the tip of the dagger menacingly. The chromed blade bit into the neck of her dress and Maeryn gripped the hem firmly with his free hand, slicing through the silk and opening the dress in two, all the way down to her navel. He pulled and tore the two flaps of fabric wide apart, leaving her chest fully exposed. Appalled, I closed my eyes and looked away, afraid of what was about to happen next.

"Do not touch me, viper! Do not dare!" Reilynn spat emphatically in Maeryn's face, struggling and pulling her arms against the heavy leather strapping around her wrists in a frenzied effort to try and break free from the rack. The queen turned to me, fixing me with her desperate gaze, imploring. "Is this an act of a king? Whom do you serve,

Duke Aiden? The time is coming very quickly when you will have to choose."

Maeryn wiped the foamy globs of spittle from his forehead and cheek, quietly fuming. The king turned away from Reilynn, sheathed his dagger, and started to unfasten his belt, with a sad resignation in his wild eyes. "I am king. I get to fuck the queen, whether she likes it or not. It is my divine right as monarch."

"Your grace?" I spluttered, blinking twice and taking a reflexive step backwards, utterly baffled and disgusted by his inexplicable logic. Even the two footmen standing on opposite sides of the rack appeared stunned.

"I will have her, willingly or not." Maeryn muttered under his breath as Reilynn pulled ineffectually against the leather straps.

"Your grace, you cannot. You must not! It would be treason, an affront to natural law." I protested, desperate for a way to avoid having to make a decision that would prove to be irrevocable. I had done many despicable things on Maeryn's order during the coup. At his behest I had killed men, women and children, including royal children, in cold blood, but the violation a woman by force was an even more grievous crime according to the tenets of my religion. Queen Reilynn had been favourably blessed by the Empress with wide, curved hips, a slender waist and glorious, cone-like breasts. As a young knight in the City Guard, I had regularly conjured fantasies about sharing a bed with the gorgeous young Princess I had seen from afar during celebration days in the city. But in those fantasies she had always been a willing participant, frequently instigating and even dominating our illusory nocturnal encounters. I could not bear the thought any man forcing themselves upon her. Not only would it be the grossest of insults to the dignity of the queen, but rape was also the most heinous act possible in the dogma of my patron deity, the Goddess. No amount of favour and patronage from the king was worth an eternity of torment in the Demesne of the Succubus for allowing such a crime to occur when I had the power and opportunity to prevent it. I abruptly realised that my sole purpose within the torture chamber was now to get Queen Reilynn out again alive and with her virtue intact, whatever the consequences might be.

"It is treason to suggest that you know better than your king!" Maeryn fumed, and he waved me away with his left hand in a clear gesture of dismissal. "Get out, Duke Companion. Your presence here is no longer wanted or required."

"My liege, please, I cannot. Some orders cannot be obeyed." I checked the position of the footmen around the room, planning which one to attack first if I was forced to fight to free the queen from the torture chamber. The soldier serfs were both young and inexperienced. I was certain they would be no threat to me in single combat, but if they chose to attack me in a group with the king, the odds of three to one were not in my favour if I wished to avoid injury.

"Then you will have to watch." Maeryn sneered, stepping forward as one of the two footmen grinned complicity, as if waiting for a tavern band to strike up their next melody. My fingers gripped the hilt of my longsword, the armoured joints of my gauntlets creaking with the tension. Maeryn took another step forward and raised his hands, as if to grasp Reilynn by both breasts. Maeryn's eyes were frenzied with rage and lust, whereas the queen was calmness personified. Reilynn looked over at me with a serene defiance. She knew as well as I did that I no longer had time to prevaricate or try and please both her and the king. Before the king was able to touch Reilynn's chest, she lashed out with unexpected speed and force, the pointed tip of her shoe striking Maeryn directly in his exposed crotch. He howled in agony and stumbled backwards, falling to the floor.

"Bitch! Show the king some respect!" The younger of the two serfs reproached Reilynn, slapping her across the cheek. Without even realising I had even made a decision, my sword flew free of my scabbard and I leapt forward, closing the distance between where I had been standing and the serf that had dared lay a finger on royal flesh without consent in less than a second. The edge of my blade sang through the air, decapitating the hapless footman with a single strike. I turned on the spot, interposing my sword between the queen and the second soldier, who stepped away from the rack, his brown eyes watering in panic.

"No, m'lord, please don't kill me!" The serf begged, lifting his empty palms in supplication. I saw he was little more than a boy, still short of his eighteenth year. "I won't say anything! Let me go! Please!"

I glanced over at Reilynn for guidance, and she signalled me an almost imperceptible shake of the head, casting her eyes downwards. I lunged again and the serf didn't even have time to scream before my sword had separated his skull from his neck. For a handful of seconds the shocked silence was broken only by the quiet drips of blood falling from the tip of my blade to stone floor. I swallowed with trepidation. There would be repercussions for having killed two soldiers from the city garrison, and none of them were likely to be pleasant. I was not given the opportunity to contemplate what they might be any further before matters immediately turned for the worst. There was a sluggish, but enraged growling behind me as Maeryn gathered his wits and regained his feet.

"You will die for that, Reilynn." Maeryn hissed, drawing the dagger from the scabbard at his belt. Reilynn screamed my name in horror, urging me to intervene. I could not let Maeryn harm Reilynn, but neither did I have the heart to kill the king, the same man who had elevated me to my position in the Royal Guard. Tactically, my options were limited. I was not in the position to interpose my body between the king and the queen. Instead we each stood at the point of a triangle, me off to the right hand side of the line connecting Maeryn and Reilynn. I stepped forward and flicked up the tip of my longsword, slashing up and across my body, from right to left. Maeryn shrieked as I knocked the dagger from his right hand, severing the first and middle fingers completely and taking off his ring finger at the first knuckle. The king's scream of pain was short-lived, as I silenced him on my backswing by knocking him insensate with a hard blow to his right temple from the pommel of my longsword. The impact of the bejewelled metal globe against Maeryn's skull sounded dull and wet, rather than yielding a sharp crack, so it seemed unlikely that I had broken the bone beneath the flesh, but the way Maeryn slumped to the floor without any resistance or attempt to protect himself from the fall told me that it would be some time before he recovered his senses. If the consequences of killing two soldiers of the Cothraine Field

Army were dire, the repercussions from maiming and assaulting the king were almost beyond imagination. I shook the droplets of blood from the surface of my blade, drew in a deep breath and sheathed my longsword before I turned to face the queen.

"You chose well, Duke Companion Aiden." Reilynn reassured me, with the merest hint of a smile. "Thank you."

"You are welcome, your majesty." I replied, bowing reverentially to the queen, glad that I had been able to defend the queen's honour, even if it meant that I had sacrificed any goodwill or standing I had enjoyed with the king.

"Release me, Duke Aiden." Reilynn commanded me, her tone urgent and forceful. "How long might we have until Maeryn awakes?"

"An hour or two at most, your majesty." I informed her, as my fingers busily tried to loosen the leather straps binding her slender right wrist to the chunky oaken frame of the torture rack. After a few seconds of fumbling, I dispensed with my gauntlets to use my fingernails, working them beneath the leather strips so that I could unfasten the knots. Reilynn's green eyes glistened with urgency and arousal, and standing so close to her, I found it difficult to not be distracted by the sweet, sensual aroma of her perfume and the pert curves of her bare chest. The temptation to kiss her was almost uncontrollable. Reilynn smiled as she looked up into my face, sensing that my attention was being diverted from focusing entirely on the task she had given me.

"Concentrate, Duke Aiden." Reilynn warned me, deliberately raising her chest into my eye line, simultaneously teasing and reproaching me as the wooden frame creaked under tension as the queen tugged against the leather bindings. "I am grateful for your aid, but not *that* grateful."

"Sorry, your majesty." I replied, chastened, keeping my eyes focused on her wrists, untangling the intertwined loops of strapping securing the queen to the frame.

Once I had freed both her arms from the rack, Reilynn braced my cheeks between her newly-liberated palms and kissed me long and hard on the mouth. The queen's breath tasted of vanilla cream and strawberries and her lips burned with the heat of a steel furnace. I swallowed nervously when she released me, unsure of what to do next. Fortunately, Reilynn was in a rather more decisive mood. "Well done, Duke Companion. We must leave this place, immediately."

"Yes, your majesty." I agreed, nodding, my eyes inadvertently drawn again to her exposed breasts as I lowered my head. I shivered involuntarily, shucking off my cloak and presented it to the queen, held wide open to block my view. She accepted the thick purple garment with a knowing smile, wrapping it over her shoulders and back, using one of her aetherium hair pins to close and secure the fabric over her chest. As Reilynn preserved her modesty, I put my gauntlets back on before kneeling by the prostrate form of the king to relieve Maeryn of his set of master keys to the citadel. "If we lock him in the chamber, it will buy us some more time before an alarm is raised."

"Excellent idea, Duke Aiden." Reilynn said, allowing herself a small smirk of satisfaction. "His injuries are no threat to him, then?"

"No, ma'am. It is unlikely that the blood loss will be mortal. But now his hobbled leg has a maimed arm to match. I doubt he will ever be capable of raising a weapon in anger ever again."

"A shame." The queen scoffed. She looked down at Maeryn with something akin to pity, squatting by his prostrate form to remove her father's signet ring from his mutilated right hand and clutch it tightly in her palm. "Even I cannot justify killing such a lowly, base snake in cold blood. Let us leave him to the tender ministrations of the Arch Mage. I can think of no more suitable a punishment for the crimes he has committed."

I ushered the queen out of the torture chamber, locking the door behind us. Silently I prayed to the Goddess that Maeryn would not regain consciousness until I had managed to liberate Queen Reilynn beyond the walls of the city. Then I guided the queen out of the palace garrison as quickly as we dared walk, exiting the garrison by the same private portal we had used to enter. Even though our arrival and departure from the dungeon had been unobserved, we wasted no time in heading directly across the citadel gardens to the Royal Palace. It surely would not be long before Maeryn returned to his senses and was discovered by one of the soldiers that patrolled the dungeon. The news of the king's assault and maiming would soon overtake the keep and the wider city, so it was imperative that we were able to get out of Clongarvan as quickly as possible. My own position within the Royal Guard was forfeit. There was no possibility of clemency after having injured the king. None of the guards or other servants thought to question the absence of the king when we reached the courtyard in front of the palace as Reilynn was never usually seen in his company. As we climbed the spiral staircase up the Queen's Tower to her personal chambers, I found my tongue and dared to venture a question.

"My queen, what would you have me do?"

There was no hint of apprehension in her eyes when she met my gaze. "I must leave Cothraine immediately. Worry not, Duke Companion, you shall accompany me. I will require a bodyguard on our journey to Fossfjall."

"Fossfjall? You mean to seek refuge with the Crown Prince?"

"Indeed. And once I am married to my true love and betrothed, we will seek vengeance upon Maeryn and remove him from the throne in righteous battle, not murder." Reilynn said with quiet determination as she rapped a coded knock on the door to her private apartments in the palace, signalling her arrival to the handmaidens waiting inside. Sìne opened the door warily, relaxing only when she saw that Reilynn and I were unaccompanied by Maeryn or any of his lackeys. Reilynn kissed her most-trusted handmaiden on the cheek. "Sìne, it is time. Tell everyone, it is time for us to pay Saoirse our respects. Then meet me in my dressing room. And be quick: time is of the essence."

"Yes, your majesty." Sìne gave Reilynn a brief curtsey and then fled up the stairs of the tower, gathering the other girls towards her as she went.

I trailed deferentially three steps behind the queen as she made her way up a final flight of steps to the apex of the tower, where her private bedroom and dressing chamber lay beneath a stained glass dome. Reilynn turned back toward me as she opened the door, placing a hand in the centre of my breastplate. "Wait here, Duke Aiden. I will admit you to my chambers when I am ready. Make sure no-one passes this door."

"By your command, your majesty." I replied with a deep, respectful bow. Across the landing two of the queen's handmaidens were ransacking their room, turning over the mattresses of their beds to reveal hidden satchels, which they duly slung around their necks before heading to the staircase. I caught the eye of Róise, a recent addition to my cadre of little mice in the Royal Palace, who despite only just having come of age was second only to Sìne in her seniority among the queen's personal attendants. I beckoned her over with a brief wave of my fingers. "Róise, what is going on?"

"We're leaving, Duke Aiden." Róise said, her common Monagealy accent betraying her nervousness.

"I can see that. To go where? What did the queen mean by 'pay Saoirse our respects'?"

"Saoirse is Queen Reilynn's private yacht. It's been docked at the palace marina ever since Maeryn confined the queen to the tower. We're taking the boat east to the queen's summer estate in Bray."

"But Reilynn said she wanted to go to Fossfjall." I said, confused.

"She does. But she can't go there with a dozen handmaidens in tow. Such an obvious entourage would jeopardise the queen's safety." Róise explained.

"So she is getting you to act as a decoy by taking her yacht?" I was unsure whether to admire the queen's foresight, or be shocked by her ruthlessness in abandoning the teenaged servants so abruptly.

"Yes m'lord, Queen Reilynn planned for this possibility. We're all trained to handle the yacht and part of our duties has been to keep it seaworthy."

"What will you do once you reach Bray?"

"We'll go to ground in one of the winery houses the queen owns on the Vine Coast. Her majesty has made sure that we're provided for. We're not going to starve, Duke Aiden." Róise opened the flap on her satchel and retrieved a plump, purple satin coin purse. She loosened the cord to allow me to peer inside. The purse was crammed with no less than fifty crowns. Each one of the gold disks was worth twenty-five sovereigns. I gasped quietly in shock. It was enough money to buy a small vineyard in Lussac. "I need to go, your grace. Keep the queen safe, Duke Aiden."

"I will. Good luck, Róise." I promised, kissing her goodbye on the cheek. Róise shepherded the girl waiting at the threshold of the spiral staircase ahead of her and they scampered down the steps with real urgency. The echoes in the staircase faded away and the tower was silent for several minutes. I was just beginning to wonder whether Reilynn had abandoned me as well when the door to her bedchamber opened behind me. I turned to the queen and bowed in relief. She had dispensed with my purple cloak and her ruined dress and was instead clad in the very antithesis of royal garb: a pair of olive green heavy cotton trousers and a loose linen shirt, worn under a tan leather jerkin and sturdy, knee-length boots with thick heels suitable for riding or walking. Her auburn hair was pinned up neatly behind her ears. Yet Reilynn still somehow managed to appear regal, despite the plainness of her clothing.

"You may enter now, Duke Aiden." Queen Reilynn stepped back from the door and led me inside. Sìne appeared seemingly from nowhere and followed me inside, wearing an almost identical outfit to the queen, having changed out of her usual handmaiden's dress. In stark contrast to the aristocratic bearing of Reilynn, were it not for the armoured jerkin you could have mistaken Sìne for a farmhand at a moderately successful baronet's estate. Sìne did not wait for instructions and immediately immersed herself in one of the queen's cavernous, carved mahogany wardrobes moving clothes to one side, clearly on the lookout for something specific. The hint of a smile tugged at my lips as I watched her work, enjoying the manner her new outfit hugged her willowy figure. Reilynn gestured for me to close and secure the door behind me, which I did, before handing her the ornate, brass key that had been in the lock. "How long do you think we still have before Maeryn awakes, Duke Companion?"

"It is difficult to know with any certainty, ma'am. A half hour, perhaps?" I ventured. "I struck Maeryn very hard, so it may be longer, but someone is bound to check the cell sooner rather than later."

"Half an hour ought to be sufficient." Reilynn said, nodding with satisfaction. She glanced back over her shoulder. "Have you found it yet, Sìne?"

"Yes, your majesty." The handmaiden nodded, pushing a pile of neatly folded dresses aside, to point at a subtle carved impression in one of the wardrobe's back panels. "Here."

"Excellent, thank you, Sìne." Reilynn smiled as she brought the signet ring she had taken from Maeryn out from a pocket of her trousers and held it up for me to see. "It may seem like a trifling thing, but this ring is our salvation. Maeryn took this from my father's dead hand without ever knowing its true purpose. I had despaired that I would not be able to reclaim it without opening my legs for the usurper. The service you have done for me today is truly beyond value."

She inserted the cut ruby and its gold setting into the depression in the wood. There was a sharp click and the back of the wardrobe rolled aside into the walls. Inside the cavity behind the false wall was a storage chest five feet wide, three feet deep and two feet tall, plus half a dozen mannequins encumbered with a spectacular array of arms and armour. The queen moved over to the hidden chamber and knelt, using the enchanted jewel on her signet ring again to open the padlock securing the chest. Reilynn removed three black leather cloaks from the depths of the wooden vessel and handed one each to Sìne and me. The linings and hems were stitched with real gold thread, and the Royal Crest was embossed on the hood of each cloak. I swallowed in trepidation when the implication of the fine detailing on the cloaks began to sink in. Reilynn shouldered her own cloak and fastened the gold chain at the base of the hood around her neck. "Welcome, Shadow Duke Aiden, to the Secret Service."

"I am honoured, your majesty." I replied. I looked down at the leather garment in my hands, feeling as stupefied as if I had drunk an entire gallon of potato vodka imported from the Fossfjall permafrost. "I am yours to command."

Reilynn liberated two heavy, woven satchels from the chest, handing one to Sìne and detaching the sling from the other so that she could wear it under her cloak. Then she dug back through the contents of the chest to lift out a waxed, waterproof field pack I was all too familiar with from my apprenticeship with the City Guard and the queen gave it to me with a wry smile. "You will carry my burdens, Duke Aiden. You will also defend me from danger with your life, if necessary. Feel free to take any weapons you feel might be useful on our journey to Lesøsnø."

Sìne had likewise donned her cloak, slung the satchel over her shoulder, and she was in the process of fastening a girdle she had taken from one of the mannequins around her slender waist. The weapon belt hosted a minor arsenal: a dagger, a rapier, a hand crossbow and a quiver of thirty steel quarrels. Sìne was wearing it with a natural confidence that indicated that she had received a substantial amount of expert weapons training. My eyes widened slightly as the petite handmaiden caressed the hilt of the rapier and raised her thin, raven black eyebrows at me provocatively. I smiled back at her with a newfound respect and affection as I put on my pack and cloak, eyeing the mannequins for arms that were of a better quality compared to the longsword and dagger that had been provided to me by the armourer of the Royal Guard. I noticed that, like Sìne, Reilynn had also chosen to take a double-edged rapier with a protective basket hilt. I estimated that the weapon's blade was some 40 inches long, with a greater reach than my longsword. The preference for long, slender weapons shown by both Sìne and the queen had me slightly puzzled. The fighting doctrine of the City and Royal Guard forces I had served in favoured broader, thicker and heavier weapons, like my double-handed longsword. As I paid closer attention to the range of weapons hanging from the mannequins, my eye was drawn to a falchion hanging from the waist of the leftmost dummy. The 34 inch, single-edged blade was exquisitely thin, less than a tenth of an inch thick, with only the merest hint of a curve from the S-shaped quillon of the crossguard on the hilt to the long, pointed razor-sharp tip. The single-handed grip was adorned with a round, spiked pommel to strike stunning blows in hand-to-hand combat. Something about the craftsmanship of the weapon appealed to my subconscious, so I took the falchion to replace my dagger, reassured that the one-handed sword was a much more versatile weapon, even though it hardly weighed more than the dagger it superseded. I turned back to the queen, feeling thrilled and fearful in equal measure.

"I am ready, your majesty."

"Good." Reilynn nodded in satisfaction, and turned to Sìne with the air of a mother bear ready to defend one of her cubs. "And you, Sìne? This is your last chance to join the others. They will not wait long for you at the marina. Are you sure you wish to join us on the trip to Fossfjall? It will be a long, perhaps dangerous journey."

"I am certain, your majesty. And you will require someone to tend to your needs." Sìne said insistently.

Reilynn gave Sìne a mischievous smile. "I can look after myself, as you well know. Perhaps you are more concerned about who will take care of the needs of Duke Aiden? I am aware that you prefer to do that yourself, rather than leave such tasks to the hands and bodies of others."

Sìne's cheeks flushed with mortified embarrassment and she lowered her head, unable to look her mistress in the eye. I chose to keep my own council, not trusting myself to speak, which was undoubtedly the wisest thing I had done in many years. Reilynn let us squirm in discomfort for almost a minute before erupting into melodious laughter. The queen embraced the handmaiden hard and kissed her affectionately on the cheek.

"There is no-one else I would rather have at my side, my beloved Sìne." Reilynn reassured her, with a tight hug around her shoulders. "Come, let us go."

Reilynn led the way deeper into her apartment, only stopping when we reached her personal library. "Your majesty, how are we going to leave the citadel? We can hardly walk out of the main gates."

"I am well aware of this, Duke Aiden. Fortunately, my ancestors had sufficient foresight to provide us with an alternative route." Reilynn said, nudging a pair of crusty vellum tomes along one of the bookshelves with slender fingertips. She reached deep into the shadowy recess by the frame of the bookcase and used her father's signet ring to unlock the hidden mechanism built into the stonework. The bookcase sank into the floor without a sound. Reilynn plucked one of the oil torches from the wall and directed us inside. Once the three of us were behind the wall, she used the ring again to seal the hidden entrance behind us and then led the way into the pitch black labyrinth. "When King Tuathal commissioned the building of the citadel he had a network of secret passages installed, so that the Royal Family would always have a way of leaving the city unseen. Unfortunately, my father was murdered before he had the chance to inform the rest of the family they were there."

"Then how did you come to learn of them, your majesty?" I asked, my senses alert for the merest sign of danger as Reilynn walked confidently ahead of us. I was not fond of cold, dark, enclosed spaces such as these.

"They are routinely used by members of the black cloaks. They maintain the network of tunnels as a contingency for situations precisely like these, but they did not have the key to enter the palace." Reilynn said, giving me a glimpse of her father's signet ring in the torchlight once again for emphasis as she led us further into the maze. She walked quickly and confidently as the tunnel branched and spiralled. I had lost all sense of where we might be, but the queen appeared to be having no such trouble. She chose turns at junctions in the labyrinth without hesitation, seemingly immune to the sense of claustrophobia I was starting to feel. "From here we can go directly to a private dock controlled by the Secret Service without anyone ever knowing we left the citadel."

"I was led to believe that the black cloaks disbanded and left the city after the coup. How do you know they still operate in Clongarvan, your majesty?"

"That ought to be obvious, Duke Aiden." Reilynn snickered with amusement. "I have led the organisation since my fifteenth birthday."

True to her word, Reilynn was able to navigate us through the labyrinth of pitch black tunnels underneath the city to the port in Clongarvan without us ever seeing daylight. By my reckoning, the walk had taken almost two hours. It was almost certain that someone had discovered Maeryn and the dead footmen in the torture chamber by now. I silently prayed to the Lady begging that our luck would hold and that word from the Royal Palace had not overtaken us. Before exiting the tunnel system, Reilynn told us to raise the hoods of our cloaks until we had boarded the Secret Service clipper she had waiting for us.

"Keep your faces hidden until we are safely at sea." The queen warned. "We cannot let word get back to the citadel that we have left the city. As long as you keep your hood up, no-one will dare challenge you. Black cloaks are rightly feared by the public. Our anonymity grants us immunity from the rule of law. While we are in earshot of the public, we must not use our given names. If you must speak, you will address me only as 'ma'am'. Are we clear?"

Sìne and I both nodded, and the three of us pulled the brim of our hooded cloaks fully forward, hiding our features in deep, impenetrable shadow. The exit from the Secret Service labyrinth brought us out into the middle of the packed storage racks of a dockside warehouse. The crates were stacked from the floor up to the ceiling in rows forty feet high and over one hundred yards long. Each wooden case bore the mark of the Shearwater Company, Cothraine's premier import and export business. Reilynn extinguished the wick on her oil torch and left in an empty wall bracket next to the warehouse entrance. It was good to see natural sunlight again after the tense hours of walking in the claustrophobic tunnels beneath the city, and even the bustle of the docks felt open and airy by comparison. Sìne and I followed Reilynn in silence, our hands never straying from the hilts of our swords, ready to respond to the slightest sign of danger. The crowds parted before us fearfully, repelled by the sinister aura of our black cloaks. Even the rowdiest groups of sailors on short leave fell silent as we approached, casting their gaze to the floor to avoid identification and scrutiny.

The queen's step never faltered, striding confidently with an even, relentless pace, leading us towards a secluded dock in the most prestigious quarter of the port. Waiting for us on the quay was an elegant clipper with three masts, a sleek vessel built for speed, rather than comfort or cargo capacity. The central mast was as tall as the ship was long, some two score yards. The smooth, carvel hull of caulked cedar planks was painted in slate grey and steel blue, the signature colours of the Shearwater Company. The bow figurehead identifying the ship was a carmine-eyed, saw-billed merganser with an iridescent black head flying beneath the steeply raked stem of the narrow hull, with its speckled black and white wings outstretched. The ship's master was stood at the top of the gantry linking the ship to the quayside, leaning nonchalantly against one of the ropes. Reilynn called out to him when she reached the bottom of the suspended walkway. "Permission to come aboard, Captain Ruarc."

"Granted, ma'am." Ruarc could hardly have epitomised the character of his vessel more eloquently: I estimated him to be about two score and ten years old, his face as was hard and angular as the clipper's prow and his body was wiry, with not even the barest hint of excess weight. The battered sabre hanging from his left hip also showed that he was no stranger to the ever-present risk of piracy on the shipping lanes of the Bay of Tides and the Abyss. "It is my pleasure to receive you."

The surety of Reilynn's step didn't falter as she climbed the swaying gantry bridge up to greet the captain on the deck of the clipper. It was another surprise. I never would have guessed that the queen had the sea legs of a telai pirate from the Reach. My own ascent up the rope bridge was far less assured. "I trust your crew is ready to depart, captain?"

"Ready and eager, ma'am," Ruarc nodded, as he took one of Sìne's hands to assist her onto the forecastle deck. "The *Merganser* is itching to stretch her wings over the waves once more. We have been in port for too long."

"Perhaps it is good we have such a long journey ahead of us then. I wish to leave for Lesøsnø immediately." Reilynn instructed.

"At once, ma'am. We shall have cleared our moorings before you are settled into your quarters." Ruarc said as he led us aft towards the quarterdeck house, barking an order to weigh anchor at his First Mate before directing us below. "You and your companions have my cabin at your full disposal, ma'am. Make yourselves at home. I shall bunk in the officer's quarters while you remain on board."

"Thank you, Ruarc." Reilynn said as she lowered her hood and accepted the large iron key to the captain's quarters into her open palm.

"It is a great pleasure to see you free from the confines of the citadel once again, your majesty." Ruarc said, with a brittle smile. "I was beginning to wonder whether this day would ever come."

"So was I, Shadow Count, so was I." Reilynn replied sadly before directing Sìne and I to lower the hoods of our cloaks. "May I introduce you to Shadow Duke Aiden? Shadow Lord Sìne you already know."

"Your grace." Ruarc shook hands with me genially enough, but I could sense a great deal of suspicion hidden behind his cold blue eyes. "I take it your appointment was a recent one, my lord?"

"Very recent." I met his gaze evenly, letting him see that I was not one to be easily cowed or intimidated.

"Come now, Shadow Count Ruarc." Reilynn chided him in a pleasant, gently mocking tone. "I am as certain of Aiden's loyalty as I am that the two of you will become good friends. After all, you will need to instruct Aiden in the finer points of the protocols expected of him as a member of the Secret Service. You will be getting to know him very well in the coming days."

"By your command, your majesty." Ruarc's eyes flickered with doubt, but he bowed deferentially to Reilynn and took a short backward step. "If it pleases you, I need to supervise the undocking. I will have refreshments sent down to you at sunset."

"Thank you, captain. May I join you on deck once we clear the port?" Reilynn asked hopefully. "It has been a long time since I felt the caress of sea spray on my cheeks."

"The ship is yours, my queen. You may go wherever you please, as and when you choose." Ruarc bowed again and retreated to the stairs leading back up to the helm and quarterdeck.

The captain's quarters spanned the entire beam of the ship as was divided into three individual cabins. A tiny privy chamber was tucked into the corner of the bedroom, which was separated from the main cabin and study by a thin oak panel and sliding door. Reilynn predictably staked her exclusive claim on the bedroom, assuring us that Ruarc would have a couple of spare bedrolls brought up from the officers' quarters before nightfall. I felt the deck creak beneath my feet and a quick glance out of the windows lining the stern of the clipper revealed that the clipper was easing slowly away from the quay. Muffled shouts could be heard from the quarterdeck as the captain gave orders to his crew.

Reilynn directed us to set down our bags next to the captain's bed, before indicating that she would like to speak with me privately in the study. "Sìne, please get everything properly stowed away for me. The Herring Coast can get rough at this time of year."

"Of course, your majesty." Sìne replied with an eager smile. I could tell that she was as relieved to be out of the confines of the palace tower as the queen was.

"Duke Aiden, please sit." Reilynn gestured to one of the study's four heavily-framed, leather upholstered chairs as she closed the sliding door behind us. The queen took the seat next to me and studied my face so intensely that I needed to glance out of the window to avoid blushing. It was also a relief to see the horizon, as the wallowing of the deck was not a sensation I was used to. I hoped I would not become seasick, as the stern of the ship had barely cleared the quay. Resurfacing the deck of the captain's study with my breakfast would not be an auspicious start to our voyage. "Have you ever taken a trip by sea before?"

"No, your majesty."

"I think you will like it, Duke Aiden, once you are accustomed to the roll of the waves. There is a freedom to the ocean that one simply cannot find on land." Reilynn said wistfully, gazing out of the window onto the water.

"I will take your word for it, your majesty." I replied diplomatically, still feeling a little queasy.

"At any rate, it will not be too long a trip. The *Merganser* is the fastest ship in black cloak inventory. We should make landfall at Lesøsnø in less than twenty days."

"I have never been to Fossfjall, but I have heard much about the beauty of the Abyss beyond Hemafjord, your majesty. It will be a privilege to see it at first-hand." I said to make conversation, relieved to know that if I was unable to find my sea legs, at least my suffering would not be too prolonged.

Reilynn stroked her neck thoughtfully as she continued to look out of the window while the ship drifted lazily further along the harbour wall towards the open sea. "She adores you, you know."

"I beg your pardon, your majesty?" I spluttered, baffled by the non-sequitur.

"Sìne, of course." Reilynn explained, transfixing me with that luminous, regal stare once again. "Given your tawdry reputation at Court, I will admit that initially I failed to see why, but your actions today have shown me that you are capable of acting with some honour and integrity. We would not be sitting here now if that was not so."

"Thank you, your majesty." I replied, flattered.

"Do not thank me yet, Duke Aiden. Sìne is my longest-serving handmaiden, my oldest confidant and one of my truest friends. If you care for her as I do, you will grant me a boon."

"Name it, ma'am, and it will be done." I pledged honestly, anxious to gain the queen's favour and trust.

"Marry her. Today." Reilynn did not smile when she saw the look of shock written across my face. "While I am yet to be convinced that you love her, I do. In many respects Sìne is the only family I have left. It would please me to know that you would be the joy of her days and nights."

I swallowed my nerves and considered the queen's request. It was not abhorrent; indeed, the notion was far from it. "I do care for her, your majesty, a great deal."

"You will do it, then?"

"I will, yes ma'am." I was not entirely certain whether the churning in my belly came from excitement, terror or the gentle rolling of the deck beneath my feet.

"Good. Thank you, Aiden. Had you refused... well, it would have been intriguing to see how long you would be able to stay afloat wearing your armour." Reilynn said dryly, her eyes twinkling with dark humour.

"I cannot swim, your majesty."

"Then it is just as well that your ability to make good decisions today has not deserted you." A subtle smile of amusement tweaked the edges of her mouth.

"I suppose so, your majesty. But how can we be married today? I have no ring to give her and I doubt there is a priest aboard."

"One of the advantages of being on ship is that we are a sovereign nation on the waves," said Reilynn, her smile widening. "The captain can conduct the service, and as for rings, I believe I can take care of that."

Reilynn retrieved a small jewel pouch from the inner lining of her jerkin and emptied its contents into her palm. Two golden marriage bands, one thick and one thin fell onto her smooth, pale skin along with a third gold ring, set with a single cut diamond flanked by three emeralds on each side. "They're magnificent, ma'am."

"They ought to be, Duke Aiden. They have been in the royal family for twelve generations." Reilynn's eyes glistened with silent laughter again as she passed me the jewelled engagement ring. The queen turned her head and called out to her handmaiden through the closed sliding door. "Sìne, would you join us, please? I believe Duke Aiden has a question he would like to ask you."

Following a brief ceremony later that night on deck, conducted by Reilynn and Captain Ruarc under the sails and the stars and witnessed by the thirty strong crew of the

Merganser, we retired back to our half of the captain's cabin, where Sìne made good on her promise of how she would make love to me once we were husband and wife, and ensured that the experience had been worth waiting for.

18 - Fiacre

After a journey of over five hundred leagues and eleven days in the saddle, I was grateful for the relief of a warm bath, a hearty meal and a sturdy bed when I reached the Croycullen garrison with my riding companion, Grand Master Malvina of Ballinlara. We had only been able to make the journey so quickly thanks to my foresight of sending messages via carrier pigeon ahead of us to the guard posts along our route, instructing them to have their fastest and most durable horses waiting for us, already fed and watered, for the hard gallop north. The turnpikes were spaced close enough together that only three of our horses had run themselves lame by the time we arrived at Croycullen. I had been impressed by the Grand Master Diviner's riding skill. Not once had she expressed any discomfort, despite the length and haste of our ride. I invited her to the chambers I had co-opted from the Field Lord commanding the garrison to join me for breakfast the next morning. During our rapid flight north, we had hardly spoken. This was primarily because riding as such a breakneck pace required full concentration at all times and neither of us felt any need for idle chit-chat. The other reason was that I had no discernible talent for small-talk, especially with powerful, accomplished wizards. Dervla was a notable exception, but only because our methods of communication relied little on the spoken word and far more on a more limited, yet expressive physical vocabulary. It had pleased me when the wizard made little effort to provoke conversation during our few breaks on the road. Apparently she was as happy in her own company as I was in mine. However, with the business of investigating Eoghan's smithy now at hand, there was no avoiding the need to converse, if only to agree a plan of action once we reached the workshop.
"Good morning, Duke." Malvina announced her presence as she opened the door, without knocking. She had dispensed with her riding outfit and was wearing her robes of office – a figure-hugging gown of cerulean silk. Malvina carried her staff with her, a six foot tall pole of living oak,

topped by the effigy of an eagle owl. The wooden raptor shuffled on its perch, flexing its wings. The wizard rested the shaft of her staff against the edge of the table as she took her seat, smoothing down the silk of her ankle-length dress. The chronomancer gave me a cordial smile as we waited to be served a cooked breakfast of pan-fried bacon, eggs and mushrooms, served with baked patties of shredded onions, parsnips and potatoes – standard fare for a frontier garrison. The wizard cut an inconspicuous figure. Flat-chested, of average height and with her chestnut hair cropped short in an unpretentious, collar-length bob, her smooth features could almost have passed for those of an adolescent boy. Only the hint of wrinkles forming around her jade green eyes betrayed her true age, but I found it hard to believe that she was only a couple of seasons younger than me. Mages, it seemed, aged well.
"Grand Master," I replied cordially. Despite the resentment I felt for Karryghan banishing me from the capital, I saw no reason for my unease to be taken out upon Malvina. While she was notionally an ally of the Arch Mage, it was still unclear to me whether her loyalty to Karryghan was idealistic or habitual. As one of the kitchen serfs poured us mugs of breakfast tea, I resolved to find out exactly what the wizard's true feelings about Karryghan were, especially since the Arch Mage had ordered the abduction and execution of her former teacher. "Did you sleep well?"
"Like a corpse in its grave." The wizard said, with satisfaction. She spoke with the broad vowels and clipped contractions of a true country girl, with none of the airs and graces I had learned to feign when dealing with the royal court. "I'll be pleased to forego the saddle today, believe me."
"Then you will be happy to know Eoghan's smithy is within walking distance of the barracks." I said, keeping my pronunciation up to an acceptable court standard. Old habits die hard. I did not know Malvina nearly well enough to let my guard down, even if my instincts told me that we would get along. "Though I still do not know what the Arch Mage expects us to find. The scouts here at the town garrison surveyed the ruins of the workshop shortly after the raid and found nothing. Surely anything valuable would have fallen prey to looters by now."

Malvina took a sip of tea from her earthenware mug and nodded silent thanks to the serf that had just set down a plate piled high with enough food to feed three people. It appeared that she had made her own breakfast arrangements with the kitchen staff, as the serving on my plate was not nearly so generous. The wizard immediately picked up her fork and began to eat with gusto, completely unconcerned by talking with her mouth full. "We're after gold of a different kind, m'lord. And with all due respect to your scouts, I doubt they cast spells like I do."

"Point." I conceded. From what I had seen since my arrival the previous evening, some of the soldiers at the outpost seemed to struggle with strapping themselves into their armour properly, so it was unsurprising that they had failed to find anything of note when they had been ordered to search Eoghan's workshop. Given the air of casual, ill-discipline among the soldiers stationed here, I was sure that I would be having harsh words with the garrison's Field Lord before the day was out. "I fear I know little about the intricacies of divination, my lady. What will you be looking for, and perhaps more importantly, how?"

"Everyone leaves behind a psychic impression in all the places they've been. I can draw on the aether to bring out these impressions, cast a psychic shadow, if you will." Malvina explained, cramming another chunk of bread into her mouth. "It's a form of second sight. Very tiring, it's why I need a good night's sleep and a big breakfast."

"I see." I said with a nod and decided to overlook her poor table manners. I picked at my own plate, though my appetite had been somewhat suppressed by Malvina's open-mouthed enthusiasm. "The Arch Mage told me you were a student of Eoghan's?"

"Yep." Malvina said with her head down towards her plate as she kept shovelling.

"Is that why he sent you? Will you find it easier than another diviner to find his psychic shadow?"

Malvina scoffed. "The Arch Mage sent me 'cause I'm the best fucking chronomancer in the Triad. That I knew Eoghan don't make any difference."

"Apologies, Grand Master. I meant no offence."

"Eh, it's a sore topic, Field Duke." Malvina set down her fork and looked at me with flushed cheeks, angry and upset. "Eoghan was my mentor. Just fucking disappeared on me when I was about to take my trials and get my wizard robes. All this time the bastard was living up here. Abandoned the Art, for a fucking smithy?"

"You want answers. You want to know why he did it."

"You bet your fucking cock I do." Malvina's distress had now been supplanted by anger. "I don't give two shits about this Nexus. If the Schemer gets his clues, all's the better. That old bastard's overdue a trip off the material plane. Gods know what straws he's clutching at."

I finished my tea and nudged my plate, still half full, across the table to the wizard, who smiled gratefully at my unexpected charity. "I need to stretch my legs. Meet me outside?"

"I'll be five minutes."

I did not count exactly how long it took Malvina to clear my plate, but it felt like a lot less than five minutes. Inwardly I shuddered at the thought as I wondered whether she had licked the plates clean or not. At least it was a fine morning for a stroll. The outpost's Field Lord had not been pleased when I forbade him to give me an escort. I had dismantled his protest that it was too risky for me to visit the ruins of the workshop on my own by asking whether his troops had done such a poor job of securing the border that we might be whisked away or cut down by a Fossian raid in broad daylight. After he rather reluctantly conceded the possibility was slight, I inquired as to whether he thought any of the local townsfolk would be stupid enough to attack a heavily armed and armoured knight accompanied by a Grand Master Wizard. When he also answered no to this question I quietly reminded him to mind his own fucking business and stop questioning a superior officer, unless digging latrines was one of his favourite pastimes. The look of horror on his face when he made his excuses and scurried away had made my week.

Eoghan's workshop was in about as good a condition as I imagined it would be. There were signs that nature was starting to reclaim the building after the months of dereliction. The chamomile lawn was completely overgrown and I could see that mosses were starting to colonise cracks and crevices in the walls. The fire-damaged roof had utterly collapsed and only the facade wall was still completely intact. I scanned the gravel of the courtyard and saw no signs of recent activity.

Malvina chucked as she studied the ruined smithy. "You didn't leave much standing, did you, m'lord?"

"When your orders say raze, you raze." I told the wizard with a shrug.

"D'you think it's safe to go inside?" Malvina asked as I pulled at the workshop's door. The metal handle came off in my hand, bringing two of the door boards with it. I tossed them aside, cursing. I peered through the gap in the wood and spotted the beam that had fallen from the floor above to block the door. The beam was compressing the door frame, preventing the door from swinging.

"Anything that wants to fall should have done so by now." I said, turning away from the door in disgust. "We need another way in, though. The door is blocked."

"Here." The wizard beckoned me over to a section of collapsed wall next to the forge. "Mind your footing."

With the roof totally open to the sky, there was plenty of light in the ground floor workshop. As expected, the place had been stripped bare of valuables by the local petty thieves and looters. Had the forge not been damaged and built directly into the walls, I suspected it would have been totally dismantled too, as all the metal fittings from the furnace had been stripped. What I hadn't expected however, was for there to be a gaping hole in the stone floor with an open safe lying next to it. The scouts hadn't reported any such thing after surveying the smithy a couple of weeks after Eoghan's abduction. "Where did this come from?"

"More importantly, who dug it up and opened it?" Malvina said, standing next to me and tilting her head to the side like a curious raven as we looked down at the safe. "Shall we find out?"

"Please." I bent down and reached out towards the safe, wanting to get a feel for the metal.

"Don't touch it!" the diviner yelled and I jerked backward in surprise. "Sorry, m'lord. You'll ruin the shadow if you touch it."

"Sorry, Grand Master. Of course, I should have thought." I apologised, inwardly cringing. "How did they get it out, I wonder?"

Malvina pointed at the fragmented remains of a broken flagstone. "Smashed the stone, and went digging. Pick-axe, maybe?"

I examined the fragments more closely and saw that the stone had been shattered with a single blow, directly in the centre – a difficult feat for even a skilled looter with a pick-axe. A quick look around the workshop revealed the true culprit. I held up the rod of splintered wood, which still had its fletching attached. "No, an arrow with a hardened point: armour piercer. Not what I would expect from a common looter or bandit."

"Curious. But more so that the safe has no lock: it has a latch, but no key. It was sealed with, and opened by, magic." The Grand Master pointed to an empty space on the floor to her left as she knelt a yard in front of the safe, lying her staff at her right side, the outstretched wings of the wooden eagle owl almost touching the safe door as it flapped and shuffled along its perch to stay standing upright. "Sit, please. It'll take a few moments for me to get attuned to the psychic aura and bring it out. And remain still. I need to concentrate."

Malvina closed her eyes and began the incantation, mouthing words I could not understand at a volume barely above that of a whisper. I remained silent, cross-legged on the floor and waited. It happened gradually at first, so slowly that I did not notice the light in the workshop dimming until it was no brighter than dusk. The sky above still shone brightly with Rionnag's blue fire, but night fell within the gutted carcass of the workshop. Before the light was fully extinguished I began to see luminous twinkling forms materialise in the space in front of us. The yellow sparkles of aether rained out of the blackness, settling along the floor and the ruined walls. Two figures, a young woman walking with the aid of crutches and an older man, stepped through the gap in the wall Malvina and I had used to enter the workshop only moments before. *So this is second sight.* I thought in wonder. I saw the nebulous figures conversing as they surveyed the remains of the workshop, but could not hear the details of their conversation. I wondered whether Malvina could hear what was being said, but was too afraid of breaking her concentration to ask. As they got closer to the flagstone that had hidden the safe, I was able to clearly see the young woman's face. The scar on her right cheek was unmistakeable. Somehow, Eoghan's daughter had survived my raid on the workshop. I cursed under my breath and was rebuked with a curt shush from Malvina. I tried to get a closer look at the male as events played out precisely in the manner we had deduced. The flagstone was duly smashed with a hardened tip arrow and I noted that the archer had retrieved the arrowhead, rather than leave it behind. The man understood the value of steel and was used to covering his tracks. I was able to study him in detail as they settled down to dig out the safe. His face was not one I recognised, but the quality of his equipment was simple to place. He belonged to the Order of Sylvan.

"Ranger."

"M'lord, be silent, please." Malvina hissed. "We're getting close to the opening of the safe."

Chastened, I settled back down and watched the ranger haul the safe out of the ground. There appeared to be a brief discussion between them as to how to open the safe when it sprang open of its own accord, to their surprise and mine. When the contents of the safe were revealed, the apparitions stopped moving and Malvina opened her eyes, blinking three times to adjust her eyes to the light. "Let's take a closer look, shall we?"

The wizard stood directly behind the apparition of the girl and looked over her shoulder. Malvina beckoned me closer with a wave and chuckled when she saw the reluctance in my eyes. "They can't hurt you." She passed her hand through the girl's image several times to illustrate her point. The yellow sparks flickered and looped around the mage's arm with no ill effects that I could see. I stepped closer and examined the five objects the girl had placed on the floor in front of the safe. The money purse and letter were unremarkable, but the other three objects I did not recognise.

"Could one of these things be the Nexus?"

"Doubtful." Malvina said, a frown wrinkling her nose. "That's quicksilver in the vial, a reagent for metallurgical enchantments. Uncommon, but not remarkable, the same of which could be said for the blacksmith's focus."

"The obsidian shell?"

"Yes, quite valuable if it's not already attuned, but there's nothing intrinsically magical about it."

"And the box?"

"Now that is magical. A set of diviner's tarot cards. The safe still has a strong residual aura from them, but not nearly strong enough to be this Nexus the Schemer is after."

"So Eoghan did not hide it here, then. And you cannot sense anything here that might say where it might be hidden?"

"No, if it was ever here, Eoghan moved it a long time ago. And since he has taken the knowledge of when and where to the grave, looks like your only lead is this girl and that letter." Malvina said, waving her hand through the psychic shadow of Eoghan's daughter again.

"And now the girl is accompanied by a ranger. They will not be easily found."

"Then you'd better start looking, Field Duke. My work is done. There are no more answers to be found here. Eoghan's aura here is weak – not strong enough to recall an apparition." Malvina said, disappointed and frustrated. "Not quite a wasted trip, but almost."

"Shall I have a carriage prepared for your trip back to the capital, Grand Master?"

"Please, though it'd be good if we could wait until after lunch before heading back to Clongarvan. I'm fucking starving."

19 – Keri

We were still several days walk short of Lesøsnø when my ability to tolerate the company of other people began to reach breaking point. Ailidh was exhausted after another long day of walking on the road north to Lesøsnø. I did not need any magical intervention to divine this because she had spent the last two scores of minutes constantly complaining about the aching of her feet and the soreness of her shoulders beneath the straps of her travelling pack. Cathal was not too burdensome a companion. The ranger was comfortable in his own company and did not require the reassurance of constant idle chatter to distract his mind from the tedium of walking. He was content just to watch the scenery and the road ahead in silence, only speaking to give instructions or warn us of potential hazards. In a certain light, or after imbibing a sufficient volume of wine, I even thought that the ranger possessed a faint shadow of the fearsome, muscular physicality of my tanar'ri consorts. Ailidh however, was starting to irk me with her incessant commentary informing us of her physical and emotional state, and her asinine observations about whatever inconsequential thing caught her interest and attention in the surrounding countryside. If she believed that her innocence made her endearing, she was sadly mistaken. As had become customary on our trek north from The Sundered Shield, when the complaints about Ailidh's aching feet coincided with the sun dipping below the horizon, Cathal led us a few hundred yards off the road into the forest to find a suitable place to make camp. Once Cathal had found a clearing among the trees large enough to safely lay a fire, we each fulfilled our party roles. Ailidh pitched the tents as Cathal dug a fire pit, before lining it with stones and cooking dinner. I conjured wine for us to drink to dull the soreness of our muscles and calm the thoughts in our minds. We ate and drank in blessed silence, the potent alcohol in the wine doing its job perfectly. I felt much less aggravated as I emptied my goblet for the fifth time that evening. Lacking the regenerative energies given to me by daeva seed and my mastery of wild aetheric power, Ailidh had unwisely tried to keep pace with me. She lounged back against the stump of a fallen tree, half-asleep, grinning idiotically at the waxy touch of ivy leaves from the vines wrapped around the trunk, which tickled the back of her neck. Cathal had abstained from drinking more wine after finishing his second glass, preferring to keep his hands occupied tending the fire, knowing that he would take first watch and would need to remain alert.

"I never imagined that I'd get a taste for fine wine." Ailidh announced, drowsy and more than a little tipsy. "I could get used to this."

"Beware, Ailidh." Cathal replied, sounding a note of caution as he nudged a log deeper into the fire pit with the tip of his stiletto. "It is an expensive hobby, and one that, without moderation, eventually leads to ruin."

I laughed at that, adding, "All of the best hobbies do."

"Such as?" Ailidh asked warily, no doubt curious as to what constituted a pastime for a mentally unhinged, demon-fucking wizard.

"Oh, the usual kind of things: food, wine, smokeweed, grain spirits, money, the power of high office, the pursuit of carnal pleasure, magic, the obsessive collection forming of shoes, jewellery or books..." I said, letting my tone become whimsical before adding, "Even love."

"Love?" Ailidh echoed, confused, in that sweetly childlike timbre she had that made me want to shapeshift her into a weasel, or perhaps a rat.

"Oh, but of course, you would know nothing about that, would you, Ailidh?" My voice took on an ugly, condescending tone. In the firelight I saw the fear sparkle in the young woman's widening eyes at my sudden change of mood.

"Keri, please. That was uncalled for." Cathal chided me quietly, igniting my temper like a torch thrown onto a bone-dry haystack. Cathal recoiled as my attention snapped to him, rightly afraid of my ire. *Both of these emotionally-stunted children need a lesson*, I thought.

"Love is the greatest ruin of them all." I snarled, clutching my staff to flood the ground beneath us with wild, aetheric energy. The dirt seethed as I bent the environment to my will. Ailidh hardly had time to scream as the roots from the stump she leaned against writhed like irate snakes, bursting from the soil, binding her around the ankles, wrists, elbows and waist, pinning her in place like a butterfly mounted into a presentation case. The ivy vines encasing the fallen tree trunk slithered around her face and neck, forcing a gag of leaves into her mouth to ensure her silence.

"Keri, stop this madness!" Cathal shouted, launching himself to his feet, stiletto in hand. He had not even taken two steps towards me before a serpentine tree root grasped his right ankle and calf, tumbling the ranger to the floor. He launched his stiletto at my face, the blade spinning in the air. Without even thinking, I force-shielded my free hand and slapped the weapon into the ground with an open palm. Before the point of the knife had even hit the turf, I aimed my staff at the ranger, encouraging more thick roots to sprout from the forest floor to bind Cathal supine on his back. The fibrous cords secured him down by his ankles, wrists, waist and neck, coiling threateningly like a constricting python whenever he struggled. "Keri, why are you doing this?"

"Your company is becoming loathsome. I cannot abide such naivety, not even from a virgin maiden. I will educate you in the ruinous folly of love." I said, stabbing my staff down into the dirt at the stricken ranger's side. I slipped my robe over my shoulders and let the sheer green silk fall to the top of my hips. Cathal's eyes widened in terror as I kicked the shimmering fabric off my legs, correctly anticipating what was about to happen next. I hung my wizard robe over the twisted aetherium prongs at the tip of my staff to prevent it from getting soiled. I placed my bare feet either side of Cathal's hips, letting him get a good look at my naked body before I bent my knees to straddle his waist. The look of anguish on Cathal's face was deliciously arousing. I was briefly distracted by Ailidh's muffled screams. The girl tried to turn her head aside, so that she wouldn't be forced to witness my lesson. I psychically persuaded another vine of ivy to wrap tightly around her forehead, insistent tendrils probing across her cheeks and forehead to hold her eyelids wide open. Tears streamed down her cheeks and I could taste her torment on the air. "No, Ailidh. You *must* see. You must see the damage that can be done by love."

"Keri. No, please. Not this. Please. This is worse than cruel." Cathal begged between desperate gasps, his breathing almost cut off by the root that gripped his throat. I watched his ineffectual and futile struggles with a growing sense of excitement as my hands worked quickly and decisively to expose Cathal's waist and thighs, opening his belt and pulling his trousers down to his knees. Cathal cried out in dismay when I took his sex into my hands and unwillingly inflamed him, caressing along the length of his hardening shaft with one hand as I massaged his testicles firmly in the other.

"Cathal, my dear ranger, you are one to speak of cruelty." I reproached him sardonically. My psychic probes laid open the deepest, most closely-guarded secrets in Cathal's memories. I sensed his repressed lust for Ailidh and the rationalisations explaining why he had chosen not to act upon it, despite Ailidh's unambiguous signals. "You cannot be so dull that you are unaware of how much Ailidh would like to share your bed. Of how much she wants to be the one astride your legs right at this moment. No, you know all too well. You would fuck her ragged too, were it not for her scars and burns."

"No." Cathal's denial was weak. The faint moan of distress leaking through Ailidh's gag showed that she knew that truth as well as I did. Cathal could not see past the disfigurement Ailidh had suffered as a young girl. She would never be beautiful or desirable enough in his eyes – Cathal was too attached to the nostalgic perfection of his dead lover, Aoibheann. I looked over to Ailidh, feeling something approaching pity.

"Look what your rejection does to her, Cathal. This girl would love you for eternity, only you cannot see past a few scars." I scolded him. Cathal moaned softly, half in arousal and half in despair, as I teased him, licking along the full length of his manhood with the tip of my tongue, leaving a moist trail behind on the taut skin. "If only she had never been burned. How different would things be?"

Ailidh choked in despair and sobbed behind her gag when I illustrated my point. I used my wild power to transform into her mirror image, only without any of her flaws and imperfections. I felt lightheaded for a moment. Wearing the body of someone else was a discombobulating experience at best. Ailidh wept when she saw how alluring she was without her disfiguring burns. I explored the boundaries of my new form with my hands, unused to such a curvaceous figure. I felt a twinge of envy when I compared the shape and firmness of Ailidh's bust to my own and I glanced over to Ailidh to make a wry observation. "Do not worry. Your tits are far too heavy for me to want to keep your form for long."

Tears welled at the corners of Cathal's eyes. "Keri, stop. I cannot bear this. Anything but this."

"Gods girl, the Succubus herself would kill for tits like these," I told Ailidh in complete sincerity as I supported their weight in my palms. "If you ever knelt for the Rite of Spring, seekers would line up to cover you with their seed from five paces."

I aligned my sex with Cathal's and moaned softly as I pressed my hips down slowly to his. I spoke with Ailidh's voice as my hands gripped his shoulders and I arched my back. "How's that feel, my love? D'you like my slit?"

"Stop, Keri, please. Please!" Cathal said in a feeble, unconvincing protest. The roots around his neck and wrists tightened further as he tried to struggle against the weight holding him down. I began to fuck Cathal slowly, claiming his desire, regardless of whether he was willing or not. Hot tears streamed down Ailidh's face as she watched, tormented, hating Cathal for not being able to resist, while lamenting that she did not possess the body ravishing him. I mocked both of them, encouraging Cathal to lose control. "Yes, Cathal, show Ailidh the lust you would have for her, if she were not so damaged. Show her the pleasure you would give her virgin cunt."

Ailidh's shriek of objection was muffled by the vine across her mouth binding her to the tree stump. Unable to hold back any longer, I felt Cathal's hips respond to the slow, sensual rolls of my sex with hard, driving strokes as I loosened the binding of the roots around his waist. I arched my back, moaning wantonly as his upward thrusts set my legs trembling like those of a newborn deer. I purred lowly as I came and eased myself off him before he reached his own climax. Tantalisingly, I brushed Cathal's panting mouth with the crests of Ailidh's magnificent tits. "You see the damage unrequited love can do, Cathal? The passion and pleasure you could have given her, rather than me? You pathetic, shallow creature."

I left Cathal on the floor and moved over to Ailidh who tried in vain to shrink away from me. I glanced back over my shoulder to address Cathal. "I could heal her, you know. Make her perfect for you."

Ailidh trembled with terror as I twisted her right wrist to expose the scar burned into her forearm. I tasted the arcane fire as I trailed my tongue along the scar, leaving pristine, healed flesh behind. Ailidh screamed behind her gag as I licked the scar on her neck, devouring the disfiguring aetheric energy marking her from her collarbone to the underside of her chin. I licked my lips and regarded her for a moment. Ailidh's panic overtook her and she pulled at her bonds manically, beginning to tear the skin on her wrists. She became frantic when I took her melted ear into my mouth, tracing the tip of my tongue along the deformed lobes of cartilage. I let out a gentle sigh of satisfaction as I sucked away the disfiguring energy burned into her flesh, repairing the damage done to her as a child. I stood and stepped back a couple of paces to admire my work. The cartilage that had been melted away from her ear was now restored; bringing balance and symmetry back to her visage. Were it not for the burn scarring her cheek and her mutated, reptilian eye, Ailidh could have passed for normal. "But that would devalue what she has suffered. I think I prefer her flawed."

Cathal tensed as I returned to him, sitting astride his hips again. I lifted the tip of his cock and ground my sex back and forth along his length, to engorge him with hot blood once more. Ailidh squealed wordlessly in protest. Her thoughts were delightfully violent and her aura flared like a furnace. She wanted to claw at my flawless parody of her face with her fingernails, gouging out my eyes. "You do not deserve the love of such a noble girl, Cathal. She risked her life and soul by defying me at The Sundered Shield. I would not have minded so much, had you honoured her love by consummating it at the inn. Instead, you denied her and yourself, and for that, you must pay the price."

I looked into Cathal's eyes, delving deep into his mind to retrieve a clear memory of his lost lover, Aoibheann. I teased the idealised recollection of her likeness and voice from his thoughts, abandoning Ailidh's form and concentrating as I shifted my flesh into a new image. The slain ranger lacked Ailidh's generous curves, but she was

still positively voluptuous compared to my own sleek, willowy form. Aoibheann was half a head shorter than my true self, with chin-length auburn-red hair and a toned physique. Her heavy chest and broad hips gave her lean figure a silhouette similar to that of an hour glass. I spoke with her common southerner's accent as I completed my reformation. "Heya me lover, did ya miss me?"
"No. No! You have no right!" Cathal screamed in anguish. "Stop this, please. I beg you!"
"I have the power, Cathal. That alone gives me the right." I corrected him harshly, my tone running colder than a winter night on the Fjord Coast. "You must stop clinging to the past, Cathal. How long have you wondered what it would feel like to fuck Aoibheann one last time? I grant you this boon."
I remounted Cathal, knowing that he was aroused but unspent. Cathal cried out in pain and horror as I rocked my hips, gripping him hard using the muscles in my pelvic floor as I rode him with a savage rhythm. A ring of bone-white spikes grew out of the crown of my skull, poking through my hair as I unleashed my full power. I growled with pleasure, a demonic yellow fire in my eyes, as inch-long razor-sharp talons extruded from my fingertips. I raked a hand across his chest, slicing open his tunic and drawing blood. The coppery tang ignited my desire even more as I fed off the terror, frustration and hatred emanating from both Cathal and Ailidh. Their screams brought me to climax and I carved a deep gash into his bare chest with my thumbnail, the first mark of a demonic rune. I whispered an incantation in the daeva tongue and began to drain Cathal, siphoning the very essence of his soul upwards through the wound on his breast into my hand. I marked Cathal again, cutting deep as I fucked him mercilessly, one slice in his flesh for each climax I extracted by force from him. After the second mark the amethyst vapours of his soul grew thicker as they condensed to form a crystal in my open palm, evaporating through the bleeding sigil I had cut into him. The colour drained out of Cathal's tawny eyes, turning grey as the soul gem began to solidify.

No, do not kill him. I have need of him yet.

I recoiled in agony at my mistress's rebuke, as if a wave of lava had washed over my entire body. The pale purple gem fell from my hand and broke on Cathal's sternum allowing his soul entry back into his body. Denied the ultimate ecstasy of stealing Cathal's soul, I settled for sating my lust instead. A quick glance over at Ailidh gave me a spasm of pleasure. I revelled in her powerless anguish. Cathal was barely sensate as his soul infused back into his body, but his base instinct kept him hard inside me. When I carved a third and final gash into his chest, he was unable to endure any more. Cathal's hips leapt and quivered as he came, his eyes screwed shut in anguish at the ecstasy of my torture. The scent of sulphur and burning flesh filled the air as the blood oozing from the cuts I had made on Cathal's breast burst into flame. The fire quickly petered out, leaving behind a jagged, cauterised scar. The rune would be readily identifiable as being demonic in origin, even to an uneducated layman. The aggressive script looked like someone had cast a handful of narrow, sharp fangs onto a platter.

"Such a shame; a man is a poor substitute for a daeva. No stamina." I sighed as I let the motion of my hips finally come to rest. I abandoned Aoibheann's body, reshaping back to my true self. Cathal had passed out in the aftermath of his ordeal, but Ailidh's muffled curses still filled my ears. I raised myself off Cathal's limp, devastated form and stretched my legs, glad to have them returned to their proper length. I walked over to the tree stump where the enchanted vines and roots still held Ailidh helplessly immobile. I squatted on the ground next to her and regarded the distraught girl with genuine sympathy. I reeked of sweat, wine, sex and brimstone. I smirked and held my hand beneath my slit. I let Cathal's seed ooze out onto my palm and fingers.

"You wanted this, did you not?" I taunted Ailidh, holding out my hand to let her see and smell the sticky, white fluid. The vine in her mouth prevented Ailidh from spitting in my face, but I was delighted to see and hear her try anyway, the utter contempt and hatred she felt for me making her aura taste bitter. I grinned like a proud parent. "It is a hard lesson to learn, my child, but you will remember it well. Consider it my parting gift. Next time you want something so badly, go and claim it."

I smeared her lips and cheeks with Cathal's seed, rubbing my palm across her face twice. "Otherwise this will be the closest you get to tasting love."

I collected my belongings and walked out of the camp without looking back. It was long the past time for me to go.

20 - Cathal

The chorus of birdsong that accompanied dawn was particularly unwelcome this morning. The barrage of chirrups and whistles had my ears ringing, an extra pain to accompany the myriad aches all over my body following last night's ordeal. I tried to move my arms, finding that the dawn's light had dispelled the magical energy that had bound me helpless to the floor. I ripped my right arm free, wrenching the tree root looping around my wrist out of the loam beneath the carpet of leaf litter beneath me. I moaned in pain as the motion aggravated the ragged tears in the muscles of my chest. With my free hand I tugged at the fibrous cord wrapped around my throat until I had created enough slack to slip the root over my head. I propped myself up on my right elbow and simply breathed deeply for a few moments to recover some kind of equilibrium. The cauterised scars on my chest smelled of brimstone and I felt nauseous at the memory of how I had acquired them. I shuddered as I recalled the sensation of my soul being drained out through the deep cuts by Keri's magic, remembering how my awareness had dulled to almost nothing as the soul gem had taken form in her hand. I knew that I was lucky to still be in my own body, rather than have my consciousness trapped with a crystal to be traded like gold for influence and power on the infernal planes, or to be sacrificed as a spell reagent. The pain in my chest flared again as I freed my left arm from its half-buried restraints. I stretched my aching back as I sat up, groaning in discomfort. I glanced over to the tree stump where Ailidh had been forced to watch Keri's punishment of my reticence to lay with Ailidh at The Sundered Shield. She was still bound to the broken tree trunk with thick tangles of ivy and was completely still, having either passed out or fallen asleep during the night. With both of my hands now free, it was a simple matter to snap the roots bracing my ankles and waist. I refastened the buttons on my trousers, closed my belt buckle and I stood, feeling revolted and unclean. I picked up my stiletto from where it had fell, the blade impaled deep into the ground, almost to the handle. I crossed the campsite gingerly, every muscle in my body protesting at the slightest motion. I knelt at Ailidh's side and used my knife to carefully slice away her vegetal bonds, starting first with the vines binding her neck and gagging her mouth.

Ailidh woke with a gasp of terror, not even registering me with her eyes before she started screaming. I shushed her like a mother comforting her baby, placing a gentle, restraining finger on her lips. "Ailidh, you are safe now. Keri is gone, be calm. Calm now."

She looked furtively around the camp, the movements of her eyes and head jerking violently like a wood sparrow on the lookout for a goshawk. Her chest rose and fell rapidly with her panicked breathing and I had to concentrate on her face as Keri's words echoed in my mind. *You would fuck her ragged too, were it not for her burns and scars.* It shamed me to admit that Keri had been right. With the scars from her neck and arm healed, and with the delicate shape of her ruined earlobe now restored, I did find Ailidh more attractive. But that was not the most shameful thing, not by far. When Keri had raped me with Ailidh's blemish-free body, I had enjoyed it and I had been disappointed when she had not let me come in her. With Keri stripping me of my agency, it was as if I had been absolved of responsibility for my pleasure, my intellect completely detached from the carnal desires of my body. The trauma of Keri's coercion had only begun to sink in when she defiled my memory of Aoibheann. Keri's misuse of the form of my soulmate had made it doubly harrowing when she started to siphon away my life force. Aoibheann had died in my arms; I did not doubt for a second that Keri had taken her image with the intention of creating a perverse symmetry in our deaths. After Keri had sliced open my breast for the second time, I had lost all sense of self and had been certain that I would die. I did not understand why she had ultimately chosen spare me, but having been given a reprieve, I wondered how to make the best of it. I had no sense of how to recover from being used so cruelly and then casually discarded. I cut the roots securing Ailidh's ankles to the ground before turning my attention to her waist and wrists. She was still hyperventilating as I sawed at the root holding her left forearm to the fungus-ridden stump at her side. "Almost there. Relax. I will free you soon."

Ailidh found her senses and her voice after I had severed the last fibrous root binding her to the floor. I reeled in pain and shock as she slapped me across the face with all of the strength she could muster, her palm stinging my cheek and sending my senses spinning. "Bastard! You *fucked* her! Came in her! How *could* you?"

Her unprovoked attack incensed me, my anger almost boiling over irrevocably. I could have taken her, right at that moment. I would have ripped open her clothes and ravaged her, bent over the tree stump, had I not realised that Keri must have intended to provoke exactly this kind of toxic discord between us. I blinked in shock, still astounded at her outburst of fury, but paused a moment to let my blood cool. I raised my open palms in supplication, trying to placate her and stave off another assault. "Ailidh, please... you saw it all. It is not like I had any choice."

The heaving of Ailidh's chest slowed as she processed my words, but her features were still twisted with hurt and hatred. "I told you that I loved you. You *knew*. And you still fucked her."

"Ailidh, we are not having this conversation now." I warned her with a raised finger. I tore the shredded remains of my tunic off my mutilated chest so that she could see the extent of my injuries. I directed her attention to the raw marks over my torso with the fingers of my left hand. "You think I wanted *this*? I almost died."

Tears appeared at the corners of Ailidh's eyes and she clutched her face in both hands, rubbing away the flaky, dried residue of my seed from her cheeks in distress. "Cathal, I...I-"

"Later. We need to go." I stood and walked over to my tent, collapsing the prism of fabric and dissembling the wooden rod frame to stow it away into my backpack. "I need to get away from here. A very long way away from here."

I glanced over my shoulder to check on Ailidh. She was still weeping quietly, but was also in the process of packing away her tent and bedroll. The jagged slashes in my chest burned like acid as I replaced my bloodstained, ruined shirt with a fresh tunic from my pack and donned my armour. I doubted that we would be able to make much progress on our journey today, but I could not bear to spend another moment in this accursed camp. I took out my frustration by kicking the charred logs over the edge of the burnt out fire pit, smearing the ashes over the ground with the soles of my boot to make sure that nothing still smouldered. I sagged under the weight of my pack, every muscle between my waist and neck aching in protest as the leather straps dug into my shoulders. This was going to be a long, painful day. I buckled my weapon belt over the top of my hips and picked up my longbow, waiting until Ailidh had likewise slung her pack and picked up Sapphire's cage. I gave her a silent tip of my head, my eyes pointing towards the west where the sun was rising. I found the trail leading us back to the road and set off tentatively, trying to assess just how much damage Keri had done. The flexing of my ribs brought agony to my chest with every breath, but the cramps in my arms and legs were tolerable as long as I didn't try to walk too quickly. The heavy, still air meant that I could hear Ailidh's quiet, reluctant footsteps following a few paces behind me over the birdsong announcing daybreak. I let the calmness of the still air envelop me like a second cloak. I had always taken solace from being surrounded by nature; the deeper into the wild the better. I feared that not even the serenity of the forest of the Western Weald would be enough to provide the merest spark of comfort on this cold, calm morning. As we rejoined the road and turned north, dark, moody clouds portending rain bubbled at the horizon to the north-east. A storm was blowing inland over The Bay of Wolves, which at this time of year would be laden with several inches of frigid rain. *Perfection,* I groused to myself. *As if the day's walk was not going to be difficult enough.* The last marker post on the road we had passed yesterday evening indicated that we were still three score and ten leagues from Lesøsnø; at least five days' walk, I judged, in my current condition. The forest thinned as we crossed the boundary from the Western Weald to the North Riding. The rolling grasslands stretched for over three hundred leagues from Drommasund on the Fjord Coast in the north-west of Fossfjall to the border with Cothraine and Sundgau to the south-east. Despite being over four hundred leagues further north than Cothraine's Breadbowl, the agricultural heart of Cothraine that lay between the towns of Siskine and Ballinlara, the North Riding was the most productive farmland in the Western Triad, thanks to the fertility of the volcanic loam that had been laid down after the eruption of the volcano beneath the Caldera. The mineral-rich fallout from the event meant that staple crops such as wheat, maize and potatoes grew faster and stronger in Fossfjall than anywhere else on the continent, giving Fossfjall a large food surplus that could be bartered for luxury goods that would otherwise be unavailable at such northern latitudes, such as wine, spices and gemstones. From here on, the road to Lesøsnø was utterly exposed to the elements as it lanced like an arrow towards the heart of the cultural capital of the Western Triad. The terrain between the forest and the city undulated like the Bay of Serpents in mid-winter. Another glance to the horizon had me muttering a prayer to the Warrior to give me strength. The slate-grey cloud was racing south far faster than I had expected, and the only thing worse than walking uphill was walking uphill into a headwind while rain or snow battered you from the skies. I estimated that we had less than two hours before the dull curtain of rain that I could see already encroaching over the ridge ahead of us would arrive. I cursed the Lady's mercurial temperament under my breath and upped my pace, wanting to get as far as I could from last night's camp before the coming storm forced us to seek shelter. I sucked air in between gritted teeth and ignored the spasms of pain in my calves and thighs that informed me of their displeasure at being overworked in the aftermath of Keri's assault. I grimaced and drove us onwards into the headwind, which was increasing in strength by the minute as the storm front drew closer. I scanned the countryside around us for a potential refuge. There was a dense copse of willows in the lee of a down roughly a league and a half from the eastern side of the road. The stiffness of my muscles prevented me from breaking into a run, so pressed forward against the wind as quickly as my aching body would let me, slower than a jog, but faster than a brisk walk. I checked that Ailidh was still following in my wake. Her head was down and her eyes did not leave the floor, but otherwise she kept pace with me without complaint or question. The first misty globes of drizzle started falling from the sky as we entered the thicket of willow trees. By the time we had started erecting our tents, a good fifty yards inside the tree line, we were already almost drenched to the bone. I helped Ailidh finish assembling her tent and took Sapphire's cage with me as I erected my own tent. There was no hope of starting a fire in such an intense torrent of rain, so we crawled miserably into our tents to wait out the storm. Ailidh caught my gaze before entering her canvas shelter. She looked simultaneously furious, remorseful and miserable. My returning glance was utterly devoid of emotion. I was still numb from Keri's assault and I absolutely had no desire to talk about it, especially not with Ailidh after her outburst this morning. I flattened my bedroll inside the canvas prism of my tent, listening to the raindrops hammering off the waterproof, waxed linen canvas. With sleep under these circumstances a distant possibility at best, I did not even bother entertaining the idea of taking off my armour. I simply lay down on the floor and unlatched the door to Sapphire's cage. She practically jumped onto my face, nuzzling my cheeks sympathetically with her chin and densely whiskered cheeks. She spoke to me in a series of short high-pitched yips and yowls, as if granting me the benefit of her feline wisdom. I hugged and stroked her with a protectiveness to rival that of a snow bear matriarch. Sapphire purred appreciatively, licking the end of my nose with her rough tongue. The hot, moist barbs tickled my skin and I couldn't stop myself from kissing the soft fur on her throat, beneath her chin. Sapphire, as fickle as the Lady herself, warned me off with a paw placed over my jugular vein. Her claws were extended, but there was no intent to cause injury. She just wanted to provide me with a gentle reminder of the boundaries of our friendship.

"Sorry, kitten." I apologised, scratching her between the shoulder blades of her forelegs in the way I knew she found irresistible. Sapphire closed her jewel-like blue eyes and purred gratefully. My fingertips traced circles and massaged the long silver and black fur over her spine in a languid rhythm, as much for my own relaxation as hers. Sapphire stood on my chest, seemingly knowing how to avoid treading on the marks Keri had carved into my torso, sniffing the air as she walked in a circle twice before lying down on my stomach, her head resting on my lap. I stroked Sapphire's neck and back for several moments before quietly lamenting to myself, "Gods, what a mess."

Sapphire transfixed me with a terrifyingly intense stare, her disapproval utterly unambiguous. The cat's body language and facial expression practically screamed '*This is your fault.*'

"Warrior's cock, Sapphire," I groaned, my voice low so that it wouldn't carry to Ailidh's tent. "Who appointed you to the office of Dark Rider?"

I immediately regretted asking, given the sharpness of Sapphire's curt mewing and yelping. I could have sworn that the cat had rolled her eyes in response to my question. I was so annoyed by the cat's condescending air that I grabbed Sapphire with one hand around her face and attacked her soft belly with the hard fingertips of my other hand. "Just you remember who is in charge here, kitten." We spent a few moments play fighting, my fingers prodding and poking harmlessly at Sapphire's yielding flanks and stomach, while she reminded me just how many sharp teeth and claws she possessed, without actually using them in anger. When Sapphire sensed that my mood was sufficiently buoyed, she clasped both of her front paws around my wrist, restraining the middle finger of my hand between her jaws.

"Ouch! Alright! You win, trouble." I said smiling, as I used the fingertips of my free hand to tickle her behind her ears. Sapphire purred and rubbed her scent glands against my face affectionately, her whiskers tickling my lips. She then put her head back down on my thigh, slumping onto her left flank between my legs. It was a clear indication that her victory entitled her to use me as a mattress to nap on until the rain stopped falling. I knew better than to disturb Sapphire from her repose. Regardless, it was not like I had anywhere else I would rather be. The canvas shell of my tent rapped and chattered to the persistent beat of falling raindrops. The percussive reports of the raindrops recoiling from the taut canvas sheet were oddly relaxing – even somatic. I closed my eyes and took slow, deep breaths, trying to dull the pain emanating from the gashes across my chest. At some point I must have fallen asleep, because I found myself back in the camp of the previous evening, bound to the dirt as Keri rode my hips. In the dream she was not wearing Ailidh's or Aoibheann's body, but her own. She was beautiful and terrible in equal measure, the demonic fire in her eyes blazing heat down into my soul.

Her crown of bony thorns grew longer as the talons on her fingers dove deep into my chest, clutching my heart. I felt my life draining away as Keri drew out my soul. Her sex tightened around me as she approached climax. Large, leathery wings grew from her shoulder blades, spreading out to envelop me in darkness. With a single hard pull she yanked my still-beating heart free from my body.

Sapphire shrieked in terror and scrambled for the corner of my tent as I woke from the nightmare, sitting up with a jolt of panic, screaming. I placed a hand over my sternum to reassure myself that my ribcage was still intact and tried to calm myself, slowing down my breathing. Sapphire stayed perfectly still, her ears tucked back as she regarded me warily, ready to duck out of the tent at any further sign of danger. For a moment there was nothing other than the sound of my breathing and a gentle pitter-patter of raindrops on the canvas. The worst of the storm had passed, it seemed. I beckoned for Sapphire to come back to my lap, whispering. "Sorry I scared you, kitten."

Sapphire's ears pricked back up and the tension in her back relaxed, but she made no attempt to move from the safety of the corner. The entrance flap to the tent rustled and Ailidh's blonde head poked inside.

"Cathal, what's wrong? Are you alright?" she asked, fear and apprehension written starkly across her face.

"Just a nightmare," I replied, waving her away. "I will be fine. What time is it?"

Ailidh scrutinised my face and body language doubtfully, but answered my question. "Mid-afternoon. We still have a couple of hours of daylight."

I eased myself out of the tent gingerly, giving Ailidh enough time to clear out of my way. I scanned the horizon in all directions, surveying the weather and the position of the sun in the sky. There was another band of rain approaching from the north-east, but I judged from the strength of the wind that it would almost be nightfall before it reached us.

"Then we should get moving. That storm has cost us a lot of time."

Ultimately, the aching of my thighs and lower back stopped us from making more progress towards Fossfjall's capital city before the fading light and incoming squall of rain did. The hot needle pricks of small spasms in the muscles were a warning sign of a more serious injury on its way if I continued to overtax my stressed body. I found a sheltered spot in the bend of an oxbow lake, where beds of tall reeds prevented us from being overlooked from the road. Ailidh pitched the tents next to the fire pit I had just constructed. The first drops of rain were just beginning to fall when the kindling glowed hot enough to ignite the pyramid of logs. The fire was well established by the time the rainfall was heavy enough to persuade Ailidh and me to retreat into the cover of our tents. Ailidh laid face-down on her belly, the cushioned mat of her bedroll beneath her, watching the dance of the flames. The slashes in my chest were still far too raw to be able to adopt the same position, so I lay flat on my back with my head facing upwards to see the smoke rising up into the sky.

Unable to bear the tension any more, Ailidh broke the silence. "Aren't you going to talk to me?"

"About what?" I asked, even though I already knew the topic she wanted to discuss.

"Last night."

"What is there to say? Keri almost murdered me and made you watch." My voice was devoid of emotion, as if I were describing events that had happened to another person; events whose details I had learned only at second hand. Not events that I had been at the centre of. "She wanted us to see how powerless we are compared to her."

"If that's what she wanted, it worked. I've never felt so humiliated, so violated. She took my body and used it to fuck you." Ailidh gagged on the words. "Just thinking about it makes me want to be sick."

I bit my tongue, rather than blurting out the retort that sprang to mind. *How do you think I felt? I almost ended up in a soul crystal!* Instead I simply remained silent. I resented the pettiness of equating her trauma to mine, as what Ailidh had suffered seemed to pale in comparison to the physical and mental ordeal Keri had subjected me to. But I conceded that her distress was genuine and that I had failed in my promise to protect her from all harm. The admission of failure made me feel ashamed.

"And then she literally rubbed my face in it. How superior she is to me." I didn't need to see her face to know that tears formed in the corners of her eyes. The anguish was obvious in her voice. "More experienced, more powerful, more beautiful. I'm nothing compared to her."

"You are a far better human being than she is, Ailidh." I reassured her. "You have a good heart."

"What use is that when those with evil in their soul always win?" Ailidh said, choking back a sob.

"Unchecked evil is by its very nature self-defeating. Evil is not immune to the destruction it leaves in its wake. Eventually it ends up consuming itself. Kindness, on the other hand, grows stronger the faster you give it away." I twisted my neck to give her a smile of encouragement. It was not returned. "Rest, Ailidh. We could both use a good night's sleep."

"D'you want Sapphire with you?" Ailidh asked, eyeing the silver tabby's cage next to the fire. The cat was snoozing with her back arched along the curve of the willow frame, getting as close as she could to the heat of the flames.

"Best not, I think. My nightmare earlier almost frightened her out of her fur."

"I'll keep her with me then. Sleep well, Cathal."

"Sleep well, Ailidh." I said back, hoping that my sleep would be untroubled by dreams.

21 – Ailidh

Time passed slowly as Cathal and I walked in silence along the cobbled road to Lesøsnø. The granite stones were treacherously slick with autumn rain, requiring us to be mindful of our footing, lest we turn an ankle. Cathal estimated that we were still a couple of days walk from our destination, as the farmland east of Lesøsnø was notoriously hilly. We passed farmhouses set back from the road every couple of leagues, thick hedgerows and islands of deciduous trees demarking the boundaries between the steadings. The fields were busy with farmhands harvesting the crops. The rows of maize, potatoes, wheat and barley stretched for leagues, horizon to horizon. It had obviously been a year well-favoured by the Earth Mother, as the maize plants made even Cathal look diminutive, standing tall and unbowed by the rain. Cathal traded small handfuls of copper and silver coins with the masters of some of the less prosperous farmsteads in exchange for cuts of salted meat, loaves of bread, butter and eggs to resupply our packs. It was a more than fair transaction. The farmers were grateful for the coin, and Cathal would be better rested if he did not to have to hunt for our dinner. He even bought a new bar of soap from a lavender farm on a whim, knowing that I would appreciate the chance to bathe in perfumed water before rejoining civilised society in the capital city of Fossfjall. The sun was just starting to set, and my thoughts were just starting to turn towards asking Cathal whether we should make camp for the night when I heard Cathal click his fingers three times. It was one of the coded danger signals we had agreed back at his cabin near Croycullen. One click was for wild beasts, two clicks was an alarm for soldiers, but three clicks meant bandits. I had been too engrossed watching my step on the slippery cobblestones to even consider the possibility of being waylaid by brigands. Fortunately, Cathal had been more alert. I drew my wakizashi as I glanced up from the slick stones beneath my feet, noticing that Cathal had set down his pack and Sapphire's cage so that he could unsheath his longsword and stiletto. Four lithe figures wrapped in scarlet, woollen cloaks sprang up from behind the hedgerow nearest the road, swords and knives in hand. I had expected the bandits to want to parlay and allow us to hand over our belongings without violence, as they did in the fairy tales my father had told me as a child, but the look on Cathal's face told me that only bloodshed would suffice for these thieves. Seeing that we too were armed, three of the bandits converged on Cathal, with the final one heading directly for me, shouting a berserker cry to intimidate me. I barely had the time to shuck my pack and lift my sword before he was upon me, swinging his longsword in wild, whistling arcs. I dodged to my left, stepping around my pack, not allowing myself to be distracted by the sound of steel parrying steel, as Cathal defended himself. The berserker continued to scream at me, almost tripping over my pack as one of his feet got caught in the shoulder strapping. I kept my eyes fixed upon the tip of his sword, as Cathal had taught me to do, raising my hands to keep the point of my sword aimed at his throat. There was a dreadful gurgling sound from behind me, that of blood bubbling from a punctured windpipe. My assailant lunged forward, slipping on the wet cobbles as he tried to take advantage of the flicker of fear that made me glance over my shoulder for an instant, hoping that the death rattle did not belong to Cathal. I gasped as the berserker's longsword flashed towards my face, recoiling instinctively. A current of wind buffeted across my forehead as the blade slashed through the air, less than an inch in front of my nose. It pushed my fringe away from in front of my right eye back over my ear. This time the berserker's cry was one of terror as he saw my mutated eye and scarred face. He stumbled for balance on the wet stone beneath his feet, his shock lasting less than a second. It may have only been a tiny hesitation, but it was long enough to be fatal. I struck out with the tip of my wakizashi, stabbing him through the windpipe and the spine at the base of his neck, before twisting my blade on its side and wrenching it free horizontally through the neck muscle and carotid artery. I turned on the spot, blood dripping from the curved blade of my sword, terrified by the thought of what I might see, as the berserker's corpse slumped to the floor behind me. Even outnumbered by three-to-one, Cathal had easily outmatched the bandits. One had been stabbed through the side of the neck by

Cathal's stiletto, and dismembered limbs of the other two bandits lay scattered over the cobbles, lying next to their bodies. Cathal knelt by the weakly gurgling bandit and used his stiletto to end his suffering with a merciful, precise blow to the heart.

"Ailidh, are you injured?" Cathal asked, his eyes studying my face intently with concern.

"No, I'm alright." I replied, breathing heavily and sheathing *Caranachd* back into the scabbard on my left hip. I looked back over my shoulder at the bandit berserker who had almost taken off the top of my skull, saw the blood still oozing from his partially decapitated corpse and promptly vomited my lunch over the slick cobblestones of the road. I fell to my knees, retching again, and began to cry, overwhelmed by my close brush with death and the horror of having been forced to kill a man, even if it had been in self-defence.

I felt Cathal's wrap a strong arm around my trembling shoulders, and he handed me a skin of water to rinse the foul taste of bile from my mouth. "You did well, Ailidh. Had you not remembered what I taught you, it would be your body lying there now. Come, we must get off the road. Look, there is an ash grove less than a league from here. We can make camp for the night once we are out of sight from the road."

Night had fallen by the time Cathal guided us into a tiny clearing between the coppiced trees, and he sat me down on the recently-cut stump of a five-stemmed ash. Cathal made camp, pitching our tents and lighting a small fire for both light and warmth.

"Would you like something to eat?" Cathal asked, sitting on the ground before me.

I shook my head. "I don't think I could keep anything down. I feel sick."

"It is no easy thing to kill a man, even if you must kill or be killed. Remember that as much as he chose a brigand's life, he also chose his death. You need not feel guilty."

"I don't. He almost spilled my brains onto the road. And for what, a few coins?"

"Desperation drives men to extremes. I have seen it many times."

"He had such rage in his eyes. What d'you think made him become a bandit?"

"Maybe he just enjoyed killing. Some people do. Rest assured that they all end up judged by a higher power." I didn't resist when Cathal clasped one of my hands in his. "I am glad you are unhurt. What kind of guardian would I be if I were not able to escort you to your destination?"

"One who tried their best." I said, with a sigh. "Cathal, I'm exhausted. Let's speak in the morning."

"Of course, goodnight, Ailidh." Cathal kissed the back of my hand and retired to his tent.

I did the same, putting on my nightshirt and lying down on my bedroll. I listened to the fire slowly burn down to flickering embers, the cracking and popping of the wood reminding me of the ticking of a clock. Unable to get comfortable, I tossed and turned on the bedroll, preoccupied by the passing of time as the night drew darker and colder. Thoughts churned and raced through my mind, preventing me from sleeping as I reflected both on the events of the last few hours, plus what I had achieved in my life so far. I had a trade, but no livelihood and no friends, having been sheltered by my father since my accident as a child with the forge. I was one score years old, but I had never taken a lover and seemed unlikely to after Cathal had rejected me at The Sundered Shield. King Maeryn had stolen my only family from me, and since my father's kidnap, I had almost been killed twice and been left emotionally devastated by Keri's rape of the man I loved. My life had served no purpose, and in waiting for purpose to find me I had lost everything I valued or desired; my home, my family and my future. Bile rose in my throat at the injustice and senselessness of it all. Was I not worthy of a normal life? All I wanted was the simple happiness of a husband and wife and their children; to experience love and passion, to be valued and needed, even if it was only by one man. Why did the Lady seem to smile on some people and give them what they wanted so easily? Why was I being hurt and punished in this way? I felt like screaming in frustration, baying at the heavens like a wolf separated from its pack. When the solution to my anguish presented itself, it took my breath away. I knew what I wanted and how badly I needed it. I just had to claim it, as Keri had told me in the aftermath of her betrayal. I took off my nightshirt and entered Cathal's tent. He was sound asleep, lying on his back and snoring as gently as a hibernating bear. I closed my eyes briefly to help me concentrate, picturing how Keri had mounted him back in the forest of the Western Weald. Cathal didn't stir when I removed the linen sheet from over his bare chest. The dying embers of the fire were still bright enough to bathe the canvas of Cathal's tent in a warm, amber glow, allowing me to appreciate the musculature of his body, and see the three jagged strokes Keri had carved into his chest, marking him with a demonic rune neither of us could decipher. The sight of him aroused me and I straddled his waist, rubbing the cleft of my sex along his manhood, feeling the shaft lengthen and harden at my touch. The sleeping ranger's eyes remained closed, but I could hear as his breathing become shallower and more rapid. I placed one hand beside the sigil scar on his chest to steady myself, groaning as I pressed my hips down to get him to penetrate me. Recalling the way Keri had rolled her hips against Cathal, I replicated the movement slowly, the initial stab of pain passing quickly, getting used to the rapturous sensations as his manhood stretched and opened my slit.

Cathal opened his eyes with a low, drawn-out moan, finally aware that he was not having an erotic dream, sucking in mouthfuls of air, like a beached salmon gasping on the keel of a fishing boat. "Ailidh, wha-"

"Don't talk." I interrupted him, grabbing his wrists and holding his arms down flat against his bedroll. "No words." There was just the sound of our breathing as I rode him, increasing the speed and depth of how I enveloped his sex with mine. One of the rune scars on Cathal's chest began to glow an infernal crimson as I began to feel my first ever climax build. I yelled in surprise as I felt the heat of my orgasm surge inside me and I arched my back, my knees quaking in ecstatic release. I put my hands underneath Cathal's armpits and shifted my feet, letting him lift me and lie me down on my back. There was a fiery glint in Cathal's eyes that matched the glow of the demonic carving on his chest. I hooked my legs around his waist and gripped his biceps, watching the incandescent scar burn brightly, illuminating our bodies as Cathal made love to me more urgently, his hands alternately holding me down to the bedroll by my hips and my tits. I moaned as he dipped his head to suckle on my nipples, grazing the hard buds between the sharp edges of his teeth, his cock driving ever harder and deeper inside me. I closed my eyes and came again, overwhelmed by the torrent of stimulating touches. I gasped for air as I trembled, barely able to process the sensations flooding into my brain from all over my body. Cathal kissed me on the lips and neck before his strong hands turned me over onto my belly. Rough, urgent fingers lifted my hips and he mounted me like a bull covering a cow. Each breath came as a cry as he fucked me hard and fast from behind, one hand holding my hip and the other grasping my shoulder, lifting my torso away from the ground, my tits bouncing with the momentum of his thrusts. I turned my head to look into his eyes and was not surprised to see the scarlet rune scar fully inflamed, glowing ominously on his breast. Cathal's arousal matched my own: it was an animal, primal coupling that left me shaking and breathless when Cathal finished me by sliding his fingertips between my thighs, stroking my sex, just above where he penetrated me. As my orgasm peaked, I was able to feel Cathal's climax the instant before his seed surged into me.

I collapsed onto the cushioned linen bedroll, and turned over onto my back, looking up at Cathal. "By the Goddess, is it always like that?"

"Not always." Cathal panted for air as he sat down at my feet to catch his breath. "It felt like I was possessed."

"Perhaps you were." I suggested, gently caressing the luminous scar on his chest with my toes. The glowing light gave out no heat at all. If anything the skin beneath the glowing scar tissue was colder than the surrounding flesh. The brightness of the demonic light illuminating the flesh from within was not fading, holding its intensity as the seconds and minutes passed. "What d'you suppose that means?"

"I do not know, and it worries me." Cathal frowned as he looked down at the iridescent mark with trepidation, touching it self-consciously with his fingertips. "But it is surely no coincidence that the script comes to life now."

"When we get to Lesøsnø d'you think we'll be able to find someone able to translate the rune?"

"We shall see. Keri left her mark for some evil purpose, no doubt." Cathal shuddered and looked away, closing his eyes. "Ailidh, why did you come to me tonight? I thought I had made my feelings clear."

"I thought I had, too. Cathal, I love you. I want you to father my children, I want to share the rest of my life with you, to love you and be loved back."

"What makes what your actions tonight any better than what Keri did?" Cathal asked, the infernal light emanating from his chest casting his handsome features with tortured shadows. "I did not ask for this."

"You had the power to stop me. You could've left and walked away. But you didn't." I said, sitting up and raising myself onto my knees before him. "You wanted me too, though you're too proud to admit it. Cathal, I could have died tonight, a maiden, never having known a man's desire. I'm not going to die as an old, bitter spinster. I won't let life pass me by anymore. I belonged to you from the moment you found me burned and broken on the lawn at my father's smithy. I knew it the moment I saw you. I came here to show you that you belong to me as well, body and soul."

I leaned forward to take him into my mouth, tasting the residue of our ecstasy on his skin and making him hard once again. The second scar on his chest began to shimmer as Cathal groaned lowly, his hands finding and squeezing my breasts. Unable to restrain his arousal any longer, Cathal tried to get up onto his knees, only for me to shove him back down flat onto his back, my hands pressing his shoulders down hard against the bedroll. Cathal's eyes blazed hungrily with unspent passion as I squatted astride his hips and let the tip of his sex graze the base of my body. I teased him as his hips leapt upward, denying him the warmth and wetness of my slit. My hands pinned his wrists to the ground and I kept my tits just out of reach of his tongue. I looked deep into his lovely tawny coloured eyes.

"Say it."

"What?" Cathal's face flickered in confusion.

"Say it, Cathal. Say what you want, what you want to do to me right now." I commanded, letting one of my nipples sway agonisingly close to his lips.

"I want you, Ailidh." Cathal whispered, the second scar now glowing like the flames of an iron smelter.

"What do you want?" I let his hard tip briefly slip in and out of me, his breath hot on my chest.

"I want to fuck you." The searing intensity of his gaze left no room for doubt.

"Then do it. I'm yours, Cathal." I said and let go of his wrists. I moaned as Cathal penetrated me with a sharp, deep thrust. His touch was simultaneously tender and wanton, his manhood driving harder and further inside me, until he had me gasping at every movement of his hips. Every caress of his fingertips on my skin was like being shocked by lightning. I closed my eyes and came again and again, unable to control the quaking of my limbs and the heaving of my chest as I gulped desperately for breath. I opened my eyes when I felt his hands grip me hard by my tits, his fingers squeezing with every stroke of his hips. My fingers encircled his wrists and held on tightly as I looked down into his face, seeing that he had abandoned any sense of restraint and self-control. Passion and desire shone in his eyes as he met my gaze without flinching, even though my disfigurement was on full view. His breathing became rapid as he worked himself to a frenzied climax. Cathal yelled in agonised pleasure as he massaged the calloused pads of his thumbs in circles over the tips my breasts, leaving my nipples swollen and sore. My spine arched and the muscles in my legs were gripped by involuntary spasms, no longer under my conscious control as Cathal came inside me again. When the sensations of rapture passed, Cathal and I were laid down side by side. I watched his ribs flexing rapidly as he tried to recover control over his breathing, his eyes closed. Even though the horizon was beginning to turn blue as Rionnag began its slow climb towards the horizon into the western sky, I put an arm around his waist and pulled him against me. "I love you, Cathal."

He looked into my eyes but said nothing in response, the silent flexing of tendons in his jaw betraying his stubborn ambivalence and inability to articulate his true feelings. I should have been annoyed, but was still too ecstatic to care. I felt changed by the coupling emotionally and physically. I had shared myself with Cathal in the most intimate way and he had responded with the kind of passion I had previously only fantasised about. I had made him mine, just as he had made me his. For the first time in my life I felt complete. I laid my head on his shoulder and slept with Cathal's arms and legs still intertwined with mine.

I woke to the smell of bread frying in butter and beaten eggs over the crackling wood of an open fire. The aching between my thighs reminded me of the previous night's lovemaking and I wondered whether Cathal had woken early out of habit or embarrassment. I poked my head out from the flat of his tent, seeing that he was already dressed for the road. Cathal kept his back to me as I scampered nude back to my own canvas shelter as silently as I could manage. Sapphire gave me a withering, accusatory glare as she was woken by the rustling of the heavy, water-resistant fabric, circling twice around her cage before trying to get back to sleep, flashing her teeth in annoyance as she castigated me with curt, muted yelps and yowls. "I'm sorry, kitten. I'll be out of your way soon enough."

Once dressed, I approached Cathal at the fire, greeting him with a tender caress on the back of his neck, tangling my fingers in his thick, dark hair. The ranger could've been made from rock, such was his lack of reaction. While I was relieved that he did not flinch at my touch, neither did Cathal turn his head to give me a smile or a kiss. I was confused by the complete absence of response, given the intensity of our coupling during the night.

"Hey, Cathal. What's wrong?"

Cathal's eyes were glassy and unfocussed. He stirred the ingredients frying in the pan mechanically, without conscious thought, flipping the slices of bread over before they could burn. His reply was equally lifeless. "Nothing."

I took the pan from his hand and placed it on one of the stones marking the edge of the fire pit. I sat next to him and cupped his cheek in one hand, gently turning his head so I could look into his face. "Obviously not true. Talk to me."

"Not now, Ailidh." Cathal said, his voice barely louder than a whisper. "Please."

"We need to talk about last night." I put my hands on his shoulders to steady him and stop him from avoiding my gaze. I needed him to see me. "It was beautiful, Cathal. I've never felt happier or more alive. And I meant every word – I want to share my life with you."

"I do not feel myself, given everything that has happened over the last few days." Cathal kept his eyes down, refusing to meet my gaze. "I need time."

"Alone?"

"Preferably."
"When you're ready to talk, I'll be ready to listen. I'm here for you, always." I gave Cathal a gentle peck on the lips, to remind him that I loved him. I let my lips linger on his, but I could have kissed a boulder and felt more of an emotional response. Cathal finished cooking as I started to dismantle the tents and pack up the camp. We ate in silence, the ranger's eyes never lifting from his plate. He brooded in silence and I sensed how futile it would be to try improving his mood with idle chatter about the weather or how eagerly I anticipated reaching the city. Instead, to keep my mind and hands occupied, I let Sapphire out from her cage and fed her some of my eggy, fried bread accompanied by a palm full of fresh water to keep her going during our first stint of walking. When Sapphire could eat and drink no more, she curled up on my lap and rolled onto her back, inviting me to tease her belly. The cat purred contentedly as my fingertips traced lazy circles through her long silver and black fur, gently massaging the warm, yielding flesh underneath. I used my free hand to carry mouthfuls of my breakfast from my plate to my lips, but I ate without enthusiasm, not even really tasting what Cathal had prepared.
When our plates were empty, Cathal sighed. "We should get moving."
Cathal extinguished the fire as I rinsed the frying pan and our two plates with a squirt of water from my canteen skin. By the time I had ushered Sapphire back into her cage and replaced all of our cooking paraphernalia into my backpack, Cathal had dismantled the fire pit, covering the ash and burning embers with a shallow layer of fresh soil that was still damp from the morning dew. The ranger picked up his longbow, slinging it over his shoulder and back. Without a word, he began trudging back down the hill towards the road that led to Lesøsnø. I picked up Sapphire's cage, scratching her forehead with a fingernail affectionately. The cat looked up at me and mewed, sounding both tired and resigned to another long day of walking. I tickled her under the chin. "I know, kitten. We're almost there. We'll reach the city tomorrow. Then we can look forward to sleeping under a roof again."
Sapphire seemed to consider this for a moment and sat in her cage, facing the road, chirping like a bird. Cathal was

already over three score yards ahead of us. "You're right, Sapphire. We should catch up. After all, what is it that Cathal always says? The road gets no shorter while we tarry. Let's go."

22 - Fiacre

No sooner had I arrived back at Clongarvan from Croycullen, I was on the road again, this time to the east. I had arrived back in the capital to find the Royal Palace in chaos. I was dumbstruck to hear that the king had been maimed by Duke Aiden, who had promptly abducted the queen, both of them disappearing from the city before the alarm had been sounded. The only aspect of the king's telling of the story that rang true was Aiden's responsibility for depriving the king of his fingers. The idea that Aiden would kidnap Reilynn was surely beyond fantasy, even for a man driven so resolutely by his rampant libido. It was undeniable that the entirety of the queen's close retinue had vanished from the palace within an hour of the king's assault however, which suggested to me that the events had been orchestrated and premeditated by some outside factor. It had been several days before anyone noticed that the queen's yacht had gone missing and another week before it had been sighted in Bray. Maeryn was so distraught at Reilynn's disappearance that he had shown no interest in what I had to report from Malvina's scrying at Eoghan's workshop. Instead he had dismissed me with orders to return with Reilynn bound in chains. The Arch Mage was utterly indifferent to Reilynn's abscondence from the palace and its affect on the king. Karryghan was only slightly more interested in hearing what Malvina and I had discovered in Croycullen. All he said was "Forget the queen, Field Duke. Find Eoghan's girl. The clock is ticking."
While the Arch Mage was confident enough in his power and position to ignore the king's wishes, I sadly did not enjoy the same level of security. So I found myself in a horse-drawn coach driving through the Belhaven gate towards Bray without even having had the time to send word to my wife that I had arrived back in the city. At least I had the luxury of being able to sleep for most of the journey, so at least I would be well-rested should a conflict arise when I arrived at the queen's summer house, where it was assumed that the handmaidens, and possibly the queen herself, had taken refuge. The queen had several

properties in Cothraine, but her Bray summer house was known to be her favourite, thanks to its location both on the coast and in the middle of one of the Crown's most productive vineyards. I had a mind to make sure my return journey to the city would be lubricated by a couple of bottles of its most celebrated red wine. My coach was escorted by a company of horse archers, which to my mind was an overbearingly large force to confront just a dozen teenage girls. Rumours around the capital tittered that the queen's attendants were members of the black cloaks, the now-disbanded Royal Secret Service, but I paid them little attention. Even a dozen black cloaks with twenty years of service each would be no match for nearly a hundred light cavalrymen. Not that I wanted an armed confrontation. I had the blood of enough children on my hands. I had given the company commander strict terms of engagement. If the situation did become hostile, the handmaidens were to be taken alive, and more importantly, unmolested. They were, after all not just young girls but also members of the Royal Household. They deserved to be treated with dignity and respect.

When my entourage arrived at the avenue leading up to the summer house I ordered the cavalry company to halt and wait quarter of a league from the house, with only the Field Knight in command of the unit following my coach to relay orders back if necessary. I had the coach stop a hundred yards from the house and I dismounted to make the final part of the journey on foot. I gestured to the Field Knight. "Wait there and do not approach unless ordered."

I considered what the appearance of a company of armed soldiers and the commander of a nation's Field Army must seem like for a young girl. My goal here was to find the queen, or information about her, not to threaten or intimidate. I resolved to make my actions and demeanour as non-hostile as I could, so hopefully I would not have to resort to violence. I walked slowly, armed and armoured, but without a helm covering my face. I stayed in plain view of the windows at the front of the house, keeping my expression neutral. When I arrived at the door, rather than demanding to see the queen, I simply grasped the brass lion's head door knocker and struck it three times. I stepped back from the door, so that I could be seen from the windows on both the ground and upper floors and counted in my head to one hundred. There was no response from the sandstone villa. No movement behind the windows, no sounds from behind the door. I stepped forward and rapped the knocker three more times. I moved half a dozen yards away from the threshold, mostly to be out of arm's reach if the door opened, but also to keep watch through the windows. I counted to a hundred again. For the second time, I saw no signs of life. I shrugged and stepped to the door a third time. This time the door opened before I had struck my second knock.

"What d'you want?" said the girl behind the door. She was only just of age, perhaps 16 or 17 years old, but she did not seem fearful or nervous. I was taken aback somewhat by her poise and determination.

"To talk: with the queen, ideally." I ventured, trying not to force a smile. "I am-"

"I know who you are." The girl interrupted me brusquely. "I've seen you at the palace, Field Duke."

"Then you have me at a disadvantage, young handmaiden. I do not know your name."

"If a name's so important to you, call me Róise."

"Róise, then, well met!" I smiled because it was a name I recognised. I had once quizzed Duke Companion Aiden as to the hierarchy of girls within the queen's retinue, and Róise was one of Reilynn's most senior handmaidens. That she had answered the door and not the queen's most trusted confidante, Sìne, was telling. The queen would not go anywhere without Sìne, and Sìne was in love with Aiden – I thought suddenly that perhaps it was not so fanciful that Aiden had kidnapped Reilynn after all. "I need to speak with the queen."

"You'll not find her here."

"Where will I find her?"

"I don't know."

"Róise, I will guarantee that you and your fellows shall not be harmed, but only if you tell me the truth. Where is the queen?"

"I don't know." Róise repeated in a toneless voice, her chin pitching upwards in defiance. I knew she was lying, and she knew that too, but her loyalty to Reilynn was absolute. The girl was a third of my size, but I respected her willingness to sacrifice her freedom and even her life for her queen. It was more than could be said for how I felt about the king.

"I cannot just take your word for it. I must search the villa. If she is not here, then I will leave and not return. My soldiers will go with me."

"And not return?"

"And they will not return."

"You can't enter wearing that." Róise said, pointing at my sword belt.

I turned my head and beckoned over the Field Knight with a shout. "Second!"

The cavalryman acting as my adjutant galloped over and pulled up his horse beside me in an instant. "Yes, my lord?"

"I am going to search the house for the queen with Róise here." I said, handing him my sword belt.

"Unarmed, my lord? Are you certain?"

"Róise and I are just going to talk and look for Queen Reilynn. I am told she is not here, I am just making certain." I said, exchanging warm glances with both the handmaiden and the knight. "It will not take longer than one hour. If I am not back in two hours, raze the villa and kill everyone that tries to leave."

Róise went pale and even the cavalryman gasped. "As you command, my lord."

As it happened, the villa did not need to be razed. Within thirty minutes I had confirmed Reilynn had not been on her yacht and had never journeyed to Bray. I returned to my coach with two bottles of the estate's finest vintage clutched in each hand. As I set them down carefully on one of the seats, the Field Knight returned my sword belt asking, "What now, my lord? Do you wish the handmaidens to be taken into custody?"

"No, Field Knight, leave them be. They have committed no crime and the queen is not with them. No good would come of it."

"As you wish, my lord. Did they at least tell you where the queen has gone?"

"They did not need to. I know exactly where she is headed: the one port in the world that will welcome her with open arms - Lesøsnø."

23 - Keri

It has often been written that Lesøsnø is the most beautiful city in the world. I was reminded of the cliché as I saw the tallest of the city's towers start to peek over the horizon when I was still a dozen leagues short of the Fossfjall capital's imposing defensive wall. The architecture of the City of Spires mirrored the jagged nature of the mountains that dominated the terrain around Lesøsnø. The city sprawled among the valleys between the peaks of two dozen mountains flanking the eastern end of the Abyss, a gash in the continent over three hundred leagues long that had been gouged out of the rock and soil by the cataclysmic explosion of a now extinct supervolcano, millennia before humans had settled the region. The outpouring of ash and minerals had turned the North Riding into the most fertile farmland in the whole of the Triad. With agricultural riches came gold, followed rapidly by an influx of men and women of culture and learning. Lesøsnø's university was the largest and most prestigious on the continent and while the Wizard's Guild here was smaller in number than the one in Clongarvan, its ranks were arguably of far greater quality, thanks to its proximity to the Great Library of the Seven Scholars held within The Scribe's Spire. For a spellcaster, there was no higher prestige than to be accepted into Lesøsnø's Wizard's Guild, thanks to its privileged access to the peerless aggregation of arcane wisdom in the Great Library. The library's name was well-deserved: it was reputed to hold a copy of every known book and scroll ever published in the last three thousand years, as well as an authoritative compilation of council records from across the Western Triad known as The Litany of Births and Deaths. For a suitably extortionate fee, it was possible to commission the one of the library's eponymous seven master scribes and illuminators to provide you with your own personal copy of any document within the library's vast archives. It was this service that I planned to take advantage of after I finally reached the city. I was looking forward to spending some time losing myself in the labyrinthine depths of the world's largest repository of written knowledge while I performed the research my dread mistress had demanded I carry out all those weeks ago at the fallen stone circle near Bray. As I approached the city, it became easier to identify the individual spires and towers from their shape, height and colour. The road from Skøgvik to the capital brought you towards the city from the south-east over the vast expanse of productive farmlands of the North Riding. The mountain range along the edge of the Abyss protected travellers from the moisture-laden anabatic winds that surged up the immense fjord from the west, which powered the violent thunderstorms the Caldera was famous for. The farmland got nearly all of its precipitation from the invariably bitter north wind, which in winter brought potentially lethal blizzards and flurries of snow in the winter months howling south from the Bay of Wolves. Today I was fortunate to be favoured by a gentle, warming westerly breeze from the rain shadow of the mountains. The sky was clear of clouds and the visibility was excellent. It had been over a decade since I had last visited Lesøsnø, so I was taken aback once again by the sheer height of the city's defensive wall. The black basalt fortification, standing at some ten score feet tall, made the city appear as if it had been carved out of a mountain. Green crystals of olivine flickered in the basalt, making the stone walls glimmer in the sunlight. If the stone palisade was impressive, the architecture inside was truly breathtaking. The spire that had attracted my attention on the horizon was the Tower of the Aether, the home of the Wizard's Guild in the east of the city. It was twice as tall as the city wall and the ivory-coloured marble and twisted spiral walls gave it the appearance of a gigantic narwhal tusk. I had often wondered what the view from the Arch Mage's chambers looked like from under the glass dome at the apex of the tower, especially at night. It was unlikely, however, that given my pariah status with the guild that I would ever be offered a tour. As I walked past golden fields lush with ripening wheat and edged closer to the city's eastern gate, other towers and spires began to poke their heads into view above the black cliff of the defensive wall. The quill-like Spire of the Scribe that held the main book repository of the Great Library was the second tower to come into view. The Spire of the Scribe was at the opposite end of Lesøsnø from the Wizard's Guild and dominated the western end of the city, standing some fifteen score feet tall. It had prime position overlooking the Abyss and was surrounded by a vast granite plaza and stood in the centre of circle of a further nine stylised towers, one for each of the Gods of the Pantheon. The north of the city hosted the university buildings and the arcades of the Artisan's Quarter, which supplied the thousands of the university's students and academics with the tools of their trade. More to my personal taste was the bustling Commoner's Quarter that sprawled over the south of the city and encompassed Lesøsnø's port and market district. With enough money and patience, almost any object you desired could be found on the vast ranks of merchant's stalls. It was also my favoured hunting ground for souls, as there were plenty of young, orphaned pickpockets wandering the narrow, cobbled streets who would not be missed by families or the city guard. I licked my lips at the thought of sharing my bed tonight with a tanar'ri as an act of public service, simultaneously making purses safer in the process by removing a pair of light-fingered hands from the shady alleys of the Merchant's Quarter. I already knew where I would be renting a room – a tavern halfway between the port and the Great Library called The Star and Sextant, which was as popular with sailors on shore leave as it was with visiting academics that had a taste for adventure, good food and strong beer. It was mid-morning when I reached the East Gate. The chief sentinel at the portal took one cursory glance at my mage staff and nodded me through the open portcullis without a word, letting me bypass the queue of commoners who were being questioned by the guards and having the contents of their wagons searched. Wizards were such revered visitors that they were not subjected to the usual indignities of Lesøsnø's strict contraband checks at the city boundaries. Once past the imposing basalt edifice of the city wall, Lesøsnø opened wide like a book falling face up onto its spine. The myriad towers thrust upwards into the sky in stark contrast to the wide open parks and boulevards that characterised the ambience of the city. The Central Boulevard ran the entire length of the city, some three leagues from the East Gate to the sea front at the edge of the Abyss. I was glad that the prevailing wind was a westerly off the coast, since it prevented the agricultural stink from the stables lining the inside of the defensive wall from lingering over the city. With the giant narwhal tusk of the Tower of the Aether on my left and the pale granite citadel housing the Royal Palace to the north on my right, I strode along the gentle downslope of the broad, pine tree-flanked avenue towards the sprawling university campus, the Cathedral of the Pantheon and the Great Library beyond. Lesøsnø's main thoroughfare bustled with activity without being crowded. Groups of students dressed in formal academic gowns streamed to and from the university to their lodgings south of the cathedral, deep in the Commoner's Quarter, holding animated conversations of questionable levels of profundity all along the way. Local farmers and traders transported their wares towards the markets in the south-west of the city while pairs of spear-wielding guardsmen dressed in stainless steel chainmail patrolled up and down the boulevard, looking relaxed and approachable. The general ambience of the city was far friendlier than the Cothraine capital. Even the slums were welcoming, with whole neighbourhoods often holding impromptu street markets, where hawkers sold some of the best cuisine available in the city from communally-maintained food kiosks built between the granite tenements. I had developed a taste for one of these street food specialities over a century ago; a bread and sausage sandwich served with pickles, caramelised onions, fried eggs, ketchup and mustard, called porilainen. I was briefly tempted to seek out one of the stalls before heading to the library, but having not eaten one for over a decade, I reasoned that having to wait a few extra hours would be no hardship. It was not long before I was stood before the central palace of the Grand Library of the Seven Scholars. All ten of the figurative spires reached up to the sky beyond the height of the city's defensive wall and stood upon giant cuboid plinths, each one as large as the Royal Palace. The towers took on the aspect of the god of the pantheon it represented. The Warrior was symbolised by a great two-handed sword; the Earth Mother was represented by the colossal sculpture of a sprawling pine tree and the Empress by a huge effigy in the form of a beautiful pregnant woman. All the towers were awe-inspiring in their own way, but it was the Tower of the Scribe that formed the centrepiece of the Great Library, the tallest of the spires in the centre of a protective ring. I adored the whimsicality of its architecture, the spire taking the shape of a goose quill resting in an ink pot. Each floor of the tower aligned with the intricately carved barbs of the feather and the vane was aligned from west to east with the prevailing wind to minimise the stress on the stone walls of the spire during the ferocious winter storms that rolled down the fjord to batter the city. Of all the buildings I had seen in all of the towns of the world, the Scribe's Spire was my favourite and all the more beautiful for the repository of knowledge contained within its white marble walls.

I paid the doorkeeper four silver shillings, double the normal entry fee, and asked, "Where may I find the Head Librarian?"

The porter's eyes flickered to look at my staff and he answered without hesitation. "Mistress Hulda will most likely be working at her escritoire in the Atrium, master wizard."

The Atrium was the central hall of the library, a cavernous volume that could easily hold a three-mast carrack. The walls of the chamber were festooned with league after league of shelving, each one crammed with leather-bound compilation tomes or arrays of scroll cases made from wood or copper. The ambient light level was barely above that of late evening twilight to preserve the texts and the smokeless oil lamps maintaining the temperature and light level gave the entire space a glorious, sweetly floral scent. In the centre of the hall was an open plan scriptorium, where the titular Seven Scholars that gave the library its name performed their meditative work, copying and illuminating the texts of books from the library's unparalleled collection in reverent silence. I approached the white-haired woman who sat in the middle of the arc of seven writing desks slowly and respectfully, not wishing to disturb her concentration. It was a joy, watching her fingers transcribe the text from one scroll to another with such precision and artistry. In comparison to her exquisite letterform, my own writing looked like it had been splattered onto a page by a drunken spider after it had gone swimming in a pot of ink. I waited in silence, observing Hulda apply her considerable skill with no small amount of awe, until the Head Librarian realised that she was being watched and she raised her head.

I had known Hulda, the Great Library's chief scribe, for more than two score years and she recognised me instantly, even though my last visit to her library could hardly be described as being in recent memory. She stood to favour me with a deep, courteous bow, her psychic aura a delighted, herbal teal. "Keri of Moonchion, as I live and breathe. There must be something in the air. I swear I was thinking about you just yesterday, wondering what had become of you."

"It is a pleasure to see you as well, Master Illuminator." I replied, giving her a heartfelt smile and an equally respectful bow of my head. A life such as mine does not allow for the luxury of friends, but I could genuinely say that Hulda was one of the few people I knew whom I liked and admired without reservation.

"How long has it been, Keri? Ten years?"

"Twelve, I think."

"And yet still you look as young and beautiful as the day I first met you, four decades ago. You must tell me the secret of the longevity of your youth." Hulda said as she welcomed me with a lingering hug of affection.

"Tanar'ri seed," I whispered into her ear as I returned her embrace.

Hulda giggled like an over-excited child, wagging an age-wrinkled finger in my face warningly. "You must not speak such heresy Keri, not even in jest. Some inquisitor might take you seriously. How you have evaded immolation at the stake this long boggles my mind."

"It is a mystery to me too, believe me." I told her honestly, amused that she had not realised that I had told her the literal truth.

"So what brings you to my library this day?"

"The Seventh Prophecy of Nevanthi, I require a copy."

Hulda tilted her skull and regarded me questioningly with her mismatched eyes. The Master Illuminator had been born with heterochromia, where an imbalance of pigments in her irises had given her left eye a pale blue colour, while her right eye was a rich jade green. In her youth, the rarity of her condition had made her one of the most striking and fiercely-courted women in the city. "Curious, it is hardly her finest work. I have always preferred the fourth and the ninth."

"Would you have a copy for sale?"

"No, but for you I can have one ready in two days." Hulda said, picking up a quill and parchment from her desk to write a commission note that a nearby porter immediately rushed off to the Hall of Scribes, where a small army of illuminators worked practically day and night to produce scrolls of texts for sale to the general public. "In the meantime, you will find our reference copy in the Divination section of the Tower of the Mystic. Come, we can find the tome together. And you can tell me more about what piqued your interest in it along the way."

I glossed over the details regarding who had commanded me to research the prophecy, instead citing a nonexistent academic interest in accounting for the discrepancies in the level of detail that separated Nevanthi's Seventh Prophecy from the other dozen she had written during her tenure as Clongarvan's Grand Master Diviner a thousand years ago. It was no exaggeration to say that Nevanthi had changed the perception of the Art of Divination from being seen as the purview of charlatan mystics and grifters wishing to separate fools from their gold to a respected school of magic. She had devised the Tarot of the Planes, being the first wizard to learn how to communicate with the all-seeing, all-knowing denizens of the psychic plane, enigmatic beings that paid little heed to the linearity of time. The incongruous ambiguities in her seventh prophecy, compared to the unprecedented level of precision and detail in her other predictions, had prompted many scholars to wonder whether it had actually been written by her at all, or whether it might have been her first work with the Tarot and that she had left it unpublished until her reputation for accuracy as a chronomancer had been fully established. For scholars in the history of the Art, it was one of the most keenly debated topics that still remained unresolved. Personally I cared little for the provenance of the prophecy, only whether it held sufficient clues to help my mistress locate and claim the Nexus. Once we had reached the appropriate floor in the Tower of the Mystic, the Head Librarian bade me to sit down at a nearby table as her eyes expertly scanned the shelves for the book containing the combined works of Nevanthi. I was barely settled into my seat when the Head Librarian gave out a quiet murmur of triumph.

"Here it is," Hulda said with satisfaction, as she withdrew a huge book bound with emerald-coloured leather from the shelving and placed it upon the table before me. "Do you think you might still need to refer to the text tomorrow?"

"That is a distinct possibility, yes."

"In that case, give the book to the curator when you leave the Library tonight. They will make sure you can collect it directly from me in the Atrium tomorrow."

"Thank you, Hulda."

"You are welcome, Keri. Once you have finished your research for the day, you should join me for dinner. I would love to hear the details of your adventures since you were last in the city."

"I have other plans for tonight, unfortunately. But I will be staying in Lesøsnø for at least a few days. I would be happy to indulge you tomorrow evening. Do you still make that divine farikal and raspeball stew?"

"Every week on Penitent's Day," Hulda confirmed. "Either you are a mind-reader or coincidence follows you around like an orphaned lamb. I already have the mutton marinating and cabbage fermenting."

"That is all well and good, but I would be happy to live off the potato dumplings alone."

"Hah! My youngest son has tried, but the lack of protein would do for you in the end." Hulda chuckled. "I will leave you to your contemplations. I need to get back to the Atrium, but do not hesitate to let me know if you need anything. My scribes and curators will be honoured to help you."

I kissed Hulda a fond goodbye once on each cheek before settling down to read Nevanthi's Seventh Prophecy verbatim from its original source for the first time. The giant sheets of parchment felt smooth under my fingertips and despite the tome being over seven centuries old, the ink looked as dark and fresh as the day the text had been scribed. There was little I found in life more satisfying than rustle of vellum while finding your place in a book. I smoothed down the page and caressed the ornately illuminated figure seven that marked the start of the prophecy that my dread mistress had taken such an interest in.

I read through the entire text twice before asking one of the curators for a quill, a pot of ink and half a dozen sheets of paper. I read through the text for a third time, making notes on the paper with my jagged, scratchy handwriting. I reflected upon Hulda's assessment of Nevanthi's Seventh Prophecy. She had been diplomatic describing it as 'hardly her finest work'. It was, in my opinion, as pungently rank as rotted shark.

Nevanthi's prophecies were rightly renowned for being exquisitely detailed and specific in their regard to identifying events, times and persons of interest. The seventh prophecy was more akin to the vague ramblings of a fairground psychic than the work of a serious practitioner of the Art. But regardless of how dreadfully the overwrought, needlessly-portentous prose had been written, hidden within the text were a sufficient number of parallels to eliminate coincidence as a factor in how the predictions in the prophecy were related to current events. The first parallel was the downfall of a long-established royal line just prior to the appearance of the Nexus. The second was the transformation and banishing of a dissenting wizard into a feline changeling for the crime of confronting an Arch Mage's ambition. The third and final parallel was the growing tension between two neighbouring states as the winter solstice heralding the manifestation of the Nexus on the material plane approached. What had confused temporal scholars for generations was that all the rest of Nevanthi's predictions ran in a sequential order detailing the history in fifty year chunks beginning a century after her death. She had never specified the limits of the time period described by her seventh prophecy, leaving it curiously unstuck in time, and the vagueness of the predictions had left its veracity in serious doubt. As I read through Nevanthi's account again, it was as if floral buds of clarity had begun to erupt through the plain uniformity of a formal grass lawn. It became apparent to me that the overzealous groundsmen curating the gardens of divination had weeded out the untidy seeds of truth from Nevanthi's most chaotic work, without ever giving their shoots a chance to allow the profound revelations waiting patiently beneath the opportunity to germinate. One of the few explicit details written in the prophecy was that the initial appearance of the Nexus on Dachaigh was exactly one score years prior to the impending winter solstice and its accompanying alignment of the planes. The prophecy also placed the first manifestation of its power on the material plane within the borders of Fossfjall, but gave no clues as to a more precise location. Neither did it provide any hints to the physical form that the Nexus had assumed upon its arrival on the material plane. Undeterred, I ploughed through the minutiae of the text once more, trying to eke more information out from the depths of the ugly prose. The account confirmed the speculative thought I had shared on the road with Cathal and Ailidh, that Arch Mage Karryghan had engineered the coup and subsequent political tension between Fossfjall and Cothraine. Nevanthi's predictions anticipated a war between the nations and warned of a period of chaos in the wake of an invasion by extra-planar beings pursuing the Nexus. It was inevitable that once it revealed itself, unless it was claimed before the weakening of the barriers between planes at the winter solstice, the Nexus would bring an influx of magicians and planewalkers from all across the cosmos to compete for the right to possess it. Karryghan clearly had his own desire to be the one that found the Nexus first, and he was ruthless enough to sacrifice whole nations in order to fulfil his ambitions. I surmised that he had studied the prophecy in far more detail and for far longer than I had, and sought to place himself at the centre of it. The text was ambiguous on the fate of the Nexus itself, making no predictions as to who or what ultimately claimed it, but it was clear to me that Karryghan would face stiff competition for the power of the Nexus, given that my mistress had already expressed her interest in it. What the Arch Mage of Cothraine wanted the Nexus for was of no concern to me. I just had to beat him to the punch, and thought that I might even be able to use him and his prior knowledge to help lead me to the Nexus itself. As accomplished a wizard as Karryghan was, I was certain that I could best him in a battle of wits and in terms of arcane mastery, though that did not mean that I would forego allies or help, if I was able to find it. Which lead me to the curious case of the changeling: it was clearly no coincidence that my path had crossed with the changeling accompanying Cathal and Ailidh. It seemed likely that the transformed diviner mentioned in the prophecy was Cathal's feline companion. The changeling had been polymorphed by the Arch Mage presumably for trying to interfere with his plans. If I could undo the spell, they would be a useful source of information regarding Karryghan's plans for the Nexus. Given the circumstances in which we had parted company in the Western Weald, it would be challenging to say the least to reinstitute myself back into Cathal & Ailidh's company, but as I re-read the passages detailing the transformation a possibility began to take form. My train of thought was disturbed by one of the custodians informing me that the library was about to close. She took the tome of Nevanthi's collected works along with my written notes, promising that I would be able to collect them from Hulda in the Atrium tomorrow morning. Darkness was rapidly falling as the twilight dusk faded on the horizon. I walked south to The Star and Sextant and rented the most expensive room in the inn before prowling the narrow alleyways of the Merchants Quarter and baiting an unfortunate teenaged pickpocket into trying to filch an enticingly heavy coin purse swinging from the sash around my waist. I caught the girl by her emaciated wrist and she meekly allowed me to drag her back to my room where I seduced her before draining her soul. Her life crystal was anaemic, pale and brittle, but still carried enough energy for me to summon an incubus and bind it for the evening to have it tend to my needs. The tanar'ri gratefully consumed the girl's body and soul in its entirety, darkly joking that next time I should remember that it preferred meals with more flesh on their bones. Suitably refreshed and energised by the daeva's seed, I woke at dawn and returned to the Great Library as soon as it opened its doors for the day. I greeted Hulda at her desk in the Atrium and she directed me to a secluded alcove where I could continue my research in private.

The Master Illuminator refreshed my ink pot and laid out a selection of half a dozen freshly-cut goose quill pens as I flicked through the leaves of parchment to where I had left off the previous evening. "You look as bright-eyed and bushy-tailed as a red squirrel buried in a sack of hazelnuts. You had a suitably entertaining evening, I trust?"

"Never a dull night at The Star and Sextant," I told her, licking my lips.

"Well, I cannot promise the same level of excitement as that esteemed establishment, but I can promise better food and finer wine." Hulda replied, her slim shoulders quivering with mirth.

"I would not miss it for the world." I said truthfully.

"I will come and collect you just before closing time. Make sure you have worked up a good appetite."

With fresh eyes I re-read the Seventh Prophecy in its entirety, paying particular attention to the references to the diviner that had been polymorphed by the Arch Mage. Divination had never been my speciality, but even I knew enough that when destiny and portent collide, there is never any room for random chance. It was definitely no accident that the changeling had ended up seeking refuge with the exiled ranger. The only mystery that remained was how significant a role Ailidh had to play in the turmoil to come. I could find no explicit or implicit references to her at all in Nevanthi's text, but I felt certain that some form of hidden connection was just waiting to be found. After all, the Arch Mage had gone to the effort of having her father abducted, so there were latent hints of some kind of connection between Ailidh's family and the location of the Nexus. During our time together on the road I had paid only scant attention to what Ailidh had divulged about her personal history, but I knew that she was a score years old, hailed from Croycullen and her parents were named Eoghan & Sigrid. I consulted the Litany of Births and Deaths, the Great Library's unparalleled chronicle of the ebbs and flows of the population in the major towns and cities of the Western Triad. The library's archivists annually collated the details from all the birth and death certificates issued by the town councils across Cothraine, Fossfjall and Sundgau into a single, unified record that dated back some dozen centuries. I spent half the day trying to cross-reference what Ailidh had told me with the records in the Litany, utterly fruitlessly, as it turned out. Not only were there no references of children born with the name Ailidh in Croycullen in the last half-century, neither could I find any record of a child called Ailidh being born to parents named Eoghan and Sigrid anywhere in the Western Triad within five years of Ailidh's approximate time of birth. While it was not impossible that her birth had not been registered, it seemed more likely that she was simply mistaken about either where she had been born or the names of her parents. It was an irksome development, but one that I chose not to dwell on, instead scribing more untidy notes on scrolls of paper until the Atrium's skylights were dark and the only light flickering in my alcove came from the sweet-smelling smokeless oil lamps.

Hulda tapped my shoulder gently and helped me gather my notes into an ivory scroll holder made from a hollow length of a sperm whale's rib bone. "Good news, Keri. Your copy of the prophecy will be ready by noon tomorrow."

"Thank you, Hulda. How much will I owe you?" I asked as I conjured a knapsack to carry the bone tube containing the notes I had made over the previous two days.

"We can discuss business tomorrow. Now is the time for farikal and wine." Hulda said and ushered me out of the Great Library with a friendly arm wrapped around my shoulders.

24 - Cathal

I was pleased to see that Lesøsnø had not changed in the decade since I had visited it last. The forest of spires behind the glimmering defensive walls gave the city a unique skyline against the backdrop of the colossal fjord of The Abyss. Ailidh's gasp of wonder as she saw the city for the first time was almost as high pitched as the cries of the falcons that quartered back and forth over the wheat fields hunting for mice and voles. I smiled and looked back over my shoulder. "Wait until you see the city from the inside of the wall."

The final few leagues to the Fossfjall capital passed quickly, but sadly the queues at the East Gate did not. At least we were able to wait in the line basking in glorious late autumn sunshine, rather than one of the frigid northerly squalls that were increasingly common at this time of year. Traffic into the city always reached a peak as harvest-time drew closer, with landowners and farmers flocking to the Merchant's Quarter to either hawk their wares directly, or negotiate deals with distributors prior to bringing their goods to the city. The sentinels at the guard posts on the main city gates were renowned for their attention to detail and the level of scrutiny they gave to all incomers to the city. I could expect no special favours after Maeryn's coup. Any diplomatic privileges that I might have had as a green cloak of the Order of Sylvan had long since been cast to the wind as the relationship between the royal families of Cothraine and Fossfjall soured in the wake of Maeryn's marriage to Reilynn. When Ailidh and I eventually reached the front of the line, the sentinel regarded me with no small amount of surprise, contempt and suspicion.

"You're a long way from the forest, tree-hugger. What business do you have in my city?"

"I am here to see the head of my Order, Lord Commander Braden."

"The Lord Commander, such an esteemed guest of the city! He's expecting you, is he?"

"I doubt it."

"How am I to be sure he'll take you in off the street? He's a personal friend of yours?"

"As a matter of fact, yes he is." I replied calmly, suppressing the testiness I felt at the sentinel's impertinence. I knew that an argument would not get us through the gate any quicker. Better to let him enjoy his power play.

"Really," the guard looked me up and down, doubtfully. "Your name and rank?"

"Cathal," I told him, drawing his attention to the silver gilt insignia of oak leaves I wore on the collar of my cloak. "Baron Ranger Cathal."

"If you say so, my lord," the border guard sounded unimpressed. "And you, what's your story, blondie?" the sentinel asked, eyeing up Ailidh lasciviously.

"She is with me." I interjected.

"I don't remember asking you." The guardsman told me with a frosty glare.

Ailidh hid her disfigurement carefully behind her hair, hooked her arm through the crook of my elbow, held on tightly and favoured the sentinel with her loveliest smile. "I'm with him."

The border guard turned back to me, with a distinctly bored air of disappointment and jealousy. "Lucky you. Be on your way, both of you. You're holding up the line."

Ailidh waited until we were through the gate and out of earshot before asking "What was all that about?"

"Gate sentries like to make their own entertainment. They need little provocation to give pretty young women a strip search, especially if they are travelling alone. Lone men are liable to get either a beating or have their coin purses ransacked on a slow day. Fortunately the queues were too long this afternoon for such shenanigans."

"That's disgusting." Ailidh said, her lips twisting. "Guards are supposed to enforce the law, not abuse it."

"Sadly, those who know the laws best are often the most inclined to break them. Positions of power frequently attract people without scruples who will hide behind the very rules they create and exploit. Often it is better to learn how not to attract their attention."

"But that won't change anything. They'll just continue to get away with it."

"So said many a prisoner and heretic hanging in manacles by their wrists from a dungeon ceiling," I lamented, leading Ailidh down the bustling central boulevard to the sea wall. I wanted to show her the Abyss before seeking out Braden at his estate in the north-east of the city. "I do not dispute that you have the moral right of it, only that it is impossible for a common individual to affect change."

"Only if everyone has so cynical an attitude as that. Father said that bullies don't prey on the weak, because they're weak too. They just exploit the attitude that no-one thinks they can challenge the way things work."

"Perhaps that is why Eoghan left the Circle to become a blacksmith." I speculated. "Maybe it was his way of rebelling?"

"That may be true, I don't know. I just think 'it's always been done this way' isn't a compelling enough reason to let people in positions of power victimise those who aren't."

"Careful, Ailidh, or you might find yourself swinging from chains attached to the walls of a castle gaol. But for all it is worth, I agree with you." I pulled my elbow closer to my side, dragging her arm along with it and bringing her hip to rest against mine as we walked down Lesøsnø's main thoroughfare. The physical contact was pleasant, but despite the extraordinary intensity of our coupling several days ago, I did not feel the unmistakeable stirrings of love in my soul for her. She had my respect and affection as a friend, but I just did not feel from her the calling of a life companion in the same way Aoibheann had become so intimately vital to my being when we had been together. I knew that I risked breaking Ailidh's heart once more, but I had also been raised to be true to myself, leaving me feeling conflicted as to how our relationship might develop in time. Ailidh clang to me gratefully, her head constantly turning in wonder as she tried to take in the magnificence of the City of Spires. I had been in Lesøsnø more than a dozen times before, and the grandeur of its scale and architecture still took my breath away. I abandoned my effort to count the number of spires breaching the horizon after I had passed one hundred. Each one had a different height and profile, and few shared the same architectural design influences. The buildings seemed to have an infinite diversity in colour, form and style, yet simultaneously managed to coalesce together into a glorious, cohesive whole. Other cities in the world were larger and more densely populated, but none were more atmospheric or aesthetically beautiful. I could understand perfectly why a veteran of the wilds like Braden would choose to spend his exile in such a place. We took our time negotiating the crowds on the central boulevard, letting the crowds overtake us as we ambled down towards the immense plaza surrounding the Great Library. Sapphire's cage attracted the attention of several luxury goods brokers who tried to bargain with me for her sale.

"A silver tabby, if my eyes do not deceive me. Exquisite and so rare in these parts! How much are you asking for it?"

"She is not for sale." I said, Sapphire yowling lowly, as if worried that I might be tempted to be rid of her.

"Come now, everything has a price! Ten sovereigns? No, thirty..." The merchant offered, trying to read my stony face. She paused for a moment, waiting to see if I would bite at her offer. "Surely I cannot offer more than fifty."

"Not for all the gemstones littering the beaches of the Jewels." I told the merchant, scratching Sapphire's ears through the willow bars of her cage. The merchant lost her interest almost as quickly as it had been piqued and she rejoined the throngs of well-dressed students and artisans milling towards the university campus.

"This is incredible, Cathal," Ailidh gasped in wonder, having had half an hour to try and grasp the enormity of the city after we had passed the immense defensive wall. It was almost impossible to see the sentries walking back and forth along its length, the basalt fortification was so tall, but I knew that over two thousand men at any one time could be expected to be keeping watch over the approach to the city. The northerly and southern borders of Lesøsnø were barred by the jagged, impassable ridge of mountains that embraced the city. The basalt edifice of the city wall closed off the city from the lush, broad expanse of the North Riding and Lesøsnø's western border was secured by the cavernous fjord of the Abyss. The placid waters were overlooked by two immense forts. The northern sea wall was bristling with giant trebuchets, cannons and ballistae, which stood ready to rain down destruction upon any force foolish enough to mount an attack on the city from the sea. The southern fort was dominated by the lighthouse, the sixth tallest spire in the city. Topped with polished glass and precision-ground lenses, the lighthouse was able to direct a searing golden beam of illumination down into the Abyss for over two score leagues, aiding ships in their navigations towards the city. The lighthouse also shone out over the North Riding, reminding the citizens of Fossfjall of the supremacy of their capital city over the surrounding region. "I thought Birlone was big when I visited it with Father, but this place is huge!"

"Clongarvan is larger, believe it or not." I said as we passed under the Portal of the Scribe, the symbolic gateway to the Great Library. "But I prefer Lesøsnø. It is somehow more elegant, better refined."

"I can believe it." Ailidh replied, her jaw open wide as she tried to take in the enormity of ten towers that formed the centrepiece of the Great Library. In the centre of the plaza was the Tower of the Scribe, as whimsically witty as the God of Words himself: The stone sail of a gigantic goose feather quill lanced upwards into the sky, drinking from the great pot of ink at its base. The base of the tower alone had as large a surface area as Ailidh's home town of Croycullen. I tried to put myself in her shoes, looking anew at the grandeur of the place. It was not difficult to be awed by the sheer scale and ambition of its architecture and construction. The Tower of the Penitent reached literally up to the heavens, a granite forearm ten score feet tall clasping a thread of prayer beads in its palm. The reaping scythe of the Dark Rider hewed across the apex of his eponymous tower and a marble image of the Goddess, unspeakably voluptuous and alluring in visage and form, graced the roof of her wing of the library, a captivating manifestation of ultimate femininity three score feet tall that had haunted the erotic dreams of all the men and women alike that had seen it.

I tugged her along, our arms still linked at the elbow. "Come, you wanted to see the Abyss. We are almost there." I led Ailidh to the far western edge of the plaza, walking us between the towers of the Empress and the Dark Rider until we reached the sea wall. I smiled at her encouragingly and took her hand to aid her ascent of the steep granite steps, ducking out of the way so as not to obstruct her view once she had reached the stability of the wooden platform on top of the wall. Ailidh's eyes widened in shock and she breathed, "By the Earth Mother's great bountiful tits..."

The vehemence of my laughter took me by surprise and I wheezed for breath, "Ailidh! Who taught you to curse like that?"

She did not answer, frozen in place, numbed into silence by the sight before her. The view was genuinely awe inspiring, even though I had seen it before. Beyond the city's protective sea wall, space seemed to disintegrate. If madness took you and you chose to leap over the sea wall, it would be over a minute before you met your fate on the clear cerulean plane of water below. It was over four leagues from the bottom of the fjord to the level of the plaza and the width of the Abyss stretched to the north and south further than the eye could see; some two score leagues at its narrowest point near the city. The Abyss was lined by mountains that had been pitched up into existence following the cataclysmic rupture of the supervolcano beneath the waters, accentuating the contrast in height between sea level and the surrounding land. The glass isle of the Caldera, the vestigial remains of the supervolcano's crater was barely visible on the far western horizon, almost five score leagues beyond the sea wall. Only the plaintive cries of hungry gulls wheeling around the fishing boats returning to port to the south and the gentle whistling of the on-shore breeze from the west disturbed the silence. I placed an arm around her shoulder, letting the moment linger as we gazed out over the giant fjord, simply trying to comprehend the enormity of the scene. I lost track of time before Ailidh turned to me and looked up into my eyes.

"That's the most extraordinary thing I've ever seen."

"Welcome to Lesøsnø." I told her, with an affectionate peck on her unscarred cheek. "We can come back tomorrow, or later in the week if you wish. The view is even more spectacular when there are thunderstorms over the Caldera, especially at night."

"I'd love to see that."

"Perhaps we will, if the Lady smiles upon us." I said, directing us back down the stairs of the sea wall. "But for now, all I want to do is take the weight off my feet at Braden's estate. He lives in the north-east of the city, in a compound between the Royal Palace and the East Wall."

"You're sure he'll welcome us?"

"No doubt," I reassured her. "He was like a father to me when I joined the Order."

"I bet that he's even fond of cats." Ailidh said, looking down at Sapphire's cage with a smile.

"Yes, but their effect on furniture and his sinuses, not so much." I laughed, giving Sapphire a cautionary glance. "You will have to watch your step, trouble, and keep your claws out of the leather."

The cat yelped curt phrases of protest, circling the perimeter of her cage unhappily. Ailidh made sympathetic noises and tickled the end of her tail through the thin wooden bars. "You'll win him over, Sapphire, I'm sure."

Braden's compound was easy to find. We had exchanged a limited amount of written correspondence following Maeryn's coup, so I knew that he had taken refuge in Lesøsnø and that the Fossian Royal Family had granted him ownership over a lodge towards the northern end of the Park of the Earth Mother, which dominated the northeast of the city and bordered the university campus and the granite citadel of the Royal Palace itself. The compound surrounding Braden's estate was several acres in size, more than large enough to be self-sufficient and avoid any false claims that the Fossian Royal Family was harbouring dissidents from Cothraine. The property belonged to the Order of Sylvan, which like the Wizard's Guild, was an organisation whose authority spanned the entire Western Triad, regardless of the nationality of an individual member. Crown Prince Sjur, the *de facto* head of state for Fossfjall, was far more politically savvy than Maeryn and had welcomed the influx of Cothraine's rangers into his country's ranks of the Order of Sylvan as soon as Maeryn had announced that he had considered them enemies of the state and made them a target for his purge. Sjur had invested a lot of time cultivating good relations with Braden in the years since the coup, and I hoped this would work to our advantage when assisting Ailidh in her quest to discover why her father had been kidnapped.

Once I had found the estate deep within the thick copse of oak trees to the east of the Royal Palace, I jogged around the dozen foot tall granite brick walls of Braden's compound until I found the entrance. Ailidh panted slightly as she re-caught her breath and I announced myself to the sentries standing guard at the wrought iron gate connecting the private estate to the wider city beyond the

tall stone walls, both palms raised and empty of weapons. "May the blessings of Sylvan be upon you, my siblings."
A dark-haired ranger in her mid-twenties behind the gate stared at me through the narrow, charcoal-coloured bars with disbelief. "Baron Cathal, is that you, my lord?"
I regarded her more closely for several moments until a name finally sprung forth from my memory to match the face. "Devorgilla, it is good to see you again. But we will have to exchange the tales of our escape from the purge later. I must speak with Braden urgently."
Devorgilla stepped forward and grasped my shoulder through the bars of the gate, as if double-checking that I was not some kind of apparition sent from the Hells to deceive her. "The Lord Commander will be delighted to see you. Please wait here. I will not be long."
She was true to her word, escorting the Lord Commander of my Order out from the front door of the secluded town house with an enthusiastic spring in her step. Braden was a tad more reticent until he saw my face through the iron bars of the gate. The wrinkles upon his brow smoothed out and he smiled broadly in recognition, directing the sentinels at the perimeter of his compound urgently, "Open the gate... open the bloody gate!"
Tears dripped from the corners of my eyes as I embraced my former master and surrogate father, holding him close to my chest. "It is good to see you again, my master."
Braden likewise clutched me to his chest. "Cathal, my boy, I feared that I might never see you alive again. I am glad to be disappointed. What brings you here?"
We held onto each other silently in a lingering hug, unwilling to let the moment of our reunion end too soon. Inevitably, I had to let go of Braden and we regarded each other at arm's length before returning to the business at hand. "I came to ask for help. Maeryn is up to foul business once more in Clongarvan."
"I have heard rumours of the usurper king's erratic behaviour. Tell me more once we are inside. But first you should introduce me to your lovely travelling companion."
"Braden, this is Ailidh. It is on her behalf that we made the journey. Maeryn had her father kidnapped and she was left for dead in the aftermath of the abduction."

Ailidh hid her scar behind her fringe as she gave Braden a respectful curtsey. "It's an honour to meet you, Lord Commander."

"Please, just Braden is fine. Any friend and companion of Cathal's is a friend of mine." Braden gave Ailidh an embrace and tucked her fringe behind her right ear to greet her properly with a kiss to both cheeks. Ailidh went stiff and I heard her short intake of breath in panic when Braden exposed her disfigurement, but my master did not even flinch, kissing her twice tenderly on each cheek. "When you reach my age Ailidh, one learns not to judge a book by its cover. It is what is inside which matters. Nothing can disguise what is in a person's heart, and my boy here would not choose to travel with an evil soul."

"Thank you." Ailidh blushed, bowing her head.

"Now then," Braden said, returning his attention to me. "We need to discuss the mammoth in the swamp, or, should I say, the cat in the cage. Since when did you start keeping pets?"

"Sapphire is not a pet." I said, frowning.

"I suppose I could make use of her as a mouser, but she is not to be allowed on the furniture. Cat hair makes my eyes swell up like watermelons from the Reach."

"She is not a mouser, either."

"Then, pray tell, what kind of cat is she?"

Ailidh answered for me, lowering her mouth to the side of Sapphire's cage and scratching her behind her ear. "She's a little princess, aren't you, gorgeous?"

Sapphire purred and rubbed her whiskers and the scent glands on her cheek across Ailidh's lips, the feline equivalent of a kiss. Braden rolled his eyes. "Another mouth to feed... The princess had better keep her fur and claws to herself and sleep in her cage until I can acquire a cat bed, otherwise she might find herself tied up in a bag and thrown over the compound wall."

"Braden, you wouldn't!" Ailidh gasped, appalled.

I reproached Sapphire with a stern glare. "You hear that, kitten? You need to be on your best behaviour."

The silver tabby mewled her understanding expressively and closed her eyes slowly in supplication. Braden harrumphed and led us across the estate to his granite brick town house. "Butter would not melt in that mouth, I am sure. Let us take refreshments in the dining room."

The house was modest for a man of Braden's rank, but then he had always felt more at ease in the wilds than in the city. Few mementos or keepsakes adorned the walls and the floors were made from simple, polished oak planks. They creaked slightly as we moved from the hall, through a well-appointed kitchen to the dining room. I recognised the skulls of a vampiric worg, a grizzly bear and a sabre-toothed arctic tiger adorning the dining room wall, hanging opposite an animated, psychic portrait of an exceptionally comely pond nymph. I already knew the stories attached to them from Braden's adventures in the wilderness before he had been appointed Lord Commander, but I hoped that he would recount them again later for Ailidh's benefit. As we sat, I noted that the dining table was large enough to seat a round dozen. "How many rangers do you have living with you here?"

"At the moment, just the seven," Braden replied. "Though I am in contact with a further three score rangers that survived the purge, and who also sought refuge with me here in Fossfjall. We aid the local Order of Sylvan with patrolling the far north and east of the country. In return, they and the Fossian royal family granted us ownership of this estate for rest, healing and training between patrols. I cannot complain, under the circumstances. We have been treated with respect and with honour."

Devorgilla approached the table and gave us a shallow, respectful bow. "What can I get you, my lords? Wine? Beer? Tea? Or just water?"

"Beer, please." Ailidh and I said simultaneously. It was too early in the day for wine, but standing out all morning in the autumn sun while waiting to pass through the East Gate had given us a thirst that could not be quenched by water or tea.

"For me too, please Devorgilla. A flagon each will suffice for now, I think." Braden chuckled, slapping his thigh in delight at our unanimity of thought. "Now, Cathal, tell me the tale of what brought you here from your exile in the forest."

Braden and I had both gotten through two flagons of beer each while I recounted the story behind Ailidh's flight from Croycullen at length. It took nearly three hours in all, with Braden interrupting me with questions and Ailidh interjecting periodically to fill in gaps she thought my account had missed. Braden had looked at Sapphire with a newfound respect when he had learned that it was she that had alerted me to Ailidh's plight. "Who would have thought: a guard cat? I ought to place her on sentry duty!"

"What do you think, master? Given the amount of time that has passed, do you think Eoghan could still be saved?"

Braden sucked air through his teeth sceptically. "It seems unlikely. Sorry to put it so bluntly Ailidh, but unless your father knows something of truly exceptional value, his chances of surviving this many weeks in the custody of the king's dungeons is remote."

Ailidh blanched but remained silent, calming herself with a mouthful of beer. I spoke up on her behalf, venturing "We are sworn to try, regardless. Whatever Eoghan's ultimate fate may be, more serious questions regarding Eoghan's abandonment of his position in the Wizards' Guild and why Maeryn targeted him remain."

"Quite so, my boy," Braden nodded. "Strange happenings always seem to occur around the solstice. And this year the timing of the winter solstice converges with a cosmic conjunction of the planes. As omens go, it is about as foul a coincidence as they come. My gut tells me that the abduction of Ailidh's father and the timing of the planar alignment is no accident."

"But what does it all mean? I can't make head or tail of it." Ailidh said, releasing Sapphire from her cage. The tabby immediately sought refuge on her lap and Ailidh let her fingertips lazily massage the cat's exposed belly fur. Sapphire purred, gazing skyward up to Ailidh's face with unreserved adoration.

Slightly irked that Sapphire had never responded to my attentions quite so enthusiastically, I joked "Should we get the two of you a private room?"

Ailidh shushed me dismissively and Braden rolled his eyes before continuing. "Alas, I am no diviner. There are greater forces at work here than the machinations of petty kings and wayward mages, I am sure."

"Could you petition the Fossian Royal Family for aid from the Guild here in Lesøsnø?" I asked, desperately trying to find options we could pursue.

"Yes, but who knows whether it would do any good." Braden shrugged. "The mages here have their own preoccupations, no doubt. Our best bet, I think, would be to go direct to the source of the conflict."

"You mean Clongarvan? To the Royal Palace, or the Tower of the Aether?" I said, my jaw falling open at the audacity of the proposal.

"One or the other, or both," Braden said, pulling thoughtfully at the greying hair on the back of his neck. "I have been waiting for an opportunity to retake the Order's rightful place back in Clongarvan. I ought to have known that it would be laid down on a platter for me by my favourite son."

"We cannot just ride back into the city in plain sight." Braden chuckled. "I knew this much already, my boy. Rest assured that we are not without resources and have friends here in Lesøsnø that are more than positively inclined to lend us aid."

"Friends like who?" asked Ailidh.

"The Crown Prince Sjur, for one: he is still apoplectic following Maeryn's annulment of his betrothal to Reilynn." Braden explained. "Were it not for the Dowager Queen's stabilising influence, he would have battered down the gates to Clongarvan already."

"Ailidh's father wrote that we might find clues explaining his abduction in the Great Library."

"You will want to speak with the Scholar best versed in the history of divination. That would be the Master Illuminator, Hulda, I believe she is called." Braden frowned. "But your queries will have to wait for now. The library will be closed for the Dark Rider's and the Empress's Day."

"Today is the Jester's Day?" I said, raising my eyebrows. "I completely lost track of the date while we were on the road."

"Easily done, my boy," Braden consoled me, emptying the last of the beer from his flagon into my glass. "I often forgot what month it was during my patrols along the Bay of Bears and in the Silkwood."

"If only I knew what happened to Gormlaith following the purge." I lamented, Sapphire echoing my regret with a soft yowl from her resting place on Ailidh's lap. "She could tell us everything we wanted to know from a single séance. Thanks to the cache Ailidh's father left behind, we even have a set of diviner's tarot."

"No matter, my boy," Braden told me with a consolatory pat upon my shoulder. "The Lady is too impatient to hide your path for too long. You are both welcome to stay here for the time being. My instincts tell me that these events must be investigated and that Karryghan and Maeryn must finally be held to account. I will send out word by falcon that all of our siblings within a week's ride are to be recalled to the city at once.

"We will set out for Clongarvan in exactly three ten-days, so that we can gather as many rangers as possible and still reach the Cothraine capital before the solstice." Braden stood and laid his palm on the back of Ailidh's hand. "Your cause is just and your need is urgent, my lady. My rangers will rally behind you without hesitation."

"Thank you, master." I replied, bowing my head respectfully and squeezing my mentor's sinewy bicep, relieved that he had agreed to lend his aid to Ailidh.

"I have waited idly here for too long. I will not forego the opportunity to right the injustice of Maeryn's coup now that it has presented itself." Braden said gravely. "But my stomach is ready to start growling like a famished wolf. We can plan more in the morning. Let me help the others prepare dinner while Devorgilla gets you settled into your quarters. She can provide you with fresh clothes – you must want to change into something that does not reek of the road. Join me back here when you have freshened up."

Devorgilla berthed us in adjoining chambers, simple rooms not dissimilar from the barracks I had grown up in at Sylvan's Dell, the headquarters of our Order in the southeast of Clongarvan. The room contained a single bed, a storage chest, a dresser, a wicker laundry basket, plus a leather-topped bureau and chair. The room was illuminated by a small lead-framed window and a pair of oil lamps, which burned fragrantly and without smoke. I placed my pack and Sapphire's cage on the floor between the chest and the desk, opening the cage door to let Sapphire stretch her legs again, after her brief release from incarceration in the dining room to cuddle with Ailidh. She made an instant beeline for the bed, leaping up onto the mattress and circling twice before laying claim to it with an emphatic meowing as she flopped over onto her side, her tail twitching in delight. "I thought you were going to be on your best behaviour, kitten. If Braden catches you, he will put you in a sack with a hundredweight of granite and throw you into the Abyss."

Sapphire considered my warning briefly before standing, walking around in a circle once more and lying back down exactly in the same place on the mattress. I snickered gently under my breath, rubbed her fur backwards up from the base of her tail to her neck and bent down to kiss the top of her head between the ears. "It is just as well that I love you, trouble."

Sapphire re-groomed herself with rapid licks of her barbed tongue, annoyed that I had deliberately ruffed up her fur, before lying back down on the bed to sleep unmolested. I rummaged through the dresser for a fresh tunic and a clean pair of trousers my size, stripping off my sweat-laden travelling clothes and throwing them in the laundry basket. The sensation of clean linen against my skin was almost as good as a hot bath. I felt instantly refreshed and having been freed of the weight of my pack, armour and sword belt I practically bounced back to the dining room.

Devorgilla was already seated at the table with two other rangers, one of whom leapt up to his feet as I entered the room. "Master Cathal, I can scarcely believe it!"

"Brother Creighton," I smiled and embraced my one-time apprentice. I had mentored him when he had joined the Order as a boy, and though we were not too dissimilar in age – I was only a dozen years his senior – he had always looked up to me in the way I had looked up to Braden. "You've filled out some since I saw you last."

"Red meat and exercise, as you always told me." Creighton said, almost on the verge of tears. "Though these days, I have too much of the former and not enough of the latter."

"It clearly suits you well, though. The boy I left at Sylvan's Dell the year before the coup was a skinny runt." I joked, turning Creighton pale with embarrassment as Devorgilla's throaty, dirty laughter echoed around the dining room. Mortified, Creighton immediately changed the subject, lowering his head in respect. "I heard about what happened to Sister Aoibheann. I know the two of you were close. You have my condolences, master."

"What is done cannot be undone, but thank you." I replied, my heart wrenching at the memory, recalling my sense of powerlessness as my lover's life had ebbed away in my arms. The most painful recollection was the look of joy on her face when she had realised that I would survive her and that her death had not been in vain. "We all lost

people dear to us during the purge. But we should not
dwell on our losses. Sit, please, and tell me everything
about what has happened to you since the coup."
We had been exchanging tales for almost half an hour by
the time Ailidh joined us in the dining room. As well as
changing clothes, she had taken the time to wash and
comb her hair, hiding her disfigurement behind an
immaculate golden blonde curtain. She took the seat next
to me, stroking the back of my hand, as if seeking
reassurance. "I haven't missed dinner, have I?"
I confirmed that we had not even started the evening's
repast, giving her hand an affectionate squeeze before
introducing her to the rangers sat around the table.
Creighton blushed as pink as coral when Ailidh turned her
gaze to him, a sure sign that he was instantly smitten with
her. The arrival of Braden and the other off-duty rangers
that had helped him cook the evening's meal scuppered
any opportunity that the more worldly-wise Devorgilla might
have used to tease Creighton for his chronic shyness.
Creighton was too young and inexperienced with women to
recognise Devorgilla's robust banter for what it was – an
expression of interest, rather than scorn – I resolved to give
him a private word of advice after dinner and save him a
few more blushes. Our evening meal was simple but
delicious: a thick cutlet of pan-fried venison served with a
mushroom, herb and cream sauce alongside a delightfully
buttery potato and parsnip mash. Our conservations flowed
as easily as the red wine Braden had chosen to accompany
the meal and we lingered at the table long after the sun
had sunk below the horizon. The younger rangers steadily
made their excuses and left the dining room to stand watch
on the compound's perimeter or go to bed, leaving just
myself, Braden and Ailidh at the table. Ailidh had been
silent for most of the evening, listening with interest to the
stories that the rangers had shared, but I had noticed her
attention be drawn periodically to the portrait of the pond
nymph. The movement of the figure in the psychic portrait
was subtle but unnerving, if you had never seen one
before. Knowing that it was being watched, the nymph blew
Ailidh a kiss and favoured her with a sensual pirouette.
Unable to contain her curiosity any longer, Ailidh asked
"Braden, where did you get that picture of the nymph? I
swear I just saw it move."

"Ah, one of my most memorable adventures," Braden smiled, taking a sip of wine and looking back over his shoulder at the picture. "I was patrolling the Lockwood, north of Siskine. I had heard rumours of an illegal logging camp overlooking the Bay of Serpents and after several weeks of searching, I found a lake that was being polluted by the run-off from the camp. The lake's pond nymph confronted me, demanding to know whether I was responsible for the despoiling of her domain. I assured her that I was not and that I was here to help.

"She tasked me to destroy the camp and kill the bandits, telling me that I would find their operation four leagues to the north-east of her lake and that I should only come back to tell her once it had been done. I agreed, because how can one refuse such a beautiful fey creature? Fortunately for me, the camp was small, though judging by the hundred acres of felled trees surrounding it; it must have been operating for at least two seasons. The loggers were no warriors, used to only hitting stationary trees with their axes. Once I had dispatched half a dozen of them with my bow and sword, the remaining men, another dozen in total, surrendered to me, begging for mercy. I warned that if I ever saw them again in the Lockwood, their blood would water the saplings springing up in the forest of tree stumps they had left behind. I had them dismantle the camp and they fled, some going north to Killcuain and the others east to Birlone. I patrolled around the area of the camp for another seven days, waiting to make sure that the criminals did not try to restart their illegal enterprise. Only once I was certain that they were not coming back, did I report my success to the pond nymph."

Ailidh leaned forward in her seat, her elbows on the table as she listened with rapt attention. "How did she reward you? With a night of passion for the brave knight that saved her lake?"

Braden laughed. "You read too many fairy stories, my child. No, she struck me blind for daring to look at her and forbade me to ever trespass upon her domain again. I stumbled around in the dark for three days until I passed beyond the threshold of her power and my eyesight began to return. I was fortunate not to have walked off the edge of a cliff or been waylaid by a pack of wolves or wild boars. It was only after that, when I pitched my tent for the night that I noticed she had conjured her portrait into my pack for me to remember her by. To this day, I have never seen a more glorious creature."

Braden retired to his chamber to sleep and I said goodnight to Ailidh, suddenly overcome with tiredness. I always felt doubly fatigued at the end of a long trip, not just because of the cumulative toll of the journey, but because of the culture shock of arriving in a big city. Cities always seemed to have a life of their own. The constant bustle of activity under the street lights gave places like Lesøsnø and Clongarvan a low level hum, which once heard could not be unheard, and a perpetual glow that washed out the starlight from the night sky. I never slept well in cities and tonight proved to be no exception. It always unnerved me to look up into the heavens and not be able to see the stars. It was well after midnight when I heard Ailidh creep into my room and wrap herself around my back, lying next to me on the narrow mattress.

"I can't sleep either. The city's so bright and loud compared to Croycullen."

"You get used to it, or so I am told. I never did." I whispered back, keeping my voice low so as not to wake Sapphire. She had no such trouble and was laid out on her back in her cage, her legs lolling about at random angles as her paws and whiskers twitched, as she dreamed her intense feline visions.

"I'm not sure I will. I don't want to be alone tonight." Ailidh said and slipped one of her hands underneath my nightshirt to caress my chest. "Can we talk now? It's been nearly a week since we left the Weald."

I turned over on the mattress to face her and Ailidh saw it as an invitation to show her desire. Her hands lifted my nightshirt so that she could kiss my torso, brushing her tongue lightly over the two iridescent scars that still glowed ominously on my breast. Her feel of her fingertips on my skin was soft and urgent. I could sense her craving to be touched, to be loved, and I almost lost myself in the provocative sensations as she offered herself to me. It would have been easy just to give in to my arousal and couple with her once more, but all too familiar doubts nagged at my conscience. Our coupling at the camp had begun with me being unaware of it until it was too late to stop. I had been surprised by the strength of my need to share her pleasure, to satisfy her passion. Tonight it was different. I felt the hunger of carnal desire that gnawed away at my soul from the loneliness of the years I had endured on my own in my forest refuge, but this time I could not dismiss the guilt I felt at betraying Aoibheann's memory, a lingering sense of infidelity, as if my soulmate's sacrifice during the purge had been invalidated by lying with Ailidh. My hands ensnared her wrists and I pulled my lips back away from hers. "Ailidh, please stop. This, this is not right."

"How can I make it right, Cathal?" Ailidh asked, upset by my rejection of her. Ailidh's hands, made strong by her apprenticeship at the forge, gripped my shoulders with a force bordering on pain. "Isn't it enough that I love you?"

"You know it is not that simple for me."

"So you say. And yet you still fucked me, the marks on your chest are testament enough to that." Ailidh scoffed. "Are you going to tell me that it was a mistake? It didn't feel like one to me."

"Ailidh, please," I said, placing one hand on her hip and the other on her cheek. I wanted nothing more at that moment than to feel the heat of her body beneath mine; to feel the moist grip of her slit around my cock; to feel the silky firmness of her tits against my palms; and to hear her breathless gasps of ecstasy murmuring my name as we made love hard and deep, long into the night. But the fear of acknowledging my own uncertain and contradictory feelings for her, of whether I dared risk becoming attached to her was too strong. The idea of opening up to her so completely terrified me, as did the unknown consequences of the demonic rune Keri had carved into my chest. "Do I regret it? No. If I had thought that I might, I would have stopped you. Ailidh, I hope you know that I hold you in the highest esteem as a friend. But was it a mistake? Perhaps, in the sense that we still do not know the meaning of Keri's mark. Nor do we know what the consequence might be if we were to continue to be intimate and activate all three marks of the rune. I cannot take the risk. And nor should you want to, either."

"You'll never love me, will you?" Ailidh asked bitterly. "You'll always find some excuse."

"I do love you. Just not in the way you desire." I kissed Ailidh's forehead and rocked her in my arms as she wept quietly. I let Ailidh intertwine her legs with mine and I held her tightly against my chest until, eventually, we both fell asleep.

25 – Aiden

It was a full six days before I found my sea legs. I had never set foot on a vessel larger than a rowing boat before we had boarded the *Merganser* in Clongarvan. Certainly I had never experienced waters less placid than an inland pond on a calm summer's day before. So it came as quite a shock when Ruarc took the ship directly north from the western coast of Finisterre Isle past the windward coast of Hrothurjökull, passing to the west of the volcanic archipelago, rather than the more sheltered, east coast. The west coast route was more direct and would take more than two days off our travel time to the Fossfjall capital, but left the ship fully exposed to the brutal westerly winds that battered the coasts like the icy breath of a white dragon. The pitching and rolling of the deck for the first three days left me bed-bound and unable to stomach neither food nor water, such was the extent of my seasickness. Captain Ruarc had been somewhat less than charitable in his assessment of my illness, branding me a pathetic, lily-livered landlubber. The queen was only marginally more generous, mocking my discomfort at every possible opportunity. Only my wife treated me with any sympathy at all, doting upon me like a mother tending to a sick infant. From anyone else I would have considered it patronising, but Sìne managed to comfort me both physically and mentally without making me feel like I was somehow at fault for not coping with the conditions as well as the rest of the crew. By the fifth day, Sìne was teaching me how to let my body sway in unison with the undulations of the deck as the waves swelled and rolled beneath the keel of the ship. The day after, I was able to keep my feet and the contents of my stomach even if I was below deck and had no view of the horizon. On the seventh day after we left Clongarvan, Ruarc was sufficiently tolerant of me that we began to spend time together so that he could start my formal induction into the Secret Service and tell me about the expectations the queen would have of me in my new role. From the beginning, he made it clear that he was only speaking with me by order from the queen.

"Let me speak plain, Shadow Duke. I know exactly who you are and I know exactly what you have done. Queen Reilynn somehow believes you have some future value to her, which is just as well for you, otherwise you would have found yourself overboard not long after we had left the docks in Clongarvan."

"I respect your honesty, Shadow Count, so let me speak equally plain: do not threaten me again if you want to live long enough to have regrets."

"Do not think for a moment that you can intimidate me or pull rank on my ship, Shadow Duke. I am both master and commander here. The only things I answer to are the queen and the wind." Ruarc warned in a tone barely more civilised than a bear's snarl. "And neither of them are as favourably inclined toward you as you would like to believe."

For day after day, as we neared Lesøsnø, I found myself having to follow Captain Ruarc around the ship like an obedient puppy, listening intently as he conducted his increasingly tetchy protocol briefings, informing me of my new responsibilities as a member of the black cloaks, whilst simultaneously carrying out his regular duties on the ship. Queen Reilynn would spend hours in the pulpit at the bow of the ship, letting the saltwater spray wet her face and hair as she surveyed the horizon, neither caring whether the conditions were fair or foul. The queen seemed happier and more at ease the longer the journey went on, though I was unable to say if this was due to her newfound freedom from her imprisonment in Royal Palace, or her anticipation of reaching our destination and being reunited with the Crown Prince. In contrast, Sìne spent most of her time in our cabin below deck, unless the weather was especially fine. Ruarc's crew, though well disciplined, still possessed the hungry, roving eyes and wandering hands of sailors, and my wife did not enjoy nearly the same level of reverence than the queen. While she was more than capable of dealing with any malign attention from the crew, my wife did not court trouble and simply chose to stay out of sight and out of mind for the majority of the journey. By the time we reached the Hemafjord Peninsula, I was almost starting to enjoy being on board the ship. Similarly to my time in the City Guard, life was simple and highly structured. As the queen's personal bodyguard, I was spared all of the regular duties and expectations Ruarc might have of one of his crew, and I grew to appreciate the rhythms of life aboard a ship. I imagined that it was more relaxed than crewing on a naval ship of the line; The *Merganser* was built for speed, rather than battle. She was armed only with hand crossbows, pikes, swords, sabres and rapiers. With a fair wind, Ruarc assured me that no vessel on the Western Ocean could hope to intercept her. So it was with some consternation when Ruarc reported to Queen Reilynn that the usual strong westerly gales that carried trade traffic east along the length of the Abyss to Lesøsnø had failed to materialise after we had cleared the Aurochs Horn. The *Merganser* floundered in the pitiful zephyrs spiralling around the great estuary for days as Ruarc took us north and then back south to each side of the Abyss, desperately searching for some kind of wind to speed us on our way. The Abyss was truly worthy of its name: a channel blasted out of the bedrock by the cataclysmic eruption of a volcano, ripping a tear in the continent three hundred leagues long, almost a hundred leagues wide where it spanned the Caldera, the simmering volcanic island left behind by the explosion, narrowing down to a still colossal two score leagues wide at its narrowest point where the great fjord met the ocean. The cliffs were so tall that even from the middle of the channel at the estuary the peaks of the mountain ranges that flanked the gash in the earth could be seen. The sheer scale of it seemed impossible, but Ruarc had told me that the fjord's walls only got taller and more intimidating the closer you got to Lesøsnø. Our progress was slow in the oddly becalmed channel, almost as if the gods wanted to delay our arrival to the city. Ruarc had the ship hug the southern wall of the fjord, where he was able to find a headwind to tack against, and our path zigzagged tortuously east. As we approached the Caldera, tension levels among the crew increased markedly. The Caldera played host to the pirate haven of Obsidian. The town was literally carved out of the black glassy rock that had spilled out of the earth following the eruption of the volcano and its inhabitants were known to be as sharp and spiky as the rock their stronghold had been hewn from. It was on our seventh day struggling against the wind that the glass isle of the Caldera came into view on the horizon, just as dusk began to turn into night. The column of volcanic gases rising from the interior of the vast crater were aglow with crimson light from the lava pool in the centre of the island, giving the impression of a luminous tower reaching many leagues up into the sky. It was an ominous omen that was not made less intimidating by the crackle of lightning sparking through the dust clouds. The walls of the Abyss amplified the echoes from the thunderclaps, making the air roll and shake with terrible violence and volume. Captain Ruarc ducked past the rigging between the sails on the foremast and the pulleys on the forecastle bulwark, joining Reilynn, Sìne and me in the pulpit over the clipper's bow, where we had been watching – enjoying would be too strong a word – the awe-inspiring display of natural power illuminating the silhouette of the glass isle.

"The Caldera, at last..." Ruarc said, his tone betraying his exasperation. "I have never known such capricious winds in the Abyss, your majesty. Provided we stay close to the Caldera's shoreline, it should make the wind more predictable. With luck we should pick up a tailwind and make landfall at Lesøsnø in two days."

"You have done well, captain. You and your crew have my thanks. There is nothing to be done about the wind." Reilynn reassured the sullen shipmaster.

"Staying so close to the shore does carry a risk, your majesty. Unless the wind picks up soon, there is a chance that the pirates in Obsidian might notice us and give chase." Ruarc frowned.

"I have every confidence that you will keep us safe, captain. And even if we are boarded, Aiden and Sìne alone are worth a dozen marines." Reilynn said, favouring her handmaiden with a smile.

"I hope so, your majesty. If I were you I would sleep in your armour and keep your weapons close to hand. I would not be surprised if we found ourselves in an ambush by dawn." Ruarc said grimly.

Sìne gave me a kiss and said "It's getting late. I think I'll get some rest while I can."

I let my lips linger on her neck below the ear, enjoying her scent. I squeezed her hand and nodded my approval, not that she needed it. "Good idea. I think I'd like to remain on deck for the first watch, with your permission, captain."

Ruarc raised his left eyebrow. "That is not necessary, Shadow Duke, but yes. By all means, I would welcome another keen set of eyes on the horizon."

"I think I will retire for the night as well, captain." said Reilynn. "Send word down to us at the first sign of trouble."

"Aye, your majesty," Ruarc agreed, bowing respectfully.

With the queen and my wife safely below, Ruarc secured the ship, running dark with no signs of artificial light. The paint on the *Merganser*'s hull seemed to devour the starlight, barely casting any silhouette. Only the pale, bubbling wake trailing behind us betrayed any sign of our passing. The coast of the glass isle passed slowly by the ship's port side, the wind swirling and working against us. The town of Obsidian was as dark as the volcanic rock that gave it its name, and I wondered whether our transit past the pirate stronghold would be noticed. Moments turned into hours and I could find no hint of activity from the port. It was almost two hours after midnight when I heard the shipmaster swear under his breath. "Shit."

The fatigue and drowsiness of standing watch for so long instantly cleared and I stepped to Ruarc's side. "What is it, captain?"

The shipmaster handed me his spyglass and pointed east, towards our destination. In the dim glimmer of the starlight, I could see the tops of four tall masts and their sails just eclipsing the horizon. "Corsair, about eight leagues away."

"Is it a pirate? How can you tell?" I asked. I trusted Ruarc's more practised eye, but from this distance the ship would just as easily been a merchantman from all I could discern.

"At harvest-time all the traffic heads towards Lesøsnø, not away from it. It is a privateer, believe me."

"Warrior's cock," I grimaced. "How long do we have?"

"No more than an hour, and there is no sign that we might catch a change in the wind. We will not be able to outrun her." Ruarc said. "You should warn the queen. Bolt the door to the cabin and protect her with your life. I will send as many men as I can spare to guard the entrance to your quarters."

I stood in silence for a moment, thinking hard, recalling everything I had read while training as an officer in the City Guard and latterly, all the texts I had been given on diplomatic protection while serving as Maeryn's bodyguard.

Without looking back at Ruarc, I focused my gaze on the pirate corsair and shook my head. "No."

"I beg your pardon, Shadow Duke?" Ruarc said, his mouth open in shock.

"I said 'no', captain. It seems to me like a poor idea. If we barricade the queen into the captain's quarters behind a wall of men, it will only entice the pirates towards her. And we would be trapped like fish in a barrel. There would be no hope of defending her." I explained. "Better that she remains mobile and able to defend herself. After all, a moving target is so much harder to hit."

"What do you propose, then? That I put her on a rowing boat and point her the way to Lesøsnø?"

"No, I have another idea. We take the fight to them instead. We let them board and kill their leaders to break their morale."

"Shadow Duke, they will probably outnumber us by three-to-one or more. What you propose is suicide."

"Ah, Captain. I never said that we would play fair. I need to warn the queen and get into my armour."

"But your armour's gilt will make you stand out like a beacon in-" Ruarc aborted his objection abruptly, a wry smile breaking out across his face as his quick mind caught up with the plan still forming in my head. "Aiden, I believe I may have underestimated you. It will be a difficult ruse to execute, however."

"The privateers probably think we are packed to the gunnels with wine and antiquities from the south. If they were made to believe I am a nobleman passenger as well, they may try to parlay and demand a ransom. When they smell the promise of gold, they will not be interested in what to their eyes will look like a pair of cabin girls."

"So when you have the pirate captain's attention and petition him for a truce to parlay..." Ruarc ventured, waiting for me to confirm his own thought.

"We spring the trap." I confirmed and rushed below to the captain's quarters while Ruarc briefed his crew. I woke my wife and the queen with the news that a ship had been sighted and that it was likely hostile. I told them about my deception to distract attention away from Reilynn in the event that we were boarded. Reilynn nodded her assent, though she was not happy that she would be unable to wear her armour. Sìne was far more concerned about the risk I putting myself at, by choosing to deliberately make myself the pirates' primary target, but she had been unable to reply when I had asked her "Who would you rather the privateers try to kidnap or kill, me or the queen?"

I reassured her with a long kiss on the lips. "I would rather that they tried to kill me, too. Nothing is more important to me than your safety and the queen's."

Sìne helped me into my armour, fastening the greaves to my shins and the leg plates to my thighs as I tightened the strapping of my breastplate at my sides. The silver-gilt metal would shine out like stars against the night, making me a very obvious focus for the attention of the privateers. After nearly three weeks at sea, it felt strange to be wearing armour again, but its sturdiness reassured me that my plan was as good as any that stood a chance of getting us through to the Fossfjall capital unscathed. I wrapped my sword belt around my waist, attaching only the lightweight falchion I had taken from the queen's armoury to it. My longsword would be too heavy to wield effectively in the frantic, close-quarters of an on-deck melee. I took a deep breath, mentally preparing myself to play the role of the nobleman, while I checked upon Sìne's and the queen's preparations. Both were now fully-dressed and ready for combat, wrapped in their black leather cloaks, with their rapiers and hand crossbows hanging ready at their waists. They took a pauldron each and settled them into position over my shoulders as I fastened one bracer and then the other around my forearms. My fingers fumbled with the straps on my right forearm and Reilynn steadied my hand with hers, looking deep into my eyes. "What you are about to do is very brave, Aiden. Utterly stupid, but very brave, nonetheless."

"Thank you, your majesty." I said, smiling at the backhanded compliment and donning both of my gauntlets. "Let us get on deck before I have a fit of sanity and change my mind."

The three of us ran back up onto the deck of the ship and met with Ruarc at the conning tower on the quarter deck. Reilynn said "Captain, we are ready. Where do you want us?"

"I hope you are not afraid of heights, your majesty?" Ruarc handed the queen and Sìne each a heavy glass phial and explained "Alchemical pitch; dip your bolts into this and rain fire down on their sails and gun deck. Nothing causes greater panic on a ship than fire. You will get the best view from the crow's nest. If you get spotted and need to make a quick escape, there is a zip line down to the anchor deck."

"How'll we know when to start shooting?" Sìne asked.

"That will be simple enough: The moment either the pirate captain or I get run through at the neck." I said, my voice trembling slightly.

"Remember, we need to get the corsair fully alongside and tempt them into boarding us if we wish to avoid being blasted apart by her guns. We will play the meek merchantman first, feinting surrender before showing the pirates that our teeth and minds are sharper than theirs." Ruarc reminded us. "Spring the trap too early and all of us will be feeding the sharks before dawn."

"Time to play the bait," I said, blowing the breath out from my cheeks in apprehension. "Where is the best place for me to be seen?"

"They will most likely try to get aboard on the main deck, near the centre mast. Put yourself on deck between the centre mast and the forecastle and you are bound to attract their attention. And if anyone takes pot-shots at you with a crossbow, you will find more cover to seek there." Ruarc advised, glancing again at the horizon on the ship's starboard bow. The corsair's captain was clearly skilled – they had used their approach to trap us between the Caldera's coast and their ship, forcing a confrontation. The black silhouette grew ominously larger on the horizon and now it was no longer necessary to use Ruarc's spyglass to identify the open cannon hatches on the broadsides of the privateer's hull. "Get into place quickly. It will not be long now."

I walked the queen and her handmaiden to the central mast. Standing at over five score feet tall, it was the ship's tallest and the crow's nest was almost at its very apex. In some respects it was fortunate that the sea was so calm, as it meant that the deck was still and the tip of the mast hardly swayed at all, which would make the climb far easier for Reilynn and Sìne. My heart didn't leave my mouth however until I saw that they were both safely seated in the wooden basket at the top of the ship. Sìne gave me a wave and disappeared behind the wooden rim of the nest, no doubt to prime her hand crossbow ready for action. I walked over to the starboard side of the ship and grasped the topgallant rail, watching the pirate vessel slowly but inexorably close the distance between us. I could almost make out the outlines of figures scurrying about the deck of the corsair, which was now just half a league away across the jet black waters of the fjord. I flinched when I saw the flash of one of the corsair's cannons illuminate the side of the pirate ship. Seconds later I heard the whistling of the cannonball flash across the bow of the ship and crash into the water a hundred yards from our port side. The blast was followed a moment later by a second shot, this one impacting in the water just three score yards from the *Merganser*'s bow.

"Lower the sails!" Ruarc shouted, starting our deception. As well as allowing the pirates to board without having a cause to perforate our hull with cannon shot first, lowering the sails also gave us a second advantage. When Reilynn and Sine started peppering the corsair's own sails with bolts tipped with flaming pitch, the pirates would not be able to use our own tactics against us. "Raise the white flag, but keep your weapons ready!"

The *Merganser* slowed now that there was no wind power to offset the friction of the water against her keel, drifting to a stop. The corsair tacked away from us and then came about to approach us from behind. The privateer bristled with a dozen cannons embedded into her gun deck on each side and three dozen pirate marines jeered and stomped eagerly on the main deck, brandishing boarding pikes, grappling hooks and rapiers above their heads, celebrating their triumph. As the bow of the pirate ship passed our stern I began to walk aft, repeatedly calling out "Parlay! I invoke the right of parlay! Let me speak with your captain!"

The crew of the *Merganser* drew their weapons and arrayed themselves out along the centreline of the ship, as Ruarc shouted instructions and encouragement. "Steady on, mates, and keep your weapons low. If the pirate captain has a brain rivalling the size of his ship, we might still avoid bloodshed this night."

"Parlay! I invoke the right of parlay!" I repeated, shouting clearly and with as much self-assurance and confidence as I could muster. The two ships were now almost fully alongside each other. The clatter of grappling hooks rang from the deck as the pirates finished their boarding manoeuvre, dragging the corsair's port flank fully against the *Merganser*'s starboard side. "I wish to negotiate safe passage with your captain!"

The pirates lowered a single boarding plank and I walked as confidently as I could toward the end on the *Merganser*'s deck. The starlight reflected from my armour, illuminating the deck around me almost as well as a torch. I heard a murmur ripple across the deck of the corsair, speculating about how much gold I might be willing to pay for a ransom. The pirates fiddled with their weapons, and I was relieved to note that none were armed with crossbows. A single pirate walked across the gangplank with the steady ease of a man used to spending more time on the waves than upon dry land. The man did not cut an impressive figure. His skin was an anaemic pale ivory and his false smile revealed that he was missing several teeth due to bouts of scurvy. The general scruffiness of his clothes and the jagged, dull edge on his sabre told me instantly that this was no pirate captain, certainly not one so successful to be able to afford to run a corsair with a crew of three score privateers. The pirate addressed me with a sneer. "Ye wanted to parlay, so parlay."

I stepped towards him, as if to shake hands, before felling him to the deck with a single punch to the middle of his forehead. "What do you take me for, fool? I will speak with the captain only, not the ship's whore!"

Hoots of delight erupted from the deck of the corsair and some of the pirates had tears of laughter in their eyes as they clutched at each other for support. The scrawny pirate raised his hands in mute supplication, blood trickling down his nose and he barely took to his feet, scrambling on hands and knees back towards the boarding plank and the relative safety of the corsair. He was met halfway by the actual captain of the privateer, who kicked him out of his way, off the plank to splash with a pitiful cry in the waters below, to the continued hilarity of the corsair's marines, some of whom were now bent double in mirth. The pirate captain was almost my equal in height and bulk and carried himself with an arrogant, brutal air, his long, thick greying beard studded with golden clips to groom the hairs away from his mouth and chin. The rapier at his waist was of the finest quality, as were his clothes. I estimated that he was about Ruarc's age, which immediately put me on guard. It was rare for pirates to reach that kind of age and that could only mean that he was both seasoned and ruthless. I could not play him for a fool, which meant that my deception would have to be convincing on every level.

"Well played, my lord! I'm tempted to let you go for the entertainment you've given us this night alone, but I can see by that lovely armour of yours, you've got a more than sovereign or two to rub together. How many of them'll be mine come the dawn, wonders I."

"I am open to suggestions, captain. After all, I will have no use for money in Hell. I would dearly like to avoid combat, but my concern is whether it can be avoided after we have handed over our valuables."

"That's a fair old dilemma, my lord, make no mistake." The pirate agreed, his eyes glimmering in the starlight. "What's to stop me from killing you all and then taking all of your money?"

"I am sure you are a canny businessman, captain, to be able to afford such a fine ship. Surely you must appreciate the value of a steady income over a single payout."

"Must I?" the captain said, raising a thick dark eyebrow sceptically.

"Why yes! My father earned his fortune with livestock. He always told me that you can earn more money from milking a cow than from slaughtering a veal calf. Would you not agree?"

The privateer considered my statement for a moment in silence before giving me a nod. "Make me an offer, my lord. I'm listening."

"Thirty percent of our cargo for safe passage now, and a further thirty percent on each subsequent trip we make." I proposed, meeting the pirate's gaze confidently. He had respected my show of strength in dispatching his lackey. It would not be wise to show any weakness or insecurity now.

"Four score percent, now and in the future." The pirate counter-offered, spreading his arms to appear reasonable. "Or I could just paint your ship's deck with the blood of its crew."

"Captain, please, it would not even be worth making the trip!" I threw up my hands and turned away from him, clutching my head in mock despair. I lowered my head and rubbed my face with my right hand, keeping it over my mouth. I looked back over my shoulder, gauging the distance between us. "Two score percent."

"Three score percent an-" The privateer did not have the chance to finish his sentence. As soon as he started talking, I grabbed the hilt of my falchion with my sword hand and turned on the spot, lashing out with a long, arching slash as I drew the thin sword from my belt. The long reach and light weight of the falchion made my surprise attack possible. He might have seen an ambush from a shorter, heavier longsword coming. Three inches of the blade bit through the pirate captain's neck, cutting clean through his windpipe and carotid arteries. A quick jab with my heel to the centre of his chest had his body tumbling overboard into the black waters.

"NOW!" I screamed, kicking the boarding gangplank off the deck with my armoured boot. I backed towards the midline of the ship as Reilynn and Sìne began to rain quarrels of fire down onto the sails and gun deck of the corsair. The members of the *Merganser*'s crew armed with hand crossbows unleashed their first volley into the massed ranks of pirates on the port flank of the corsair, killing a third of the marines in under a second. I helped other members of the crew cut the grappling lines holding us to the side of the privateer, as others began to raise our sails.

"Put those fucking fires out!" the First Mate of the pirate ship screamed above the chaos, only to be struck in the face by a fiery bolt swooping down from the crow's nest. My eyes traced the bolt back to its source and my wife blew me a kiss before reloading her crossbow. With the pirate ship in utter disarray, its crew had abandoned all thoughts of boarding us, their only concern now being to extinguish the fires taking hold on their vessel. The sails on all four of their masts were alight and had lost so much of their fabric that the ship would have trouble outpacing a rowing boat. Ruarc ordered a second volley of crossbow bolts from his crew to cut down a second group of pirate boarders and then he had everyone focus on raising the *Merganser*'s sails. As we began to put clear water between us and the pirate ship, Reilynn and Sìne continued to pelt down bolts like flaming meteorites onto the corsair, this time concentrating their fire on the gun deck, hoping to ignite the gunpowder stores next to the cannons. We were three score yards clear of the corsair, at the very limit of hand-crossbow range, when Sìne's last fire-tipped quarrel fell through the bow-most cannon hatch. No more than a dozen seconds later the entire bow exploded as the incandescent pitch caught a pile of black powder next to the cannon, fatally rupturing the ship's hull. Ruarc and the *Merganser*'s crew cheered as the water erupted with a fountain of fire and splintered wood, the corsair beginning its dive to the bottom of the fjord.

"Gods, did you see that shot!" shouted one of the crew, dumbstruck by what she had seen. "Someone marry that girl!"

"The Shadow Duke already did," another crewman observed dryly.

Ruarc appeared at my side by the forecastle and clapped me on the shoulder. "Remarkable, you did it, Aiden!"

"We did it." I corrected him, momentarily overcome with self-consciousness. "Did you lose anyone, captain?"

"No, not even any wounds to speak of, either." Ruarc said, blinking in disbelief at just how lucky we had been.

"Aiden!" Sìne jumped the last half dozen feet from the central mast's rope to the deck and sprinted across the deck to leap into my arms. I clutched her back and we kissed long and hard. "Are you injured?"

"Not a scratch, my love." I reassured her. "And you are an evil shot, as we used to say in the City Guard."

Sìne blushed and hugged me tighter. "I have always been good with a crossbow."

"But not many can claim to have sunk a ship with one." Reilynn said, similarly in awe. Her approach across the deck was rather slower and more dignified than my wife's had been, but her eyes also glowed with appreciation, not just for her handmaiden, but for me as well. "You see, captain? I told you that you would not regret bringing these two with us."

There was a great flapping noise from the sails and Ruarc raised his head. "Indeed, your majesty. We have even caught a change in the wind. A westerly, at last! The Lady of Luck truly smiles down upon us tonight."

The next day was the very definition of plain sailing. Like her namesake, the *Merganser* spread her broad wings across the swelling waters of the fjord and as the glass isle disappeared over the western horizon the spires of the city of Lesøsnø appeared to the east. As we approached the Fossfjall capital, the walls of the Abyss grew taller and narrower making it appear like the ship was traversing a channel carved out of the rock by a colossal plough blade. Snub-nosed porpoises cavorted in the ship's bow wave just for the sheer joy of it as the tailwind impelled us towards the city at some eighteen knots. Reilynn delighted in their show, as one porpoise after another leapt clear of the water, spinning over at least twice before landing on its back. "Look at that, Sìne! I wish I felt so at home in the water."

"At least you can swim, your majesty," my wife replied. "I float like a stone."

Ruarc joined us on the anchor deck, greeting me with a shake of the hand and bowing in respect to the queen. "Unless there is a change in the wind, we will make landfall tomorrow just after daybreak, your majesty."

"You have done brilliantly, Ruarc." Reilynn took one of his hands in hers and gave it a heartfelt squeeze of gratitude. "To get to Lesøsnø in less than three ten-days, given the unfavourable winds, is nothing less than remarkable. I will forever be grateful for this service, Captain."

Ruarc, improbably, blushed as crimson as a ruby and bowed. "You give me too much credit, your majesty. Were it not for Shadow Duke Aiden's cunning and ingenuity, we never would have sailed past Obsidian."

"Let us be fair, Captain," I began magnanimously, "The ruse would not have succeeded without all of us doing their part. Without you and your men we could not have hoped to prevail against that privateer."

"True," Ruarc conceded with a grateful nod. "And let us not forget our petite guardian deva, Sìne – the wickedest shot in the west! I do not think I will ever forget the beauty of how that flaming bolt fell through that cannon port *just so*."

Sìne giggled when Ruarc kissed the back of her hand. "It was lucky, nothing more."

"Lucky? The Warrior himself could not have done it better!" Ruarc scoffed. "I will be sad to say farewell to you tomorrow, despite having to navigate some choppy waters with you to begin with, Shadow Duke."

I embraced the shipmaster warmly, accepting his apology. "I will miss you and your ship, too. I never thought I would say this, Shadow Count Ruarc, but I think I might envy you for spending so much time with such open skies and open waters."

We shook hands again and as Ruarc turned to resume his place at the conning tower, he looked back over his shoulder at me slyly. "You will all sleep well tonight, I think. Since it is your last night aboard, I have made sure that it will be one you will not be able to remember."

His cryptic words made sense when we retired to the captain's quarters and I discovered two flagons of rum standing on the dining table. The small, hand-written note pinned beneath the base of one of the bottles read: *For your heroics with the privateer – from my personal supply. Ruarc*

A closer inspection showed that the bottles were not filled with a common sailor's rum, but were instead highly-prized flagons from the island of Tiva in the Jewels, easily worth five sovereigns apiece. The clear, colourless liquor was distilled from coconuts: sweet, fragrant and powerfully alcoholic. I had never personally developed a taste for rum. The preferred brain-number in the City Guard had tended to be grain alcohols such as whisky, vodka or akvavit. I sniffed the sweet vapours from the neck of one of the bottles, wondering whether I would be a convert before the night was done. As the light faded a midshipman brought us dinner and I sat down with Sìne and the queen for our final meal on the ship. Sìne divided up the roast pork belly and vegetables between our plates and I opened one of the bottles of rum to share between us. Sìne took a tiny, bird-like sip from her glass, closing her eyes as her face contorted with pleasure. She leant across the table and whispered into my ear "Not too much of that for me, love. It makes me really fucking horny."

Reilynn pretended not to hear and lifted her own glass to her lips, her eyes sparkling as she savoured the rich array of flavours from the sweet spirit. "Now that is very good indeed. Delicious!"

As usual for our evening repasts, the queen led our conversation deftly, miraculously finding topics that were neither banal nor incomprehensively intellectual. I wondered whether such an innate talent for small talk had been selectively bred into royal family lines over thousands of years. I would have struggled to make conservation for

an hour had it been my responsibility to marshal our chatter from one end of the evening to the other. I emptied the first flagon of rum, pouring each of us another large glass – our fifth of the night. Sìne's eyes were slightly glazed over, but her speech was still crystal clear. She whispered in my ear again, licking my earlobe sensually.
"My love, are you trying to get me drunk?"
Reilynn smiled, again pretending not to notice, with all of the diplomatic elegance you would expect from a queen. I resisted the temptation to touch my wife somewhere indecent and tried to move our discussion on to a new topic. "You must be looking forward to finally making landfall again in Lesøsnø. It must be what, nearly five years since you were here last?"
"Too long, Aiden, far too long," Reilynn lamented, supping another mouthful of rum from her glass. "The Crown Prince and I were first betrothed to each other ten years ago, when I was just thirteen. Two years after that we became lovers and the unification of our houses seemed assured – not just as a political marriage, but one based on love as well. Maeryn's coup four years ago ended that dream, until now."
"You and Sjur were lovers?" I spluttered, unable to contain my surprise. "I thought tha-"
"That what, princesses and princes live a celibate, virgin existence until they marry?" Reilynn interrupted, cackling in delight like a drunken pirate. "Far from it, Aiden – who do you think taught Sìne her tricks?"
"Reilynn, I didn't want him to know!" Sìne's face blushed crimson with mortification, appalled that her one secret had been revealed. Reilynn leant across the table and kissed my wife passionately on the mouth, by way of an apology.
"To know what?" I asked uncertainly.
"That just as you have been the joy and comfort of Sìne's nights, so has she been mine." Reilynn said, looking into her handmaiden's eyes as her fingertips stroking my wife's forearm affectionately. There was literally nothing I could say to that. Reilynn was the queen and answered to no-one but the gods of the Pantheon. We were both her subjects and by divine right she could treat both of us however she saw fit. The idea that my wife had been intimate with the queen provoked a pang of jealousy, but I would not have

been honest if I had said that it did not arouse me as well. "Nothing to say, Aiden – has a cat got your tongue? Or should I say a little mouse? I know Sìne is your favourite."
"She is – I love her." I said honestly, smiling as I raised her chin with my fingertips and planted a kiss on her lips. Her hands gripped my collar and she kissed back manically, leaving us both breathless. We looked into each other's eyes, and I did not question whether it was the effect of the rum or the effect of me expressing my love for her in front of the queen that made Sìne's gaze so adoring. "I would do anything for her."
"I am glad to hear that. It is exactly what I had hoped when we left Clongarvan." Reilynn smiled. "But before we reach Lesøsnø tomorrow, I have one last service that I would demand from you."
"Name it, my queen, and it will be done." I said, as earnestly as any oath I had sworn in my life. Sìne giggled and I wondered for a second whether she truly was drunk or whether she simply knew something I did not.
"I need you to... *service* me."
"Your majesty?" I stammered, not daring to dream that she meant what I thought she did.
Sìne drained all three of our glasses of the sweet coconut spirit, bit my earlobe and chuckled. "I warned you, Aiden... Rum makes me fucking horny – and not just me."
"It has been over four seasons since the Crown Prince and I shared a bed. I cannot meet Sjur as dry as the Nagyjik desert and as tight as the drawstrings on a miser's purse." Reilynn said, her eyes sparkling with mischief. "Come."
Unable to believe my eyes and ears, I let Sìne steer me into the bedchamber and watched in mute fascination as she let Reilynn disrobe her. My wife returned the favour, letting her lips nuzzle Reilynn's breasts as the queen stood by the bed, her eyes regarding me with the kind of predatory hunger a wolf might have for a young lamb. Sìne eased Reilynn's silk knickers over the curve of her broad hips, and the queen stepped her long legs out of them elegantly, rewarding her handmaiden with a kiss on the lips and a gentle caress over her chest. In her glorious, naked majesty, Reilynn was easily the most beautiful woman I had ever seen. I kept perfectly still as the queen joined my wife in stripping me, my breath quickening and arousal stirring as my pulse raced with excitement.

"You are a very handsome man, Aiden." Reilynn said with satisfaction, taking both of my hands and drawing me up onto the mattress along with her. We knelt upright, facing each other at arm's length, unable to take our eyes off each other.

"Thank you, your majesty." I replied and searched for a suitable compliment as Sìne joined me by my right side, her dark eyes wide with love and erotic anticipation.

"And, as Sìne has told me on many occasions, you are a very fuckable man." Reilynn licked her lips, revelling in her ability to shock me with her very un-regal choice of words. "Would you like me to fuck you, Aiden?"

"Very much, your majesty," was all I was able to stammer as Sìne wrapped an arm around my waist and placed a palm on the queen's hip. Sìne's lips brushed the back of my neck, hot and wet, making it clear that whatever happened in the next few hours, she would not be a passive bystander. The thought had me harder than the tempered steel of an oriental katana. "I have never wanted anything more."

"Good." Reilynn smiled, flashing her pristine white teeth. The blaze of passion in Reilynn's green eyes was both intimidating and alluring in equal measure as she leaned her body closer to mine. I could smell the sweet vapours from the rum on her breath and I was gripped by an overwhelming desire to kiss her. I waited for her consent, my heart pounding so hard I thought I might die. I cried out as Sìne took me into her eager mouth. "Then we should make an immediate start. Do not forget to enjoy yourself, Aiden. We will not be doing this again."

"Goddess be praised!" was all I could gasp before Reilynn took my head into her hands and she kissed me fully on the lips.

26 – Keri

In a city as large and populous as Lesøsnø, news travels fast and it is remarkably difficult to keep secrets. The arrival of a Ranger of Sylvan was a rare enough event to attract the notice of all the information brokers and busybodies that kept track of all the comings and goings through the city walls, so once I had completed my research at the Great Library and paid their scribes a stupendous amount of gold for copies of all the scrolls I wanted to keep at hand for future reference, it had been a simple matter to find out not just whether Cathal had arrived in the city, but also get a report of the company he kept, plus the details of where and with whom he was staying. A few discreet inquiries lubricated by more handfuls of gold sovereigns had revealed that Cathal and his host were not the only Cothraini rangers in the city. More had been arriving every day for the last week and rumour had it that Lord Commander Braden was gathering as many men and women from the Order of Sylvan to the city for an expeditionary force that he would lead south to retake Clongarvan and depose Maeryn. It was a fanciful conspiracy theory, but one that I thought was worth investigating. Though in truth, I had a much more pressing reason for visiting the Duke Ranger's residence in the city, and it had striped silver and black fur, blue eyes, four legs and a tail, and was shockingly adept at resisting having its mind read.

I was not expecting a warm welcome when I arrived at Lord Commander Braden's modestly-sized, but well-appointed, town house. The compound was tucked away discreetly between the East Gate stables and the Tower of the Earth Mother. A copse of mature oak trees provided an extra level of privacy around the estate's tall, granite walls. I declined to give my name to the ranger standing guard behind the wrought iron gate, which did not endear myself to her when I politely, but firmly requested to see Braden and Cathal. At first she refused point blank to acknowledge that the estate belonged to the exiled lord commander and feigned deafness when I favoured her with one of my least sincere smiles and repeated my request for an audience. This standoff continued for some three hours, and I gradually wore her patience down to the bone, asking the same pair of questions of her, once a minute.

First I would query, "May I see Lord Commander Braden please?" before adding "How about now?" precisely fifty seconds later, after the initial rebuttal. Then I would wait another fifty seconds before starting the process again.

I could sense from the exasperation radiating from her bitter chartreuse aura that she wanted to kill me by the time she threw up her hands in defeat and stomped off to the house, muttering under her breath "For fuck's sake. Wait there."

"What exactly do you think I have been doing?" I asked after her guilelessly. When she turned her head to look back at me the scowl on her otherwise lovely face could have curdled milk from ten paces. I was relieved to see that she was still unarmed when she returned to her post with Braden and Cathal following a few steps behind her.

I tasted the sweet, fuchsia panic in Cathal's aura and heard his heart race when he recognised me through the bars of the gate. His fingers flexed for a non-existent weapon at his belt. "What are *you* doing here?"

Braden turned to his protégé. "You know this woman?"

"Allow me to introduce myself, my lord." I interjected, before Cathal could speak. "I am Keri of Moonchion."

Braden's cheeks turned as white as his hair and he stabbed a finger at me, accusingly. "You dare to come here, after all you have done? You have some brass-neck on you, demon-fucker. Leave now, before I decide to remove that pretty head of yours from it."

"You think my head pretty?" I snickered in delight. "How sweet, I am flattered."

"What do you want? Why are you here, Keri?" Cathal demanded in a tremulous voice full of anger and fear.

"You have no reason to trust me, I know, but I have come to grant you a favour."

"I think you have done quite enough already, sorcerer." Braden snarled, signalling to the house for his sword and bow. "Be gone. I will not warn you again."

I ignored him and turned my attention to Cathal, sensing his curiosity. "The changeling – I can free her."

"What did you say?" Cathal raised his hand to stop Braden from doing anything irrevocable and he blinked incredulously.

"Your cat; I can release her from her torment. I know who she is and how to reverse the spell."

Braden scoffed loudly. "Do not believe her lies, Cathal. Let us be rid of her, permanently, if she is too dull to take a hint."

"Master, wait a moment," Cathal said, turning back to study my face, trying to judge my sincerity. "Why should I believe you? And why should I care, anyway?"

"You have no reason to believe me, none at all." I conceded. "I am not here to beg forgiveness for what I have done, nor am I here to make amends. As for the changeling, you should care very much. You see Cathal, Sapphire is your sister."

"Impossible." Cathal gasped, anguished at my evocation of his missing sibling. The ranger pointed at me with a quavering, accusatory finger, scoffing in disbelief. "No. Impossible."

"Well, if you say so... In that case, I will take my leave. Farewell, Cathal." I gave the ranger a resigned shrug, stepping back from the gate and beginning to turn away.

"No Keri, wait!" Cathal called out. I sensed his conflict. He did not believe me, but neither could he risk letting me leave if I was telling the truth. His love for his sister was too strong. "If you are lying to me, I will choke the life out of you with my bare hands."

"Give me five minutes with her, and you will see the truth for yourself. That is all I ask of you."

Braden frowned as he watched Cathal's resolve waver before his eyes. "Cathal my boy, this, this is not wise. It is like letting a fox into a chicken coop."

"Braden, I- I have to know. I *need* to know." Cathal said, tears of fear and hope wetting the corners of his eyes. The lord commander grimaced and shook his head. "Devorgilla, please open the gate."

I gave the shapely, brown-haired ranger a false smile of gratitude as she slid back the heavy iron bolt and pulled away the bars blocking my entry to the estate. The muscles in Braden's jaw clenched and he gave me a final warning. "One false move from you, wizard, and it will be your last."

I saw no need to reply and let Cathal lead me into the house, where Ailidh was seated on a cavernous leather armchair in the sitting room, quietly reading a manual on the flora and fauna of the archipelagos of the Reach and the Jewels. Silently, I rested my staff on the door frame. "Planning a fall-time holiday? The Jewels has the best beaches at this time of year."

Ailidh shrieked in shock and abject terror at the unexpected sound of my voice, dropping the book. She hurled herself at me before Cathal could intervene. I stood firm as she slapped me across the face with all of her strength, the blow from the heel of her hand cracking a cheekbone and causing the flesh of my cheek to instantly bruise black and blue and swell with inflammation. She continued to yell incoherently in fury and she tried to strike me again. I scooped Ailidh up in a bear hug, trapping her arms immobile at her sides and I hooked a leg around the back of her knees to stop her from kicking. I shushed her like a mother calming a distraught child as she struggled futilely to escape my embrace. Her soul felt harder, more mature. I could smell the change in her. She was no longer a maiden. Aroused by this unexpected revelation, I moved one hand to her hip and another to the back of her neck, holding her fast against me and I tightened the grip of my leg around the back of her knees like a snake constricting its prey. I kept my right cheek pressed against hers, so that she could not spit in my face. I held her until she stopped struggling and I gave out an almost inaudible sigh of pleasure. I smiled and whispered into the restored lobe of her right ear. "You took my advice. I am proud of you. Now calm yourself. I am not here to hurt you. But remember, my child – my first lesson is free, it is the second one that will cost you."

Ailidh shivered in horror and whimpered, but any thoughts of further violence vanished from her mind. I released her from my grip slowly, letting her look into my face, sensing her wonder as I suffused my cheek with wild aetheric energy, healing the damage from her blow while she watched in just a few seconds. Bemused by my sudden reappearance, she turned to her lover. "Cathal, what's going on?"

"I will explain later. Please Ailidh, fetch Sapphire and bring her. She is probably asleep in my room." Cathal said. He waited until Ailidh had gotten out of earshot before rounding on me angrily. "Do not touch her again, do you hear me?"

"Keep better control of your woman, and I will not need to." I retorted, testing the extent of his feelings for her.

"Mind your tone." Cathal hissed as the echo of soft footsteps approached from the corridor outside the lounge. I was intrigued by the ambiguity of his response. It was neither an acceptance nor a denial of a relationship, but I could sense that they had definitely laid together. I set the thought aside as Ailidh placed Sapphire's cage onto the cushion of the armchair and concentrated on the matter at hand. The silver tabby started hissing and yowling the moment she saw me, resisting Ailidh's calls to calm her. I knelt in front of the armchair and Sapphire shrank towards the back of her cage, ears flat and back arched.

I regarded the changeling with genuine pity and instead of trying to read its mind, opened my own to her. *I know what happened to you and who did it. I know who you are and how to free you. I am here to help you.*

The changeling hissed again, her body language still defensive, her tail thrashing with agitation. Remarkably, the changeling sent back a coherent psychic message. *I do not believe you want to help anyone other than yourself.*

I swallowed a cackle of delight, amused by her insight. *If in helping myself I help you, where is the harm?*

The changeling stood tall, lifting her head and twitched her whiskers in contempt. *With creatures like you, one never knows until it is too late.*

It seems unlikely we will ever be friends, but you have my respect, Gormlaith. I opened the door on her cage and patted the leather seat cushion between us. *Come.*

The changeling hesitated for a moment before treading forward warily, still fearing that I was trying to trick her. When she was clear of her travelling cage, I set it down on the floor and removed her collar, placing it on the armrest of the chair. "You will not need this anymore."

"Cathal, what's all this about? I can't believe you let her near the house." Ailidh protested, still clueless as to why I was here.

I stood to fetch my staff and explained. "I came across a strange account of a changeling when I was researching Nevanthi's Seventh Prophecy in the Great Library. The details were vague, as most prophecies are, but from the clues I was able to deduce who was responsible for their transformation, the changeling's true identity and most importantly, the key capable of unlocking their prison."

I sat cross-legged back down on the floor in front of the armchair and pricked the end of my left index finger using one of the sharp, twisted aetherium barbs on the end of my staff. I let a few drops of my blood pool on the pad of my fingertip and proffered it to the changeling. *Drink.*

Distrust soured her aura, but the cat lowered its head, her rough, barbed tongue lapping away the crimson droplets, ingesting the regenerative aetheric energy I had infused into it. I touched the back of her neck with my other hand and spoke a Word of Power. Using the vague clues embedded in the text of Nevanthi's seventh prophecy, I had deduced which reagent and Word would undo the changeling's polymorph spell. The transformation was instantaneous. Cathal's sister fell into my arms, naked as a baby, her weight almost knocking me to the floor. Ailidh cried out in shock as I lifted Gormlaith back into the seat behind her and let her rest against the warm, welcoming leather. I cupped Gormlaith's face under the chin and raised her head, checking that the spell had fully undone the effects of the polymorph. Cathal took the woollen shift from the backrest of the divan in the sitting room and used it to cover his sister's modesty, a look of unbound joy written across his face. "Gormlaith? It is actually you! I cannot believe my eyes!"

The former changeling sucked in a huge lungful of air and opened her eyes with a loud gasp, still reeling from the shock of the returning to her true form. The sapphire blue irises flickered as she adjusted to the light and she looked up at me, her aura honey sweet with profound gratitude. The chronomancer reached out for my wrist, clasping it weakly and whispered "Thank you."

"I have intruded upon you long enough. I will leave you to get reacquainted in peace." I stood and left the estate without another word, ignoring Cathal's pleas for me to stop. I knew that it was better to let him eventually come to me and I honestly did not want to be a distraction to their reunion.

It was some six days later when Gormlaith found me in the dining room of The Star and Sextant tavern, while I was enjoying a hearty lunch of stewed venison and a carafe of red wine. Without being invited, she took the seat opposite me at my table. The diviner was dressed in a simple white linen wizard's robe fastened by a sash of golden silk and she wore the gemstone from her former collar around her neck on a chain of silver. The sapphire jewel failed to match the clarity of her eyes, which were regarding me coolly. She kept a hand on the shaft of her mage staff to stop it falling away from where it rested against the curved edge of the table. It had been freshly carved from jet-black ebony and I noted with amusement that the figurehead was distinctly feline. Its triangular, prism-shaped ears swivelled back and forth expressively. I nodded a greeting to her politely and took a sip of wine. "Gormlaith of Monagealy, I hope you are well?"

"I am, thanks to you, Keri of Moonchion." Gormlaith replied, returning my formal greeting courteously. Her voice had a surprisingly dusky, breathily sensual tone that matched her lightly tanned skin, not unlike the women I had known from the Reach. It was not hard to deduce that she and Cathal did not share the same mother and that their common genetic inheritance was paternal. "Why did you do it?"

"Because I could." I replied enigmatically, not knowing for certain whether she was referring to her restoration to humanity or the horrors I had inflicted upon her brother and Ailidh. Regardless, the answer was true for each case. I conjured a glass, filling it with wine from my carafe and slid it across the table towards her.

Gormlaith accepted it with half a smile and raised it to her lips to get a taste. "Bray Crown Estate; you have fine taste in wine, at least. The last thing I would expect from a demon-loving witch."

I laughed, almost spilling the scarlet fluid from my own glass. "Are you trying to provoke me, Gormlaith? I have killed for lesser slights than that in the past. Since it is you I will let it pass, but only this once. I doubt that you would want to wear the pelt of a cat again."

"Cathal said that I should not seek you out, but I had to know. Why did you do it? What do you have to gain by freeing me?"

"Permit me to answer a question with a question: why did the Arch Mage Karryghan imprison you in the first place?" I felt a tingle of trepidation from Gormlaith's aura and she drank half of her glass of wine in a single swallow, as if to bolster her courage. "Because he could."

"No need to be flippant, it is the crux of this matter."

"It happened three months after Maeryn's coup. I had spent the previous two years deep in preparation for my Master Trials and not paid any attention to the political intrigues gripping the palace. I had not been overly concerned by the deposing of the Royal Family. Provided it did not interfere with my research or advancement within the Guild, I cared little. It was only when the more sordid details of the purge reached my ears via my friends within the Tower that I began to piece together a broader picture, linking the current events with some of the lesser-known prophecies I had been researching."

"The seventh prophecy of the Seer Nevanthi." I said, using my fork to spear one of the last remaining cubes of deer meat from my bowl of stew. I placed the warm chunk of venison in my mouth and chewed thoughtfully, listening with my full attention as Gormlaith continued.

"Indeed. It has long been ignored for its apparent detachment in time from the rest of her predictions and its dreadful phraseology. Many chronomancers consider it to be an aberration compared to the rest of her work. Nevanthi often went to great lengths to divine the precise names, places and times for the events she wrote about. But the seventh prophecy is an exception, more akin to the work of a charlatan medium than a scholastic diviner. It is only the source that lends it any credibility at all.

"But the parallels were clear in my mind, once I was made aware of all the atrocities that had been committed during Maeryn's coup and the subsequent purge. The manifestation of a planar nexus is always accompanied by a time of strife and turmoil upon the realm in which it appears - its power is a prize worth beyond measure in gold. Had I not been distracted by my concern for Cathal's safety in the wake of the disbanding of the rangers, I might have realised that I was the one destined to become the changeling." Gormlaith finished her glass of wine with a shudder of terror. I refilled it to the brim and motioned for her to continue. "Instead, I was too hasty. I took my concerns directly to Karryghan in his private chambers, not realising that he was the architect of the coup. He transformed me on the spot, but not before laying clear his own plans for the Nexus. He could not risk slaying me outright, not within the Tower, but it was convenient for me to go missing, tormented by the knowledge of what he intended to do, but being incapable of doing anything to stop him."

"So you sought out your brother."

"Yes. With my strength in the Art and our shared blood, I was able to find him using instinct alone. The desperation and longing for him I felt after my transfiguration was strong enough to allow me divine that he had survived the purge. And the rest I believe you know." Gormlaith's shoulders quivered and she gulped down another large mouthful of wine, self-consciously stroking the dark blue jewel resting in the clavicle of her neck. "I have answered your question. Now answer mine. Why did you free me?"

"The appearance of a planar nexus is the greatest peril this world has known for ten thousand generations. Magicians and celestial beings from all of the cosmos will flock to its power like thirsty vampire bats upon a herd of cattle if it still remains on Dachaigh when the planes align on the winter solstice. The Nexus must be found before that happens and be kept away from those with malign intentions, like Karryghan."

Gormlaith's glorious blue eyes narrowed with mistrust and she regarded me like a deer watching a wolf through the massed branches of a bracken patch. "Beware, Keri. If I have one superlative talent as a diviner, it is in the knowing when I am being lied to, or when I am not being told the whole of the truth."

"Our goals are aligned, suspicious one." I chided her gently, whilst simultaneously and imperceptibly bolstering my psychic defences, letting Gormlaith only see in my mind what I wanted her to see. "You wish to see Karryghan be denied control of the Nexus, and rightly so. It is far too dangerous to be left in the hands of a mortal, especially one as ambitious as him. And neither of us wants to see Dachaigh laid to waste by a war between celestials and planewalkers."

"You speak the truth, Keri, but only in part." Gormlaith emptied her glass and stood, her aura tasting a pale, umami grey with disappointment. "Will you not tell me the whole of it?"

"Not yet."

Gormlaith sucked air through her teeth in exasperation. "You make it hard for others to place their faith in you, Keri of Moonchion."

I chuckled and sat back in my chair, swirling the last dregs of wine around my glass, watching the viscous red droplets cling to the side of the crystal goblet before their weight dragged them down into a shallow pool above the thick, colourless stem. "Ultimately, I find it makes life easier if one does not allow the expectations others have of you to fly too high."

"Little wonder then, that you choose to live your life alone." Gormlaith said, with a resigned sense of pity.

"Never have I ever crossed a bridge that I have been unwilling to burn." I admitted with a cynical smirk.

Gormlaith remained silent for a moment, before giving me a nod of grudging respect. "Will you be staying in the city much longer?"

"Another ten-day, perhaps two, should I find sufficient material in the Grand Library to keep me entertained."

"As untrustworthy as you are, I am convinced that you may well prove to be an ally in our future endeavours. I agree that our goals overlap, but I will need to persuade Cathal of that before I can say any more."

"You will be able to find me either here, or at the Grand Library for the time being. And I will send word to you at Lord Commander Braden's estate the day before I leave the city."

"Thank you, Keri." Gormlaith smiled, leaning down to touch the back of my hand in gratitude. Her palm was soft, warm and dry. "If we do not meet again, know that despite the crime you committed against my brother in the Western Weald, I am unable to bear an irrevocable ill will against you. I shall always be grateful to you that my mind and body is able to visualise and articulate thoughts as complicated as these once again."

"We will meet again, I am certain of it." I rose from my seat and crossed the breadth of the table to give her a hug of heartfelt affection. "And you are welcome. You will know by now that I am a woman of few virtues, but once I deduced the truth behind your treatment at the hands of Karryghan, I could not let such an injustice stand."

"You tell such sweet lies." Gormlaith told me sadly. "But I will send for you if Cathal and Braden agree with me that we cannot achieve our goals without your help."

I embraced the young diviner again and kissed her goodbye twice on both cheeks. "Farewell, Gormlaith of Monagealy. May the Lady always smile down upon you and may the Mystic forever empower your spells."

Gormlaith regarded me with a frown of deep contemplation before wrapping her arms around my shoulders and kissing me once delicately on the forehead. "I would grant you the same benediction, but I know that you pray to very different gods than I do. Goodbye for now, Keri of Moonchion."

27 - Gormlaith

We had been lodging with Braden at his compound in the city for two weeks and I was still getting used to walking on two legs rather than four. I had lost all the natural agility I had inherited from my transformation into a cat as well much of the acuity I had gotten used to from my sense of smell and hearing. Back in my own body once again, I felt huge and clumsy, but I was happy to regain the full use of my sense of vision. One of the most disconcerting effects of being transformed was that I had lost much of my colour and depth perception. It had taken me nearly a year to get used to my new view of the world after Karryghan had polymorphed me and now that I had been restored to my true self, I hoped that the readjustment period this time would be much shorter. I compensated for my reduced dexterity by keeping my movements slow and Cathal had observed that it seemed like time did not run quite so fast for me when I walked. I still could not quite believe the mirror when I checked my reflection following my evening ablutions. I stepped out of the bath, droplets of warm water infused with fragrant lavender oil clinging to my skin. I looked at my reflection, pleased to see that I had reclaimed the full sleekness of my form. I turned side on to the mirror and ran my hands over my smooth skin, sweeping away the skein of water cooling my flesh. I dried myself with a thickly woven cotton towel and slipped into a nightshirt made of sky blue linen cloth. It was a pleasure to sleep in a proper bed once again, but I had found that I could not let the night take me unless I curled up into a protective ball, my limbs tucked tightly to my chest, as if I were still a cat. At least tonight my sleep was mercifully untroubled by dreams. Keri's reversal of Karryghan's spell had brought back memories I had tried hard to bury. In the days since my restoration, I awoke midway through the night more often than not, screaming from visions of being polymorphed by the Arch Mage back in his chambers at the Tower of the Aether in Clongarvan. The trauma of my transformation into Sapphire still ran deep. The next morning I dressed in the simple wizard's robe I had worn when I met with Keri in The Star and Sextant. I joined my brother, Ailidh and Braden in the dining room for a hearty cooked breakfast. My stomach was delighted to get reacquainted with a varied diet of foodstuffs fit for humans, rather than scraps of raw meat. As we cleared our plates, I glanced over the table at Ailidh. "How would you like a trip to the market, Ailidh? I need some new clothes. No offence to you, lord Braden, but my nethers prefer the feel of silk or satin to that of hemp or linen."

Cathal hid his amusement behind his hand, the skin around his eyes creasing as he tried to contain his laughter. Braden chuckled to show that he was not upset. "Rangers are made of sterner stuff than wizards, it seems." Ailidh seemed taken aback by the frankness of my admission for a preference of luxury fabrics when it came to my underwear, but her eyes lit up at the prospect of going shopping and I could taste cloying, sweet vanilla excitement in her aura. By far the best thing about being back in my own body once again was the full restoration of my aetheric affinity and abilities with the Art. "I'd love to see the Merchant's Quarter."

"Gormlaith will teach you how to haggle properly, no doubt." Cathal said, handing me his coin purse without hesitation and before I needed to ask. "Try not to buy everything you see, we need to save some money for contingencies."

"Thank you, brother." I opened the drawstrings of the purse and peered inside. Inside were two dozen gold sovereigns and a good handful of silver shillings. It was enough to outfit both myself and Ailidh three times over and still have more than half of our gold to spare, I reckoned. I returned to my room to fetch a satchel, slinging it over my shoulder and placing the purse securely inside, before collecting my staff and knocking on the door to Ailidh's chamber. "Ailidh, are you ready?"

"Just a moment," she said, nudging open the door to invite me inside. Ailidh rummaged through her pack and pulled out her father's coin sack, dipping her strong, slender fingers inside to retrieve half a dozen gold sovereigns. She handed them to me, urging me to add them to our shopping budget. "I've never owned any fancy clothes. Would you help me choose something? You can buy something for yourself as well."

"It would be my pleasure." I told her, giving her left cheek a kiss. Ailidh gave me a hug of appreciation and gave out an adorably tiny, high-pitched squeal of excitement.

It was a fine autumn day, the sky blazing blue with sunshine as Rionnag climbed towards its zenith in the heavens. A gentle breeze wafted in from the coast, setting the leaves of the trees rustling as we walked south from Braden's estate through the Park of the Earth Mother to the city's main boulevard. The base of my staff crunched on the tightly packed gravel as we made our way westwards past the Shrine of the Pantheon and the university campus, turning south before we reached the ten towers that dominated the plaza overlooking the Abyss. The finest fabrics in the world could be found in the Market of the Lady, which adjoined the city port's warehouse quarter. I had a personal preference for the featherlight, warming silks from Kyotka and exquisitely glossy cotton-based satins from the Jewels. Textile importers frequently hired couturiers from across the Western Triad to run their own in-house boutiques and the most famous, highly respected – and therefore most expensive – designer in Lesøsnø was called Célestine, a Sundgovian woman who had moved to Lesøsnø from Masevaux on the Vine Coast, a town world-famous for its hot, humid summer nights, outrageous fashions and flexible morals. After spending four years trapped in fur and then having the good fortune to be freed from my curse in the same city as her, I was not going to buy clothes from anyone else. I wanted to wear something that would make me feel human again and, more importantly, feel like a woman again.

Célestine was attentive without being overbearing, letting us browse her sensual creations without interruption. The Sundgovian, like most women from her country, was tall and lean, wearing her greying hair simply in a shoulder-length bob. The quality of her gown spoke for her, instead of a practised sales pitch. It was impeccably stitched, hugging her svelte figure perfectly and the woven brocade detail drew your eye to the subtle curves of her femininity without making you feel like you were leering. She had a discreet, understated beauty and elegance, matched by the mellifluousness of her accent. As Ailidh looked around her workshop she could hardly keep her jaw off the floor. It was unlikely that she had ever seen garments of this quality during her sheltered upbringing. Célestine used a tape to measure us at the shoulder, bust, waist, the hip and down the inside of our legs before personally selecting a range of pre-made garments in our size, including dresses, gowns, robes, jackets and, critically, underwear.

Ailidh and I shared a private dressing room and I felt no self-consciousness in baring myself before her. After all, I had sat on her lap as a cat, where her fingers had caressed me to edge of delirium. After a moment of reflection, she saw how at ease I was with her and Ailidh forgot her inhibitions. We assisted each other in choosing and trying on a range of bras, bustiers and knickers. I sighed with satisfaction as I settled my hips into a girdle of blood red silk and pulled an impossibly soft and narrow string up to the top of my thighs. I adjusted the placement of the whalebone cups of the matching corset so that they pushed my tits up and together to form a deep, dark crevasse of cleavage. I loved the feel of the fabric and when I checked my reflection in the full-length mirror, the contrast between the colour of the silk and the tone of my skin made my eyes glister in delight.

"You're so beautiful, Gormlaith." Ailidh said. "I wish I was as tall and tanned as you. Put me out in the sun for too long and I turn as pink as a boiled lobster."

I turned my head toward her and appraised Ailidh honestly. With her magnificent bust held firm by a skin-tight bra of emerald green satin and her sex hidden behind a matching frill of fabric that sat high on her waist, exposing her sharp hip bones, I thought she was one of the most stunning creatures I had ever seen. I was glad that my olive-toned skin hid the flush of arousal on my cheeks. I could not have cared less about the scar she hid behind her long blonde fringe. I felt the urge to pull her to the floor and see what she tasted like. Instead I embraced her and gave her a delicate kiss on her unblemished cheek. I took her into my arms, letting the warm, toned flesh of our bellies touch.

"You look incredible, Ailidh. If I were Cathal and saw you wearing that, I would marry you on the spot."

Ailidh blushed and kissed me briefly on the lips. I crushed my desire to respond as I truly wanted to, knowing it would only complicate matters. Ailidh loved my brother. She barely knew the real me. "That's the nicest thing anyone's ever said to me. Gormlaith, will you be my sister? I always wanted one. It was so hard growing up alone, especially after my accident."

"Ailidh, you *are* my sister." I brushed aside her fringe and kissed her scar. "I felt it from the moment I saw you."

"You don't know how happy that makes me." Ailidh said, tears forming in the corner of her eyes. I kissed them away, tasting salt, as she hugged me tightly. My heart raced as I felt the heat from her chest against mine. I had to let go before I was tempted to do something irreversibly foolish. I turned my attention back to the racks of clothing Célestine had provided for us and we helped each other choose more underwear to try on, delicately folding and setting aside our current outfits for purchase. Ailidh picked out two nightdresses while I opted for a matching set of camisole and knickers in black and crimson lace that clung to me as if it were a second skin and a sheer cerulean silk nightgown that flowed from my shoulders to my ankles like a wave washing over a rock on the beach.

With the question of undergarments and nightwear settled, I urged Ailidh to pick out a gorgeous evening dress made from turquoise-coloured silk I thought would suit her. It hung from thin shoulder straps and the floral patterns stitched in gold thread just beneath the bust pulled the fabric in at the waist, curving over her hips and thighs before flaring back out like the petals of a lily below the knee. I settled the seams correctly along the lines of her legs and gasped. "That is stunning, and a bargain for just three sovereigns."

"I've never spent so much money before. Not on anything, never mind a dress." Ailidh looked at her reflection seemingly shocked by how perfectly the dress flattered and enhanced her figure.

"Do not even think of backing out now. We are buying it." I told her sternly. I felt envious that I did not have the same kind of curves to wear a similar cut myself, but just being able to look at Ailidh wear it was compensation in itself. "Ask Célestine to find you matching shoes and you can wear it home."

For myself I picked a heavy robe of thick, wine red silk more suitable for the working garb of a wizard. The chest piece was embroidered with a posy of rose petals, flecked with razor-thin fragments of obsidian rock mounted into the stitching. The gown clung, shimmering, to my figure and I felt fully human for the first time since my transformation. Four sovereigns seemed like a fair price to pay to recapture my sense of self and sensuality. Célestine brought me a pair of thick-soled, knee-length riding boots made from supple leather that had been dyed a deep, stygian crimson. The heels gave me an extra two and a half inches of height and ensured that I would not trample upon the hem of the robe as I walked. The couturier appraised me with her cool, pale green eyes and nodded, satisfied that I did her work justice. "You look ravishing, my lady."

I settled our bill without haggling – it would have been an insult to the quality of Célestine's garments - and folded our old clothes back into my satchel. Ailidh trod back and forth in the dressing room experimentally in her pair of turquoise suede demi-boots, slowly putting one foot before the other. They too had a heel tall enough to prevent her from stumbling on the hem of her dress, but it was clear that Ailidh was only used to wearing flat-soled shoes. "I feel like I'm learning to walk again for the first time."

"You get used to it." I said and offered her my elbow. Ailidh hooked her arm through mine and we walked back to Braden's compound, hip to hip. We attracted scores of admiring glances along the way, making me feel like one of the most desirable women in the city, but any unwelcome attention was discouraged by my wizard staff. Even the most drunken, lecherous sailor on shore-leave has the common sense required to resist propositioning a wizard without their explicit invitation and consent.

My brother's former apprentice Creighton was standing on guard duty in the mid-afternoon sun when we arrived back at Braden's estate and he stared at us with wide eyes and flushed cheeks when he opened the gate for us, muttering under his breath. "By the Goddess..."

I found Cathal seated with Braden in the lord commander's office, drawing up a list of supplies to be purchased for the coming expedition. Even Braden did a double take when he saw me in my new outfit. I tossed the coin purse back to Cathal and he raised a silent eyebrow as he felt its weight. Clearly the shopping expedition had not cost nearly as much as he had anticipated. "Are you not even going to ask how much I spent?"

"No," Cathal shook his head with a half-smirk of contained mirth. "You seem happy, sister. That alone makes it worth every copper. And you look fabulous."

"Just wait until you see Ailidh." I replied, as much in warning as to pique his curiosity.

My newly adopted sister was reading in the lounge and I made a pot of tea for us to share as the afternoon gave way for the evening. She had taken off her new shoes, but spent as much time stroking the fabric of her new dress as she did reading from her book. I noticed it was a tome on the history of Fossfjall. She thanked me with a caress on the back of my hand when placed a mug of tea on the side table next to her chair. I took a place on the couch and watched her read in silence until Ailidh realised that I had not taken a book of my own. "What's wrong, sister?"

"Nothing, I just had an idea. Your father's tarot deck, may I see it, please?"

"See it? You can have it. It's of no use to me." Ailidh put the thin leather strap of a bookmark in her tome to keep her place, set the book down on the cushion of her chair and went to her room to retrieve the tarot deck. She returned a few moments later with a tan leather box embossed with runes of real silver. The markings were tarnished with age and it was obvious that the cards had not been used in many years. Ailidh set the card case down on the low table in front of the couch. "Here you are. Cathal recognised what it was, but didn't know how to open it. Not that it matters, since neither of us can read the cards anyway."

"A tarot case is not difficult to open. You just need to know a little of the ancient nagyjik tongue." I explained, tapping three of the runes in sequence, speaking the names of the letters as I touched them. "A-va-ta. Open."

The lid of the box detached from the tray underneath and I separated the two halves to retrieve the cards inside, which were protectively wrapped in a purple satin bag. I could sense the impatience of the cards as I removed them from their pouch and spread them face up across the table. They had lain idle for too long and were anxious to be used once more. Ailidh admired the artwork but seemed reluctant to touch or pick up any of the cards. I wondered if she was able to sense the psychic ripples from the cards as they practically begged to be used. "They're gorgeous. Was it difficult to learn how to read them?"

"Not as difficult as you might think. The Tarot of the Planes does most of the work. The cards are alive in a way. They are a method of communicating with the watchers on the psychic plane. They exist outside of what we would call linear time. For them everything that has ever happened or will ever happen has already occurred. So in a manner of speaking, reading the tarot is not divination. It is reportage, from the point of view of the watchers."

"So you can find out about anything? Any event, anywhere, any when?"

"Within reason, yes," I nodded, restacking the cards into a single pile. "Though sometimes the watchers will choose not to give an answer, or give an ambiguous one. The skill of the diviner is in interpreting the meaning of the card given the context of the question and the querent asking it."

"What do you want to use them for?"

"We could save ourselves a lot of time in the Great Library if I conduct a séance first to narrow down what we need to look for regarding the situation we find ourselves in. After dinner tonight, we should carry out a divination with Cathal and Braden." I placed the cards back into their pouch and box, reassuring them psychically that they would be needed again before midnight. "I already know the major driver behind events – the manifestation of an aetheric nexus coinciding with the alignment of the planes this winter solstice – but much still remains unknown to us: Karryghan's motivation for the kidnap of your father; whether your father still lives; whether it is possible to bring Karryghan and Maeryn to justice for the coup and the purge; the form and location of the Nexus itself."

"Braden said it is unlikely father still lives." Ailidh said, her voice cracking slightly with grief.

"Unlikely does not mean impossible. But if Eoghan is truly dead, better that we know before reaching Clongarvan. It fundamentally changes the objectives of our expedition."

"If my father cannot be saved, then he must be revenged." Ailidh said with an ugly tone that did not suit her.

"Be careful what you wish for, Ailidh," I cautioned her. "Karryghan is too powerful to challenge directly. The last time I confronted him I came away with fur and a tail. I would surely not survive another encounter without help and the only wizard I know that might possibly be able to best the Arch Mage in battle is no friend of ours."

"Keri." Ailidh spat out the name, as if it was a mouthful of rancid milk.

"Yes. Maeryn, on the other hand, is another matter entirely. He must be removed from the throne. If we could find some way to infiltrate the royal palace, he could be made to answer for his crimes."

"But if Karryghan was the architect of the coup, what would stop him from simply arranging another?"

I paused for a moment, considering the question. "That, as an acquaintance of ours might say, is a bridge we can burn after we have crossed it."

At this point Cathal entered the room, taking a break from planning with Braden. His mouth fell open when he saw Ailidh in her new dress. "Goddess's tits, I should have encouraged you to spend more."

Ailidh stood, gave him a twirl and stepped across the room to let him see her in motion and take him into her arms. She kissed my brother tentatively on the mouth and asked "D'you like it?"

"Like it? You look like you have fallen from the heavens." Cathal said, appraising her once more from arm's length. I saw a shiver of arousal run down his body and I thought to myself, *for the love of the Empress, tell her what you feel!* Instead he turned to me, noticing the box of tarot cards on the table. "What are you two up to? Telling fortunes?"

"No, Ailidh and I were talking about our objectives once we reach Clongarvan. A séance would clarify matters immensely. Do you think Braden would participate in one after dinner tonight?"

"I imagine so, but I will have to ask. Regardless, we have planned enough for one day. I am going to assist in the kitchen. I will fetch you when the evening meal is ready." Cathal said, running his eyes up and down Ailidh's figure once again, an almost imperceptible tremor quivering his shoulders before he retreated out of the lounge.

"What did Cathal mean, 'telling fortunes'? You can use the tarot to do that?" Ailidh asked.

"You can," I replied hesitantly. "But I do not recommend it. I think it is better if you do not know some things in advance."

"Things like what?"

"Whether you will marry or have children, how you will die, or what age you will be. It stops you from living in the moment."

"I think I'd rather know." Ailidh said frowning, obviously preoccupied by Cathal's reluctance to reciprocate her love for him.

"Trust me, sister. When people have asked me to tell their fortunes in the past, no good has ever come of it." I told Ailidh as I gave her a supportive hug.

"I do trust you, Gormlaith. I'm so glad to have you." Ailidh's arms clutched me to her tightly, making my pulse race, though I was careful not to let my arousal show.

We took our seats again and finished our tea, reading in silence until Cathal came to collect us for dinner. It was easy to tell that Cathal, rather than Braden, had led the preparations for the night's repast: he was by far the better cook. The game stew he had prepared had been slow-cooked for hours with wild boar, venison, diced bacon, red wine and root vegetables, which he served with fondant potatoes that would not have looked out of place on the menu of a restaurant in Lesøsnø's artisan's quarter. I had not eaten this well even in the Tower of the Aether in Clongarvan and told him so. "If you ever wish to move to the city, brother, rest assured that you would make a fortune as the head chef of a gourmet restaurant. The Wizard's Guild would hire you in a heartbeat."

"She's not wrong," Ailidh agreed, resisting the temptation to lick her plate, instead scouring the last drops of sauce away from the stoneware with a large chunk of bread.

Braden dismissed the other rangers once they had finished eating and I retrieved the tarot box from the lounge, sitting at Braden's left hand side, near the head of the table. Cathal cleared the table of everything other than our wine goblets and refreshed the carafe with another bottle of red wine before taking his seat opposite me at Braden's right. Ailidh sat next to me on my left and she squeezed the back of my hand reassuringly as I prepared the cards. Unlike the séances carried out by charlatan mystics and fake clairvoyants, a true divination did not require any rituals or ceremony. Just a flat, clean surface and having clarity of mind and purpose was enough. The lord commander spoke first. "I have not attended many diviner's readings in the past, Gormlaith. Is there anything in particular you want us to do?"

"Only try to avoid distractions and focus very clearly on the questions you have regarding our mission and objectives in Clongarvan. The Tarot will do the rest." I advised, handing the deck to Ailidh. "Concentrate on your father, Ailidh. There is no need to shuffle the deck. Just ask the tarot what you want to know."

Ailidh closed her eyes and the hint of a smile curved at the edges of her lips as her thoughts recalled her father and all the memories of his devoted, paternal love for her. "I have my question."

"Give me the deck, please." I retrieved the cards from Ailidh and placed them face down on the table before me. "What is the exact phrasing of your question?"

"Is my father Eoghan dead or alive?"

I nodded in approval, silently confirming that the way the question had been worded would yield a clear answer. I took the top three cards from the deck and placed them face down in an equilateral triangle, representing the Northern Triad, the constellation that pointed towards the pole star, the principle reference point for sailors and navigators across the entire northern hemisphere of Dachaigh. I turned over the card at the apex of the triangle first, explaining the role of each card in relation to the question as I carried out my divination. The first card was the eighth major arcana card, The Mystic. "Card number one represents the object of the seeker's question – here The Mystic clearly represents Eoghan. He was a Master Diviner and wizard after all."

As I spoke, the painted image of a white-haired, bearded sage dressed in purple robes and seated at a desk in a library dissolved before my eyes, seemingly melting from the card and reforming inverted, with the scrolls that had littered the desk at the bottom of the image now appearing at the top. My eyes widened and my jaw dropped open in astonishment. "What in the five hells?"

"Gormlaith, what is wrong?" my brother asked, the concern clear in his voice.

"This, this simply should not be possible." I said, picking up the card and turning it over three times to confirm that the image was truly reversed compared to the reference pattern on the back of the cards. I glanced around at my companions, almost lost for words. "Major arcana cards in the tarot are not permitted to present as being reversed. But then neither is the tarot ever mistaken. I know of no other account of a reversed major arcana card in the recorded history of divination, ever. This is unprecedented. The reversal of the card must represent Eoghan's abandonment of magic."

A wave of psychic pressure from the tarot deck told me that my supposition was correct, but also that it was not the first time this deck had been forced to reverse a major arcana card. I blinked again in utter astonishment and turned over the second card. "The second card represents outside factors that may have an influence on the question. Zero: The Aether."

As soon as I laid the card down on the table the image began to invert again, the painted nebula swirling chaotically and the maiden of The Aether, wearing a crown of laurel leaves in her long raven-black hair tumbling head over heels. I snatched my hand back from the card, whispering to myself. "What *is* this?"

I flinched when Ailidh put her hand on my arm. "Could there be something wrong with the cards?"

I stared mutely into her mismatched eyes for a moment and shook my head. "No, no. You do not understand. It is literally impossible for the Tarot to be mistaken. To have one reversed major arcana card in a spread is freakish. To have *two* is... unconscionable. The watchers are infallible. This is beyond my comprehension."

"But what does it mean?" Braden interjected, looking disturbed that the séance appeared to have gone awry so quickly.

"It can only be related to the coming appearance of the planar nexus. There can be no doubt that Eoghan abandoned his position within the Guild of the Art after discovering something about the manifestation of the Nexus at the planar alignment this winter solstice. As to what he found out, it is impossible to know, but the timing cannot be coincidental – according to the account in his letter to you Ailidh, Eoghan abandoned his office the day after he met your mother."

"What could induce a mage to break their vows of service to the Guild?" Cathal asked, resting his chin in his hand. "What could have possibly happened that day?"

"Perhaps he simply fell in love and could not leave her." Ailidh ventured, recalling the account Eoghan had written in his farewell letter.

I turned to Ailidh and kissed her on the forehead, adoring her for her naivety. "Bless you, Ailidh. If that were the case he simply would have married her and taken her to live as his wife at the Tower of the Aether. No, I find it impossible to believe the answer could be that simple."

Braden bristled irritably and motioned for me to continue the reading. "The Nexus might be a concern for the Arch Mage Karryghan, but it is of no relevance to us in our aim of retaking Clongarvan and the throne from the usurper."

"Apologies, lord Braden." I bowed my head and turned over the third and final card in the spread. Like the previous two cards, it was also a major arcana card, but this one showed no sign of reversing after I left it resting on the table without comment for over a minute. Cathal covered his eyes and turned his head away from the table, as did his former master. My brother was no expert on the tarot, but this card needed little in the way divinatory prowess to interpret. Only Ailidh looked at me expectantly as I swallowed, announcing the name of the card. "The outcome: number thirteen, The Executioner."

Ailidh's eyes flickered between the table and my face, glowing expectantly in the lamp light for good news. I pitied her ignorance for a moment before putting myself in her place and thinking about how I would feel if our roles had been reversed. I pulled my sister to me and wept into her long blonde hair, whispering into her ear. "I am so sorry, Eoghan is dead."

Despite Braden's pre-emptive warning for Ailidh to lower her expectations when we had arrived in the city, she deflated like a spinnaker deprived of a tailwind, the confirmation of her surrogate father's death utterly devastating her. We cried into each other's hair as the lord commander and my brother shifted uncomfortably in their seats, taking refuge in their wine glasses, rather than in words or gestures. Eventually Ailidh mastered her grief, wiping her eyes clear and emptying her goblet of wine. Cathal refilled it to the brim as soon as its base came to rest upon the oaken dining table. She immediately took it off the table again and emptied half of it in a single, long swallow. Ailidh hand trembled as she set her glass back down on the table and croaked weakly, "Oh, daddy."

I re-gathered the cards into the deck and handed them to Braden, comforting Ailidh by holding one of her shoulders as I instructed Braden, "Focus for a moment and think upon what you want to achieve upon your return to Clongarvan. When you are ready, place the deck onto the table and summarise any questions you would like the tarot to answer."

As the Lord Commander of the Rangers closed his eyes and pondered the phrasing of his questions, I caressed the back of Ailidh's neck, drawing her scarred cheek down onto my shoulder, and whispered an oath to her. "Justice will be done, my sister, I promise. We will make Karryghan pay, I swear it."

"I am done." Braden declared a few moments later. He placed the tarot deck onto the table and gave me an affirmative nod to continue my divination.

"Tell me what you asked please, lord commander."

"My exact words were: is it possible for us to remove Maeryn and Karryghan from power."

With Braden's query clear in my mind, I began to retrieve and place cards. For a less exact question like this, a more detailed spread would be needed. I chose the Sword of the Heavens spread, laying out ten cards face down before me on the table from left to right, the first two cards to represent the handle, the third and fourth cards placed above and below the second to represent the crossguard. The remaining six cards formed the blade. I explained the significance of each card's placement in the layout as I began to turn cards over and started my divination.

"The first card represents you and your aims, lord Braden. The Six of Virtues, minor arcana – Justice – the interpretation here is self-evident, I think. You wish to restore order to Clongarvan by removing Maeryn and the Arch Mage from their positions."

"For all the suffering they have wrought, I wish to remove them from the material plane." Braden growled and took a sip from his wine.

I let the remark pass uncommented, concentrating instead on the divination and turning over the second card in the spread. "This card represents obstacles to the goal. Minor arcana, the Ten of Sins, reversed. Deception, ill-dignified –

you fear that your goals may be interfered with by outsiders."

"Correct." Braden nodded. "I would prefer to keep this expedition in-house within the rangers if at all possible."

"Card three, the ideal desired outcome: Five, major arcana – The Warrior. Again, the divination is not difficult here. You wish to see Maeryn and Karryghan vanquished by force of arms." I turned over the next card. "Card four, subconscious concerns regarding the goal – there is a clear link here to the second card. Major arcana, seventeen – The Trickster – you are worried that our enterprise is doomed before it even begins; that word of your return to Clongarvan may already have reached the ears of our enemies."

"Hence why I want the absolute bare minimum of people involved. My rangers can be trusted. Everyone else is a potential foe."

"Card five, past influences that affect the goal." I turned over the card representing the bottom of the sword blade, where it joined with the hilt. "Minor arcana, the Eight of Sins, reversed. Revenge – in the context of the spread, here the reversal is an intensifier. Your motivation is clear here, my lord. To right the wrongs committed against you personally and against Cothraine by Karryghan and Maeryn."

"Indeed, I will not be at peace until they are both dead."

"Card six details influences that are yet to occur that will affect the goal. Minor arcana – the Fifteen of Virtues – Knowledge: Interesting, this could have a great number of interpretations. A scholar or writer, perhaps, though more likely the direct or indirect assistance from a mage. We may find help from within the Tower of the Aether itself. Many of the wizards there are no friends of Karryghan." I had my own thoughts as to the identity of who this helpful mage might be, but kept them to myself, not wanting to start an argument in the middle of a divination. "Card seven represents outside factors that will provide help towards the goal. Four, major arcana – The Empress – this represents a powerful benefactor, most likely a woman in a position of considerable power, perhaps even a royal family."

"Since the Empress is the patron of families, could this not represent help from my fraternity of rangers?" Braden asked.

"With all due respect to your brothers and sisters of Sylvan, my lord, the Three of Virtues would have been a more appropriate card for that, and we cannot exactly consider them to be an external factor in our expedition."

"You mentioned that Sjur might be sympathetic to our cause, master." Cathal interjected. "Perhaps this is a sign that we should ask him or the Dowager Queen for assistance."

"I will consider it, but remember that every extra person we involve with our preparations is a potential source of a rumour that might reach Clongarvan before we do. Please continue, Gormlaith."

"The eighth card shows outside factors that oppose the achievement of our goal." I explained as I turned the card over. Ailidh's cheeks flushed at the explicitness of the imagery on the card. A giant, extraordinarily attractive demon with huge, leathery wings and long scarlet hair was shown on the card riding a captivated man with her slit, his hands reaching out imploringly to touch her statuesque body. "Number fourteen from the major arcana, The Succubus – this makes no sense at all in the context of the rest of the spread. I will need to mediate upon it."

Cathal glanced at Braden and took a sip of wine from his glass. "Maybe it is a warning not to camp too close to any whorehouses along the way to Clongarvan, master."

"Always good advice, my boy," Braden snickered as Ailidh covered her mouth, giggling.

"Card number nine shows the seeker's prediction for the outcome. Here we have the One of Sins, reversed and ill-dignified: Violence, but with no satisfactory resolution, either a partial victory or no victory at all."

"That is indeed what I expect. Our chances of success seem to be low, but I am getting too old to wait any longer and let Maeryn and the Arch Mage both continue to defile and destroy my country. I would rather die in the effort, rather than let matters continue on as they are."

"And now, the tenth and final card, the actual outcome itself," I turned over the card at the tip of the sword's blade. "The Twelve of Virtues, Power – but reversed and intensified. We will indeed reach Clongarvan and enter battle with both Maeryn and Karryghan, a literal power struggle for the heart of the nation."

"Does the spread say who will win?" Braden asked, leaning forward in his seat.

"Not explicitly, no. But it does allude to there being only a single victor, and that they will assume a role of greater power and influence than they ever had before."

"Well at least it does not predict a total catastrophe." Cathal sighed with relief, emptying his goblet of wine.

"I need to think more upon the meaning of the eighth card." I mused, turning it over in my hands.

"Then I will leave you to it, Gormlaith. It is getting too late for my old bones." Braden said as he stood. His demeanour was ambivalent, neither buoyed by the divination, nor discouraged. "You can tell me more in the morning."

"I think I'll turn in as well." Ailidh said, pushing her seat back from the edge of the table, the feet squeaking on the floorboards.

"Ailidh, are you alright? The news about Eoghan, it is a lot to take in." I put an arm around her shoulder and kissed her cheek.

"I don't know how I feel right now. I need to sleep on it." Ailidh hugged me back, on the verge of tears again. "It shouldn't be so much of a shock – we all suspected it. But my heart feels empty all the same."

Cathal followed Ailidh out of the room with his eyes and I reproached him silently again for being so reticent in confronting his feelings for her. *Comfort her, you fool!* Instead Cathal emptied the carafe of wine into our glasses and he stared at me in silence, taking repeated sips every few seconds until his glass was empty. When he made to stand I stopped my brother from rising from his seat by reaching over the table and placing a firm hand on his elbow. "Go to her. Take her to your bed tonight. Ailidh needs you." I did not add what I really wanted to: *if you do not, I will.*

"Gormlaith, you know I am fond of her, just not that fond. And even if I was, there is a problem. I dare not." Cathal opened his tunic and bared his chest to me. Two luminescent scars on his breast glowed ominously with an infernal crimson light. They were accompanied by the third dull scar Keri had left behind following her marking of him in the Western Weald. "The sigil began to glow when Ailidh and I coupled after Keri abandoned us. I am not sure I want to know what might happen if all three were to be activated."

"Why did you not tell me about this before?"

"I was ashamed. Ashamed that Keri had done this to me, and ashamed that I had let my passions cloud my better judgment when it came to Ailidh." Cathal told me in a low, confessional tone. "The last thing I would want is to hurt her. I hope you know that."

"I know, brother. But by design or not, you already have. And there is only one way in which you can make amends."

"I cannot, not while Keri's curse burns in my chest."

I scoffed loudly, frustrated by his stoic stubbornness. "By the Penitent's celibate cock, if only you had been so abstemious on the road to Lesøsnø, Ailidh would not think that she might still be able to convince you to be her husband."

"Rangers cannot marry, as you well know." Cathal retorted hotly.

"But they do fall in love. You and Aoibheann did not need legal confirmation from a piece of paper to know that the two of you were married." I snapped back, cupping Cathal's jaw with my hand and looking up into his eyes. "You two could bring so much joy to each other."

"Perhaps, but it is just a fantasy until I know the threat posed by Keri's mark. Can you help me?"

My shoulders fell, disappointed by my brother's reticence. He seemed totally unable to recognise the blessing Ailidh represented by coming into his life. I opened Cathal's tunic wider, tracing my fingers across the scars to memorise the shape of the demonic rune on his chest. "I will research the mark tomorrow at the Great Library. If there is a way it can be deactivated, I will find it."

Cathal embraced me in a tight hug worthy of a snow bear alpha and I returned it, my slender arms barely able to wrap around the length of his waist. "Thank you, sister."

I sat back down as he left the room and drained all the wine from my glass in a single gulp. I resisted the temptation to vent my frustration by hurling the glass into the fireplace. Instead I picked up the card of The Succubus, turning it over and over in my hands, hoping to deduce its meaning in Braden's spread. An hour later, when I finally went to sleep alone in my own bed, the significance of its appearance in the divination still eluded me.

28 – Aiden

Just as Captain Ruarc's gift of coconut rum had backfired in its intention to make my final night aboard the *Merganser* forgettable, the sight that greeted us the following morning was undoubtedly the most awe-inspiring natural view I had seen in my life and likewise made certain that I would never be unable to recall its full splendour, even if I tried. The forest of stone towers that dominated the Fossfjall capital stood shining proudly in the pale blue light of the post-dawn sun on a plateau almost exactly halfway between the calm rippling waters of the Abyss and the towering peaks of the mountains embracing the city limits. The scale of the place was almost beyond comprehension. Spanning more than eight leagues from the waters of the fjord to the apex of the tallest mountains above, it was impossible from this perspective to take in the magnitude of the whole city at once. Lesøsnø's docks were even broader than those in Clongarvan, with berths for over a thousand ships, spanning over two leagues in breadth. When you also considered that it was almost four leagues as the fulmar soars directly up from sea level to the city, the sheer size of the harbourage alone was extraordinary. A winding, stone-cobbled road climbed the wall of the fjord and a constant stream of carts climbed and descended along it. For those able to afford the fees, the road could be bypassed using an elegant array of cranes and winches, which looked like a siege of grey herons gazing down from the edge of the plateau into the clear water below, as if hunting for particularly large and juicy fish. Ruarc had told me that taking a crane, rather than the road, cut hours off the transit time from the dock to the city, making the toll worth paying if you had a particularly fragile or perishable cargo. I could not envisage Queen Reilynn wanting to waste time or suffer the indignity of taking a cart up to the city, so I hoped that the crane platforms and the ropes holding them were suitably robust. I was not fond of heights. Standing on the battlement of a city wall was one thing, but swinging from a rope three leagues above a windswept fjord seemed to me like quite another entirely.

Ruarc embraced each of us when we said farewell at the bottom of the jetty where the *Merganser* was berthed. As we left the ship Reilynn, Sìne and I were dressed identically to how we had boarded it: cloaked, armoured and armed. We concealed our faces inside the shadows cast by our black hoods as Reilynn led us to the crane marked with the sigil of the Fossian Royal Family. The guardsmen standing sentry at the entrance to the crane's enclosed platform crossed their pikes as we approached, blocking our path with a silent warning. Reilynn pulled back the right sleeve of her tunic and showed her engagement ring to the senior guardsman – identifiable from the golden filigree on his epaulettes. The narwhal ivory disk was carved with the personal insignia of the Crown Prince Sjur. The soldier gasped in shock, withdrew his pike and bowed reverently.
"Your majesty!"
Reilynn lowered her hood and favoured the sentinel with a luminescent smile. "I would like to see the Dowager and the Crown Prince, immediately."
"I will send word to the palace at once, your majesty!" the guard ushered his companion out of the way and unlocked the door to the elevator car, ushering us quickly inside. "Take your seats, please. Your ascent will begin shortly." The platform lurched as the sentinel pulled a waist-tall lever standing proud of the wooden decking a few seconds after the door was closed. I gripped the armrests of my chair hard and gulped as my stomach churned uncertainly.
"Your majesty, are you sure this thing is quite safe?"
Reilynn laughed melodiously. "Perfectly sure, Shadow Duke, this is the fastest and most secure way of making your way from the dock to the city, believe me."
Sìne tittered affectionately and leaned over to clasp my knee. "Listen to yourself, Aiden. Just two nights ago you were brave enough to face down a pirate corsair singlehanded!"
"Pirates I can fight, my love. Gravity, I am not so sure." I told my wife, my eyes drawn to the movement of a messenger falcon flitting past the window next to me. I turned eyes back to the queen, eager to avoid any reason to gaze out onto the fjord rapidly falling away beneath us.

"How long will it take for us to reach the city, your majesty?"

"Less than two hours, long enough for that falcon to reach the palace and for a welcoming committee to be sent to greet us, I would think." Reilynn said. "I am anxious to see my betrothed again."

A sudden gust of wind set the platform swinging languorously. "I am anxious that I might see my breakfast again."

"My poor darling," Sìne said and sat on my lap, distracting me with sweet, featherlight kisses. I put my arms around her and did not let her stop until the lift car came to rest in the courtyard of the Royal Warehouse in the city. When I sensed that the swaying motion of the platform had stopped, I opened my eyes. My wife favoured me with a smile of such compassion and beauty that my pulse began to race. "Feel better now, my love?"

"Immeasurably," I replied, squeezing her tightly to my chest. I stood and exited the lift quickly, glad to be back on solid ground and took one final look out over the Abyss. The view from the city plateau was undeniably and dizzyingly spectacular, but I was grateful to be seeing it from the security of stone, rather than the fragility of wood suspended from rope.

As Reilynn predicted, a delegation from the Royal Palace awaited us once our trip on the crane was completed. If she had hoped that the Crown Prince Sjur would be among it, she was destined to be disappointed. The leader of the group was a grizzled warrior easily into his mid-seventies who resembled a dire wolf alpha male far more than he did a human. The silver-haired giant was almost seven feet tall and almost as broad. Despite his age, I was uncertain as to whether I would be able to best him in single combat if I had to. Reilynn lowered her hood and the grey wolf's face lit up as he grinned terrifyingly. "When the falcon announcing your arrival at the docks reached at palace, I did not believe a word of it. I told Sjur not to come, so that he would not have to see me spill the guts of the liar claiming to be his love over the floor. I have never been more pleased to be wrong than I am now, my little vixen."

"Torulf, you old son of a bastard!" Reilynn embraced the Fossian Royal Guardsman as if they were family. I recognised the name from the diplomatic briefings I had been given when I assumed the leadership of the Purple Cloaks – Torulf was both the supreme general of the Fossian Land Army and the lord commander of the Fossian Royal House Guard.

"Reilynn, the gods have delivered you back here, at long last!" Torulf swept Reilynn from her feet and whirled her around twice in a bear hug of pure, adolescent delight. "I cannot wait to see Sjur's face when he finds out it is truly you! Come, you must join me in my carriage – and your travelling companions too, of course."

It was just the four of us in Torulf's stagecoach, with Reilynn, Sìne and me taking up one bench while Torulf seated himself upon the bench facing us alone, with hardly any room to spare. Once we were in motion Reilynn introduced us formally and I was unnerved when Torulf recognised my name. His huge fingertips flexed against his palms ominously. "Aiden, the same Aiden that served as Maeryn's head of security?"

Reilynn leant forward and placed her palms over Torulf's giant hands. "Yes, but do not rush to judgment, my old friend. I would not be here without his aid."

At length, Reilynn recounted my deeds both within the king's dungeon and on the waters by the glass isle and as she told her tale, I saw the lethal hardness of Torulf's gaze towards me soften. By the time Reilynn finished her story, he looked like he wanted to adopt me. "You have some balls on you, Duke Aiden, to hoodwink a privateer corsair so. If only our Fleet Admirals were so bold!"

"Thank you, your grace." I replied modestly, with a deferential bow of the head. I knew that I was on sketchy ground due to the circumstances surrounding my elevation within the Cothraine Royal Court after Maeryn's coup. Having burned my bridges with Maeryn, I certainly could not afford to make a poor first impression with the Fossians. While Maeryn and Karryghan lived, I would not be able to safely set foot into Cothraine again. My immediate, if not permanent, future was in Fossfjall. "The safety of my queen was my only concern. The risk to me was secondary."

"And rightly so!" Torulf exclaimed, leaning across the gap between us to slap my shoulder in agreement. It was like being struck with a battering ram, but somehow I managed to smile. "When our duties are complete this night, Aiden, we will drink to your boldness and cunning!"

Having overcome my initial poor impression with him, I charmed Torulf further by relaying an account of Sìne's key role in the sinking of the pirate corsair, subtly letting the detail slip that we were married. You could have marched an army through the gape of Torulf's open mouth when I told him of Sìne's now legendary shot onto the corsair's gun deck. He looked at Reilynn with utter disbelief, waiting for her to contradict my account. Reilynn shrugged her slim shoulders phlegmatically. "It is true - every word of it."

"You two will sire warriors able to conquer nations!" Torulf declared, appraising Sìne in an entirely new light. "I am pleased that they will be born in Fossfjall – now that I know your pedigrees there is no way in Hell that I would let you defect to another nation."

Sìne stood briefly to kiss Torulf on the cheek. "You're too kind, your grace."

"Ah, my girl... If only I were two score years younger! You and I would breed an army like this world has never seen!" Torulf exclaimed. I coughed my objection politely and the grey dire wolf tipped his head back and howl-laughed straight from his belly. "You did well to claim her first, my lord."

It took our carriage less than quarter of an hour to traverse the length of the city from the docks to the Royal Palace and the blue sun was approaching its apex in the sky when our carriage stopped on the gravel courtyard between the Granite Citadel and the parterre garden within the high-walled palace compound. Torulf dismissed the honour guard waiting for us outside the citadel's main gate with an expressive sweep of his right hand, leading us beneath the raised portcullis into the central keep. With practised ease Torulf negotiated the twists and turns of the citadel's corridors and within moments we found ourselves in the throne room of the Fossfjall nation. Reilynn broke into a run as soon as she saw her beloved. The Crown Prince Sjur, unable to believe what he was seeing, stood stupefied and open mouthed as the Dowager Queen gazed down from her raised vantage point upon the throne, a beatific smile on her face.

Torulf grasped the pauldron on my left shoulder with one of his huge, wrinkled paws and whispered into my ear, "Those two might need some time alone. How about we find you a guest room?"

Torulf settled us into a suite within the Royal Palace fit for a visiting king and queen – a chamber far larger than I had been entitled to even as the king's personal bodyguard. Torulf assured me that we would be sent for when we were needed and that we should make ourselves at home. Refreshments were provided to us every two hours during the day, and the suite was fully equipped with hot and cold running water and a flushing privy to cater for every need we might have for our daily ablutions. One wall of the suite was covered with fully-laden bookshelves and one corner of the room was dominated by an immense and ornate writing desk. There was a dining table and chairs near the granite and marble hearth, plus a pair of gold-framed sofas upholstered in iridescent purple silk. The polished oak floorboards were arrayed with luxurious woven rugs collected from around the world and the huge white pelt of a snow bear guarded the space before the fire.

Sìne was especially keen to try the bed. It was almost as large as the elevator car we had ridden from the docks to the city and the mattress was stuffed with soft, warming duck down. Sìne stripped off and beckoned for me to join her on the thick, wielding mattress. "Reilynn and Sjur'll be fucking for days before she needs us again – d'you want to see who can break the bed first?"

With little else to keep ourselves occupied, Sìne and I indulged our most intense carnal desires for each other between bouts of rest and reading. We both surprised each other with our enthusiasm for the written word, both of us having come from backgrounds that would generally be assumed to be illiterate. Through our service to the Crown we had both developed a passion for reading, but our tastes differed markedly. We took time out between intense sessions of lovemaking to work our way through the dozens of books available to use in the suite's miniature library to read to each other and share our interests. It was during one of these periods of intellectual reflection that Sìne broached a literally life-changing subject. "Aiden, I should've bled last week - normally I'm more regular than an astromancer's clockwork orrery."

"Forgive me for being dull, but what does that mean, my love?"
Sìne pulled my hand to her naked belly. "It means that a miracle grows within me, right here."
"You are with child?" I asked, incredulously.
"Yes."
"My child," I stated, already knowing it as the truth.
"Yes, my love." Sìne nodded, clasped my head between my hands and kissed me as if her life depended upon it.
"By the Goddess, I adore you, Sìne." I gasped between kisses and we made love until the night fell.

When we were finally called for some four days later, Sìne was proud to tell me that our mattress had needed to be changed twice compared to just the once for Reilynn and Sjur. The queen glowed at the Crown Prince's side, as beautiful and as happy as I had ever seen her. Reilynn gave both of us a bear hug of affection when we reported to her in the Granite Citadel's throne room. "You have been treated well, I hope, while Sjur and I reacquainted ourselves?"
I let my wife answer for us, "Impeccably, your majesty."
Reilynn took Sjur's right elbow into her palm and protectively drew her betrothed to her side. The Crown Prince was almost as tall and broad as his Supreme General and Chief of Royal Security. Sjur was just shy of thirty years old and his thick ginger locks gave him the powerful air of a Fire Giant. I would not have fancied my chances against him in single combat. Fortunately, he beamed down at me with gratitude, thankful for the role I had played in returning Reilynn to his embrace. The Crown Prince stepped forward and clasped both Sìne and me to his side. "My ravishing, russet vixen told me all about your exploits on the journey from Clongarvan. Without your help, I am certain I would never have seen my love again. Know that you both have my eternal thanks."
"Thank you, your grace." I said, offering him a deep, respectful bow and snaking an arm around my wife's slender waist to feel the reassuring warmth of her hip on my thigh.
"Today will be momentous day, my friends." Reilynn told us. "The sham marriage arranged by Arch Mage Karryghan and the usurper Maeryn will be annulled."

"And then the preparations to unify the nations of Fossfjall and Cothraine may begin." Sjur said with satisfaction. "A chronomancer from the Wizard's Guild will be here within the hour to conduct an inspection and repudiate the validity of Maeryn's marriage to Reilynn. Once they confirm that their arrangement was an unconsummated sham, we shall honour the betrothal promised to me by King Connell."

"What do you mean by an 'inspection'?" I asked with my heart in my mouth, worried how Sjur might react if he was told the Reilynn and I had coupled on our last night aboard the *Merganser*.

Reilynn stepped away from her beloved and took my arm, leading me away from the others, her voice barely audible as she reassured me. "A magical determination, using second sight: To see whether Maeryn has claimed his husbandly right to inseminate me – both Sìne and I can assure you that he did not."

"Will they be able to see that we coupled?" I whispered to her, concerned about how the night of passion Sìne, Reilynn and I had shared on the *Merganser* might inadvertently affect the future of two nations.

"It is irrelevant – the inspection is not a test of chastity – it is a legal matter regarding Maeryn's claim to the throne of Cothraine." Reilynn explained; her voice barely more audible than a whisper. "Were I to demand a similar inspection, I would find that Sjur has had his fair share of whores, no doubt. But none of them are of royal blood, so do not constitute grounds to annul our betrothal. And now that I am here, he will neither need nor want them anymore."

The inspection itself was a relatively simple affair. The Master Diviner from Lesøsnø's Tower of the Aether joined us in the throne room. She was a tall, elegant woman in her early sixties, with long, fine silver hair that cloaked her slender shoulders. She wore a simple, luxurious robe of yellow wool and the figurehead of her ivory staff took the form of a white-tailed eagle. Reilynn took her place on the seat at the Dowager Queen's left hand side and simply waited for the wizard to cast her spell. The diviner knelt on the floor before Reilynn and dipped her hand into the leather pouch that sat against her left hip, attached to her waist by a thin cord strap. The wizard closed her slate blue eyes and chanted silently under her breath. The light appeared to be sucked out of the throne room and luminous golden apparitions of Reilynn and Maeryn coalesced before the throne. The shadow golems exchanged silent words and Maeryn was sent reeling by a slap across his face. The figures flickered and reformed as the chronomancer accessed a different memory and I saw Maeryn get surrounded by the queen's handmaidens on the parterre, their lethal needles at his neck. Reilynn's apparition brushed off Maeryn's hand dismissively with a stinging blow from her garden shears. The scene flickered again to the palace dungeon and Maeryn's abortive assault of the queen. I saw a shadow of myself step into view and cleave off the fingers of Maeryn's hand when I disarmed him. Light flooded back into the chamber and the wizard raised her head. "The marriage was not consummated, your majesty."

The Dowager Queen, Sjur's mother Vigdis, stood and placed her hand on the mage's shoulder. "Thank you, Grand Master Nilsine. I had not doubted it, but protocol dictates that it must be confirmed legally. You may go, with my most profound gratitude."

The wizard used the support of her staff to retake her feet and she curtsied to the Dowager Queen. Torulf escorted Nilsine from the throne room as Vigdis turned her attention to Reilynn and her son. "Sjur, I am delighted that there are no more barriers standing between you and the throne. It will be the proudest day of my life when you are married and I cede the throne to you. When the news of the coup reached me four years ago I feared this day would never come.

"But the nightmare is over and my late husband's dream of unifying the royal families of Cothraine and Fossfjall lives once more. By sunset tonight the usurper's claim of marriage to Reilynn will be annulled. Maeryn will be made to answer for his crimes and your firstborn son will take the throne in Clongarvan." Vigdis pronounced and embraced Reilynn, who hugged her back. "And I will be honoured to welcome you into the family as my daughter."

"I will begin preparations for the wedding immediately, mother." Sjur said, kissing Reilynn on the cheek. The Crown Prince then turned to me. "Duke Aiden, Torulf will want to speak with you today, regarding the composition of forces in Clongarvan."

"I am at your service, your grace." I said and bowed. Reilynn plucked Sìne off my arm and they disappeared deep into the bowels of the Granite Citadel, chattering excitedly about Reilynn's upcoming nuptials. Torulf's giant meaty paw tapped my shoulder and I accompanied the Supreme General to his office on the top level of the keep. The view over the city was truly spectacular, the mass of spires cast into sharp relief by the dark backdrop of the Abyss. We spent the day discussing Clongarvan's defences and I held back no details, regardless of how inconsequential I might have found them. By sunset we had drawn and annotated maps of the city as a whole and of the royal palace itself.

Later that night, after Sìne and I had reunited over a late supper, I was enjoying an exceptionally lurid dream reliving the evening Reilynn, Sìne and I had spent together making love in the Captain's bed on the *Merganser*. The boat pitched unexpectedly and I jerked awake, sitting upright before my eyes even opened, anticipating danger. It took a few seconds for my eyes to focus and I was relieved to see that Sìne was still asleep on the bed, lying on her side facing me, with her left arm draped over my waist. I blinked to clear my vision and it was only then that I noticed two things. The first was that we were not alone in the room. My second realisation was that the starlight twinkling through the window was glinting off an exceptionally fine, narrow blade being held just inches before the tip of my nose. Belatedly, I realised that a firm hand was gripping my right shoulder, holding my torso still and upright. I blinked again to make sure I was not still dreaming. As my eyes began to adjust to the dim starlight, I recognised the visage of the interloper holding a knife in my face. "Your majesty?" Reilynn was seated next to me on the edge of the mattress, dressed entirely in black linen. Reilynn's long auburn hair was tied back behind her ears and braided into a single plait, and her regal features were marred by conflict and uncertainty. "Do not move, Aiden. You will live so long as you remain still."

"What is wrong, your majesty?" I asked, even though feared that I already knew the answer. I tried to remain calm as I appraised the blade coruscating in the feeble light. It was the signature weapon of an assassin: the pointed blade was less than an inch broad, razor thin and eight inches long, worn on a spring-mounted bracer beneath the forearm, concealed by the sleeve of her shirt. I felt lightheaded, knowing that it would just need a tiny flick from her wrist for Reilynn to slit my throat.

"I never should have allowed myself to become fond of you, Aiden. And I certainly never should have taken you into my bed. It only makes this harder." Reilynn said, a single tear trickling down her cheek. "I was grateful for your help in freeing me from Maeryn's insanity and giving me the opportunity I had been waiting for to flee the city, and I let sentiment cloud my judgment. If Sine had not been able to convince me of her love for you, you would not have lived to board the *Merganser*."

"Are you going to kill me, then?" I said, stroking the lovely raven-black tresses of my wife's hair away from her face. Sine stirred, waking gently. I wanted to see her gorgeous, dark eyes one more time.

"Your usefulness to me is at an end, Aiden." Reilynn explained as Sine woke, holding my palm against her cheek. I saw love and sadness in my wife's gaze, but no sense of surprise. I found it oddly reassuring the Sine was not shocked. After all, Queen Reilynn had always been her first love. It was natural that she would have already known. "The crimes you committed against my family are too grave to be allowed to pass without consequence. You stood by as Maeryn stabbed my father, your rightful king, in the back. You helped butcher my sisters, my cousins, my nieces and nephews. The spectres of my kin scream for vengeance. And they will not rest in peace until I have justice."

Sine knelt beside me and stroked my face. "For all the ill you have done during the purge, I still love you and I forgive you, even if the queen cannot. Our child will earn your redemption and ensure that you have brought some goodness into the world. A father has the right to name their child if it is a son. What name would you choose?"

My eyes drank in every detail of Sine's naked form as I considered the question. I wanted my memory of her to be perfect before I was condemned to an eternity of damnation in the afterlife. I had no illusions that the balance of my actions on the material plane tipped the scales of my ledger disproportionately to toward the side of evil. "Sìne, my life's regret will be that I cannot bring joy to more of your days and nights. If we have a son, he should be called Connell."

"A fine choice, my love," Sìne's eyes began to well with tears, but she would not turn away. If this was to be my end, she would not let it pass unwitnessed. I clutched her hand in mine, awed by her strength. Had our roles been reversed, I would not have been able to watch.

Tears were also on Reilynn's cheeks when I faced her for the last time. "Reilynn, your majesty... if it takes my life to earn your forgiveness, then that is the price I must pay. I am sorry."

"I know, Aiden." Reilynn said, closing her eyes and looking away. "But in these circumstances, sorrow alone is not sufficient a reparation."

There was a moment of silence before I heard a sharp, metallic click. I flinched as the queen flexed her fingers and retracted the assassin blade back into the sheath hidden behind her sleeve. Sìne supported my shoulders as she lowered me back against to the headrest of the bed quickly, while the queen let out a short sob of anguish before briefly covering her mouth with both hands. Reilynn took at deep breath before looking me in the eye, fixing me with a pitiless, unforgiving stare. "You are a killer, Aiden. But I am not. Even your death at my hand would not atone for your crimes against my family. And justice would not be served by depriving Sìne of the love of her life, not now I have seen how happy you make her with my own eyes. I cannot break the heart of my dearest friend. You will help Sìne raise your child and restore honour to your family name. Your penance will be to love and adore her with every fibre of your being until your dying day. I will hear of it if you do not."

My voice trembled as the realisation that the queen had spared my life set in. The weight of the implicit threat behind her edict was not lost on me, either. "It will be as you command, your majesty."

"You will leave tomorrow for Drommasund. The town is in need of a new Lord Protector able to keep the trade routes of the North Riding open and defended from barbarians, wild animals and worse. Life in the permafrost is hard, but there are worse fates than banishment. Serve well, and you will be richly rewarded. Serve very well, and one day you might be welcome once again in my court." Reilynn wiped away the tears on her cheeks and kissed her handmaiden fiercely on the mouth. "I will miss you, Sìne."

"I'll miss you too, Reilynn." Sìne replied, hugging her mistress hard with both arms. "Send word if you ever need me. I'll be there for you, always."

"When we see each other next, my beautiful Sìne, you will have a son to marry one my daughters." Reilynn said, crying.

"And a daughter to marry one of your sons." Sìne kissed Reilynn on the cheek, still holding on tight. "I'll look forward to that day."

Reilynn eased herself out of Sìne's arms and kissed the backs of both of her hands three times each, a sign of her unquestionable love and respect. Unable to trust herself to speak any further, the queen disappeared silently into the shadows without another word, bereft at having cut the final ties binding her to her past life in Clongarvan. I embraced my wife, thankful that I had been granted a chance to repay the queen's mercy. Sìne straddled me and put her arms around my neck, resting her head on my shoulder. I could feel her heart pounding against my chest and I felt a sudden rush of panic as the realisation of how close I had come to losing her. "Sìne, I love you. Can you forgive me?"

"Forgive you for what?" Sìne asked, her soft lips nuzzling my neck and her tongue tracing around the folds of my earlobes.

"For getting you exiled to the other side of the continent from your home? And estranging you from your oldest friend?" I suggested.

"Yes I can, because we're going to have a long life together." Sìne said, her fingers playing sensuously in the hair at the nape of my neck.

"Even so, days on the Bay of Wolves are cold and hard."

"Then we need to make sure the nights are warm and tender, my love." Sìne kissed me and let her sex leave a slick, molten trail along my manhood. "I'll need plenty of children to help me occupy my days."

"How many were you thinking of?" I asked, letting her mount me, guiding her with my hands on her hips.

"Five," Sìne replied, nipping my collarbone with a brief, sharp bite of passion as she used long, tantalising strokes of her hips to keep me engorged. "Sons to honour the Warrior and the Penitent; daughters to bless the Empress, the Goddess and the Earth Mother."

"Five is an auspicious number." I conceded, moving one hand between her shoulder blades to press her against my chest and let my lips suckle on the tips of her pert breasts. "I will do anything for you, my love."

"Anything, my lord?" my wife asked, the playful glistening of starlight catching in her eyes.

"I am yours to command, my sweet little mouse."

"Then shut up and fuck me."

I did as I was told, happily, for many decades to come.

29 - Cathal

The night after the séance I invited Ailidh to spar with me in the training yard behind Braden's town house. I had always found sparring to be the best way of releasing pent up anger, aggression and frustration. Following the confirmation of her father's death at the hands of King Maeryn's torturers - the iconography on the card of The Executioner had made it all too clear the manner of Eoghan's death, even to my untrained eye for divination - I imagined that Ailidh would be feeling plenty of those emotions that could be exorcised today. Braden provided us with blunt training swords and padded armour that protected our chests, forearms and thighs. The edges of the battered training blades were thick and dull, but could still leave a bruise underneath the padding if you were struck too hard.

Braden helped us into our armour and I strapped him into his own cuirass as he gave Ailidh our terms of engagement for the session. He demonstrated the flick of the wrist we should use at the last second to reduce the power of our strikes, without sacrificing their speed. "These swords cannot cut, but they can still hurt unless you roll your hands like this to take energy away from the strike."

"Like this?" Ailidh did a couple of practice cuts in the air trying to replicate what she had seen and Braden got to her to keep repeating the motion, using his fingertips to limit the flex of her wrist until he was satisfied with her technique. "I think I've got it."

Gormlaith watched our preparations from the back door of the house before beckoning me over to her with a wave of her ebony staff. I trotted over and gave her a quick hug. "Can I tempt you to join us, sister?"

She scoffed loudly. "I am a wizard, not a gladiator. The Great Library calls to me, as do the many mysteries within its walls waiting to be uncovered."

"Keri's mark?"

"Among other things - I would like to review Nevanthi's Seventh Prophecy again. There is no doubt in my mind that Eoghan's abandonment of his duties within the Guild of the

Art are linked to the Nexus, but I still have no clue as to what this has to do with Ailidh and her mother. There may be answers buried deep within the text. I have taken a couple of sovereigns from your coin purse in case I need to lubricate the library's illustrators with gold to gain access some of their more esoteric services."

"It is as much your gold as mine, sister. I know you will spend it wisely." I cupped Gormlaith's cheek and kissed her farewell on the lips.

When I rejoined Ailidh and my master, Braden was using the tip of his sword on Ailidh's armour to identify the acceptable targets for our sparring session, placing the blunt point of his practice sword on each part of her body in sequence. "Only strike at the following places, otherwise you risk injuring your partner; the forearm, just above the wrist; the outside of the upper thigh; the centre of the chest; and on the side of the body, halfway between the ribs and the hip bone. Clear?"

"Clear as crystal, my lord!" Ailidh saluted him with her sword.

"Good! Remember, focus your attention on the tip of your opponent's sword and keep your own aimed here, at the base of your adversary's throat, unless you are striking." Braden tapped the hollow between his clavicles at the base of his neck with the fingers of his free hand for emphasis before beckoning me over to stand between him and Ailidh. "Cathal and I will demonstrate first. Watch closely, not just our swords, but our hands, head and feet, too."

Braden and I raised our swords in a two-handed grip, raising them in a salute over our heads before settling into a combat stance. Two heartbeats ticked by before we began to spar, our arms and upper bodies held still as our feet moved, our wrists flexing almost imperceptibly to test each other's focus, our sword tips drifting in a leisurely dance, presenting fractional openings in our guards to tempt a strike. Our short, rapid steps had us advancing, retreating and circling each other as we assessed our relative strengths and weaknesses. It had been many years since we had last sparred, but I was not lulled into a false sense of superiority by my relative youth to my former master. His reflexes and decision-making were still as lightning fast as a viper. I tempted him into several strikes towards my chest and legs, relying on my greater mobility and longer stride to get me out of trouble as I tried to gauge his true reaction time.

My old master repaid me the honour, intentionally leaving his guard infinitesimally open to a strike at his forearm. I feinted towards the proffered target, knowing that it was a trick, switching my grip to slash down at his thigh. Braden side-stepped my attack and lanced out a thrust towards the centre of my chest, which I parried on my backswing, retreating several steps to restart our dance once again.

"So Cathal, what would you say are my vulnerabilities?" Braden asked, for the instructive benefit of Ailidh, who watched us, utterly engrossed.

As I answered we continued to exchanges feints and parries, neither of us reaching our intended mark. "Few. Your eyes and hands are as quick as ever, master. But your left knee is stiffer than the right and hampers your mobility when turning and dodging to your sides."

"The onset of arthritis, my boy, age catches up with us all. How should you exploit it?" Braden asked, while slashing at my thighs and making me jump over his blade.

"Attack from one side and then the other: Keep you turning, until an opportunity presents itself to attack either the chest or your side." I replied, demonstrating to Ailidh exactly what I meant, using wide arcing slashes to strike at Braden's legs and forearms in turn from left to right, angling my cuts randomly up and down relative to his waist. Braden parried again and again, looking to counterattack, but I used my greater agility and strength to try and bludgeon my way past his defence. My eyes lit up as his left foot seemed to slip on the gravel of the training yard and the tip of his sword fell low enough for me to lash out at his left side. Before I could execute my strike, Braden adjusted his grip on the hilt of his sword and whipped the blade upward and outwards, crashing the dull edge into the inside of my right bracer. Pain lanced down my forearm and I dropped my sword, cursing loudly. "Fucking daeva shit! I thought you were pulling your strikes!"

Braden's laugh was utterly without sympathy. "You can withstand a few more bruises, my boy. After all, it is your own fault. I cannot believe that you fell for that old trick again."

I stripped off the padded bracer and there was already a blue and purple bruise forming where Braden's sword had struck, directly over the scar he had accidentally given me in a similar sparring exercise at Sylvan's Dell before Ailidh had even been born. I rubbed my forearm tentatively, feeling glad that at least this time I would not need a healer. The bruise would be sore for a few days, but at least that gave me an excuse to indulge in an extra glass or two of wine until it had faded. I turned to Ailidh and gave her a cautionary wag of my finger. "Never ever trust an old swordsman Ailidh, even their bodies can deceive."

"How does the saying go?" Ailidh asked, squinting in concentration as she tried to remember. "There are old swordsmen and there are bold swordsmen, but there are no old, bold swordsmen."

"That is exactly so, my fair Ailidh. Guile and cunning will succeed where brute force and bravado cannot. Most battles are fought with brainpower, not muscle power." Braden explained. "The strongest and bravest swordsmen might have the most songs written for them, but that is because they inevitably find themselves in the grave far too young. No bards will ever write about my battles because there is no perceived glory in exploiting the preconceptions your enemy might have about you. The strongest weapon you possess is not the sword you have in your hands, but the wits you have in your skull.

"Be decisive in your thoughts, commit to them quickly and without hesitation. Self-doubt kills more warriors than the plague." Braden said, beckoning Ailidh forward to take my place. "It is your turn now. Do not hold back in your attacks, Ailidh. Your enemies will not. Show me what you can do."

As Braden led Ailidh through her initial sparring session I leaned my training sword against the back wall of the house and went to the kitchen to wet a linen cloth and wrap it around my arm to sooth the inflammation of the bruise my master had inflicted. I found a suitably-sized tea towel and soaked it in iced water and looped it several times around my forearm, securing it against my aching flesh with my padded bracer. I then retrieved a flagon of ale from the cold store and brought it back out onto the training yard for us to share. I took a swig from the bottle as I propped myself up on the back wall of the house, watching closely as Braden instructed Ailidh. I smiled when my former apprentice joined me, watching them both keenly.

I did not need my sister's magical affinity to see that Creighton practically swooned over Ailidh as he watched her spar with Braden. He was only a couple of seasons older than her, and had it not been for Ailidh's firmly declared love for me, I might have encouraged him to take a more active interest in her. Even though I did not consider myself romantically attracted to Ailidh, I doubted that she would have appreciated Creighton's interest complicating things further. Besides, I knew that someone else hid their own interest in him under a bushel due to the regulations on interpersonal relationships within the rangers, and that he was more likely to be successful if he directed his attention there. Creighton's eyes followed Ailidh's every move closely and he mused under his breath. "Her form is excellent."

"Are you referring to her sword-work or something else?" I asked provocatively, a sly smile tweaking at the edges of my mouth.

Creighton blanched as I took another swig of beer. "Her sword-work, of course..."

I laughed and put a hand on my former apprentice's shoulder. "Of course... you do not have much experience with the fairer sex yet, do you?" I asked, seeing the look of horror on his face and adding quickly, "There is no shame in that, Creighton. We all start from a blank slate."

Creighton gulped, swallowing any defensive pride he might have been tempted to respond with. "No, Cathal, I don't."

"Then let me give you the benefit of my experience. Ailidh has already set her heart upon someone else. Your attention would not be welcome from a romantic point of view." I explained, passing him the flagon of beer in consolation. Creighton took at long chug from the bottle, quietly distraught. "There are others who would be interested, though."

Creighton handed the flagon back to me, wiping his mouth and looking quizzical. "Really? Who?"

"Devorgilla."

"But she hates me! She is constantly making fun of me." Creighton lamented.

"Trust me, my old apprentice. She does not hate you, far from it." I reassured him. "Just be sure that you are alone and have some privacy when you choose to speak to her about it. Provided that you are interested in her, of course... But her form is... excellent."

"The Order forbids relationships between rangers." Creighton protested.

"It does, but that does not prevent them from happening. Aoibheann and I were more than friends, much more." Creighton reappraised me with slightly less innocent eyes, frowning. "Thank you for the advice, Cathal. I will think upon it."

As he turned to go I reached out to grab his bicep. "See that you do, and that you do it quickly. If the purge taught me anything, it is that you cannot rely on the apparent permanence of any relationship. In the blink of an eye someone you thought you might be able to rely upon forever can be gone."

"I understand." Creighton replied before ducking back inside the house.

I frowned and waited until I was sure he was out of earshot before mumbling under my breath, "Time will tell if you truly do."

I directed my attention back to Ailidh and Braden, who were duelling furiously. Braden was taunting Ailidh into striking at him with all the speed and power she could muster, parrying and deflecting her strikes as he skipped around her like a dancer at a midsummer festival, his practice sword glittering and swirling in the sunlight. I choked on a guffaw as Ailidh crudely let her frustration show. "Fucking stay still, you old bastard..."

"No, get faster, you young whippersnapper!" Braden laughed, smacking her across the rump with the blunt fuller of his blade. Ailidh yelled in fury at the indignity of his stinging strike and lunged at Braden's chest. My master thrust the length of his blade forward and sideways, using the crossguard of his sword to interlock with hers, pushing downwards to get Ailidh to overbalance and stumble to her knees. The tip of her sword stabbed uselessly into the ground, her neck nearly resting on the dull edge of Braden's training sword. Had this been a real combat, Braden's next move would have been to decapitate her on his backswing as he brought his sword back up to a guard position. Braden left Ailidh on her knees for a moment to contemplate her mistakes. "How did I defeat you?"

"You were too fast for me, too strong." Ailidh said, panting to recover her breath.

"No, think again." Braden actually stamped a foot, frustrated that Ailidh had missed the point of his previous lesson.

"You goaded me. You played on my emotions and made me angry and frustrated."

"Indeed, I got you to defeat yourself." Braden nodded, smiling gratefully when I approached to hand him the flagon of beer. Braden gulped down several mouthfuls as Ailidh clambered back to her feet wearily. When she stood upright Braden passed her the ceramic bottle and she drank deeply as Braden continued his lesson. "Mental weak spots are often simpler to find than physical ones, and are always easier to exploit. When battles are fought in the mind, victory will arrive faster if you can stop the mind of your enemy from functioning properly."

"That is all well and fine, but you were still too fast and too strong for me." Ailidh protested.

"No! N-" Braden exploded before seeing the devious grin on Ailidh's face. He looked at me ruefully, raising his index finger, placing it diagonally over his lips and turning between us, both annoyed and delighted. My old master locked eyes with me and said, "She is a faster learner than you ever were, my boy."

We spent the rest of the day conducting sword form drills and taking turns as the aggressor and defender in one-versus-one and one-versus-two melee engagements, always keeping Ailidh as one of the combatants to try to compress several years worth of training into a single day. As dusk fell we called a halt to our sparring drills and I helped Ailidh out of her armour. The sight and the smell conjured memories from my post-patrol evenings I had spent with Aoibheann and the recollection made my body tremble briefly with arousal. Aoibheann had always preferred us to make love before bathing for the night so that we could better remember each other's scent. I had not noticed it before until the memory had struck me, but the smell of Ailidh's sweat on her skin was practically identical to Aoibheann's. Ailidh noticed my hesitation and asked, "Is everything alright, Cathal?"

"Yes, it is nothing, an old memory." I said unfastening the straps on my thigh pads as she took off my padded breastplate. Ailidh looked up into my eyes and frowned, unconvinced that I had told her the whole truth. My pulse quickened as I glanced down from her face and my gaze found the dusky abyss of her cleavage visible between the open buttons of her tunic. Every unconscious instinct I had screamed for me to kiss her, to take her to bed, to surrender myself to her love and give her the devotion and pleasure she deserved.

"I'm going to take a bath and get changed. Could I persuade you to join me?" Ailidh asked, placing a hand in the centre of my chest and looking up into my eyes.

A shiver trembled down my spine. Once again the lingering fear of the unknown consequences of Keri's mark on my breast prevented me from having to confront and acknowledge the full extent of what I truly felt for her. "I do not think that would be wise. I will wash after stowing our training gear in the armoury."

"I will see you at dinner then." Ailidh's disappointment was palpable, but she smiled bravely.

I held on to Ailidh's hand tightly as she turned to go. "Ailidh, I really enjoyed spending time with you today. I wanted you to know that."

"I did, too." Ailidh kissed my cheek and left to get freshened up for dinner.

By the time I had packed away our training equipment, taken a bath and changed into fresh clothes, the evening meal was well underway and Gormlaith had returned from communing in the Great Library with her books and scrolls. The dining room was noticeably busier than it had been when we had first arrived at Braden's estate. More than a dozen rangers had answered Braden's summons and the house was getting so busy that a makeshift camp of tents had needed to be pitched on the front lawn. The room bubbled with excited chatter about our expedition to bring justice to Maeryn and the Arch Mage and retake our rightful place at Sylvan's Dell in Clongarvan. After four years of exile, many of the rangers, including myself, were anxious to see our home once again. I noticed that Creighton was sat at the opposite end of the table from Devorgilla, studiously ignoring the frequent glances she gave him. Obviously my former apprentice had not taken my advice to heart quite yet. I shrugged inwardly as Gilleonan, one of the freshly-arrived rangers, graciously gave up her seat at the table to allow me to sit next to my sister. I kissed Gormlaith once on each cheek in greeting and nodded my thanks to Gilleonan. "Good evening sister, have you seen Ailidh?"

"Been and gone. She was not hungry and did not feel comfortable around so many new faces." Gormlaith replied. My sister rubbed the back of my hand consolingly. "You will just have to put up with my company tonight."

"You say that as if it is some kind of chore."

"Maybe it is. You have to listen to me tell you about everything I learned at the Great Library today." My sister chuckled, taking a sip of wine from her glass before reaching beneath her seat to retrieve her satchel.

There was a heavy tap on my shoulder before I had a chance to reply. I turned my head and gratefully received a plate of food and a large goblet of wine from a ranger I had not seen in more than six years. I placed my meal on the table and stood to give him a brotherly embrace. "Torcall, it is not often that I have seen you being reduced to waiting upon the table."

"We all have to do our duty, brother Cathal." Torcall said, hugging me back. "How have you been, my lord?"

"Until recently, mostly bored I would say. My exile in the Weald was fearsomely dull until a few months ago." I laughed, before turning his attention to my companion at the table. "You met my sister Gormlaith before in Clongarvan, I believe?"

"Still looking as lovely as ever, my lady," Torcall ventured and kissed the back of her hand gallantly.

"And still not interested whatsoever in men, my lord," Gormlaith replied with her warmest, most dismissive smile. "But I am flattered nonetheless."

Torcall laughed generously, a wistful look on his handsome, weather-seasoned face. He had held a candle for my sister ever since meeting her during one of her visits to Sylvan's Dell as a teenaged apprentice over ten years ago. "I will have to content myself with that, lady Gormlaith. But please, do not let me interrupt. More of my brothers and sisters need feeding and watering. I hope we can speak later, Cathal. I have the night watch: perhaps you could join me for a time?"

"I would love to." I said, squeezing his shoulder. "Gate duty?"

Torcall nodded and made his way back to the kitchen. Gormlaith watched him leave, her eyes lingering on his legs and the sway of his hips. "A genuinely charming man, such a pity for him that I am immune to it: if only he had been plumbed in slightly differently."

I was glad that I had not been eating or drinking when she said it, as I would have redecorated the table with the contents of my mouth. Instead the only thing that passed my lips was a guffaw of air and I covered my face with a hand as I tittered like a coy maiden, mentally processing the image she had conjured. "Truly sister, that would be a sight for sore eyes."

"It is good to see you smile once again, brother."

"It is good to have a reason to." I said, squeezing her hand firmly. "So much has happened in the last few weeks. I have not felt this hopeful about the future since the coup."

"It is the influence of the planar alignment due to coincide with the winter solstice. Events of great importance always seem to cluster around the time of a planar alignment. But what makes this one so exceptional is the added factor of the manifestation of an aetheric nexus." Gormlaith explained, laying out scrolls from her satchel onto the table before us. "Seer Nevanthi anticipated all of this in her Seventh prophecy, but it stands alone from her work in its imprecision and crudeness of prose. It is almost as if either she or the watchers on the psychic plane, who helped Nevanthi author her greatest works, did not want the precise truth to be known ahead of the actual events."

"Why is that?"

"There are several theories. One is that the outcome of the planar alignment and manifestation of the Nexus is so cataclysmic that even the watchers, who exist outside of what we would consider linear time, refuse to acknowledge it. Another is that if the watchers were to allow the fate of the Nexus to be known ahead of its ordained time it might discourage action from beings whose intervention is needed for the Nexus to end up in its proper place, or worse, encourage action from those not meant to get involved." Gormlaith said, stroking the paper scroll copy of Nevanthi's seventh prophecy that she had purchased from the library's illuminators, tapping her fingernail against several paragraphs in the text for emphasis. "Nevanthi left many gaps in her predictions, such as the exact form the

Nexus takes, the precise date and location it forms and its ultimate fate. All of this is in direct contradiction to the detail and precision of her other predictions."

"All that happens occurs as is meant to be." I quoted from the dogma of the Dark Rider.

"Indeed, brother." Gormlaith nodded. "I know that you are about as religious as I am, but in this case it seems that we must place some trust in powers that exist on planes higher than ours."

I pushed aside my plate, suddenly not hungry anymore, instead reaching for my wine glass. "Did you make any progress on deciphering the meaning of Keri's mark?"

"As it happens, I did." Gormlaith said, laying smooth more of her scrolls of research upon the table. "Though the illuminators took some convincing that my interest in demonic script was more urgent than just purely academic - I hope that you were not expecting any silver in change."

"I trust that your discoveries were worth the gold?" I asked dryly, not really caring about the money.

"Judge for yourself, brother." Gormlaith said, using our wine glasses and plates to hold down the corners of a scroll some five feet wide and three feet tall. It was covered in the aggressive, jagged marks of the demonic alphabet and I could see where Gormlaith had annotated the reference work with her own observations, combining demonic letters together into the runes that formed the sigil Keri had carved into my chest. "Contrary to what you might expect from creatures of such limited motivations, demons have a remarkably sophisticated system of writing. It is a runic system using symbols from a vocabulary of marks using two to seven strokes, with the sigil taking its meaning from not just the number and types of mark, but also their relative size and angle of orientation. Sigils can be constructed from anything between two and seven marks, but depending upon the order in which they are written, the relative weight of the mark and its angle to the vertical, the meaning of each mark and the overall rune it is within can vary widely."

"I suppose it would have been too much to ask for simplicity where daevae are concerned." I said with a resigned shrug. "Did you manage to deduce the meaning of Keri's mark?"

"I believe so, but please bear in mind that I am neither a demonologist nor a linguist." Gormlaith cautioned me before drawing my attention to three of the marks on the paper she had outlined with a charcoal pencil. I recognised them as the cuts Keri had left on my chest. "Finding reference to the each of the individual marks was simple enough. Your sigil has one mark of three strokes and two marks of four strokes, symbolising a relatively sophisticated concept. A sigil of a single two stroke mark would be among the simplest concepts in the demonic script, while a sigil of seven marks of seven strokes would represent one of the most difficult concepts in the demonic language."

"So what does it say? And more importantly, what does the glowing of the marks mean?"

"Given the orientation of the marks, the best translation I can find is 'soul drain' or 'soul anchor'. Given the context of when Keri marked you, I think the most fitting meaning would be 'soul drain'. It is a sigil used by daevae to siphon the life force of a being into a soul crystal."

"Which is exactly what she did to me," I shivered involuntarily, placing a hand over my sternum, where the demonic lettering was hidden by my tunic. "Were you able to find out why the marks glow in the way that they do?"

"The first runic mark of the sigil made from three strokes pertains to lust and sexual desire. Your coupling with Ailidh appears to have activated it. It seems likely that some residual power was left in the marks after Keri abandoned her effort to drain you."

"Can you disarm the sigil?"

"I cannot, sorry my brother. I do not have the knowledge required and even if it was contained within the Great Library, it might take many months for me to uncover it. But I would guess that any danger it might have posed to you has passed. When Keri changed her mind and let you keep your soul I suspect that whatever grip the sigil had upon you dissipated."

"But you cannot say that for certain."

"The only thing I can say for certain is that everything which has been born will someday die and that the Crown will raise taxes next year." Gormlaith shrugged. "If you want a more definitive answer than that, the only person you could ask is the one that gave you the markings in the first place, but I doubt you want to do that."

I emptied my wine glass, shuddering at the thought. "Indeed not."

"Then get on with your life, before the opportunities before your eyes pass you by."

"You are not nearly so cryptic or profound as you would like to believe, sister." I said, flagging down Torcall for a refill of wine. "I know you would love to play the matchmaker between me and Ailidh, but it is not that simple. I am not going to blindly activate the rune without knowing the consequences just to satisfy your romantic aspirations for the two of us."

"But you would make such a good pairing. You should not let your fear hold you back."

"Easy for you to say, sister, the marks are not upon your soul."

"I just want you and Ailidh to be happy, brother. To be loved is gift – you should embrace it."

"I did once, and you know the heartache that cost me."

"I do. And I know the joy it gave you, too. Do not turn your back to love, brother. Otherwise you may never have the opportunity to feel it again." Gormlaith said, her fingers encircling my wrist.

I placed my hand over hers and squeezed tightly. "It is good to have you back, sister. I have missed your wisdom and advice."

"I have been giving you the benefit of it for the last three years and you seem about as likely to listen to it now as you did when I had fur." Gormlaith said, with deadpan sarcasm.

"At least then you were easier to ignore." I retorted playfully, kissing her cheek. I saw a smile die on her lips as I stroked her arm affectionately. "Are you alright, sister? Did I say something wrong?"

"No, no." Gormlaith looked away and she attempted to put on a brave smile that did not quite reach her eyes. "I am glad to be back too, despite the cost to you." She added, tapping the sheet of demonic writing on the table before us.

"If there has been one good outcome from making Keri's acquaintance, it is your freedom from Karryghan's curse." I said, stroking the back of her hand. I could sense the

traumatic toll of her transformation, which was hidden in the aura behind her bright, inquisitive eyes. "You have not spoken about what it was like, being Sapphire I mean."
"It is not something I wish to talk about. Having your body ripped away from you and your mind implanted in an alien form; retaining your thoughts but having another set of instincts and behaviours placed in primacy over your own. It may be some time until I can truly call myself me again – if that makes sense?"
"It does, after a fashion." I said, tilting my head over to one side, pondering to myself curiously for a few moments before asking her "So when a cat purrs does that mean-"
Gormlaith interrupted me by placing a finger over my mouth, a look of abject horror on her face. "No, stop. We are not having that conversation. Not now, not ever. Just let me say this – never allow yourself to be polymorphed."
"I love you, trouble." Laughing, I kissed my sister on the cheek and I let her retire to her chamber to sleep without asking her any more embarrassing questions.

30 – Reilynn

My beloved entered my chambers with a sour look on his face. "What is wrong, Sjur my love?

"Torulf tells me that there has been some unusual activity in the city. Over the last two weeks there has been an influx of Rangers of Sylvan from the wilds." Sjur said, taking the seat next to me, his thigh jiggling unconsciously in the way it always did when he felt agitated. My father had shared the same involuntary habit, which my mother had delightfully described as having a leaky foot. "He thinks that they are assembling a warband. They have hired ten carriages and fifty horses, horses that I had wanted to use in our wedding procession, I might add."

"But there is no Sylvan's Dell in the city. I thought that Fossfjall's Order of Sylvan is based out of Rundalen in the Pineholm."

"They are. These green cloaks belong to the Order from Clongarvan. Lord Commander Braden took refuge here after the purge. Mother granted him an estate in the Park of the Earth Mother."

"Duke Braden still lives? That is excellent news, indeed." I clapped my hands together in delight. I had met the grizzled chief of Cothraine's rangers several times before the coup and he had been a fierce supporter of my late father. "Summon him to the palace, beloved. I would speak with him."

It was mid-afternoon when Torulf escorted the lord commander and his Second, a taller, dark-haired ranger about Sjur's age who I did not recognise, into my temporary office in the Granite Citadel. As they entered I stood up from behind the bureau I was working at, managing the logistics of the banquet to be held in the Grand Hall, the night before my marriage to Sjur. When Braden recognised me from halfway across the room, he rushed forward to kneel at my feet. I proffered the back of my hand and he kissed my fingers reverentially. "Queen Reilynn, how did you ever manage to escape from Clongarvan and make it here to Lesøsnø?"

"With a little of bit of help from my friends in the black cloaks," I explained, with a pang of grief in my heart. By now my loyal handmaiden Sìne and her husband Aiden were well on their way to Drommasund so that Aiden could make reparations for his part in Maeryn's coup by acting as the frontier town's Lord Protector. I would have loved for Sìne to have acted as my Maid of Honour, but she would not be separated from her husband and despite my growing fondness for him, I could not condone his continued presence at court. Sjur's youngest sister Astrid had instead been given the duty, cementing our bond as sisters by marriage. "I am surprised you did not know already, lord commander, my reunion with Sjur and our upcoming nuptials have been the talk of the city for the last week."

"Forgive me, your majesty, but I have been rather preoccupied of late and have not had chance to keep myself up to date with current events in Lesøsnø." Braden said as I silently bade him to stand and take the seat opposite mine at my desk. "But it is wonderful to see you again free of the confines of the palace."

Braden waited respectfully for me to take my seat before sitting himself. His brooding Second stood without complaint behind the lord commander's chair. "Yes, Duke Braden, I understand that there has been a great deal of activity in and around your estate in the last two weeks. I am curious to know just what you are up to. Some of the more nervous souls in the citadel are concerned by the gathering of so many elite troops within a stone's throw of the palace."

"May I introduce you to Baron Ranger Cathal, your majesty?" Braden raised a hand to his shoulder to point at his deputy, who bowed respectfully. "It was his arrival in the city that alerted me to the deteriorating situation in Clongarvan."

"Cathal, now where have I heard that name before?" I wondered, rapping my knuckles on the desk to jog my memory. The spark of recall brought a flash of joy to my lips. "Of course, you are the one who gave Maeryn his limp and had him invalided out of the rangers as a trainee. He does not remember you with any fondness, Baron Cathal."

"Neither I for him, your majesty," Cathal replied, his gaze frigidly cold.

"Tell me this please, was the sparring incident truly accidental, Baron?"

"Even as a boy, Maeryn was spoiled, privileged and looked down upon people of common birth, or people like me who were orphaned as children." Cathal said, standing still and proud, unapologetic for what he had done. "He believed that the circumstances of his birth made him superior to the other trainees. I simply showed him that superiority is a matter of talent and application, not breeding. Sometimes I wonder whether I made a mistake in doing so. Would he have fallen prey to the manipulations of the Arch Mage and led the coup if I had not humiliated him so?"

"Baron Cathal, you should not blame yourself. The only person responsible for Maeryn's actions during the coup and purge is Maeryn himself. He chose to commit such evil and be the Arch Mage's pawn. Regardless, even if you had not maimed Maeryn as a trainee, Karryghan would have found another proxy willing to do his dirty work." I said, reassuring the ranger and feeling a sympathy and kinship for him. "But we should look to the future not the past. Now that the sham marriage to Maeryn has been dissolved, an opportunity presents itself to retake control of Clongarvan from the usurper and his patron. Both Maeryn and Karryghan must be brought to justice and then my father's original vision to unify the thrones of Cothraine and Fossfjall can finally be realised."

"How can we help you, your majesty?" Braden asked.

"I would ask two things of you, lord commander. Firstly, I understand that you have been gathering a force of rangers into the city in recent weeks. I would like them to represent Cothraine as my honour guard at my wedding to the Crown Prince next week."

"It would be a privilege and our pleasure, your majesty."

"Secondly, when Sjur ascends to the Fossfjall throne after we are married, we will leave the city by ship to retake the Palace via the Royal Marina in Clongarvan. Before we dock at the marina, I would like your rangers to lead a force to secure the sea fort and the ballista towers overlooking the Bay of Tides. Once the threat to our ships is neutralised, Sjur's marines will secure the palace grounds and depose Maeryn."

"Your majesty, my rangers are not shock troops." Braden said with a sharp intake of breath.

"But you are elite. And you know the city far better than Sjur's commandos. I would not place you and your people in more danger than I thought reasonable. All I need you to do is to lead Sjur's men to their objectives as quickly as possible. They will handle the majority of the fighting. You will also have some help from inside the palace grounds."

"Help from whom, your majesty?" Braden asked, raising a silver eyebrow.

"I have two score black cloaks embedded throughout the palace and the city at large. Once you make contact with their leader at the city docks, they will provide you with the intelligence you need to overtake the sea fort and the towers on the sea wall as quickly as possible before reinforcements can be summoned from the city garrison. How many rangers do you think you will have at your disposal by the end of next week?"

"Perhaps as many as fifty, your majesty," Braden replied. "I have no objections to your plan to retake the palace in principle, my queen, but it does leave one rather large issue unanswered: what is to be done about the Arch Mage Karryghan?"

"My primary concern is eliminating Maeryn and reclaiming the throne. Once the city is secure, Karryghan will be dealt with. As powerful as he is, the Arch Mage cannot hold his position without the support of the Crown. If the Guild of the Art seeks to protect him, I will have the Tower of the Aether razed to the ground. Karryghan will be held to account for his crimes."

"There may be one complicating factor at play here, your majesty." Braden's Second interjected. "The Arch Mage precipitated the coup to take possession of a powerful arcane artefact, an aetheric nexus, the appearance of which will coincide with the planar alignment this winter solstice."

"This is not news to me, Baron Cathal. Maeryn told me as much himself. But surely it is nothing more than a magical fantasy."

"I can assure you, your majesty. It is no fantasy. My sister Gormlaith is a wizard of the Guild, a chronomancer, or diviner. After the coup she was assaulted by Karryghan for discovering his plans and was lucky not to have been killed outright." Cathal explained. "And more recently the Arch Mage ordered the kidnap, torture and murder of a former

Master Diviner living in hiding near the Fossfjall border in Croycullen. The Arch Mage believed he had knowledge either of the Nexus's form or location. For him to co-opt the Field Army into such crimes leads me to believe that the Arch Mage will stop at nothing to possess the Nexus, whatever it is. I know not what he stands to gain from it, but the idea that Karryghan engineered the murder of the Royal Family and would be willing to precipitate all out war with Fossfjall is enough for me to believe that he should be denied access to it at all costs."

"Then let us make sure we either find it first or liquidate him before he has a chance to use it." I said, my voice hardening like steel being quenched in a water bath. "The slaughter of my family will be revenged, one way or another."

"We will do everything possible within our power to aid you, your majesty." Braden said earnestly.

"I am glad to accept your support, lord commander. Supreme General Torulf will brief you on our current plan to retake Clongarvan and the Royal Palace. I look forward to hearing your thoughts on it in the coming days." I stood to dismiss the rangers as Sjur entered the room.

"Please come with me, Master Rangers." Torulf gestured to the door. "We will take refreshments and discuss how to bring the hammer of justice down on the heads of Maeryn and the Arch Mage."

Both Braden and Cathal bowed in respect to the Crown Prince as they exited and once the door closed Sjur kissed me full on the lips and backed me up to edge of my desk.

"It sounds like your meeting went well."

"Very well, my polar bear," I slipped my hands underneath his armpits and drew him closer to me. "The assistance of the rangers could be a decisive factor in retaking the Royal Palace in Clongarvan."

"I look forward to seeing their prowess on the battlefield for myself." Sjur said, his lips nuzzling my neck beneath the ear. "My berserkers will learn much from them, no doubt."

"The art of subtlety, perhaps?" I teased him, nipping the tip of his nose with my teeth.

"An overrated virtue." Sjur growled, amused. His hands found my hips, gripped hard and he pulled the full length of our bodies together. "Remind me, how many children did the Arch Mage say you would sire?"

"Seven sons and seven daughters."

"Fourteen children, over how many seasons do you think?" Sjur mused, his lips still busy on my neck. "A score, perhaps?"

"I do not fancy the notion of giving birth in my forties. Hopefully we might have a few sets of twins along the way."

"Even if that were so, you would be cutting it fine."

"All the more reason to make an early start, I would think. But not right now, we have business to attend to." I said as my fingers pried his hands away from my waist.

"You can be such a tease, my sensuous scarlet fox." Sjur groused, but took the hint. He smoothed down his cloak as he sat down in the chair Braden had just vacated.

I returned to my seat and opened one of the half-dozen scroll cases littering my desk. I withdrew the vellum sheet from inside and spread it over the desk. Illuminated upon it was a detailed map of Clongarvan. Sjur drew his chair closer to the desk as I pinned down each corner of the map with the weight of one of the scroll cases. "If we leave for Clongarvan immediately after the wedding, how long will it take your fleet to get there?"

"Thirty to forty days, depending upon the wind. We would definitely arrive before the solstice."

"Forty days, plus another ten-day until the wedding, that is good." I nodded with satisfaction. "More than enough time for the *Merganser* to make the trip and for Ruarc to distribute orders to the black cloaks in the city."

"Taking the sea fort prior to making landfall will be key. Its siege weapons will wreak havoc on our fleet, otherwise."

"Yes, my love. I have three black cloaks infiltrated into the fort's command staff. They will ensure that the rangers are able to take the fort without too much resistance."

Sjur flexed his fingers as he envisaged the battle to come. "My berserkers will make short work of any guards. All they need is an axe in their hands and ground beneath their feet."

"I will not permit a wholesale slaughter, Sjur." I reminded my husband sternly. "Those troops are my subjects, not my enemies. Save your bloodlust for those that deserve it."

"As you wish, my vixen. Though I fear Maeryn will not give me a fight worthy of song."

"His name is not worthy of remembrance, my husband. He will be forgotten quickly once he is dead. As will the rest of the ringleaders of the coup. Once the palace is secure, Maeryn and Karryghan's lackeys must be liquidated quickly."

"Your black cloaks are watching them, I assume?"

"All of them, save Karryghan." I said, nodding. "It will be difficult to bring the Arch Mage to justice. Not even the black cloaks can break into the Tower of the Aether. We will need support from the council of Grand Masters."

"I have spoken with the Arch Mage here in Lesøsnø. They will not support hostile action against the Guild in Cothraine."

"Unsurprising, I suppose." I looked down at the map, my fingertips tracing circles around western quarter of the city, where the Tower of the Aether was the most prominent landmark, standing proudly in the centre of the Park of the Mystic. "The Guild has long prided itself on its political neutrality, until the coup, at least."

"Could we keep him confined to the tower? It would be simple enough to garrison the park." Sjur suggested.

"Unlikely. My spies tell me the Tower of the Aether contains portals that connect it to many other parts of the city, and Karryghan is powerful enough to disguise his appearance with glamour spells. If he chose to flee the city, we would not be able to stop him."

Sjur's breath hissed through his teeth in concern at the thought of the Arch Mage escaping. "Then we need to hope that he has made enemies on the council who will help us."

31 – Ailidh

When Cathal had rescued me from the lawn of my father's smithy, if I had been told then that I would end up being a guest of honour at a Royal Wedding just a few months later, the notion would've struck me as being beyond fanciful. Yet here I was, sat in the Shrine of the Pantheon on the front row of the crowd alongside my adoptive sister Gormlaith, dressed in the fine turquoise gown she had helped me choose in Célestine's boutique only two weeks ago.

In the week following Braden's initial summons by Queen Reilynn, the rangers had been working closely with her husband-to-be, Crown Prince Sjur, and the Supreme General of the Fossfjall Army, Torulf. Using information Torulf had gleaned from a defector among the King's Companions, they had put together a battle plan to retake the Royal Palace in Clongarvan. Braden would lead a vanguard of Sjur's berserker commandos in securing the sea fort overlooking the Royal Marina before sending a signal to Sjur and Torulf to initiate the assault on the Royal Palace itself. Once Maeryn was eliminated, Reilynn would summon the heads of the army and the City Guard to ensure a peaceful transition of power and prevent fighting from engulfing the whole city. Then our attention would turn to the Tower of the Aether and the Arch Mage. Gormlaith had warned that persuading the Guild Council to turn over Karryghan would be difficult, only for Reilynn to assure her that she would tear down the Tower and execute every wizard inside until Karryghan was made to answer for his crimes against her family. It had also been agreed that the rangers would leave the city separately from Reilynn & Sjur's force. Once married they would board the flagship of the Fossian Navy, notionally to go on a honeymoon cruise. Thirty ships carrying over ten score warriors each would escort Sjur & Reilynn down the Abyss and then south to the Cothraine capital. Cothraine's Navy had been decimated following the purge and would be no match for Fossian flotilla if it chose to engage it in battle.

Both Torulf and Sjur judged that such action was unlikely, as the superior quality of our ships and the experience of our captains meant that even a surprise attack on our fleet stood little chance of inflicting even minimal losses against our armada. Maeryn's diplomats and spies would surely pass word of the wedding and the departure of the fleet from Lesøsnø, so it was necessary for the rangers to depart the city using the land caravan Braden had already acquired. Reports of Cothraini Sylvan aboard Fossian ships would surely alert Maeryn and the Arch Mage that an attack was imminent, and we all knew that maintaining some element of surprise was key to minimising casualties on both sides. So it had been decided that the rangers would proceed with their original plan to cross the border on land, before hiring a ship in Moonchion to join Reilynn's flotilla on The Herring Coast at Monagealy Sound. But before any of this plan could be executed, there remained the small matter of the wedding itself.

The Shrine of the Pantheon was packed with nobles and commoners that had flocked to capital for Crown Prince Sjur's marriage and coronation. The Dowager Queen and the High Priestess of the Empress already sat next to the Altar of the Divinity, where both ceremonies were due to take place. The wedding rings, thick bands of pure gold, sat upon cushions of purple satin alongside the regal crowns of Fossfjall, which Vigdis herself would place upon the heads of her son and daughter-in-law after she announced her abdication. Gormlaith and I sat on the front row of pews next to the altar, at the explicit invitation of Reilynn herself. Other than the diplomatic legation from Cothraine that was resident in the city, Reilynn had no-one else to call upon to represent her at the wedding, given that she had already co-opted Braden and his rangers to be part of her wedding entourage. From our position next to the central aisle of the cathedral, both Gormlaith and I had a perfect view of the altar, the aisle and the road approaching from the east. Brassy horns and sweet strings sounded as Crown Prince Sjur's chariot turned onto the main city boulevard from the avenue leading towards the Granite Citadel. Sjur was flanked by an honour guard of his sworn berserkers, all of whom rode immaculately groomed war horses. The procession covered the half-league between the palace and the shrine in moments. Sjur's eagerness to be formally bonded with his love was almost tangible on the air. The berserkers formed a protective shield around the entrance to the shrine, standing firm against any threat to the king-in-waiting, whether it be perceived or real. Sjur was accompanied on his walk up the aisle to the altar by Torulf, Fossfjall's ferocious Supreme General.

They took their places to the left of the altar, waiting with baited breath, while Reilynn's procession made its way up the city's central promenade. My heart sang as I picked out Cathal from the swarm of cavalrymen cantering their steeds alongside Reilynn's horse-drawn carriage. The crowds lining the city's central boulevard shrieked in happiness and excitement, throwing cascades of fragrant rose blossoms into the path of Reilynn's stagecoach, their heady perfume being carried up to the church by the wind as the carriage's wheels crushed the carpet of petals to the floor, releasing their delightful scent into the air. The cheers grew louder as Reilynn's carriage drew closer to the Shrine of the Pantheon, reaching fever pitch as it came to a stop and the Queen of Cothraine stepped out onto the granite stone plaza surrounding the shrine.

Even though she was heavily veiled, the sight took my breath away. Even Gormlaith's jaw dropped open at the unparalleled beauty of her wedding dress. It was a vision of ecstasy in the finest, pure white sundgauvian cotton lace. The train of the gown was exquisitely brocaded and some ten yards long. As Reilynn took her place next to the altar my sister gasped, "That may well be the most beautiful woman in the whole of the Western Triad."

I could only nod my head silently in agreement. If I had ever doubted that royalty ruled by divine right, the notion had been dispelled the moment I laid eyes on her. Seeing Reilynn from this close, in person, I thought that she had a splendour and serenity that would shame devae – that she had the kind of beauty that could cause men to lose their minds. My attention was distracted from her as Braden and Cathal took their places as honour guards behind her. My innards melted as Cathal caught my eyes with a subtle smile, his gaze flickering briefly along the length of my dress. Cathal was a paragon of masculinity in his battle gear and I would have happily let him ravish me on the floor of the cathedral, but I put the idea aside – the notion of upstaging a queen on her wedding day with such a profane act was unconscionable. Little did I know that Sjur and Reilynn had already pre-empted my thoughts. As soon as the marriage rites were concluded, Sjur stripped away Reilynn's veil, kissed her deeply, and in a clearly premeditated coupling, they publically consummated their marriage on the top of the altar. The Dowager Queen watched on proudly as the Crown Prince inseminated her new daughter-in-law, tenderly stroking Reilynn's face and holding her right hand as her son made love with his new wife and queen. The Priestess of the Empress, far from appearing shocked, took Reilynn's left hand in hers and placed her free palm on Reilynn's bare stomach, chanting a fertility blessing to sanctify their union.

I watched the whole episode open-mouthed, gasping in horror to Gormlaith. "That surely isn't normal for a royal wedding."

"No, absolutely not..." Gormlaith confirmed with wide eyes, equally as shocked as I was. "I suppose it is one way of ensuring that the marriage cannot be contested on grounds of non-consummation."

When they were done, Vigdis wasted no time and ceded the throne, appointing her son to succeed her as King and welcoming her new daughter-in-law as Queen. "Sjur, my son, I could not be a prouder mother this day. Not only have you become a husband, you have also become a king. One day soon you will also become a father and sire a dynasty that will lead the nations of Fossfjall and Cothraine for generations to come."

"Thank you, mother," Sjur kissed the Dowager Queen's cheek, his heart radiating pure joy and pride. "It is my life's honour to accept the gift you have preserved for me so diligently and for so long. It is my vow to you that I will not squander this blessing you have worked so hard to give us."

"I am glad to know that the future of Fossfjall is secure in your hands, my son." Vigdis said, smiling contentedly and turning to her successor as Queen of Fossfjall. "Queen Reilynn, it is an honour to welcome you into my family. The children you will carry for my son shall unify our nations for a thousand generations. Cothraine and Fossfjall will know peace and prosperity once again."

"It is a grievous tragedy that my family did not live to see this day, but their loss will be avenged." Reilynn pronounced loudly to the gathered crowd. "Maeryn and Karryghan will soon rue the day they chose to interfere with the destinies of our Royal Houses."

The entire cathedral erupted with noise as the wedding party cheered their support, waving clenched fists in the air and Sjur's berserkers added to the cacophony by howling louder than a hunting pack of dire wolves.

"Well said, my love!" Sjur shouted above the din, applauding. "Their days are numbered!"

The noise was deafening as the crowd clapped with joy, chanting the names of their new king and queen, who walked arm in arm back down the central aisle of the cathedral, waving their gratitude for the outpouring of love and devotion. The honour guard of rangers stood side by side with Sjur's berserkers, Torulf and Braden each leading a column of soldiers in the wake of Fossfjall's royal couple. Gormlaith wiped a tear from her cheek, overcome by the emotional outpouring of hope and delight from the massed celebrants. I steadied her with a hand on her elbow and kissed her gently on the side of her neck. "Are you alright, sister?"

"More than that, I think I could burst." Gormlaith laughed, enveloping me in a hug. "In the days following my transformation, after I had learned the truth about the coup from Karryghan himself, I never thought I would live to see this day come. What we have witnessed here is the beginning of their downfall, and it cannot come quickly enough."

We followed the wedding party out of the Shrine of the Pantheon, walking down the city's central boulevard towards the sea. The road was lined by thousands of noblemen and commoners alike, who showered the congregation with grains of uncooked wheat, which had been soaked in fruit or vegetable juices to give the grains colours of a rainbow - raspberries for red, carrot for orange, apples for yellow, nettles for green, woad for blue and beetroot for purple. Gormlaith and I laughed in delight the whole way to the sea wall, where Sjur and Reilynn boarded the lift that would take then down to the Royal Marina at the bottom of the Abyss. The rangers and Sjur's berserkers formed a protective cordon so that the enthusiastic throng of Lesøsnø's citizens could not get too close to the workings of the lift. The whole city appeared to have turned out for the wedding and as the lift began its descent to the king's flagship docked below, the air around the lift carriage was surrounded by glittering coloured grains of wheat, making it look like the royal couple were being transported down a column of multicoloured light. It was an extraordinary sight, cast against the magnificent backdrop of the Abyss. A giant flock of screeching gulls and gannets, always on the hunt for an easy meal, swarmed around the lift, snatching grains of wheat from the air, wheeling around the thick cable suspending the platform like a feathered funnel of wind. Eventually they dispersed as the crowd ran out of rainbows to throw and the happy throng of citizens gradually started to thin out as the lift carriage disappeared out of sight, returning to their daily business, gossiping about the ceremony. I heard fragments of their conversations as Gormlaith led me over to where Braden and Cathal still stood guard at the top of the royal lift with Torulf and the rest of Sjur's berserkers.

"-the queen is so beautiful-"

"-it's good to have a king again-"

"-and then he fucked her, right on the altar!-"

"-they never did!-"

"-for a moment I thought the Dowager might join in-"

"-those two will sire some divine-looking children-"

Cathal greeted us both with a hug and steered us through the crowd to where Braden was deep in conversation with Torulf. The Fossian Supreme General was a colossus of a man, seemingly more dire wolf than human and even more terrifying in appearance than the armoured brute that had kidnapped my father in Croycullen. He favoured me with a grin of ferocious charisma when he noticed me on Cathal's arm. "You keep fine company, Baron Ranger."

"Thank you, your grace. May I introduce you to my sister, Wizard Gormlaith of Monagealy and our companion, Ailidh? It was the abduction of her father, Eoghan of Ballinlara that alerted us to the current situation in Clongarvan." Cathal said, unconsciously drawing me a little tighter to his side. I bowed my head respectfully to the general, tightening my grip around Cathal's elbow.

"My condolences to you, child," Torulf said, his liquid grey eyes full of empathy. "Lord Commander Braden informed me of your loss. There is seemingly nothing the Arch Mage and his puppet will not stoop to. I look forward to the day my troops will sweep their filth from Clongarvan and make them face the Dark Rider's Judgment on the fugue plane."

"Thank you, your grace," I replied, shuddering at the intensity of his declaration. Torulf was such a force of nature it seemed to me that trying to deny him his goal would be about as futile as trying to hold back a high tide.

"I could not agree more, Supreme General," Gormlaith ventured carefully. "But prising the Arch Mage out from his Tower will not be as easy as plucking an oyster from its shell."

"If need be I will simply smash the shell." Torulf replied with a nonchalant shrug of his giant shoulders.

"I hope that will not be necessary, your grace," Gormlaith said, swallowing in trepidation. "Karryghan does not have unanimous support on the Grand Masters' Council in Clongarvan."

"Time will tell, Wizard Gormlaith. I will not give your Grand Masters long to find their consciences." Torulf said, watching the last dregs of the crowd filter away into the side streets and away from the sea wall. He turned to Braden and clasped his hand affectionately. "Our work is done here, my old friend. I must check progress on the loading of our ships and report to the king and queen. We should make sail before sunset. I bid you a safe journey, Lord Commander. I will look forward to seeing you again on the waves at Monagealy Sound."

"May the Earth Mother grant you favourable winds and calm waters, Supreme General," Braden said and smiled, both of his hands dwarfed by Torulf's mighty paw as he bid him a fond farewell. "Boats are not my preferred mode of travel, but I look forward to seeing you again on your flagship."

Torulf whistled sharply and the berserkers formed a rectangular cohort, which followed the general as he jogged away, leading the soldiers down the sea wall to one of the largest cargo cranes that had been reserved for his use. Braden glanced around to make eye contact with each of his rangers and nodded the way back into the city. "Let us go."

Cathal was in a philosophical mood as he walked back to Braden's estate, with his sister on one arm and me on the other. "What do you think? Is today the beginning of the end for Maeryn and Karryghan, or the end of the beginning for Sjur and Reilynn?"

"Can't it be both?" I frowned.

"It is definitely both," Gormlaith concurred. "The more pressing question is how long these periods last and what happens afterwards."

"Maeryn is surely doomed." Braden said, falling into step beside us and adding his insight into our conversation. "Now that the legality of his claim to the throne in Cothraine has been thrown out by the Guild of the Art, he cannot survive the coming storm Sjur and Reilynn will bring down upon him."

"And Karryghan?" Cathal asked.

"There things are less certain." Gormlaith said with a worried frown. "The Arch Mage is more than a match for any of the Grand Masters on the Council and could do considerable damage to any force threatening the Tower of the Aether in an open assault."

"Surely you are not suggesting we leave him be?"

"Not at all, but a direct conflict would risk many casualties, including innocent bystanders around the Tower. We should consider our options carefully before moving against him."

"You mentioned Karryghan does not have complete support on the council." Braden said. "Could they be persuaded to turn him over to Sjur and Reilynn?"

"It seems unlikely, but it is possible."

"Then how would you eliminate him?"

"I have a suggestion, but you will not like it."

I saw Braden's shoulders tense beneath his armour. "Go on."

"Keri."

"No, absolutely not!" Cathal interjected hotly, dropping his sister's arm as if it were a venomous snake.

"Brother, I know how it sounds." Gormlaith squeezed Cathal's hand between both palms, her sapphire blue eyes looking up imploringly into his face. "Our best chance of toppling Karryghan is with the element of surprise. Attack him in his chambers at the Tower, before he has a chance to entrench himself with layers of acolytes between him and any threat. To oppose him any other way risks thousands of deaths. He is that powerful, that ruthless. And the only spellcaster I know that might have any hope of defeating him in single combat is Keri. You all know what happened last time I stood against him. I cannot defeat Karryghan without her."

"Sorry Gormlaith, but I will not have a demon-fucker in my warband." Braden spat.

"This is a matter beyond any of us." Gormlaith protested. "If Karryghan should get his hands on the Nexus, the consequences would be dire, not just for Cothraine, but for the planes themselves. Keri understands what is at stake. She would not have freed me otherwise."

"You are biased towards her." Cathal said, freeing his hand from her grip.

"You are biased against her, and quite rightly, too. But we have to look beyond ourselves. Karryghan wants the Nexus so that he can try to depose the Mystic. Imagine if he succeeded. It would be like turning one of the heavens into a new hell. Magic itself would become corrupted." Gormlaith said, with tears forming in her eyes at the thought. "We cannot allow that to happen. I cannot. And I would take help from any quarter to prevent it."

"I agree." I said, hugging Gormlaith to show that she was not alone in her convictions. "We've got to consider every option. Cathal, I know that Keri wronged us, hurt us badly in the past. But she did free Gormlaith, and though I wouldn't go so far as to say her heart is in the right place, if Gormlaith thinks she can help us avoid a slaughter in Clongarvan when we bring Karryghan down, we should at least see if she would be willing to help us."

"We can set conditions, take precautions." Gormlaith continued to press her case. "Forbid her from casting spells until we reach Clongarvan. Having her join us is a risk we can manage. The benefits of having her aid outweigh the dangers."

"What do you think, my boy?" Braden asked Cathal. "You know the witch better than I do. Can she be controlled?"

Cathal stopped walking, rubbed his face and scoffed. "You might as well try to command the wind."

"But could she best Karryghan?" Braden pressed, his opposition wavering.

"Judging from what I have seen of her ability? Without a doubt," Cathal frowned. "But why would she endanger herself in opposing him?"

"Come with me, and ask her yourself." Gormlaith pleaded. "She does not wish to see Karryghan gain control of the Nexus. That alone is reason enough."

"We should speak with her, at least." I said, touching Cathal's cheek with my palm. Cathal closed his eyes and nodded, with a sense of defeat, worn down by his sister's persistence. "Then let's go, now, before you change your mind."

"Ah, we should go home first." Gormlaith said with a dry smile. "You will want to change before we go to her lodgings."

"What's wrong with the way I'm dressed?" I asked, nonplussed.

Gormlaith took my arm and began to lead me back to Braden's estate once more, chuckling. "If you enter the Star and Sextant wearing that, you will either walk out with all of your holes violated, or be carried out with several extra ones. For your own sake Ailidh, before we speak with Keri we should dress you for battle, not a ballroom gala."

32 – Keri

It was the evening immediately after the Royal Wedding when I was finally revisited by Gormlaith at the Star and Sextant, confirming my prediction that we would meet again. This time she did not come alone, which was fortunate, given the amount of attention she was attracting by wearing an extraordinarily lovely wizard robe of thick, wine red silk. Ailidh also drew plenty of glances from the inn's rowdy clientele, though for a very different reason. She was dressed identically to Cathal in a ranger's leather jerkin and walking boots. Gormlaith's staff and the sword belts worn by Ailidh and Cathal gave the group an unspoken aura that sent a message very much along the lines of *fuck with us at your peril*. I attracted Gormlaith's attention with a wave of my hand, watched the sway of her hips as she led Ailidh and her brother to my table and thought that I would very much like to fuck with her, albeit in the privacy of a bedroom. The prospect seemed remote however, as she and her guardians sat down with me at my table. They all, very politely, declined my offer to share some wine together. Cathal looked the most ill-at-ease of the three and let Gormlaith do most of the talking. With the pleasantries quickly dispensed with, Gormlaith got straight down to business.

"I imagine you know why we are here. Is your offer to assist us in retaking Clongarvan from Maeryn and Karryghan still open?"

"It is."

"Will you join us?"

"I will."

"Even if that meant having to face Karryghan in battle?"

"Gormlaith, my dear, I would be disappointed if we did not!" I chuckled, taking a sip of wine. "I assumed from the start that preventing the Arch Mage from taking control of the Nexus meant he would need to be slain."

"The prospect does not scare you at all?" Gormlaith asked, incredulous. "You know what he did to me."

"On the contrary, I look forward to finally meeting someone able to rival my skill in the Art."

"I hope your words are not ones of misplaced confidence, Keri. I am not looking forward to meeting the Arch Mage again, not in the least."

"As I said last time you were here, Gormlaith, it is imperative to keep the Nexus out of Karryghan's grasp. The balance of the planes must be preserved. If that means getting my hands bloody, so be it." I set down my glass on the table, carefully watching the mage's face. Gormlaith took a deep breath and nodded. "So, when do we leave?"

"Hang on a second," Cathal interjected, raising both palms. "Let me make one thing clear first. Your inclusion into the warband is conditional. After what happened on the road to the city, I would rather you did not travel with us at all."

"State your terms, Cathal, and I will abide by them."

"Until we reach Clongarvan, you will not cast magic within our camp, unless you are required to aid in its defence from wild beasts or some other threat."

"That is acceptable."

"You will also keep your contact with the rest of the party to a minimum and sleep separately from the rangers."

"That is also acceptable, and probably in the best interest of everyone." I said with a dry smile.

The journey south from Lesøsnø was far swifter than my journey north had been. Cathal's band of green cloaks had made the most of the unexpected assistance of the Dowager Queen and Crown Prince to assemble ten horse drawn carriages and enough supplies to construct a small village when we made camp each night. During the day I rode in a carriage with Braden and six of his lieutenants, and I had been given a private tent, which kept me segregated from Cathal, Ailidh, Gormlaith and the rest of the party. I appreciated the solitude and understood the suspicion the warband treated me with. As we departed the city, Cathal had taken me aside and warned me that my presence was a tolerated necessity and that any trust between us would need to be rebuilt from scratch, despite my assistance in breaking Gormlaith's curse. I accepted his scorn and wariness without complaint. In light of the events surrounding my abandonment of Cathal & Ailidh on our journey to the city, I was surprised that I was not being kept under a constant armed guard. Perhaps Braden and Cathal knew that I had the will and the means to break any shackles placed upon me if they tried. It was eight nights before my privacy was imposed upon. I was lounging on the simple cushioned bed roll of linen the rangers had provided me with, reading one of the scrolls I had purchased from the Great Library by candlelight when the silence was broken by the rustle of fabric at the end of the tent. Cathal announced his entry with a soft voice. "Keri, I saw the light. You are still awake at this hour?"

"It is only an hour beyond midnight. Reading is almost as good as rest." I said, gesturing with the scroll.

"What are you reading?"

"Refreshing my memory on Nevanthi's seventh prophecy; some of the finer details still elude me. But you did not visit me at this hour to talk philosophy and portent." I set down the parchment, sliding it back into its protective tube, before giving the ranger my full attention. He appeared furtive, even humiliated, his aura slippery and evasive. "To what do I owe the honour of this visit?"

"I wished to speak to you."

"Alone? About what, I wonder?"

"The mark you gave me. Gormlaith translated the rune. She called it a soul drain."

"Soul drain, soul siphon, soul tap – the daevae might call it all of these things and more. What of it?"

"Can it be undone?"

I laughed at the question. "Not in the sense that you would like. The spell was interrupted."

"You were going to kill me." He said it as a statement of fact, rather than an accusation.

"Yes." My reply was equally succinct, devoid of any emotion. "And I would have used your soul gem to summon a tanar'ri to rape and murder Ailidh."

"Yet we both still live. Why?"

"Because I changed my mind. Perhaps I do not find your company as loathsome as I claimed." I said, regarding him coldly. "What do you want, Cathal? What is done cannot be undone."

"The spell is still active. And I suspect you know how to stop it."

"Still active, you say? Impossible. Show me." I commanded him. Cathal took off his armoured jerkin and unbuttoned his shirt reluctantly, opening the fabric to let me see the glowing from the runes. I drew in a sharp involuntary breath, unable to stop myself from touching the pair of iridescent scars. Immediately I realised what had happened. When the Succubus had intervened in the soul drain, she had used our bond to form a connection with Cathal's soul. If the demonic sigil was fully activated, my mistress would be able to use it as a marker to form a link to the material plane. "What caused the runes to light?" Cathal lost his tongue, stammering with shame and embarrassment. "It began when Ailidh and I..."

"Fucked?" I interjected into his hesitation.

"Coupled." Cathal corrected me, a flash of anger briefly crossing his face.

"Ah, I understand." As the Succubus is the matriarch of lust, it was only natural that her magical anchor would feed on carnal energies. "Ailidh has matured since you inseminated her. I like the change in her."

"Can you deactivate the runes?" Cathal asked, his eyes pleading for good news.

I shook my head and lied without hesitation. "No. But you have nothing to fear from them. Completing the spell will not cause your soul to leave your body. The time for that has passed. If anything, it will strengthen your link between body and soul. The interruption of the original drain left it weakened. Did you feel stronger during the coupling?"

"Yes." Cathal admitted, lowering his head in mortification and avoiding my eyes.

"Then you know what you must do. Literally nothing would make Ailidh happier." I said with a knowing smile, but before I could take my hand off Cathal's chest and step away, his strong fingers encircled my wrist. Instantly understanding his intent, I tipped over my head to meet his gaze and subjected him to a withering stare of contempt.

"Cathal, you abject wretch of a man, you put your seed into her belly and yet you still do not love her."

"No... I do not." Cathal said, his voice breaking with his shame. "You did this to me. You must stop it. And she must never know."

"You ask too much." I told him, playing upon his fears to manipulate his emotions. If I could induce him to take me by force, it would strengthen my mistress's grasp on his sigil.

"Do you want to make me beg, or demand?" Cathal said with a snarl. I waved my free hand and the air just inside the canvas lining of the tent began to shimmer in a coruscant quicksilver membrane. Cathal let go of my wrist and looked around the tent in alarm. "What did you just do?"

"A sonic baffle. No-one outside will hear what happens now." I replied while pulling my robe off over my head and tossing it onto the ground next to my bed roll. I could feel the hunger of his eyes on my flesh, smell his yearning to be freed from my spell and see the repressed scarlet lust he harboured for me in his psychic aura. "Do you want to punish me for what I have done to you? Take your revenge on my body? It would be a fitting manner in which for you to complete the spell."

Cathal remained still for three breaths before he stepped forward and grabbed my hair, pulling back my head savagely. I gasped as I felt his teeth bite hard at my neck and tits. My hands worked at his waist to free his manhood as he fingered me roughly, making me yelp in pain and arousal. Our eyes locked. I stared at him imploringly and whispered, begging, "Ruin me."

The third scar on his chest began to scintillate as he spun me around and threw me onto the floor, pinning me face down onto the dirt with his weight. I moaned loudly to inflame his rage and passion as he buggered me with long, hard stabbing thrusts. My fingers clawed at the dirt, leaving deep gouges in the ground as I cried out, turning my head to look into his eyes, nodding encouragement and inciting with him further with my gaze. I spread my thighs and groaned lowly as Cathal pressed me down into the ground with one hand between my shoulder blades, the fingernails of his other hand digging deep into my hip. My tits scraped painfully against the ground as Cathal slammed his hips hard again and again and again into mine. He grabbed a handful of my hair and pulled as I came with a yell, unable to control myself any longer. The rune scar on his chest began to burn with infernal fire as he hurled me sprawling onto the bedroll, incensed that I was feeling more pleasure from my punishment than him, the abrasions on my chest and limbs seeping blood into the linen cover. Cathal turned me onto my back and he mounted me again, his hands gripping my ankles to open my legs wide. The look on his face almost matched the frenzied ardour of one of my

tanar'ri consorts. There was no tenderness as he ravaged me, as I wanted him to. This time I didn't have to fake my cries of pleasure and pain. The urgent brutality of his coupling left me in raptures. I shuddered and came again, my fingernails raking across Cathal's shoulder blades and back, leaving long, deep scratches that tore at his skin. He snarled in pain and held me down, fingers clamped tightly around my throat, depriving me of air with almost murderous intent. His other hand wrenched and twisted the flesh of my breast hard into the depths of his palm as he ground my body savagely against the bedroll. My eyes rolled up to the back of my head as I struggled for breath, though I did not feel any fear. We both knew I had it in my power to stop him if I wished it. Instead I submitted to his lust, my back arching and legs thrashing as I climaxed yet again. I tore the thin linen covering my bedroll involuntarily with my nails, my fingers clawing desperately at the fabric until Cathal came deep inside my sex. The three-lobed sigil I had cut into his chest sparked blue like a flash of lightning, casting our entangled shadows across the canvas of my tent. Abruptly, the light from the scars vanished into the darkness, the final element of the anchor spell now complete. Cathal collapsed onto me, breathless and gulping for air. I hooked my legs around his back, trapping him inside me. I closed my eyes, panting with satisfaction.
"Better."
"Yes, I do feel better." Cathal wheezed, misunderstanding my statement. "The light is gone, and I still have my soul."
"That is not what I meant." I chuckled, gently stroking the dulled scar tissue on his chest. "Work on improving your endurance and I would consider taking you as a lover."
"What? No, this was just to break the spell, nothing more." Cathal looked down at me in puzzlement, appalled by the purple bruises and bite marks he had left on my neck and breasts and at the raw, bleeding abrasions covering my flesh where he had shoved me down into the dirt. He tried to withdraw from me, but I held him fast with my thighs, teasing him with slow, rocking motions of my hips.
"And now that the spell is broken, you would tell me that you did not enjoy it?" I taunted Cathal, rolling him over and pinning him beneath me. Cathal groaned lowly as I took him deep into my mouth, tasting our combined passion. His hand went to my neck again, this time to guide my mouth

and tongue gently, rather than to choke. "Do you want me to stop?"

"No." He croaked, broken of any notion of resistance. I had his seed on my tongue in minutes, so complete was my power over him. As he moaned in ecstatic defeat, I reflected that there was more than one way to steal a man's soul. Cathal looked down at his chest. The scars remained dark, despite his arousal and climax. Cathal touched the marks tentatively. "It is truly over then."

"Yes." I rolled off him and tapped into my wild aetheric affinity, suffusing my body with a regenerative glow and healing the bruises and bloody scratches marking my skin. "Now get out, before you are missed."

I lay back, luxuriating on the linen mat, my senses still glowing from the intensity of the coupling, as Cathal dressed in silence and left my tent with no small amount of haste, shame and regret. It was still over an hour before dawn when my dozing was interrupted by unexpected warmth surrounding my body, and an insistent probing by damp, tumescent flesh against my thighs. Thinking that it was Cathal returning for another coupling, I spread my legs before opening my eyes. The violation was inhumanly fast and deep, fully awaking me with a scream. Before my eyes adapted to the dim pre-dawn light I recognised the smell and knew I was lost. The warmth was accompanied by a reptilian musk, tinged with brimstone, the tell-tale scent of a lust daeva. Yet I could tell from the creature's aura that this was no common demon from the Second Circle. The bittersweet psychic tingle surrounding her carried so much power and confidence that it could only be my mistress, the Succubus herself.

And, terrifyingly, she was pleased with me.

Indescribable ecstasy washed over my entire being as she injected her venom into my belly. I was instantly paralysed by the intoxicating fluid and was left utterly at her mercy. She could have taken my soul in that moment and I would not have cared. It was all I could do to keep my eyes open and air circulating in my lungs. The Queen of the Daevae caressed my face with genuine gratitude and tenderness as she leaned down to brush my lips with hers. Her face was the most beautiful thing I had ever seen. Her lips did not move as she spoke to me telepathically, our minds joined as one.

Keri, my servant, once again you have surpassed my every expectation. It is a joy to speak to you in person once again. I have not visited the material plane in decades.

I live to serve you, dread mistress.

So do all of my agents, but none serve as well as you do.

The Succubus knelt over my comatose body, her huge, leathery wings mantling around us like a protective cocoon. My aura trembled in fear and adoration as she stroked my neck and chest with an obscene delicacy. The claws on her fingertips were longer and sharper than spearheads. A mere flick of her slender wrists would be more than sufficient to disembowel me. She allayed my fears with another kiss on the mouth. Her luxurious hair was a livid, scarlet mane that fell down to her shoulders and was studded by a bone-white crown of a dozen twisted horns sprouting from her skull just above the level of her temples. The mere sight of her flawless skin and exquisitely feminine figure inflamed my devotion and love for my mistress. I knew that she would be the death of me, but that it was worth the price of eternal damnation just for the enjoyment of a few brief moments in the presence of her endless, effortless sensuality.

Our pursuit of the Nexus draws to a close, my servant. I can sense it nearby, dormant and elusive. Tell me of your discoveries at the Grand Library.

Nevanthi left no clues as to the form of the Nexus, but all the other elements of her prophecy have proven to be true. It manifested in Fossfjall almost exactly one score years ago and was discovered by accident by a diviner who abandoned their office to hide it. I know that the girl who accompanies us was fathered by him, but know nothing of the mother. The girl, Ailidh, was not kept privy to the diviner's secrets and has no knowledge of the Nexus's location.

And the business with the changeling? That amused me greatly.

She and the Nexus are connected in the prophecy, but it is not clear how. I dare venture that we will learn more when we confront the diviner's killer in Clongarvan. The Arch Mage has ambitions for the Nexus and is crucial to its appearance.

You must prevent the Arch Mage from taking possession of the Nexus, at any cost. I have my own plan for the Nexus. I will use its power to destroy the Executioner and take his place as the Lord of the First Circle. If you continue to serve me well, you will replace me as Queen of the Second Level.

You honour me greatly, dread mistress.

Then, once Hell is under our control, we will use the Nexus to lay waste to Heaven and end the Celestial Conflict once and for all. But all depends upon finding the Nexus first and learning how to control it. I sense it hinges on the diviner and his daughter. Find out how.

It will be as you command. I will speak with her again about her origins. She must know more than she has spoken of so far. I could find no record of her in the Litany of Births & Deaths. Blondes are rare in Cothraine. It seems impossible that the birth of such a girl in Croycullen would pass unnoticed by the town council.

Keri, my sweetling, you never fail to please me, but I must go now, before the dawn breaks. I have preparations I must make.

The Succubus kissed me again and the barbed sting in her tail injected me with such a large dose of her orgiastic venom that I thought I might die from ecstasy. My dread mistress was gone when I awoke and only the trail of her venom across my belly and thighs convinced me that I had not hallucinated the whole episode. I conjured a glass vial and scraped the viscous green liquid off my skin, sealing the immensely potent paralytic toxin inside with a thick cork stopper. The poison would keep indefinitely and I had little doubt that I would find a use for it sooner rather than later. Sunlight seeped through the canvas of my tent and I heard the bustle of activity as the rangers began to dismantle the camp. I dressed myself and picked up my staff and knapsack before stepping out into the bright blue morning sun, glowing with pleasure and feeling like I had experienced several lifetimes of carnal delight in a single night. I was certain that today would be a fine day.

33 – Cathal

"Did you see Keri this morning?" Gormlaith asked. "She looked like the cat that got the cream. No, more like the entire creamery."
"You would know all about that." I scoffed, tugging on a rein to steer our carriage around a divot in the road surface.
"Come to mention it, you are looking far too pleased with yourself as well." Gormlaith said, regarding me with a frown. We were sat together on the driver's platform of our wagon, the third time in as many days I had shared the duty with her. Ailidh was riding with the scouting party at Braden's request, learning more fieldcraft from Torcall and Creighton, two of the most talented trackers and rangers in our warband. "Did something happen last night?"
"No, nothing." I said, looking away to concentrate on the road ahead.
"Brother." Gormlaith's tone was affectionate but warning. The sapphire gemstone inlaid into her necklace glistered in the sunlight as she shook her head, sadly. "You have never been able to lie to me. Not even when I was a cat."
"Honestly, Gormlaith, Sapphire was less judgmental." I deflected.
"Do not try and change the subject." She parried. "What are you two up to?"
"Nothing!" I protested, far too defensively. Realising my error, I tried deflecting again. "Define 'something'."
"Oh, I would not presume to know." Gormlaith responded with deadpan sarcasm. "Not given your predilection for redheads."
"That is unfair, and bordering on slander."
"So I was right. You did see her last night. And this morning you both look like you were given a ten-day of first class service in a Masevaux brothel."
"It was not like that." I said, deeply uncomfortable with the direction in which the conversation had turned.
"Then what was it like? Will you tell me, or should I consult the tarot?" Gormlaith transfixed me with one of her most disapproving stares, which had me squirming in my seat.

"Sister, please."

"It was nothing you are proud of, that is for certain." Gormlaith said as I stopped the carriage, lest my lack of attention run us off the road and break an axle on the embankment.

"Sister, I swear, one day your divine intuition will be the death of me." I sighed, looking up briefly to the heavens. "I spoke with her about the soul drain. About why it was still active and whether it could be dispelled."

"And?"

"We came to an arrangement. Keri completed the spell and my scars are nothing more than that: marks from an event I am only too keen to put behind me and never speak of again."

Gormlaith's perceptive blue eyes narrowed with suspicion. "What kind of arrangement?"

"Gormlaith!" I cried in exasperation, throwing up both of my hands into the air. "It is done, and the matter is over with. My body is healed and my soul is where it should be. I have no love for Keri, you know that."

"Did you lay her?" Gormlaith demanded, verging on fury. My mouth opened and closed twice, but no words would come. Gormlaith slapped my cheek hard in her frustration. "Cathal, you idiot! Whatever will Ailidh say?"

"Sister, please. She cannot know. It was the only way to dispel the soul drain. Keri incited me." I bowed my head, feeling ashamed as I confessed, "Gormlaith, I- I was not gentle."

"I will keep your secret, but not for you." Gormlaith hissed, utterly aghast. "Ailidh deserves better. You laid with the girl, knowing that she loves you. You cannot toy with people's feeling so! It is not right."

"I never asked for her love. It is my fault that I cannot return it, that much is true. But would you have me live a lie?"

"If she carries your child in her belly? Yes." Gormlaith said, her cheeks were flushed with anger and she was adamant in her resolve. "Time will tell if your coupling impregnated her. And I would expect you to do the honourable thing."

"I would. You know I would." I said, lowering my head once more, my eyes closed in remorse. "I have sworn to defend her with my life, and I will."

"That is not the same thing as being a good husband." Gormlaith reproached me as she rose from her seat, ducking back into the rear of the wagon and delivering a final, devastating admonishment. "You should have found a better solution. When one makes deals with a demon-worshipper, the price is rarely what is agreed. But I suppose it is your soul to lose."

Gormlaith's disapproval haunted me for the rest of the day, so I was glad to be able to concentrate mindlessly on the road, chivvying the horses to find and follow the easiest path as we caught up with scout troop. An outrider met the caravan of wagons an hour before sundown, leading us to a small clearing in the Western Weald. We were a day's ride from Sylane, where we would take the road south past the Mouth of the Dragon and through the village of Killcuain to rendezvous with Reilynn's fleet south of Moonchion in the Bay of Serpents. Based on our progress so far, Braden had estimated that we would be in place to meet the queen's flotilla with a full two days to spare. Though true to form, the Lord Commander of the Rangers had insisted that we maintain our original daily target of leagues travelled, in order to compensate for any unforeseen delays we might still encounter along the way, especially since it was not utterly certain that a suitably large ship would be available for us to hire when we reached the harbour in Moonchion.

Once I had parked my carriage in its place in the camp's defensive circle, I dismounted from the driver's seat and secured the horses, giving them troughs of hay and water to recuperate from their hard day of walking. By the time I had finished Gormlaith was already helping our contingent of rangers unpack our wagon and assemble their tents. My sister waved me away when I silently gestured an offer to help her pitch the tent we shared with Ailidh. I took her wordless hint that she was still disgusted with me and instead made my way over to the centre of the wagon circle, where Braden was conferring with Creighton and where Ailidh was chatting animatedly with the scout riders she had been paired with for the day. She greeted me with a hug and a kiss on the cheek.

"You look like you enjoyed yourself." I said, returning the hug, but not the kiss. "Not too saddle sore?"

"I might need to lie down in the back of the wagon tomorrow." Ailidh laughed. "But it was much more fun than walking or driving."

"Creighton took good care of you, I hope." I said, just loudly enough for him to overhear, knowing that my former apprentice had a soft spot for Ailidh.

"Ever the perfect gentleman." Ailidh glanced over at him, with a smile. The introverted ranger's cheeks flushed at the compliment and he quickly broke eye contact, concentrating furiously on Braden's orders for the night watch. "I'm learning so much from riding with the scouts."

"Good, we will make a green cloak of you yet." I said as Ailidh looked up at me, beaming with pride. "Are you hungry?"

"Ravenous. D'you have time to join me before your watch?"

"Yes, I have the graveyard shift tonight." I led Ailidh across the camp towards the mess tent. A dozen rangers were already busy brazing large joints of meat and peeling vegetables for the colossal stew pots already blackening on the fire.

"I wish you wouldn't call it that. It sounds like tempting fate." Ailidh said with a shiver. "And you should never test the Lady's temperament."

"Ailidh, nothing ever happens in a graveyard at night." I laughed, taking her hand and giving it a reassuring squeeze as I steered her to an empty table. I sat next to her on one of the benches, enjoying the feel of her hand in mine. There was a murmur of several concurrent conversations as a handful of junior rangers filing into the mess gave us respectful nods and smiles, though they clustered together on tables at the other side of the tent, neither wishing to impinge upon our privacy, nor wanting to have their own conversations overheard.

"Not according to the stories father read me as a child."

"Fairy tales? Or horror stories?" I asked, raising an eyebrow.

"Both." Ailidh smiled as she scooped a long strand of her golden hair behind her right ear. Since spending time with Braden and Gormlaith in the city, she was noticeably less self-conscious about showing the burned side of her face, knowing that she was in the kind of company that would never judge her by appearance alone. Keri's observation that Ailidh had changed since she had begun her stay in

Lesøsnø was an accurate one, though I was unconvinced by her reasoning for it. "Though, I enjoyed the fairy tales the most."

"I preferred the horror stories."

"Why am I not surprised?" Ailidh grinned, leaning over to kiss my cheek. I smelled the sweat on her hair from her day in the saddle and once again I was reminded of Aoibheann's scent when we shared a bedroll after a long day patrolling the hills and forests near the Dragonspine. I looked into Ailidh's face and I felt a nervous fluttering in my stomach when the sight of her disfigurement did not unnerve me. I cupped the back of her head in one hand and returned her kiss tentatively on her lips. Ailidh sighed with surprise and satisfaction when my courage failed me and I drew back to gauge her reaction. "What was that for?"

"An apology. You have always been forthright about your feelings for me, and I fear that I have not."

"Cathal, what are you trying to say?" Ailidh asked with a frown, her question tinged with apprehension.

"That I have been a fool; that I am not worthy of your adoration; that I have not always been honest with you or myself about us. And that I should beg your forgiveness for the mistakes I have made." I said earnestly, holding her gaze without flinching.

"What mistakes?" Ailidh asked, regarding me closely as she stroked my face and neck affectionately.

I glanced around the increasingly full mess tent, wary of the attention of curious eyes, ears and chatty mouths. "Not here. Come with me."

I stood and beckoned for Ailidh to follow as I led her back to our carriage, finding that after Gormlaith and her assistants had erected our tents, they now pursued other duties, either standing guard on the perimeter or joining the rest of the off-duty rangers at the centre of the camp. I led Ailidh into the three person canvas shelter I shared with her and my sister. Double checking that we were alone, once I was assured of our privacy, I kissed Ailidh on the mouth and began to undress her as soon as we were hidden behind the translucent paper partition screen surrounding my personal section of our tent.

"Cathal, what has possessed you?" Ailidh asked breathlessly as I pulled her down to the bedroll. She gasped my name as I showered her face, neck and torso with ardent kisses. My lips and tongue caressed every square inch of her below the chin until she opened her sex for me and let me taste her. Ailidh's soft groans became more urgent as my tongue explored her, her fingers gripping the hair on the back of my neck and tremors shaking her legs as she came. Our lovemaking was long and tender, part seduction, part penance, as I sought atonement for not reciprocating her desire until now. It was only after night had fallen and we had raised each other to another mutual climax that Ailidh noticed that the demonic sigil carved into my chest had lost its ominous glow. "My love, your scars..."

"Are no longer of any concern." I reassured Ailidh as we held each other close. I could not have been more content as I let her lie on top of me. "I realised something this day, something I have denied but something you have always known. I am yours. I would do anything for you: Everything for you."

"And what caused this epiphany?" Ailidh asked with an unfocussed smile, still half-delirious.

The sounding of alarm horns from the camp's perimeter pre-empted any opportunity I might have had to answer her. We both leapt towards the pile of clothes we had abandoned at the side of my bedroll, covering our modesty and donning our chest armour and boots in frantic seconds as distressed bawls of panic erupted from sentries all across the camp.

"Hell hounds!"

"Demonspawn!"

As I fastened my sword belt over my waist, I checked that Ailidh's boiled leather jerkin was settled properly around her torso. "Forget the rest! Just take your sword!"

I grasped Ailidh's wrist and ran out of our tent, my sword already unsheathed. Several tents were already ablaze, thanks the mindless hell hounds spitting fireballs at every enemy and structure that they could see. I heard Braden's commanding shouts over the chaotic din of the battle.

"Rangers! Form up! If you cannot see the whites of their eyes, get closer!"

"Ailidh, stay close, keep behind me." I ordered her, getting her to draw her sword. I dared to waste a second to kiss her full on the lips, as if it would act as a protective ward against the evil ransacking the camp. "And do exactly as I tell you."

My eyes swept the chaotic battlefield that had once been our camp, and I identified a handful of hell hounds tearing apart a tent that had been adjacent to my own. The three demonic war dogs were sufficiently isolated from the rest of the camp that I was confident that I could kill them before attracting attention from the rest of the infernal raiding party. I gestured my intent silently to Ailidh and she nodded, running in after me as I charged the pack of demonic hounds. The first fell before it realised it was under attack, my precise blow decapitating the fel beast in a single stroke. A similar fate befell its companion, which turned its head just in time for my strike to bisect its skull from jawbone to spine, exactly midway between the fel beast's eyes as I whirled my blade around a full circle on the follow-through from my attack on the first demonspawn and brought it down with all of my strength onto the hell hound's head. Alerted by the fall of its companions, the third hell hound snarled and leapt towards my throat. I dove beneath its attack in a forward roll, quickly regaining my feet to see that Ailidh had backed up my attack with horizontal slashing strike that had decapitated the upper skull from the hell hound's lower jaw and torso. I gave my lover an encouraging nod as she rejoined me at my side. Our sense of victory and satisfaction was short-lived, however as a psychic demand thundered through the clearing.

WHERE IS THE GIRL? FIND THE BLONDE AND BRING HER TO ME, NOW!

Ailidh and I were forced to our knees by the sheer force of the psychic call, a terrible mental onslaught neither of us had experienced before. She looked at me in horror, not quite comprehending the nature of the threat. I gripped my sword's hilt tighter, realising with a growing sense of despair that Ailidh was the only one in the camp with blonde hair, and that the voice we had just heard could not have come from any ordinary demonspawn. The only being I knew of that was capable of such psychic power was the avatar of a full-fledged prime daeva. Of all the rangers in the camp, only I had a weapon capable of besting a daeva in single combat, and while my sister and Keri were already sorely pressed engaging the swarm of hell hounds wreaking havoc in the camp, only I could stand between the daeva and its prey with even the smallest chance of success. I recalled my argument with Gormlaith from this morning. I had sworn to defend Ailidh's life with my own. There was no question that I would be true to my oath. I grabbed Ailidh's jerkin by the shoulder pad and looked deep into her eyes. "Ailidh, find Gormlaith. Find Keri. And run."

"No, Cathal! I can't do that. I love you. I won't!"

"You must. In the name of all that is holy, you must!" I implored her, tears running down my face as I kissed her lips for what I already knew would be the final time. The ground shook with heavy footsteps as I heard my destiny approach. "Flee! Do it now, if you ever loved me. And do not look back."

"No! Cathal, I can't leave you." Ailidh begged, clasping my knees as she wept on the floor, utterly bereft as I stood to meet my fate.

"You have to. This is not a fight that we can win." I lifted Ailidh onto her feet as the daeva stomped past the tree line into view. I gasped both in fear and awe. The statuesque daeva was twice my height and had a wingspan of over thirty feet. Luminescent, acid green venom dripped from her serpentine tail and she was possessed of a terrible and majestic beauty. Her gorgeous features twisted malevolently when she saw Ailidh by my side. The daeva unleashed a petrifying, primal bellow and the taut muscles on her long, slender legs rippled as she began to charge towards us with long booming strides that made the ground tremor. I pushed Ailidh away from me with a shove in the centre of her back, urging her to flee. "Run! Now!"

I yelled my own war cry as I met the daeva's charge head on, rolling underneath her slashing talons as she swiped at me with one hand and then the other, the blows coming just a fraction of a second apart. The tip of my sword bit out in a broad arc, nicking through the tendons on the back of her left leg, drawing blood and severing sinews to hamper her mobility. I ducked and rolled again, trying to avoid the rapid flurry of strikes from the daeva's arms, her clawed feet and the talons on her articulated wings. Knowing that I was badly outmatched in terms of speed, dexterity and power, I dove between the demon's legs in desperation, slashing at her other thigh, attempting to hobble her completely. My blade cut deep into the muscle, thanks to the enchantment Ailidh had endowed the sword with back at my cabin, but no sooner was I back on my feet planning my next attack, the daeva's regenerative powers had begun healing the wounds almost as speedily as I could inflict them. A quick glance over my shoulder informed me that Gormlaith had reached Ailidh and that she was pulling her reluctantly away from my battle. Taking advantage of my momentary distraction, the daeva tried to trip me with a sweep of her long, horse-jointed leg. I leapt over the three-clawed hoof only to be knocked off my feet by a swing of the daeva's vast right wing. I tumbled across the ground, barely managing to keep hold of my sword. Both Gormlaith and Ailidh screamed my name in horror as I came to rest on my back, momentarily stunned. There was no time to react before the daeva plunged the spear-like talons of her left hand through my torso, just below the heart. The coppery taste of blood erupted into my mouth as I coughed up ichor from my ruptured lungs and guts. There was no sensation in my legs as the daeva sneered beautifully, bringing my face up to hers, as if for a kiss.

VALIANT. BUT NOW YOU DIE, BRAVE ONE.

"You first." I spluttered, lashing out with the final dregs of my strength to thrust the tip of my sword into the daeva's amber, glowing eye though the black vertical pupil, pressing forwards until *Dìcheall's* crossguard rested on the demon's cheekbone and the tip of the blade stabbed clear through the back of the daeva's skull. The demon's avatar shrieked in rage and pain, collapsing to the ground in a quivering heap. With the daeva vanquished and its strength dispelled, the ground pulled me down into its final embrace, my body falling through the air and crumpling like a sheet of paper when I hit the dirt. My vision began to blur and fade. There was no feeling from any of my limbs and I knew the remaining span of my life would be measured in seconds, not minutes.

Ailidh screamed with anguish as she ran to my side, falling to her knees and cradling my head on her lap as she wept. "Cathal, no, please. Don't, don't die."

Tears also ran down Gormlaith's cheeks as she stood guard at Ailidh's side. "Ailidh, it is too late. He- he is gone."
"No, no, no. Please, gods, no." Ailidh sobbed, kissing my lips, forehead and cheeks, her hot, wet tears dripping onto my face. Faced with the moment of my own oblivion, I understood why Aoibheann had smiled when I had cradled her in my arms as she died. My sacrifice had not been in vain and Ailidh would survive me. I tried to smile, like Aoibheann had. Where there still is life, there is hope. I gasped a final breath and looked up into the face of the woman I had come to love.
"I-" was all I had the chance to whisper before my world fell into darkness.

34 – Gormlaith

The sound of Ailidh's howl of torment when Cathal's life left his body would haunt me to the end of my days. She looked up at me, as she cradled his corpse, utterly distraught. "Do something. Heal him."

Tears of my own rolled down my cheeks. "I cannot."

"Why? Why not? You have magic! You have power! Please! Bring him back. He's your brother!"

"I would. If only I could." I knelt at Ailidh's side next to my dead sibling, enveloping her in my arms and letting her cry against my neck. "Even the Dark Rider could not bring him back."

"What's the point of magic then, if you can't help people? What's the point?" Ailidh raged, overtaken by her grief, clasping her head in her hands. Her lower lip quivered as she grabbed my robe and looked me in the eye, lashing out. "What's the point of you?"

I knew that Ailidh's grief matched my own, that I was not the true target of her rage and pain. But Ailidh's words still cut me to the bone, reflecting my own sense of helplessness and loss. With no clever words of comfort that I could conjure to salve our agony, I burst into tears and collapsed onto the ground next to Cathal, weeping uncontrollably. I took my brother's head into my hands and screamed impotently, regretting that our final conversation had ended poorly and that I would never be able to tell him how much I loved him or that I forgave him. Ailidh stood and fled the scene. I let her go and stroked my brother's bloodied cheeks, closing his now lifeless eyes, whispering in utter desolation "Cathal, brother."

Soft footsteps rustled behind me, but I kept my forehead pressed against Cathal's as I wept for him. A leather gauntlet settled gently on my shoulder and a sympathetic voice whispered my name. "Gormlaith, I am so sorry."

I placed my hand upon his and squeezed gratefully. "Thank you, Braden. Is the camp secure?"

"For now, all the hell hounds are dead. A daeva, on the material plane," Braden's voice shook as he regarded the corpse of the demon. "I never thought that I would see such a thing. The size of it! It could have slain us all."

"Would have slain us all, had Cathal not intervened." I corrected him. I studied the remains of my brother's killer closely. "This is no ordinary devilkin. This is the avatar of a prime daeva - Second Circle. It came for Ailidh. You heard its call?"

"We all did." Braden confirmed with a nod. "The Second Circle? The Succubus?"

"Look at it. Have you ever anything so beautiful?"

"No, never," Braden swallowed in trepidation as his eyes traced the outlines of the daeva's glorious curves. He blinked and looked away, as if afraid that looking at the demon for too long would corrupt him. "But why did it come here? What interest could the Succubus possibly have in Ailidh?"

"I have not the faintest clue." I confessed, rising slowly to my feet. I turned to Braden as Keri ran over to us across the clearing, accompanied by Creighton and half a dozen of the surviving rangers. "We cannot linger here long. This is a temporary victory at best. Once the daeva's essence reforms on the demonic plane, it will gather its strength so it can return."

"How long do we have?" Braden asked.

"Your guess is as good as mine. I am not an expert in demonology." I shrugged. "The longer we tarry, the greater the risk becomes. If the daeva is hunting Ailidh, it will surely come back soon."

Braden turned to his lieutenant. "Creighton, tell the men to pack up the camp immediately. Consolidate everything we have onto the remaining carriages, even if it means that some will have to walk."

"Yes, my lord." Creighton nodded.

"How many horses did we lose?" Braden asked.

"One score and seven." Creighton grimaced. "But enough remain to drive the remaining carriages and provide us with a half-strength scouting party."

Braden sucked air between his teeth. "Fuck. I suppose that will have to do."

"We can try to acquire more horses in Sylane." Creighton suggested.

Braden nodded before dismissing his new Second. "Go. Time is of the essence. We must conduct a burial ceremony for Cathal before we leave."

Keri raised her eyebrows in surprise. "Is that really necessary?"

Braden turned to the sorcerer, quietly furious. He stepped toward her menacingly, his nose just inches from hers. "Cathal was like a son to me. His flesh is tainted by the daeva's touch. We cannot take him with us. But I will not leave his body out for the wolves, demon-fucker. He must be buried and Cathal's sacrifice will be honoured, the risks can be damned. Your opinion has no weight in this matter."

"I apologise, my lord." Keri stepped back, lowering her head meekly. "You are correct, of course. I meant no offence."

Braden stooped to pull Cathal's sword free of the daeva's corpse. "Then make yourself useful packing up the camp, wizard. If I find out that you had a hand in this attack..." Braden aimed the tip of Cathal's sword at the base of Keri's throat, the threat unspoken, but clear.

I stepped between them, hoping to defuse the conflict. "Braden, please, there has been enough killing for one day."

The ranger lowered the sword reluctantly, not taking his eyes of Keri, his suspicion plainly written across his face. "Not enough; too much."

"On this we can agree." Keri ventured in reconciliation, her tone subdued as her gaze flickered between the two bodies on the floor in front of us.

"I will call for you when the ritual is ready." Braden gave Keri a glare of absolute, venomous distrust before stabbing Cathal's sword into the ground next to his body. Braden stalked back into the wreckage in the centre of the camp, beckoning his rangers around him to give commands that would impose order again over the devastation that had been left in the wake of the attack.

I looked back down at my brother's corpse, my heart breaking once again. I crouched beside him to kiss his bloodstained lips farewell. His body was already cold, but an involuntary twitch of his left arm drew my attention to the weapon still holstered at his side. I detached the scabbard from his sword belt, reattaching it to the silk sash gathering the material of my wizard robe around my waist. I removed the enchanted ever-sharp stiletto from its leather sheath and felt the weight of the delicate weapon. Daggers had long been a traditional alternative to spells or staff as a magic-user's last resort offense. I had never developed the arm strength to properly wield a sword and it seemed fitting that I should inherit my brother's off-hand weapon. I clutched the leather-bound grip as tears welled in my eyes, thankful that I would have a memento of our final adventure together. I placed the stiletto back into its scabbard and sobbed gently. "Goodbye, brother. May the Dark Rider protect you."

"May the Dark Rider protect him." Keri echoed with a whisper. My head snapped around at the sound of her voice. I had not realised she was still here. When I surveyed her angular features I found something unexpected: something akin to grief, or perhaps remorse. "Gormlaith, we need to talk."

"About what?"

"About this." She gestured towards the bodies of my brother and the Succubus's avatar. "Join me. My tent still stands."

I followed the sorceress warily, but her demeanour only gave me sensations of sorrow from her psychic aura, not an impending threat. We entered her tent and sat down facing each other, cross-legged on the dirt. Immediately I began to feel uncomfortable, noticing the bloodstains and rips in the covering of her bedroll. I had not wanted to believe it when he told me, but I could not deny the signs in front of my own eyes. I gathered my thoughts for a moment before breaking the silence. "Cathal raped you. Last night."

Keri shook her head. "No, Gormlaith. It is worse than that."

"What could be worse than that?" I asked, open-mouthed and appalled.

"I *wanted* him to." Keri scoffed when she saw the look on my face. "Do not look at me so. I lie with daevae, Gormlaith. Do you think that tanar'ri just want to be held?" Keri said, her psychic aura souring with the mocking sarcasm of her reproach. "No, I welcomed it, for him to take revenge for what I did to him and Ailidh in the Weald outside Lesøsnø. Not for his benefit or Ailidh's, nor for mine; but for my mistress. She stopped me from draining Cathal so that she could use the sigil I cut into him as a portal to the material plane."

"Your mistress... surely you do not mean-?" I cut off my question in mid-sentence, my jaw falling open in shock. Bile rose in my throat as the full realisation of the truth became evident in my mind. I closed my eyes, suppressing the urge to vomit, my hand over my mouth. "Your mistress is the Succubus?"

"She needed Cathal as a planar anchor. But I did not learn why until tonight: Ailidh. Ailidh is not just connected to the Nexus. She *is* the Nexus."

"Oh gods," I covered my mouth, feeling lightheaded, as if I had breathed a lungful of surgical chloroform ether. The contents of my stomach spewed out onto the ground as I wept in despair, finally realising of the depth of Keri's deception. I had been blinded by the apparent selflessness of her breaking of my curse. I had suspected that she might have an ulterior motive in reinstating herself into our group, but not in my wildest nightmares had I considered that it might be so depraved and terrible. My lack of insight had cost me the life of my brother and now might cost me the life of my dearest friend, too. But that was only the beginning. If a creature like the Succubus gained control of the planar nexus, the order of the heavens and hells themselves would be pitched into chaos. Suddenly the meaning of the Succubus's tarot card in Braden's séance back in Lesøsnø made sense. The Queen of the Daevae was literally working against us. I had been trying so hard to divine a figurative interpretation from the card that I had missed the literal interpretation before my nose. And Cathal had died as a consequence of my mistake. I vomited and retched again, even though my stomach was empty.

Keri took a cloth from the knapsack by her bedroll and wiped my lips and cheeks clean with unexpected tenderness. She held my face and looked into my eyes with genuine sympathy and sorrow. "Gormlaith, please believe me... if I had known... I would have deactivated the sigil."

"What is done cannot be undone." I sobbed, doubly remorseful because my talent told me that for once she was telling the whole truth. "You brought a prime evil into our camp. Give me one good reason why I should not ask Braden to have his men kill you."

"I will give you two." Keri said, raising the sharp point of her chin proudly. "One, I could murder every single man and woman in this camp without losing a single drop of my blood. Two, I know more about the Succubus and her abilities than anyone on the material plane. No-one can defend Ailidh better than I can."

"My brother lies dead because of your scheming. I have no reason to believe that you would protect Ailidh from a demon who is, by your own admission, your mistress."

Keri gave me an inscrutable smile and tilted her head to acknowledge the soundness of my logic. "True. Personally, I stand to gain much should my mistress assume control of the Nexus. But even as selfish a soul as mine can recognise that giving a prime daeva the ability to access all of the planes is a poor idea. The balance must be preserved, and that means keeping Ailidh safe not just from the Succubus, but from Karryghan as well. And you cannot do that alone."

My legs trembled slightly as I stood, either though fear or fatigue – I could not tell. I stared Keri down as my blood ran cold. "I do not trust you. But you are correct. I cannot hope to keep Ailidh and the Nexus safe from the Arch Mage and the daevae without your help."

"We have an accord, then?" Keri asked, remaining seated.

"For now. If you put the camp at risk again, however-"

"Both you and Braden will try to kill me." Keri interrupted me with a smirk, utterly confident in her ability to defend herself.

"Will you join us for the interment?"

"Of course," Keri replied with a nod. "I know you believe that I treated your brother poorly, but I was fond of him, in my own way."

I left Keri to let her dismantle her tent with the assistance of a pair of bloodied and scorched rangers, searching instead for Ailidh. I found her curled up defensively into a ball beneath our carriage, quietly sobbing, her sword and armour lying on the ground by her side. I rested my ebony staff against the frame of the wagon and sat at her feet.

"Braden is preparing a service for Cathal. You should join us. Cathal would want you there."

"Leave me alone." Ailidh mumbled between sobs. "Go away."

"Ailidh, you will not get another chance to say goodbye." I cautioned her, my own voice quaking with anguish. "You will regret it later if you do not."

"I can't... I can't do this anymore, Gormlaith. Not without him." Ailidh said, sounding utterly bereft and broken. My heart ached with sympathy for her, as I felt exactly the same.

"You can, sister." I placed my hand on her shoulder to reassure her. "And you must. There is no other choice."

Ailidh raised her head and regarded me with wet, swollen eyes. Her baleful reptilian eye was bloodshot and gave me a shiver of terror. Ailidh's jaw chattered as she trembled in the emotional torment of her grief. I opened my arms and she accepted the invitation, embracing me hard. We clung to each other in the cold and the dark, weeping into each other's hair.

Eventually we ran out of tears and I kissed Ailidh's forehead. "Come with me, Ailidh. Come."

Ailidh allowed me to lift her to her feet and I wrapped an arm around her shoulders to lead her back into the middle of the circle of wagons where Braden was wrapping Cathal's body in the partially-burned remains of a tent canvas. A long, shallow trench had been dug and Cathal's sword, bow and quiver rested upon a wood and stone cairn marking the grave at the head of the channel in the ground. The bodies of the eight rangers that had fallen during the hell hound ambush lay head to toe along the edge of the trench. Ailidh's chest heaved at the sight. "Oh, gods..."

I steadied her with a second arm around her waist, drawing her to my chest. I gave her a kiss on the cheek and Ailidh reached back to clutch my thigh. "Courage, sister."

Braden beckoned us towards him as he finished closing Cathal's makeshift shroud. My brother's face had been left uncovered and Braden had cleaned his visage respectfully. He might have been asleep, were it not for the paleness of his skin, which was pallid from the blood loss. "Good timing. I was just about to send for you."

"Thank you for this, Braden." I said, giving the lord commander a respectful bow.

"Cathal deserves no less." Braden said before lifting a horn from his belt and blowing a seven note signal to call the entire camp to gather for the internment ceremony.

The surviving rangers immediately stopped what they were doing and formed a column along the length of the burial trench, kneeling in respect for the fallen. Ailidh and I took our places next to Cathal's body. Keri kept her distance warily, unwilling to antagonise Braden, but mirrored the formality of the ritual, taking the knee and bowing her head.

"Sons and daughters of Sylvan, we gather to honour the passing of our brethren." Braden said, in a clear but anguished tone. The rangers began a low guttural chant, using a language I did not recognise. "We commend these bodies to the ground. Our lives are a boon from the Earth Mother and we repay her generosity by returning our flesh back to her in death."

"Amen." I said, in synchrony with the rest of the funeral party. The green cloaks resumed their dirge. I tightened my embrace around Ailidh's shoulders when I felt her breathing become ragged as she struggled to contain her emotions.

Braden and Creighton took each body by the shoulders and ankles, placing them reverentially into the funeral trench. Braden announced their names as he laid them to rest. "Brother Cathal. Brother Torcall. Sister Gilleonan. Brother Luthais. Sister Devorgilla. Sister Ciorstaidh. Brother Arailt. And Brother Seocan, may you all rest for eternity."

"Rest for eternity." I echoed with the lamenting rangers. Ailidh cried as Braden cast the first handful of dirt into the burial trench. I scooped up a clod of loam into my palm and scattered it onto Cathal's burial shroud. "Goodbye, brother."

Ailidh remained on her knees, weeping bitter tears as Braden came over to sit with us, next to Cathal's resting place. He stroked her hair affectionately and gave her a bear-like hug. "Ailidh, my child, I have something for you."

Ailidh wiped the tears from her eyes and kissed Braden's neck in supplication, meeting his gaze and trying to put on a brave face. "What is it?"

Braden presented her with Cathal's sword *Dìcheall*, which he had retrieved from the body of the Succubus and thoroughly cleaned before reuniting the blade with its custom-built leather scabbard from Cathal's sword belt. "This. I feel that you will need it in the days to come."

"Braden, no," Ailidh blanched and shook her head. "I don't want it. I don't deserve it."

"It is not yours to give or refuse, my child." Braden smiled without humour, still processing his own grief at Cathal's death. "It is yours by right and yours by need. Cathal would have bequeathed it to you and if the daeva returns, no other weapon is capable of defending you."

"But I'm no swordswoman." Ailidh protested. "It would be better left in your hands than mine."

"The blade is attuned to you. You enchanted it, and when Cathal slew the daeva's avatar, some of its power was drawn into the aetherium. You are correct to say that martial prowess alone will not save you. But if you wield this sword, you will not need to rely on swordcraft alone. The power it absorbed from the Succubus will enhance your speed, your strength and will be the bane of any daeva you might encounter. It may be your only hope in the trials that you will surely face."

"Cathal gave his life willingly to protect yours." I interjected. "Take his sword and honour that sacrifice. He would want you to take advantage of every possible factor that can enhance your chances of surviving this ordeal."

"I never wanted him or anyone else to die for me. I'm not worthy of such a sacrifice." Ailidh protested, on the verge of being overwhelmed by her grief once again.

Braden leaned forward and kissed her on both cheeks, reaffirming his love and respect for her. "It is not your place to determine what others choose to value. Like your father, Cathal placed the value of your life above his own. If you want to honour him, the best thing you can do is take his place. *Dìcheall* belongs to you, just like he did, even if he was reluctant to admit it. Wield it in his name and in his memory. And know that you always have a place of honour among my rangers."

Ailidh clasped the sword to her chest, tears welling into the corners of her eyes. "Braden, I- I don't know what to say."

"Then say nothing." Cathal's mentor replied with a bittersweet smile before kissing her forehead, his own heartache plainly written across his lined features.

"Sometimes silence speaks far more eloquently than words ever could. Ready your carriage. We leave for Sylane as soon as the graves are filled and the camp is packed."

"Come, Ailidh." I urged, placing a hand on her elbow to lead her back to our wagon. Ailidh held Cathal's sword close to her chest with both arms, as if holding a baby, still stupefied by the evening's events.

"Gods have mercy, sister." Ailidh lamented as we passed the crew of rangers shovelling soil back into the mass grave, tears running down her face.

I set her down in the rear of our wagon, which was packed to the gills with supplies recovered from the ruins of the camp. I helped Ailidh remove her boots and retrieved her armour and wakizashi from underneath the carriage, setting them down beside her. I stroked her neck tenderly before telling her "Try to get some sleep. Let me deal with the carriage."

Ailidh grasped my hand before I could drop back down to the ground. "How d'you do it, Gormlaith? How d'you stay so... composed?"

"I don't." I blurted, letting the facade of my court accent slip. With all my self-control momentarily abandoned, I bawled my grief loudly. Ailidh's hands found my neck, drawing me towards her face. I kissed her full on the lips and she responded passionately. My fingertips cupped her breasts through her tunic and I pawed at her like a newborn, just for a second, before I recovered my senses. I broke away from the kiss, sobbing in misery, yet laughing at the absurd inappropriateness of my desire. "Sorry. I need to get away from this place."

"Gormlaith, I – I..." Ailidh stammered, unsure about what had just happened and equally confused as to how she ought to react to it.

I pre-empted whatever she might have been inclined to say by embracing her in a desperate hug. I kissed her neck beneath the ear and whispered "Not now. Sleep. There will be plenty of time for talk later."

I slipped out of her embrace reluctantly, jumping out of the back of the carriage and onto the ground without looking back. I wiped the tears away from my cheeks and drew in a long breath with a soft whimper of distress. I ground my teeth and grimaced, tilting my head back and wanting to scream to the heavens.

"Gormlaith," Braden miraculously appeared at my side and gently wrapped his fingers around my right elbow. "Join me."

I said nothing as he walked me in silence across the camp to his carriage, urging me to take a seat on the driver's platform as he retrieved a large bottle made of green glass from a duffel bag in the rear of the wagon. Braden sat next

to me, uncorked the bottle and took a long swig of the potent spirit within. Braden proffered me the bottle.
"Akvavit from the Silkwood: it will not make you feel better, but it will numb you for a time."
The harsh grain alcohol burned my throat as I chugged almost a third of the bottle in a single swallow. I handed the bottle back to Braden and fell forward onto his lap, sobbing. Braden comforted me by caressing my neck and back sympathetically. I heard the bubbling of liquid as he took another gulp of the akvavit for himself. I let the magnitude of the consequences of my brother's death hit me in their entirety for the first time and my being simply dissolved with anguish. My elder brother had always been a constant in my life, albeit often a distant one. The thought of his absence tore at my soul and I wailed in despair, my fists beating against the wooden frame of the carriage with impotent, dull thumps.
"Let it out, Gormlaith. Let it all out." Braden whispered into my ear, his own tears wetting his cheeks. I yelled a primal scream of grief until my lungs ached while my brother's mentor embraced me. "Even the strongest tree must know when to bend in the face of the fiercest wind. It is better to suffer and bend than it is to break."
"Cathal... my brother. He's dead." I moaned pathetically.
"I will miss him too, Gormlaith." Braden said, stroking the back of my neck in reassurance, as if I was still a cat. The remembrance of being polymorphed almost made me flinch, but I suppressed the reaction, knowing that Braden was only trying to provide me with solace as best as he could. "No-one has the strength to carry the burden of the entire world on their back. It is only natural to fail and fall. It is how we retake our feet that counts."
"What if I do not want to get up?"
"You will always discover a need to find your feet: be it love, duty, or ambition. It matters not." Braden said, running his slender fingers self-consciously through his short, grey hair. "That you stand again, that is the only thing that matters, not the reason why."
"The Succubus came for Ailidh. When she returns, and sooner or later she will, I do not know whether we will be able to repel her."

"Then you need to either find a way of preventing the daeva's return, or nullifying the cause of her interest in Ailidh."

"I do not know if that is possible."

"You are a diviner, are you not? I suggest you find out." Braden's reproach was a kindly one, delivered with a wry smile. I stared at him mutely for a moment, before laughing and then erupting inexplicably into tears again. Braden wiped the salty drops away from my cheeks with his thumbs. "Whatever happens, my rangers will fight by your side for you and Ailidh. We are committed to you until the end. Cathal's death does not change that. If anything, it strengthens my resolve to support your goals. Your brother was my finest student. I trust that he would never commit himself to an unworthy cause."

"Thank you, Braden." I said, with my arms around his waist as I leant my head against his chest, glad to know that his commitment had not wavered in the aftermath of the Succubus's assault on the camp. I regained my composure and sat up, declining Braden's offer of another sip of akvavit. He shrugged silently and tipped back his head, gulping as he drained the bottle of the remaining spirit. He threw the empty bottle as hard as he could and I heard it smash on the ground when it eventually landed, almost two score feet away. "Can I help with the pack up? What would you have me do?"

"Nothing, my child. Sleep if you can. You can have my place in the back of the wagon."

"I should watch over Ailidh." I said, starting to stand. Braden restrained me with a gentle hand on my forearm. "Both of you should be alone for a time. I will have Creighton attend to her if she needs anything. But solitude to grieve is the only thing you will both want for the time being, I fancy. It is all I desire too, but the men require leadership."

Braden assisted me into the back of the carriage and I laid my head down on his bedroll reluctantly. He covered me with a blanket and stroked my hair with a heartbroken smile before he dismounted from the wagon silently. I drew my knees up to my chest, closed my eyes and cried until I slept.

35 – Fiacre

Maeryn had completely lost his mind in the two months since Queen Reilynn had inexplicably escaped the Royal Palace. He still wore the bandages on his right hand where Aiden had maimed him, but there were no medicines or bindings that could be applied that could prevent the ongoing disintegration of the king's sanity. It had always seemed to me that given the circumstances of Maeryn's ascension to the throne that his professed love for Reilynn was unlikely to ever be reciprocated. Now that any possibility of Maeryn maintaining the legitimacy of his claim to the Crown of Cothraine had been comprehensively undermined by Reilynn's disappearance, Maeryn spent his days rocking on his throne like a disturbed, abandoned toddler, drinking his own weight in wine every day. Following Aiden's betrayal, Maeryn had disbanded the Order of Companions and I had been co-opted into a dual role, acting both as bodyguard to the king and head of the armed forces. To say that I was displeased by the development would be a masterwork of understatement. I do not have the temperament of a bodyguard and every hour I spent with the king subtracted away from my ability to do what I considered my real job and carry out my duties in the headquarters of the Field Army. In less than a week I had learned to simply report to the king first thing in the morning, wait for a couple of hours for him to get too drunk to notice my absence and then return to the garrison for the rest of the day.

It was just before noon when Maeryn's head started to droop towards his chest, too heavy with wine for his feeble neck muscles, and I was just about to take my leave when Viscount Tadgh, Cothraine's ambassador to Fossfjall, entered the throne room, looking flustered. I silently cursed the timing of his arrival. Judging from the look on his face, the news Tadgh was about to deliver to the king was not going to please him and I was likely to lose another hour to one of the king's unhinged rages.

"What is it, ambassador?" Maeryn drawled, not realising that he was about to be given arguably the worst news of his life.

"Grave news from Lesøsnø, sire." Tadgh began, wringing his hands in distress. "Queen Reilynn has been received as a guest by the Dowager Queen and the Crown Prince. She arrived in the city last month, reportedly by boat. At the Dowager Queen's request, Reilynn submitted to a magical inspection, which found that there was no legal impediment to annulling your marriage to Reilynn on the grounds of non-consummation."

"What?" Maeryn exploded like a keg of black powder, hurling his wine glass at Tadgh, who remarkably had the mental and physical alacrity to dodge the incoming crystal goblet. It flew past his left shoulder, shattering on the floor behind him. "Lies! Slander and falsehood!"

"The legality of the declaration from the Guild of the Art is unimpeachable, your grace," Tadgh continued, his voice quavering uncertainly. "Furthermore, the legality of your ascension to the throne in Cothraine has been contested. Fossfjall has declared that they will no longer recognise your sovereignty as king and that Queen Reilynn is the sole monarch of Cothraine."

"Reilynn would be nothing other than a princess with no path to the throne without me, the ungrateful bitch!" Maeryn spluttered, bashing the armrest of the throne with his maimed hand, leaving the bandage bloodied and seeping. Fortunately, he was too drunk to notice. "I will post her head on the palace gates for this indignity!"

"It gets worse, your grace. Reilynn married the Crown Prince Sjur three weeks ago. Dowager Queen Vigdis immediately abdicated following the wedding, appointing Sjur King and Reilynn Queen of Fossfjall. They are said to be intent on unifying the Crowns of Fossfjall and Cothraine."

"Traitorous whore, how could I have ever loved her?" Maeryn staggered up to his feet and fixed me with a belligerent stare. "This is your fault, Duke Fiacre. Your failure to deliver me the Nexus has undermined everything the Arch Mage and I have tried to achieve in the years since the coup."

I knew that it was an unjust accusation, spoken in drunken anger and that I was simply the most easily available target for his impotent rage, but I almost reached out to strangle him. It was not as though anyone in the room would have been able to stop me. I raised myself to my full height and growled "I suppose your failure to bed Reilynn is my fault as well."

"What did you say?" Maeryn blinked, stunned at the temerity of my disrespect.

"That I have better things to do than play your whipping boy, your grace." I turned my attention to the diplomat and he shrank beneath my gaze. "Viscount, where is Sjur now, still in Lesøsnø?"

"No, your grace, Sjur and Reilynn left the city on the flagship of the Fossfjall fleet for their honeymoon cruise. Their destination was not declared, but the flagship was accompanied by a significant flotilla of thirty ships."

"That represents almost half of the strength of the Fossfjall navy. They are probably already on their way. I must see to the city's defences." I said, making my way to throne room's door.

"You have not been dismissed, Field Duke!" Maeryn said, with his face full of crimson, drunken fury. I pulled my arm out of the king's reach when he attempted to grab at me.

"Try and stop me, your grace." I sneered down at him, resisting the temptation to kick his legs out from beneath him. Maeryn fumed silently, knowing that he was utterly outmatched physically. I snorted in derision and left the usurper to his wine and solitary misery.

Once I was back in my office in the Field Army Headquarters my respite was short-lived. I had barely sat down at my desk with a flagon of ale and the current deployment plans for the northern border and the capital city when an apparition of shimmering silver walked out of thin air to stand opposite my desk. I hardly needed to look up from my work, as there was only one person it could possibly be. "Arch Mage, to what do I owe this honour?"

"Sarcasm does not become you, Field Duke." Karryghan said, chiding me gently with his ever condescending tone. "I understand the king received some unwelcome news today."

"If you mean that Maeryn's claim to the throne has been thrown out by the Royal Family of Fossfjall and that their newly crowned King Sjur has all but declared war on Cothraine, yes, I would suppose he has had better days."

"This was inevitable the moment Reilynn escaped from the palace. It seems a shame that palace security was left in the groping hands as someone as feckless as Duke Aiden. A friend of yours, I understand?"

"A friend of circumstance only, Arch Mage, you will recall that both you and Maeryn had a hand in appointing us to our positions." I replied testily. I would not be allowed to be made a scapegoat for Maeryn's failing legitimacy as the country's monarch.

"Indeed, Field Duke. I am beginning to think that we may have made some poor choices. Aiden abducting the queen, your failure to return the Nexus... it is not a record to be proud of."

"None of this would be an issue if you had done a better job in choosing a puppet to install on the throne with the spine to break Reilynn to his will."

"A shame that you were already married, then, Duke Fiacre. I know you have no issue with bedding young girls."

It was a reference to Dervla, of course. Karryghan had persuaded her to become my mistress before she came of age. Dervla had lied to me about it, only revealing the truth several months after I had first coupled with her. The Arch Mage had then used the threat of exposing my affair with an underage girl to blackmail me into aiding his coup and the following purge. "If you wish to say something important, Arch Mage, I would recommend that you get to it. I have work to do. No doubt you would like the capital to be prepared for when Sjur tries to smash down the city walls?"

"I could not care less about the city. It can all burn, provided I find the Nexus in my hands." Karryghan scoffed. "See to your defences if you must, but you will double the number of search parties crossing the border. If war is inevitable at this point, it does not matter how many skirmishers you send north into Fossfjall. The Nexus must be found and be in my hands before the turning of the solstice."

"And if I refuse to carry out your request?"

"Then your secret will be the talk of the Western Triad by nightfall tomorrow. You would not even be welcome in as permissive a country as the Jewels." Karryghan said with a cruel smirk. "Oh, one last thing, Field Duke, I will be meeting with King Maeryn tomorrow morning. You will be there, too."

I was not given the chance to voice my dissent before the Arch Mage's apparition dissolved into the air. I took the flagon of ale from my desk and chugged the entire bottle in a single slug, tossing the empty ceramic vessel onto the city map spread over the table. Dregs of beer leaked from the mouth of the flagon, staining the paper and smudging my immaculately inked notes, but at this point I was beyond caring. Thoroughly disgusted with matters of state and with the way my day was turning out, I closed the door of my office with a frustrated slam that almost broke the doorframe out of the mortar holding it into the wall and headed home to see my wife.

"What're you doing home so early?" Brighe frowned as I announced myself at the door to our townhouse. I should have known better than to expect a warm welcome, but on some level I did still love my wife. We had been childhood sweethearts, growing up together in the same village just outside of Sylane near the northern border with Fossfjall. We had married almost as soon as we had both came of age and we had moved together to the capital city after I had joined the Field Army. Our first few years together had been happy enough, as I had risen in the ranks quickly due to my size and skill with sword and crossbow. Things had fallen apart when Brighe had miscarried late in the pregnancy of our first child. The trauma of labouring a stillborn son just a few weeks prior to full term had left her infertile and unable to conceive. Brighe blamed the bad air of being in the city for the loss of our child and resented me for taking her out of the countryside and the forests of the Western Weald. Our marriage had never recovered and despite my elevation at court and within the Field Army, she accused me of forgetting where we had come from and faking nobility in my speech patterns. She did not understand the protocols required of working within the Royal Court and it was only the money I bought to the marital home that prevented her from moving back north. "Please Brighe, it is surely not so beyond the realms of possibility that I simply wanted to see my wife?" I said, taking off my sword belt and hanging it on the coat rack next to the front door.

"Why, has that petite curvy witch gotten rid of you?" Brighe snapped. After the coup I had told Brighe about my affair with Dervla, reasoning that I would rather she heard about it from me, rather than via rumour and that if she knew about it, it was one less thing that Karryghan could hold over my head. Brighe had not been in the least surprised, as we had stopped coupling following the failure of seven seasons of trying to have another child. When it became apparent that she was barren, Brighe had expected me to annul the marriage and was almost hostile to the notion that I would want to stand by her, knowing that I had wanted children as much as she did. "Six years you've been fucking her now, and her belly's still as flat as a pane of glass. Maybe you're the one whose seed won't germinate."

"Brighe..." I placed a palm over my eyes, sighing wearily. I did not want another bitter argument with my wife. "Can we please not do this again? It has been a bad enough day already."

"All you ever do these days is complain, Karryghan this, Maeryn that..."

"Because the country is falling apart!" I snarled back. "And somehow I am supposed to keep it together when the two most powerful men in the land are actively working against me!"

"I didn't hear you complaining when they promoted you to Field Duke."

"They never asked me to do the impossible then." I cut Brighe off with sharp gesture before she could open her mouth for her next retort. "Stop, I cannot talk to you when you are in such a mood. Do not bother cooking dinner for me tonight - I will not be sleeping here." I retrieved my sword belt and opened the front door to leave my home and wife behind me.

She continued to berate me until I closed the door, "That's right! Run away like a coward to your magical little whore!"

I walked west from my townhouse midway between the Field Army HQ and The Warrior's Guild past the city's reservoir and the gatehouse to the Royal Palace before turning north past the Guildhall Market. I maintained a tiny apartment on Mummer's Row, which lay between Fate's Theatre, the University and the Tower of The Aether. It was little more than a three room squat, with a bedroom, a privy and a sitting room, but it was cheap, discreet and more than adequate for the uses Dervla and I had for it. I gave a couple of coppers to one of the local message runners, scrawny youths too young or infirm to join the armed services or one of the many street gangs that populated the slum district in the north of the city. He sprinted off to pass word to Dervla in the Tower of the Aether that I wanted to see her tonight. She duly arrived just after sundown, her intelligent eyes glistening with mirth and a hint of malice. "The Arch Mage said you might call for me this evening."

"No mention of that bastard tonight." I told her, a threatening finger held at the tip of her nose warningly.

"Poor Fiacre," Dervla sniggered filthily. "If I had known you were in one of *those* moods, I would have brought a friend. You will make sure I can still walk come the morning, yes?"

"No promises." I told her, locking the door to the flat and taking her arm, leading her with carnal intent towards the bed. Dervla laughed and pulled her robe off over her head. She was almost two feet shorter than me, but the heaviness of her chest and hips were more than ample compensation. I enjoyed watching Dervla straddle me and the bouncing of her firm tits as she rode herself to a climax before I pressed her down into the soft mattress with my weight. She put her hands on my shoulders as I fucked her long and hard, using her willing body to drain me of all my frustrations and doubts, listening to her moans and feeling her shiver as she arched her back, hooking her short legs over my waist and clamping me between her thighs. I let her rest on my chest, her weight almost inconsequential against my bulk until her petite, insistent hands told me she was ready for another bout.

Later, long after midnight, I felt Dervla stir by my side, sighing contentedly. Sensing she was awake, I voiced a question that had been stirring at the back of my mind for more than two years. "Do you love me, Dervla?"

"I love that thick, long dragon of yours." Dervla tittered, still drowsy.

"I am being serious, Dervla." I frowned, beginning to regret having asked. "If I left Brighe, would you marry me? Bear my children?"

"Oh, by the Empress, no!" Dervla laughed callously, her eyes now wide open.

"Then why are you here, if not for love?"

Dervla looked into my eyes, seemingly genuinely confused. "To gain favour with the Arch Mage, of course... Why else? Surely you did not think- oh, Fiacre, you truly are a romantic if you thought..."

Her laughter turned my blood cold. "Gain favour?"

"Your wineskin is not the only one I have sucked, but Karryghan's seed tastes like ash and air, and he is too old to pleasure a woman like you can." Dervla stroked my face, her eyes full of pity and false tenderness. "As much as I enjoy our ruts, love is not a factor. A fast-track to Masterhood within the Guild however, that is very much a strong motivation."

"So you knew. You knew he wanted to blackmail me into supporting his coup. And you did it anyway; courted me, coupled with me, even though you were not of age." I said, aghast, feeling utterly repelled by her, almost corrupted by the touch of her flesh against mine.

"Yes, and we have both done very well out of the arrangement. Do not pretend you are an innocent party here. We are equally complicit. With the Arch Mage's patronage I will cut years from my apprenticeship and the advancement to Master Elementalist, and you stepped straight from a regional command to being the head of the Field Army."

"My wife was right when she called you a magical little whore." I pushed Dervla away from me, sitting up on the bed. Dervla laughed and sat cross-legged on the mattress. In the dim light from the oil lamps filtering through the shutters on the bedroom window, the heavy globes of her tits suddenly seemed a whole lot less alluring.

"What does that make you, Fiacre?" Dervla taunted me, tilting her head gently to one side as she regarded me sadly with knowing, gleaming eyes. "Perhaps Karryghan would not have your balls in a vice had you not been so eager to get your cock inside my slit."

"I thought that novyroyan sellswords were the most ruthless mercenaries in the world, but they have nothing on you, Dervla. Get out. And do not come back."

"My poor grizzly bear," I flinched when Dervla kissed my cheek goodbye and gave my manhood a farewell stroke with her sharp fingernails. "It can be lonely at the top. Remember me if you find that you ever want company. I really do love taming your dragon."

It was impossible to sleep after Dervla had revealed just how little she really felt for me, that our affair had been nothing more than a ploy by the Arch Mage to gain support for his insurrection. I was feeling angry enough that for a moment I honestly considered visiting one of the city's less reputable inns such as The Man-At-Arms or The Crimson Cutlass to find some unfortunate criminal to beat senseless, but I instead headed directly for the Royal Palace grounds and found a quiet pew in the Palace Chapel to pray to The Warrior for guidance and strength. By dawn my prayers were still unanswered, though I had not truly expected a divine intervention. I was not by nature a terribly pious man, but I did leave the chapel feeling slightly more at ease than when I had entered it.

My armoured boots crunched reassuringly on the gravel of the driveway that bisected the palace grounds from the gatehouse to the facade of the keep. The palace guards recognised and admitted me directly into the keep, where I made my way to the throne room, took a seat on the supplicant's bench before the throne and waited. Hundreds of long nights on sentry duty had given me the ability to sleep while sitting upright, appearing to be alert, even with my eyes partially open. I must have dozed off as the light filtering down into the throne room through the skylight was much brighter and at a much steeper angle compared to when I had sat down. A courtier announced the entry of the king. I stood and welcomed him with a bow.

"You are here early, Field Duke." Maeryn said, his eyes narrowing with suspicion, paranoid as ever.

"Arch Mage Karryghan informed me yesterday that he would meet with you this morning, your grace, and that I should be here."

"I see. Did the Arch Mage state the purpose of this meeting?"

"He did not, your grace."

"Perhaps he has some good news relating to the Nexus, at last." Maeryn sat down on his throne and signalled with his good hand for a courtier to fetch his first carafe of wine for the day.

"We can but hope, my liege." I replied, though given the nature of recent events, I rarely expected good news anymore.

It was not long before Karryghan swept into the throne room, his robes billowing in the wake of his purposeful stride. My cheek twitched involuntarily when I noticed Dervla follow him into the room, four steps behind his right shoulder, in an unspoken reminder of his power over me. I was careful to guard my thoughts, knowing that the Arch Mage's psychic powers could see through me as if I were made of crystal. With typical arrogance, Karryghan stood before the king without so much as courteous word and he certainly did not stoop to a bow. He simply waited in silence until Maeryn acknowledged him.

"Arch Mage Karryghan, to what do I owe this pleasure, so early in the morning?" Maeryn asked, feigning courtesy.

"I have received word from the Guilds of the Art in Fossfjall and Sundgau that they have rescinded their recognition of your claim to the throne in Cothraine. I have no choice other than to follow suit. To not do so would cause a schism in the Guild, which I simply cannot allow."

Maeryn's face was briefly hidden by a scarlet mist of wine droplets as he sputtered in shock. "What?"

"Your sorry reign is at an end, Maeryn." Karryghan said, as if explaining something as obvious as daylight to a backwards child. "Since you have no heirs and Reilynn is no longer a resident of the palace, it falls to me to assume the regency, as set out by the Law of Succession. In the absence of a natural heir from the Royal line, the Guild will not accept anyone else."

"You wanted this from the start, you traitorous worm." Maeryn leapt up from the throne as indignantly as his hobbled leg and maimed arm would let him. It was a genuinely piteous sight. Even Dervla looked away, embarrassed. "This treachery will not stand, Arch Mage. Arrest him, Fiacre."

"You have no authority here, Maeryn." Karryghan gloated, the smile hideous on his glistening, bald head. "The Field

Duke has been entirely my creature for years now. Perhaps now that the charade of your pathetic rule has been ended, I might finally be able to make progress retrieving the Nexus."

"I will have you killed for this, Karryghan!" Maeryn shouted, furious and impotent.

The Arch Mage slammed the foot of his staff into the stone floor, the echo stunning Maeryn into silence. The wyvern's head at the top of the Karryghan's staff bristled with hostility. "Enough! Every word out of your mouth simply serves to humiliate you further. Field Duke Fiacre; confine Maeryn in the King's Tower. He will be a guest of the Crown until I can find some use for him. And be thankful, Maeryn, that I do not find a less hospitable place in which for you to rot. But Fiacre, make it clear to your guardsmen, if he tries to leave the tower, my order is to kill him. I will not permit a rogue element at large in the capital, not this close to the solstice."

"By your command, Regent," I said, swallowing hard as I realised that whatever hopes I had of saving my country from chaos had now surely slipped away. I saw that Dervla was in my mind, reading my thoughts. The look on her face was one of sympathy and pity. She had been right when she told me that it was lonely at the top. I had not felt this isolated and alone even when standing watch overnight at a solitary guard post on the northern frontier.

36 - Keri

The last time I had visited Moonchion, the place of my birth, was more than a decade before Braden had been a babe swaddled in diaper cloth. As our battered and ramshackle caravan of wagons entered the outskirts of the port town I was disappointed but unsurprised to see that nothing had changed for the better since I had last walked Moonchion's streets. Indeed, nothing had changed since I had left as a child to start my apprenticeship at the Circle of Mages in Clongarvan two centuries ago. The dirt gutters bracing the badly paved roads still reeked of piss and human excrement, and the facade wall of the harbourmaster's mansion – the largest building in this gods-forsaken town – was still riddled with woodworm and had more paint peeling from it than was still attached to the salt spray-battered planking. While I was not pleased to find myself in Moonchion again, I was at least glad that soon we would abandon the claustrophobic wagon train for the open skies of the ocean. As well as costing the warband almost a fifth of its warriors, the attack by the hell hounds had also killed half of the group's horses, destroyed three caravan wagons and wrecked more than a third of the tents. I had decided to give over the use of my tent to the remaining green cloaks as a gesture of goodwill, choosing instead not to sleep at all for the remaining days of the journey. In the wake of Cathal's death at the hand of my dread mistress, I had tried as much as was physically possible to stay out of everyone's way, especially Gormlaith's, Ailidh's and Braden's. A handful of the surviving rangers had heard of my talent for felbinding and treated my presence with a suspicious, passive aggression. I did not resent them for it, knowing far better than they did what my role had been in the death of eight of their brothers and sisters of Sylvan. The rest, wisely, ignored me completely, but Braden's new Second, Cathal's former apprentice Creighton, having perceived his brethren's antipathy toward me, had taken it upon himself to improve my standing within the camp by lavishing me with compassion and attention. One night, after too many cups of akvavit by the campfire under a romantic starlit sky, he had even found the temerity to invite me back to his tent. I had enough empathy not to laugh in his face. Instead I gave him a withering look of contempt and told him honestly, "Child, I would destroy you."

Creighton had kept his distance after that, but I still saw him stealing glances of repressed desire at both myself and Ailidh in the days that followed. I hoped that once we were aboard ship and on our way back to Clongarvan that a cold sea breeze would dampen his ardour until he found a more receptive and realistic target for his unrequited passion.

I had always enjoyed the sea air and travelling the world's oceans. I had crossed half the breadth of the world by boat, so it would be a relief to have the privacy of my own cabin again, or the freedom to sleep out under the stars on the rolling deck of a ship. Braden had negotiated the lease of the largest ship in the port, a battered but sleek-hulled corsair that appeared to be over a century old. A wooden effigy of Lady Luck thrust out over the prow of the vessel, a two-faced figurehead symbolic of the ocean's fickle winds and currents. The Bay of Serpents beyond the port at Moonchion was named for its fearsome rip tides, which were as fast and sinuous as a sand viper on the hunt for its prey. They had been known to claim the lives of dozens of overconfident children swimming off the coast's fine beaches, as well as those of the parents that dived in after their progeny, hoping to rescue them. The rapid flows of water posed a significant hazard to ships close to the shore, too. It was the main reason why Moonchion struggled to maintain its viability as a port town, despite the wealth and variety of sea life off the coast and that the town had been established for several centuries. If you walked ten leagues along the coast west and east of the port, you could find the rotting hulks of a hundred wrecked ships that had failed to safely navigate the swift tides of the bay. The corsair's captain seemed almost as old as the ship and he expertly guided the ship safely away from the shore, barking short, efficient orders to his crew of a three dozen sailors. With the captain's permission, I stood on the forecastle of the ship, watching keenly with interest as the corsair glided smoothly out to sea. Small gangs of sailors hoisted the fore sail, then the smaller rear sail and finally the giant, triangular main sail from the ship's tall central mast. The hull creaked, seemingly in gratitude, glad to have slipped its moorings and returned to the ocean where it belonged. I was alone among the members of the warband in taking an interest in the undocking. As soon as our supplies had been transferred from the wagons to the ship's cargo hold, Braden and the other members of the ranger warband had immediately retired to their cabins. Perhaps all the time they spent in the forests and mountains gave them little affinity for the sea. I however, had regained my sea legs the instant I stood upon the corsair's gangplank. I closed my eyes, basking in the late evening sunlight and breathed deeply from the salty sea breeze, sighing lowly in pleasure. It was good to be on the waters once again.

I smiled as I watched a huge flock of gulls chase the ship's wake, cawing loudly for food and attention. The captain dug a small chunk of bread out from the pocket of his breeches and threw it over the stern of the ship. The seabirds swooped and squabbled and the largest gull, with a black back and a wingspan of two yards emerged from the melee with the titbit in its beak, which it swallowed quickly, beating away would-be thieves with its yellow, webbed feet. The captain saw my amusement and called out to explain himself, retrieving another hunk of bread from his pocket and hurling it into the swarm of gulls. "For luck!"
The captain ceded his place at the wheel to his First Mate, a broad-shouldered albino giant who appeared to be from the volcanic isles of Hrothurjökull. He ignored me as I tried to catch his attention with an ostentatious toss of hair over my shoulder, instead choosing to keep his red eyes fixed studiously on the horizon. Disappointed, I wondered whether his proclivities extended only to cabin boys. The aged captain joined me on the forecastle, keeping a friendly, respectful distance as he grasped the weather-worn balustrade with both hands, favouring me with a smile before looking out to the open ocean."Don't mind Einar, he doesn't like anyone."
"His loss," I said with a shrug, flicking my hair away from my eyes as the stiff on-shore breeze blew copper strands across my face.

"You look like a natural on deck. This is not your first sea voyage, I take it."

"Far from it."

"Where is the farthest you have sailed, if I may ask?"

"Kyotka." I said and smiled at the look of surprise on the captain's face.

"Truly? I'm impressed. Even I have not been that far east."

"You should go, if you can. The women there are exquisite." I told him, glancing over my shoulder briefly at the muscular First Mate. "The men, less so..."

The captain chuckled, his paunch rippling underneath his tunic and jacket. "I fear that my ship wouldn't make it past the Reach. Besides, I am told that the food in Kyotka is fit only for animals."

"It is not as bad as that, though an acquired taste, to be sure. Much like the women." I confirmed, smirking pleasantly at the memories.

"If you say so, master wizard."

"Keri." I introduced myself, offering my open palm. The captain gave me a respectful bow, and accepted the courtesy, shaking my hand. His grip was firm and the rough calluses on his palm and fingertips from many years of hauling miles of salt-laden ropes through pulleys felt like dry sand on my skin. The sensation was not unpleasant.

"Murchadh." The captain replied, seemingly pleased to have met a kindred spirit. "Pardon me mistress Keri, but I must attend to my duties if we are to reach Monagealy Sound by noon tomorrow. The prevailing currents here are as mercurial as the winds. If we are not careful, we might find ourselves back in Moonchion by the dawn."

"We certainly do not want that: And I would know. I was born there."

"I never would have guessed." Murchadh said, genuinely astonished. He gestured at my staff. "A Master of the Art from Moonchion? I hail from there myself – I never imagined such a thing would be possible. You are full of surprises, mistress."

"Do not let me belay you, captain. May I stay on deck a little longer?"

"Of course, you look surer of your feet than some of my crew. Stay as long as you wish. I will ensure you are not harassed."

I gave Einar a furtive look and said wistfully, "Perhaps you ought to warn me not to harass your crew."

Murchadh's laugh was long, loud and straight from the belly. "You missed your calling, Keri. You should've been a pirate, not a landlubbing spell-chucker."

"Who knows? Perhaps one day I might consider a change in career?" I replied, smiling at the captain's imaginative and affectionate jibe. It was certainly preferable to being called a witch.

"I trust you will warn me beforehand if you do." Murchadh cackled and returned to the con on the quarterdeck, leaving me in peace to look out over the gentle swell of the ocean before our sails.

Night had fallen by the time I finally made my way below decks to find my cabin. I placed my staff securely in the weapon rack next to the cabin door before stripping off my robe and hanging it on a wooden armature in the wardrobe built into the wall by the bed. There was a basin of cold water by the privy. I took a linen flannel from the pile next to the enamelled water bowl, soaking it thoroughly and began wiping the salt spray from my face, arms and hair. My ablutions were less than half done when I heard a knock at the cabin door. I rinsed the cloth and continued to wipe down my face as I walked over to the door, just as the wood rapped with a second, more urgent knock. "Who is it?"

"Ailidh. May I come in?" came the muffled reply.

I unlocked the door and opened it wide, laughing silently to myself at the look of shock that spread across Ailidh's face. Standing there nude with glistening salt crystals starting to form in my hair, I must have looked like an ocean nymph. "What do you want?"

Ailidh looked me up and down, clearly perturbed by my nakedness. I could not have cared less. Finally she spluttered "Gormlaith said I should talk to you, about the attack on the camp."

"Very well," I said, standing back from the doorframe and waiting. Ailidh's feet shifted uncertainly, though it had little to do with the languid rolling of the ship's hull in the swell. She stared at me mutely from behind her blonde fringe until my patience finally snapped. "Are you coming in or not?"

Ailidh's hands covered her eyes, too embarrassed to look at me, but entered my cabin reluctantly. My berth was too small for comforts like a divan or chairs, so Ailidh sat on the end of my bed, facing the door. "Keri, will you cover yourself, please?"

Enjoying her discomfort and simply wanting to be contrary, I sat at the opposite end of the bed, facing her with my back upright against the headboard and one of my legs draped lazily over the side of the mattress so that she could not look at me without noticing that I was fully exposed. "No." Ailidh glanced over her shoulder and immediately looked away, mortified. "Gods, you're impossible."

"You wanted to talk, so talk." I said, coiling my hair around my neck and brushing away tiny cubic plates of translucent white salt, scattering them over the bed linen like a dusting of fine snow.

"We'll be arriving in Clongarvan soon. Gormlaith said I had to know something about why the Succubus attacked the camp before we confront Karryghan, but that it was not her place to tell me and that I should ask you." Ailidh said, gabbling her words awkwardly as she tried to meet my eyes, repeatedly flinching when she saw I was still naked. She stood, pulled one of the sheets off the bed and threw it over my legs and torso. "I can't talk to you like that. Please."

I contemplated tossing the sheet aside, but the sensations of distress emanating from her aura warned me that it would be a poor idea. I gazed into her mind for insight and saw that she was reliving my marking of Cathal in the forest south of Lesøsnø. The unexpected shock of seeing me nude when I had opened the door had triggered her memory of event. I instantly felt a pang of remorse for making her go through the trauma of my assault on her fallen lover again, and tucked the bedsheet securely around my chest. An apology, however, would have been a step too far and simply would have sounded insincere, so I did not offer one. "What did Gormlaith tell you?"

Ailidh settled back down on the mattress, facing me, now that I had covered myself to her satisfaction. "Not much, just that you knew why the Succubus had come for me."

"I do. But that is not all, Ailidh. How much do you wish to know?"

"Everything – it's time that we stopped keeping secrets from each other."

"Even if the knowledge might hurt you and make you think less of people you thought you knew?"

"Keri, my love is dead. How much worse can it get?"

"Oh, my child... you should not ask such questions." I said, my heart breaking for the loss of innocence I was about to inflict upon her. "You have no idea."

"Don't patronise me! I'm not a child. I'm one score years old. I'm a grown woman."

"Ailidh, a solitary handful of ruts do not make you a woman."

"Fuck you, Keri." Ailidh spat, her temper boiling over into her psychic aura, making it taste as acidic as incubus seed. I was overwhelmed by a hot flash of arousal and I was tempted to show her exactly what it meant to be a woman on the mattress of my bed, but I managed to control myself. Now was not the time.

"You have matured, I will grant you that. Just not as much you would like to think." I smiled enigmatically and raised a palm to discourage the retort I sensed was forming on her tongue. "But this bickering gets us nowhere. Very well, I will tell you the truth – all of it – though I cannot guarantee you will be pleased by it.

"As you know by now, I was expelled from the Guild of the Art for seeking the forbidden knowledge of Wild Magic. It has been eleven score years since I left the Tower of the Aether in Clongarvan and I have explored much of this world since. It was in the ruins of Nagyjik where I discovered that I have a unique talent among all the wizards of this world: I can bind demons to my will. Over decades, my power over daevae grew to the point where I attracted the attention of the Succubus herself and she made me her servant.

"She was the one that ordered me to Lesøsnø and research the seventh prophecy of Nevanthi, to discover the location of the planar nexus. And it was she who ordered me not to kill Cathal when I drained him in the Western Weald."

"Why, for what purpose?"

"My dread mistress wishes to depose and succeed her master, the Executioner. When she controls the hells, she will use the aetheric power within the planar nexus to invade the planes of Heaven. Not even the Silver Citadel would be safe, should the Nexus fall into her hands."

"What does this have to do with Cathal?"

"The soul drain rune: it has a second meaning in the demonic tongue. It can anchor one soul to another across the planes. The Succubus used me to anchor to her to Cathal when I marked him."

"That's why the sigil glowed when we made love. She fed on our passion." Ailidh correctly deduced, wide-eyed in horror. "But there were three parts to the sigil and we only activated two. They had gone out before we made love on the night of the attack. Cathal didn't say how the rune had been deactivated."

"Do I have to spell it out? Draw you a diagram, perhaps?" I said, raising one of my eyebrows, barely able to conceal my contempt for her naivety.

"No, no... Cathal wouldn't have done that. He loved me in the end, I know it."

Inwardly I scoffed, but I did not disabuse Ailidh of her delusion. I had done enough damage already. "I would not presume to know his state of mind that night. The facts speak for themselves. The Succubus used Cathal's anchor and journeyed across the planes to assault our camp."

"But I still don't understand why."

"Neither did I: until she called for you. I fixed the anchor to Cathal, knowing that my dread mistress would use it to traverse to the material plane and claim the Nexus. But had I known then what I know now, I would have disarmed the rune." I bowed my head, implicitly asking her for forgiveness I knew I did not deserve.

"What? What is that you know now?"

"Ailidh, the planar nexus is in you. The Nexus *is* you. You were not born in Croycullen. That is why there is no record of your birth in the Litany. You were born in Fossfjall, and conceived at the exact moment in the exact place where the Nexus started to manifest on the material plane." I placed my palm on the back of Ailidh's right hand.

"Eoghan's plan to hide the Nexus was brilliant in its own way. Your foster father hid you in plain sight."

"But if the Nexus is as powerful as everyone says, why can't I feel it inside me? Why can't other people tell where it is?"

"This, my child, was the biggest stroke of genius of all." I said, brushing back Ailidh's fringe to reveal her scarred cheek and mutated eye. "Your childhood brush with the arcane fire on your father's forge was not an accident."

"What?" Ailidh drew back from my touch, as if she had been burned all over again.

"Have you never thought it curious that such a dedicated craftsman would let his only child, a toddler, get so close to a forge lit by arcane fire? How could such a devoted father ever be so careless to allow his beloved daughter to come to harm in such a manner? There is only one explanation. Eoghan disfigured you deliberately."

"No, that can't be true. That's impossible." Ailidh's eyes filled with tears as she relived the years of loneliness and isolation that she had suffered because of her scars. I could sense in her how unbearable the notion was that her beloved father had purposely hurt his own child. "Why would he do such a despicable thing?"

"Eoghan was a wizard. He knew that your body would learn to suppress magical power if he could expose you to arcane fire and make you allergic to aetheric energy. But it had to be done while you were still very young, while your immune system was still malleable enough to prevent any undesirable side effects that could kill you outright." I explained, full of admiration at the ingenuity of Eoghan's subterfuge and the lengths he had been willing to go to in order to protect his adoptive daughter. "Your scars have shielded you from the power of the Nexus and prevented it from fully manifesting within you. My mistress only began to get a faint, elusive sense for the location of the Nexus after I consumed some of the arcane fire from your body, weakening your magical immunity and allowing the latent energies of the Nexus to begin to coalesce. For you to be able to defend yourself from Karryghan and the Succubus, you must unlock the full power and potential of the Nexus within you. And that requires you to be completely healed."

Ailidh gasped in shock when I held her head still between my palms and kissed her face, licking along the scar disfiguring her right cheek, just as I had done on the night I had marked Cathal. The taint of arcane fire crackled on my tongue as my lips nuzzled gently up her face from chin to brow, lingering over the eye socket and restoring Ailidh's true face. "There, now you are truly beautiful in every sense."

Ailidh caressed the newly smooth skin on her cheek with her fingertips, wishing that she could see herself. Reading her thoughts, I conjured a small hand mirror and held it up to her face. Ailidh tucked her hair behind her ears and wept in bittersweet joy. "Thank you."

"Do not thank me, Ailidh. Had I not chosen to torment you at the camp in the Weald, it is likely that no-one would have ever discovered the truth about the Nexus, perhaps not even you. Instead, I chose to indulge my petty, sadistic whims. Now Cathal is dead, I have placed you in unspeakable peril and my dread mistress threatens to unbalance the order of the planes. I am not proud of what I have done."

"What happens now?"

"The Nexus will form itself quickly now, in hours, perhaps days. The solstice and the conjunction are near. Once the planes align every ambitious being in the universe will descend upon you to try and take your power. You must master it quickly."

"How will I do that?"

"I confess that I do not know. There is no time to school you in the Art of Planewalking. We must hope that your mastery of the Nexus comes instinctively."

Ailidh nodded, with a barely audible whimper of apprehension, as she tried to process the implications of everything I had told her about Cathal's marking, her childhood injury, about how the object of the search that had led to her father's abduction and murder had been within her all along. "Keri, d'you ever feel that you've got no control over your life? That the fates blow you from one place to the next, like a boat on a lake with no sail, no paddle and no rudder?"

"Is that how you feel?"

"Yes. That fate is playing a trick on me. Every time I feel like I have some happiness or some control in my life, something happens to take it away. Don't you ever feel that way?"

"No, I do not believe there is such a thing as fate." I replied after pausing for a moment's thought. "The only reason a thing happens is because that was the most probable outcome. Fate is an illusion."

"Then why do people worship the Lady? She is even the figurehead for this ship."

"Oh, the Lady is real, like all the gods. But that is not the same thing as fate."

"Then why is the Lady's favour so changeable, so fickle?"

"Because she is like a bored kitten: she likes to toy with her prey. Whenever kittens tire of a game, they change the rules." I explained. "That is why people believe in fate. The Lady makes sure that the most probable outcome for an event is never the same twice."

"If you don't believe in fate, what do you believe in, Keri?"

"I believe in destiny."

"How's that different from fate?"

"You can choose your destiny. You simply need to decide what it is and make it happen."

"So what's your destiny?"

"Ailidh, my child, believe me, you do not want to know." I replied with a cryptic smile.

37 - Reilynn

By the time our fleet met up with the boat carrying Braden and his warband of green cloaks, I already could feel that I was pregnant. I had not bled in the months since making landfall in Lesøsnø and when I had broken the news to Sjur, he had climbed the main mast of our flagship up to the crow's nest at the top and howled his delight like a lost wolf rejoining his pack. The sailors of the flotilla had returned his call, which echoed along the towering cliffs of the Abyss, probably all the way back up the length of the great fjord to the capital city. The news of my pregnancy had not dampened our ardour in bed at night. We still rutted enthusiastically every evening, making up for years of lost time. The only thing preventing me from feeling ultimately and unequivocally happy was the thought that Maeryn and Karryghan still controlled my country. But every time I took to the deck of Sjur's giant flagship, the *Black Kraken*, and saw the immensity of the fleet at his command, I knew that our final victory was at hand and my sense of optimism built by the day. That feeling of hope was dented somewhat when I learned from Braden why he was half a day late in making our rendezvous at Monagealy Sound.

The Lord Commander and his representatives were ashen-faced when their skiff nestled alongside my ship, and I could see from their expressions that it had nothing to do with seasickness. As they climbed the rope ladders up to the main deck, I noted that Braden's Second was missing from the group. Instead his place was taken by three women: a young blonde ranger and two wizards. The girl and dark-haired wizard I recognised as companions of Braden, to whom I had been introduced before the wedding, during preparations for our expedition, but the third woman, a tall, svelte redhead dressed in a wizard's gown of sheer green silk, I had not previously met. The blonde also appeared to have been changed since our last meeting. She no longer hid half of her face behind her fringe and her lean, full figure almost seemed to crackle with a faint aura of supernatural power that had not been evident when I had spoken with her before. Feeling slightly alarmed, I reached down to assist the leader of the rangers to the deck, wrapping my fingers around his forearm.

"Welcome aboard, Lord Commander. You seem, well, disturbed, if I may say so."

Braden bowed silently, looking bereft. "Yes, your majesty. I fear matters have become rather more complicated since I saw you last."

I ushered Braden and his companions to the wardroom on the galleon's quarterdeck where we sat down alongside Sjur and Torulf before I asked Braden to elaborate. "What has become complicated, Duke Braden? Explain, please."

As the story tumbled out of him, I felt bile and panic rise in my throat. I called a teenaged midshipman over to bring a carafe of water. The silence and tension in the room was palpable as the boy poured me a glass. My hands shook as I raised the crystal goblet to my lips. I washed the taste of vomit out from the back of my throat and swallowed. "A prime evil, you say."

"Yes, your majesty." Braden nodded. Sjur and Torulf had scoffed loudly in disbelief when the ranger had mentioned that detail when he had described the attack that had claimed the life of so many of his troops, including that of his Second, Cathal. But I could tell from the look on Braden's face, and those of his companions, that he was telling the truth. "Like Karryghan, it wants possession of the Nexus."

"I still do not fully understand what this Nexus is, nor why it is so important." I said, frustrated.

"Allow me to explain, your majesty." Gormlaith, the dark-haired mage, began. "The cosmos is structured in tiers of matter and energy that we call planes. Normally it is impossible to move from one plane to another, unless you have mastered the Art of Planewalking. There is a form of energy we call the aether that binds all of these planes together in the cosmos.

"Once every ten thousand years, the aether spontaneously forms a Nexus, a convergence of aetheric energy that can be used to move from one plane to another. It is referred to in prophecy as either a planar nexus or an aetheric nexus, though in fact they are both one and the same. The manifestation of the Nexus almost always occurs during a planar alignment, like the one due to happen at the solstice this winter." Gormlaith continued. "During the conjunction of a planar alignment, the barriers between the planes are at their thinnest, and chaos usually results as beings from one plane take advantage of the conjunction to visit planes they normally would be barred from. The Celestial Conflict between the devae and the daevae always peaks during a conjunction.

"This time, the Nexus has formed on Dachaigh, and come the solstice, beings from across the planes will flock to its power, seeking to take possession of it. Karryghan wants to use the Nexus to cheat death and depose the Mystic, effectively becoming the new god of magic."

"So Maeryn was not simply raving into his wine cup after all," I mused, taking another sip of water. "The Arch Mage precipitated the coup, murdered my family and all but destroyed a kingdom for this Nexus?"

"In Karryghan's hands the Nexus would be a weapon of unspeakable power. As the new god of magic he could wreak havoc on an unimaginable scale. He must be denied it, at all costs." Gormlaith said, with a shudder of terror. "Likewise the Succubus must be denied it as well. In her possession it would irrevocably tip the balance of power in the Celestial Conflict."

"How can we do that if we do not know what this Nexus is, or where it is?" I asked, furrowing my brow.

"There we do have an advantage over Karryghan and the Succubus, your majesty."

"We do?"

"Yes, the Nexus is in this very room." Gormlaith said, placing her hand on the blonde girl's shoulder.

I turned to the blonde ranger, puzzled. "You have it?"

"No, your majesty, Ailidh *is* the Nexus." Gormlaith said, as if that was an explanation.

"I do not see how that is possible."

This time the redheaded mage spoke. "Ailidh was conceived at the precise moment the convergence formed on Dachaigh, in the exact place it started to manifest on the material plane. By a freak of coincidence her nature was divined by wizard who became her adoptive father to protect her. Only now is Ailidh coming into her power, as the solstice approaches. Like her father, we have sworn to keep Ailidh safe from those who would harm her and use the Nexus for their own ends."

"And who are you in all this? Braden and Gormlaith I know, you I do not." I asked the mage. Something about her made the skin on the back of my neck tingle with suspicion. I was not sure whether it was her manner of speech, or the way her eyes always seemed to elude contact with the others around the table, but I found her presence unnerving.

"What makes you so invested in protecting this Nexus?"

"I have my reasons, your majesty. The balance must be preserved."

"Keri is one of the most powerful wizards in the Western Triad. Our best chance of defeating Karryghan lies with her at our side." Gormlaith interjected, coming to her fellow spellcaster's defence.

"And how do you plan to do that?"

"With the greatest of respect to your warriors, confronting Karryghan with martial power alone will only guarantee hundreds, if not thousands of dead soldiers." Keri said. "Our best gambit is to dangle the prize of the Nexus before his eyes, just before plucking them out of his head."

"We cannot hope to defend Ailidh indefinitely from Karryghan and any other extra-planar threats that will come for her after the solstice. Attack is the best form of defence we have. I have divined that Ailidh will only master the true extent of her powers after confronting Karryghan." Gormlaith explained. "Once Karryghan has been neutralised and Ailidh unlocks the full potential of the Nexus, we hope that she will be able to defend herself from any further threats, including the Succubus and the other prime evils."

"You *hope*."

"Yes, your majesty." Gormlaith conceded, rolling her shoulders uncomfortably. "There are still a great many unknowns that cannot be divined. The watchers of the psychic plane never allow all the details surrounding a manifestation of the Nexus to be known ahead of time. We have to hope that Ailidh masters her powers quickly, otherwise once the solstice has passed every ambitious demon, planewalker and celestial from across the cosmos will converge on Dachaigh and lay it to waste in the battle to control her."

"I see." The taste of bile rose again in the back of my throat and I subdued it with another sip of water. "How will you defeat the Arch Mage, if he is so powerful a threat to our soldiers?"

Seemingly out of thin air a vial of luminous green poison appeared in the slender fingers of Keri's right hand and she placed it on the table with an almost reverential delicacy. "By using this venom; it is potent enough to paralyse a raging mammoth, your majesty. I will imbue it into a swarm of magical darts, large enough to overwhelm his defences. Once the venom has taken effect, the Arch Mage will be easy prey."

"Venom from what creature, exactly, has such power?"

"It is distilled from ettercap and giant spider venom, plus other monsters." Keri said, her eyes evading my gaze once again. "The source is of less importance as its effect."

From the frown on Gormlaith's face, I knew I was being lied to, or being told a half-truth, but my instincts told me that perhaps it was better for me not to know precisely what the whole truth was. I let the evasion pass without further comment. "And if it works as well as you expect?"

"I will not have to worry about spending another four years in the form of a cat." Gormlaith said, deadpan.

"I beg your pardon?" I blinked.

"Sorry, your majesty," Gormlaith smiled ruefully. "The last time I confronted Karryghan regarding his plans for the Nexus he polymorphed me on the spot. Until Keri freed me from the spell a few weeks ago I had to get used to having a tail and fur. It is why I sometimes talk out of turn and why I currently have the urge to curl up on your lap."

Braden's face turned white in mortification and I felt my own cheeks flush as Ailidh giggled and Keri smirked behind her long, elegant hands. Torulf's laughter echoed around the wardroom and Sjur grinned, whispering in my ear, "Now that I would like to see."

I slapped my husband's wrist gently to reproach him, wondering whether I had just been propositioned. I paused for a moment as I regained my composure and let the heat radiate away from my face, letting a smile reach the corner of my mouth as I joked, "I regret to say that I was always more fond of hounds than cats."

"In all seriousness, if the venom works as well as I expect it to, the only outstanding question regarding the Arch

Mage's fate will be where to carry out his execution." Keri said, spiriting away the vial with her sleight of hand.
"It is enough for me to know he is dead. Karryghan's crimes against my family and country are too grave to grant him the ceremony of a public execution. Kill him quickly and leave his body out in the gutter for the rats. He must not be given an opportunity to evade the reckoning that awaits him on the fugue plane." I told the wizards, a lump of ice forming in my heart as I remembered the purge Karryghan had ordered against my family, and the nephews and nieces I had seen cut down in cold blood before my eyes. Their screams would plague my nightmares to my dying day.
"The Arch Mage had my father murdered too, your majesty." Ailidh said, looking at me with her large, empathic eyes. "I'll make sure our kin get the justice they deserve."
"See to it that you do, Ailidh. You will all be well-rewarded if we can avoid unnecessary deaths once we reach Clongarvan. Remember well, the people in the city are my subjects, not my enemies. Only the ringleaders of the coup and the purge, and any who put up active resistance should be killed." I told my war council, who nodded. "It is agreed, then. Braden and Torulf will lead the advance force to secure the Royal Marina and the sea fort in the hours before the main fleet makes landfall. Gormlaith, Keri and Ailidh will infiltrate the Tower of the Aether and eliminate Karryghan, while Sjur and I retake the Royal Palace from Maeryn and any guards he might have with him."

That night I failed to sleep, disturbed by Braden's report of the Succubus's assault on his camp outside Sylane. Sjur stirred as I tossed and turned on our bed, opening one eye and draping a strong arm around my waist. "What ails you, my precious vixen?"
"This business with the Nexus," I sighed, putting my hand on his forearm, my fingertips teasing the hairs rhythmically. "The idea of battling an Arch Mage is bad enough. Having to contend with a prime evil as well... imagine the carnage if it got loose in the city."
"What was it the copper-headed wizard said? We should be safe until after the solstice. Without an anchor, the demon is trapped on her plane. Only when the barriers weaken will

she be able to make the transition again to the material plane."

"There is something strange about that woman. I am not entirely sure she can be trusted. Did you notice that Braden did not explain what the anchor was that allowed the Succubus to invade the ranger camp? None of them did, almost as if it was something they wished to hide." I said, becoming increasingly agitated. "And at the end of the meeting, she just looked through me and congratulated me on our twins. How could she know I was with child? And that I carried twins, a son and a daughter?"

"A lucky guess, perhaps? Or maybe she is as powerful as Gormlaith claims?" Sjur turned onto his side and stroked my belly and neck, soothingly. "She is a funny one, too. I can just imagine her on your lap."

"I am sure you can." I rolled my eyes, though the idea was an enticing one. I liked the sensuality of her deep voice and the dusky tone of her skin. Idly, I wondered how strikingly my husband's seed would appear in contrast against her tanned, flat belly and how the sweat of her passion might taste.

"I have always found stroking a pussy to be relaxing, too." Sjur said, his fingertips wandering up the inside of my thigh.

I laughed and ensnared his wrist, encouraging him upwards towards the base of my body. "I would be your cat, but if I tried curling up on your lap, I would find myself impaled upon it."

"And that would be a bad thing?" Sjur asked as I reached across him and confirmed with my palm the suspicion that he was already stone hard.

"Perhaps not," I said with a purr.

The remaining journey south to Finisterre Isle and then east towards the Bay of Tides passed quickly and we made it into position just beyond the horizon to Clongarvan with five days to spare before the solstice. As expected, we encountered no resistance from Cothraine's Navy. As we passed the naval ports along the Herring Coast, travelling south past the Heartwood and the West Riding, it became clear that none of their ships had ever left port. With our fleet moored ten leagues south east of Clongarvan, Torulf had transferred onto Braden's ship with half of Sjur's berserker commandos. They were already on their way to main city harbour in the east of Clongarvan, where they would be met by Ruarc and a contingent of my black cloaks, who would lead them to their targets on the sea wall and the sea fort via the tunnel network I had used to escape the palace grounds. The rangers and commandos would assault their targets in a coordinated strike at midnight, securing the *Black Kraken*'s approach to the Royal Marina. Sjur's flagship already flew the Fossfjall flag alongside my personal ensign on its main mast, a clear sign for anyone watching in the city that the rightful ruler of the country was returning to retake the crown. I had to hold the rail on the quarterdeck with both hands to stop me from pacing nervously up and down the ship as we waited for the flame at Clongarvan Point Lighthouse to be extinguished and relit twice, a message that would tell us that the sea fort and defensive wall overlooking the Bay of Tides was neutralised. Midnight came and went, and still the lighthouse fire burned.

"How long do you think Braden and Torulf will need to secure the sea fort?" I asked my husband.

"If resistance is light, under an hour; if resistance is heavy, perhaps three." Sjur replied. "They have the element of surprise. Your man Aiden said discipline is lax among the night watch. I do not think we will have to wait long."

Sjur's prediction proved to be a good one. Just over thirty minutes after midnight the lighthouse fire went out. A minute later it was relit, burned for a minute and was extinguished again. Another minute later the fire flared up once more and did not go out.

"That is it. There is the signal." Sjur turned to the *Black Kraken*'s shipmaster. "Admiral Hjalmar, take us in to the marina and order the fleet to follow."

Lamps flickered along the flanks of the ship as the Admiral passed on Sjur's orders to his ship captains, who acknowledged with coded flashes of light of their own, making it seem like the fleet had been briefly surrounded by fireflies. The *Black Kraken* lurched forward as the sails were raised and they caught the wind, a brisk on-shore easterly, rushing down the Bay of Tides from the direction of Bray. A pang of distress briefly twisted at my heart, as I thought about my handmaidens, who I had sent to the Bray Crown Estate to act as a decoy during my escape from the palace. I had not received word about what had happened to them. Once our business in the palace with Maeryn was over, I resolved to learn their fate and return them to the royal household if they had survived. Sjur wrapped an arm around my shoulders supportively, kissing my cheek as I mused under my breath, "Full circle."

"What was that, my love?"

"I have come around the full circle. I left the city by sea, I am returning to the city by sea." I looked down at my armour and weapon belt. "I am even wearing the same clothes in which I left."

"It is a good omen." Sjur grinned, baring his teeth, which glittered in the starlight. "Before the sun is up, Maeryn and Karryghan will lie dead at our feet and our nations will be united in joy."

I kept my own council, not wishing to jinx our luck. The weapons on the sea fort remained silent as the *Black Kraken* sped towards the royal marina, the momentum of the huge flagship seemingly unstoppable. Admiral Hjalmar ordered that the sails be dropped just before we passed the marina's protective sea wall, letting the ship drift towards the largest jetty, where several dozen men already stood waiting for us. Even from this distance, it was easy to identify Torulf from his sheer size and the dire wolf pelt he wore over his armour as a battle cloak. Less than an hour had passed since the signal from the lighthouse. The crew docked the galleon in complete silence. They all understood the need for speed and stealth and were so well-drilled that they could perform their jobs without the need for shouted guidance by their petty officers.

As soon as the ship was lashed to the jetty, Sjur rushed down the gangplank to embrace Torulf, who greeted his friend and king with a deep bass, victorious growl. Braden stood behind the giant general and gave me a respectful bow as I took my first steps back onto the land of my birth in many months. I felt conflicting emotions as I stood on the palace marina I knew so well, this time as an invader, rather than a resident. Behind me came Gormlaith, Ailidh and Keri, as well as a steady stream of Sjur's berserkers, who formed up on the quayside in cohorts of a hundred men, waiting for orders. Gormlaith and Ailidh rushed over to speak with Braden while Keri remained enigmatically aloof, neither with one group nor the other. It reinforced my suspicion that there was more to her involvement in events than she was willing to divulge, but I set aside my concerns, joining my husband as he spoke with Torulf about the infiltration and subjugation of the sea fort.

"How many casualties did you have?" Sjur asked.

"None at all, my king! These Cothraini are as meek as sheep!" Torulf crowed. "Most of them were asleep at their posts, and the rest preferred to surrender than have their guts spilled. Your black cloaks were invaluable, my Queen. They got us into the city unseen and we have complete control of the sea fort and sea wall. No-one in the rest of the city knows we are here."

"Let us keep it that way." I said. "At least until we have control of the palace and Maeryn is eliminated. Once the royal standard of my family flies again over the keep, we can bring in the leaders of the Field Army and City Guard to ensure a peaceful transition of power. The last thing we want is bloodshed on the streets."

"I agree absolutely, your majesty," Braden said, walking over with Gormlaith and Ailidh to join our conversation. "I did not come back to Clongarvan to fight the City Guard or Field Army."

"Where are your rangers, lord commander?"

"I have most of them guarding the prisoners in the sea fort. They will be more cooperative if they can see they are being held by their own countrymen. The rest I have keeping watch on the sea wall. They know the protocols of the city guard and can exchange messages with the other watchers around the city walls without alerting them to our takeover of the sea fort."

"Good thinking, lord commander." I nodded my approval of his initiative, as we had not considered how to guard prisoners if the sea fort was taken with no resistance at all. I turned to Gormlaith, beckoning over a black cloak agent who was standing guard over us a few yards away. "It is time for us to part ways, Wizard Gormlaith. Good luck with the Arch Mage. If you are successful, come and find me in the throne room of the Royal Keep. If I do not hear from you by nightfall, I will have to resort to less subtle methods to deal with Karryghan and the Guild."

I was about to give my instructions to the black cloak when I heard Braden arguing with Ailidh. "Please, let me accompany you to the Tower. Cathal would not have left your side."

"It's too dangerous for you to come, Braden. You wouldn't stand a chance against the Arch Mage. And the queen can make better use of you here, at the palace."

"She is right, lord commander. I need you to help guide Sjur and his berserkers through the keep and the palace grounds."

"Braden, not even the trickery and guile of your swordplay can help us defeat Karryghan." Gormlaith said, her blue eyes regarding him sadly, her hands gripping the shaft of her staff tightly. "Even my brother would have told you that. The Arch Mage is a completely different kind of enemy, and not one that you have the ability to fight. Cathal would not have you throw away your life needlessly. Ailidh, Keri and I will do this alone."

"Gormlaith, what you plan to do, it is tantamount to suicide." Braden told her, visibly upset.

"Then better to only lose three lives than four." Gormlaith kissed her late brother's mentor twice on each cheek. "Have faith, Braden. This will work. It has to."

I felt sympathy for Braden, understanding how it felt to be so completely out of your depth and helpless when people you loved around you were dying. I attracted the attention of the black cloak again and identified his charges.

"Shadow Lord, escort these three women to the Tower of the Aether, as quickly and as quietly as you can."

"Take them out into the city through Sylvan's Dell." Braden interjected, in one last effort to aid Gormlaith and Ailidh. "The grounds will not be watched by the City Guard anymore."

The Secret Service agent turned to me in askance and I silently nodded my approval. Then he turned to Gormlaith and gestured to the western wall of the marina with his hand. "Ladies, follow me. This way, please."

They disappeared into hidden entrance on the buttress supporting the ballista tower overlooking the marina and I touched my forehead, whispering them a blessing. "May the Lady and the Mystic be with you."

Two more black cloaks miraculously appeared at my side, as if they had taken form from shadows and the night. "What are your orders, your majesty?"

"Take Supreme General Torulf and his commandos to secure the gatehouse and the barracks at the palace garrison. No-one is to enter or leave the palace grounds until we have secured the keep and Wizard Gormlaith has dealt with the Arch Mage at the Tower of the Aether." I turned to Torulf and warned him with a stern look. "Defend yourself if you must, you old son of a bastard, but keep any bloodshed to an absolute minimum."

"By your command, my queen," Torulf nodded and whistled to alert his troops. "We go immediately."

"The same goes for you and your berserkers, my love." I reminded Sjur as Torulf waved his battle axe in a broad circle over his head and ran with his cohorts of commandos north towards the palace grounds. "Only Maeryn and the other ringleaders need be killed. The servants in the palace are to be incarcerated, not harmed."

"My skull is not so thick that I did not remember the first time you told me, my sweet." Sjur chuckled.

"Lead the way please, lord commander." I instructed Braden. "Maeryn should be in his chambers in the King's Tower. Everyone barring the sentinels ought to be asleep by now. With enough stealth, haste and luck, by the time everyone wakes in the morning, we will already have full control of the palace."

Braden pointed the way to the terrace staircase adjoining the marina with the palace grounds and we set off at a steady trot, so that we would not interfere with Torulf's troops already silently ascending the broad limestone steps, like a giant pack of predatory wolves. Sjur's berserkers were ready and eager for action, having spent three weeks cooped up on the *Black Kraken*. They fingered the handles of their axes and hand-crossbows edgily, but they made no sound at all as Sjur divided them up into two groups. We would approach the keep from the rear, Braden leading one cohort of berserkers to sweep around the keep to approach the courtyard entrances to the keep and twin towers of the palace from the east, by the Queen's Tower, while Sjur and I took the more direct route along the western wall of the keep by the King's Tower. A dozen of Sjur's best warriors surrounded me at all times in a defensive square behind the main cohort, to protect me from harm, making me feel as if I were encased in a second suit of armour. We waited just out of sight of the courtyard, at the edge of the parterre while we waited for Braden to get his men into position. The canny old ranger imitated the call of a female tawny owl three times to signal that the ambush was ready: *too-whit, too-whit, too-whit!* Sjur replied, as Braden had taught him to, with a single whistled *too-woo* to spring the trap. The berserkers swarmed into the courtyard with remarkable speed and stealth. Braden led the charge, his green leather cloak flapping behind him. The dozen sentinels guarding the portals to the two towers and the keep, seeing that they were overwhelmingly outnumbered, sensibly dropped their weapons, fell to their knees and placed their hands on the tops of their heads. Braden approached them alone, a finger over his lips to signal to the guardsmen that they needed to remain silent.

"Keep your mouths shut and your hands empty and you will not be harmed." Braden announced, in a voice just loud enough to fill the courtyard. "My name is Braden, Duke Ranger and Lord Commander of the Order of Sylvan here in Cothraine. I am here with your queen to restore rightful rule to the throne."

That sent a murmur of disbelief rippling through the surrendered guards until I stepped forward and showed myself. One of the soldiers recognised me and gasped, "Queen Reilynn! The Empress be praised, it's really you!"

I shushed him gently and stepped closer, still flanked by my bodyguards. "Yes, I have returned to bring Maeryn to justice. Is he in the King's Tower? How many Companions does he have guarding him?"

"The purple cloaks are no more, your majesty." The sentinel said, pausing to consider his next words carefully. "Maeryn disbanded them after- after you left the palace. He trusts no-one, especially now that the Arch Mage has appointed himself Regent. The only person he lets near him is his cupbearer, Dagna."

"Karryghan is the Regent, you say?"

"Yes, your majesty," the soldier nodded. "After news of your marriage reached the Wizard's Guild they threw out Maeryn's claim to the throne."

"The Schemer is clever, I will grant him that." I said, grimacing. "What about the keep? How many guards are inside?"

"Barring the serving staff, it is practically empty, your majesty. Field Duke Fiacre has taken up residence in the throne room. These days he spends more time in the keep than he does at the Field Army Citadel."

"Fiacre," I spat the name, turning to Braden. "He too must be held to account for his actions during the purge. Take these men and hold them in the Queen's Tower. Then secure the keep. We will deal with Fiacre once the King's Tower has been cleared."

Braden nodded and I addressed the surrendered guardsmen once more. "You will be released once my business in the palace is concluded. Be patient, do not try to leave the tower and do not try to send any messages. If you attempt to do either the consequences will be bloody. I hope I have made myself clear."

The sentinels allowed themselves to be shepherded into my former residence in the Queen's Tower, which had been largely abandoned following my escape from the city. Once the guards had been locked inside, Braden posted two score of Sjur's berserkers to stand watch over the courtyard and ensure that no-one went in or out. Then he led the remains of his cohort into the keep to trap Fiacre in the throne room and subdue any resistance inside.

Sjur and I then turned our attention to the King's Tower. We left most of Sjur's cohort outside, taking only my elite bodyguard with us. We were met inside the tower's portal by one of my agents who apprised us of the situation. "Your majesty, the tower is secure. Maeryn is asleep in his chamber at the top of the tower. The only other person here is his personal servant girl, Dagna. She is in her quarters outside Maeryn's bedchamber."

"Thank you, Shadow Baron. Wait here for now. I may have need of you later."

Sjur and I ascended the stone spiral staircase in silence, trying not to create noise. My bodyguards followed closely behind, their hands ready on the hilts of their battleaxes. When we reached the apex of the tower, I gestured to Sjur and the berserkers, identifying the door to Maeryn's chamber and the servant quarters. Floorboards creaked gently as we shuffled into position, ready to give Maeryn the surprise of his life.

Unexpectedly, a thin, high-pitched voice called out querulously in the darkness. "Master, is that you?"
The door to the servant's quarters swung open and a tiny, pale figure dressed in a thin white cotton nightgown stepped out onto the landing. The berserker nearest her stepped forward and scooped the girl up in his arms and covered her mouth so that if she screamed, her cries would not be heard. Dagna tried to shriek and struggle free, but her feet were no longer in contact with the floor and she quickly sagged against the berserker limply, realising she could not break out of his grip. I hurried over to the girl, letting her see my face. I shushed her and stroked the hair out of her eyes tenderly, watching her pupils widen in shock as she recognised me. "Quietly now, Dagna, no-one will harm you."
She whined piteously behind the berserker's palm, as if she had seen a ghost. "Promise me you will not scream and that you will not run. If you do that, my friend here will put you down. Can you do that for me, Dagna?"
The girl nodded, still clearly terrified half out of her wits. I signalled with my eyes to the berserker and he carefully set her down on the floor. I knelt before Dagna and opened my arms. When the berserker let her go, Dagna sobbed quietly and threw herself into my embrace. "Do not be scared, my sweetling. You are safe now."
"Your majesty, I never thought I'd see you again." Dagna whispered, crying into my hair.
"I am here now, Dagna. Everything will be alright." I stroked her neck and cheek affectionately, looking into her wide, pleading eyes. "Did Maeryn hurt you? Touch you?"
The girl trembled in horror. "No, your majesty, but he'd always get angry and throw things. Sometimes they'd hit me."
Sjur growled under his breath menacingly as I hugged the girl to me again, kissing her forehead. "He will never bother you again. Do you understand? There is a black cloak downstairs. He will take good care of you."
I turned to the berserker who had stifled her when Dagna had stepped out onto the landing. "Escort her downstairs and tell the agent there to take her to the keep's kitchen and give her refreshment, whatever she wants."
"Yes, your majesty." The berserker dropped to one knee and looked down at servant girl with unexpected

compassion, opening his arms for her. "Come, Dagna, let me carry you."

The girl allowed herself to be swept up again, this time willingly, and she wrapped her tiny arms around his muscular neck, her bare feet braced on his hips as he descended the steps. I turned to my husband, a sensation of rage building in my heart at Maeryn's mistreatment of the young girl. "I believe it is time to wake the usurper, husband."

Sjur nodded in agreement, hefting his battleaxe with both hands. My bodyguards likewise readied their weapons as Sjur smashed the door to Maeryn's chamber out of its frame with a single mighty kick. A reedy wail of horror emanated from inside the chamber as Sjur and my bodyguards swarmed inside, surrounding the bed in seconds. There was enough starlight coming through the windows to see that Maeryn cowered on the mattress on his knees, a knife held in his left hand. "What is the meaning of this?"

My teeth grated at the sound of Maeryn's voice, which I had detested for the last four years of our sham marriage. "Is it not obvious?"

"Reilynn, is that you?"

"Who else would it be? I have returned home to watch you die, snake."

"Get up, Maeryn." Sjur said, with a snarl of pure hatred. "I would rather kill you on your feet, rather than butcher you like a pig in your bed."

"No, wait!" Maeryn begged pathetically, putting his hands together in supplication. "I will give you everything, everything I have!"

"There is nothing you can give me except your life." Sjur scoffed and he glanced over at me proudly. "I already have everything else that I could ever want."

"No! Please! No! I beg you!"

His patience for Maeryn's snivelling exhausted, my husband lashed out with his axe, slicing through his left arm at the elbow. Maeryn's knife and good hand dropped to the floor and he screamed, clutching at his stump with the remaining fingers on bandaged right hand. Blood poured onto the mattress as Maeryn shrieked in agony. Sjur followed up his strike with a sadistic blow to Maeryn's groin. My husband had been revolted by Aiden's account of

Maeryn's intention to rape me in the palace dungeon and he had sworn to take an appropriate revenge. Maeryn's scream abruptly stopped, his agony too intense to articulate, his eyes wide open with shock. But it was Sjur's third and final cut that proved to be the fatal one, as he buried the full length of the blade of his battleaxe deep into Maeryn's stomach, spilling his intestines out onto the bed. Maeryn slumped forward, the bedsheets slick with his blood. "It is a shame to ruin such a sturdy mattress."
"I would have had it burned anyway, my love." I said, linking arms with my husband. "There is no way in the five hells that I would sleep in a bed that viper had once coiled up on." I spat on Maeryn's corpse and led the way back down the staircase. The clean up could wait until Fiacre and Karryghan had been dealt with.

Sjur's troops rejoined us as we crossed the courtyard to the entrance of the keep. Braden had left guards posted at every intersection between the corridors and chamber doors, which Sjur doubled using his own berserkers. I steered Sjur and my bodyguards through the anterooms and chambers leading to the throne room, finding Braden waiting outside with a score of Sjur's men. The ranger bowed a greeting and whispered, "The keep is ours, barring the throne room. Fiacre is inside, alone. And fast asleep. But be warned, he is a formidable warrior in melee. I would not give him the chance to fight."
Sjur turned to his berserkers. "Ready your crossbows, but wound him only. His life is mine."
Braden eased open the throne room door and the berserkers filtered inside, streaming as fluidly as a stream of water trickling down a cliff face, lining one wall and then the other, flanking the chamber and ensuring that Fiacre had no chance of escape. When the final berserker was in position, a silent hand signal invited Sjur into the throne room. I followed him, again held safe in a pocket of armoured leather and steel, my dozen bodyguards alert and armed with loaded and cocked hand crossbows. As Braden had said, Fiacre was asleep, snoring, with his head lolling down onto his shoulder as he lounged disrespectfully on Cothraine's throne, as if he were the king. Incensed by the sacrilege of the killer of so many of my kin dozing on

the seat of power, I yelled as loudly as my lungs would permit. "Get off my throne!"

Fiacre woke with a start of confusion and panic, his eyes widening in horror when he saw Sjur and the two scores of armed berserkers standing between him and the throne room's door. "Oh, fuck!"

He lurched to his feet, snatching the sword from his belt into his huge, paw-like hands. Fiacre did not have the chance to make it more than two steps toward me before Sjur's commandos unleashed a volley of hand crossbow bolts, aiming for the joints between the plates of his armour. Several quarrels punctured the weak points at the shoulders, elbows, knees and the top of the thighs. Fiacre grunted in pain, stumbled and dropped his sword, bleeding profusely from his arms and legs, but not fatally. Sjur stepped forward and kicked Fiacre's sword across the floor, out of reach, though Fiacre could not have picked it up again if he had tried, his arms hanging uselessly and insensate by his side. Sjur gripped the bald pate of Fiacre's head in the palm of his gauntlet and wrenched backwards to expose his long, broad throat. Fiacre yelled in wordless horror as Sjur showed him the shining crescent of his axe blade and snarled, "This is for killing children."

Sjur struck downwards with the razor-sharp cutting edge, taking Fiacre's head clean off his body with a single stroke. The Field Duke's huge corpse fell to the stone floor in almost exactly the same place Maeryn had stabbed my father in the back, four years ago. Sjur dropped the skull with disdain and hung his axe back onto his war belt. Tears flowed from my eyes as I took my place beside him and we kissed, having finally freed the spectres of my kin from the palace by bringing their murderers to justice. "It is done. What now, my love?"

I wiped my cheeks and gasped with unbounded joy, feeling like the weight of a world had been lifted from my shoulders. "Now we wait for word from the Tower."

38 - Gormlaith

Queen Reilynn's black cloak set a swift pace as he led us across the royal marina to the sea wall, where it adjoined the southern tip of the enclosure of Sylvan's Dell. The wall was at its thickest here, supporting one of the defensive ballista towers overlooking the bay. The agent used his signet ring to unlock a hidden door in the buttress wall and led us inside. Keri imbued her staff with a light charm to illuminate the passage so that we did not have to feel our way blindly through the blackness, which I was grateful for. I had lost the night-vision I had become accustomed to as a cat and the dark still invoked fearful memories from the time Cathal and I had lives as orphans together on the streets of Monagealy. We walked a few hundred yards beneath the western city wall before the black cloak found another secret door and directed us back out under the starlight into Sylvan's Dell. The archery range had been partially reclaimed by weeds and shrubs that had self-seeded throughout the dell in the years following the purge. Huge clumps of ferns ran rampant around the walls of the four-storey wooden-framed hall where Cathal's Order had been based. In the four years since Maeryn's coup, the hall had been abandoned and thoroughly ransacked by looters. All of the windows had been broken and the top two floors showed signs of fire damage, where part of the vaulted roof had collapsed. The whole site had been left to be reclaimed by the Earth Mother, which was why Braden had recommended we enter the city from the dell. No-one would be watching for signs of activity from this derelict quarter of the city.

It was an hour after midnight and there was nary a rat or urban fox to be seen on the city streets. It felt strange to be back in Clongarvan after my extended exile, but even to me the streets felt uncannily quiet. The queen's operative hurried us north past the Astronomer Royal's Observatory and the glasshouses of the Botanical Gardens, before turning east along Mummer's Row at Fate's Theatre House, finally turning back north at the Museum of Natural History on the avenue leading towards the Tower of the Aether. My old home dominated the skyline of the north of the city, standing nearly quarter of a league tall. The windows of the Arch Mage's apartment at the apex of the tower burned brightly: Karryghan was in residence, and still very much awake. The black cloak used another one of his secret doors to slip us past the wall of the compound and into the Park of the Mystic that surrounded the tower. "I must bid you farewell here, ladies. Good luck and may the Lady and the Mystic smile upon you all this night."

I did not even have a chance to thank him before the black cloak vanished into the shadows silently like a wraith. I clutched my staff tightly and pointed the way towards the tower's main entrance. "This way, let us go."

The enchantment on the tower's main portal recognised me and opened at my psychic command. I led Ailidh and Keri through the doors to the sky-lit lobby where a young apprentice mage was struggling to keep awake, leaning for support on the lectern that stood in the centre of the reception chamber. It was doubtful that he had expected to receive visitors to the tower at this hour of the night. The apprentice blinked five times, not quite believing his eyes and I smiled inwardly at the opening line of a half-remembered joke my father had once told me as a young child: *A blonde, a brunette and a redhead walk into a bar...*
The boy was no older than fifteen. From his perspective we must have looked like a vision from one of his wet dreams. Flustered and still half asleep, he ventured uncertainly, "Ah, hello?"

I gave the boy one of my most alluring smiles to put him at ease. "Greetings and well met, apprentice. What is your name?"

"Niall of Belhaven, mistress. I am sorry, but I was not told we were receiving guests overnight."

"I am no guest, Niall. I am a member of this Guild."

"Forgive me, mistress, but I do not recognise you, or your companions." Niall swallowed nervously. I could sense his fear beginning to build in his aura. "Who are you?"

"My name is Gormlaith of Monagealy." I told him, watching his eyes carefully.

"Gormlaith of Monagealy?" Niall's aura surged with cold terror and his hand began to reach for the amulet on the top of the reception lectern. He gasped and his hand stopped in mid-air as Keri, quick as lightning, pressed the tip of her staff underneath his chin, directly over the carotid artery and jugular vein.

She tut-tutted disapprovingly. "Now, now, Niall... Do not do something you will not live to regret."

I took the amulet from the lectern and placed it in my satchel. Niall sagged visibly, his only method of communicating with the rest of the tower remotely denied to him. "Let me give you a piece of advice, Niall of Belhaven. Whatever you think your duty to the Guild might be, tonight you owe it to yourself to return to your dormitory, get a good night's sleep and worry about the consequences in the morning."

Ailidh stepped forward and took the youth's hand in hers. "Do what Gormlaith asks, please. As serious as this situation might seem right now, it'll be trivial come the dawn. Don't let your life be wasted trying to change something you have no hope of understanding or affecting."

The boy's aura wavered, fear mixing with hope in response to Ailidh's unexpected compassion and he ran for the staircase to the basement, where the apprentices slept in their subterranean dormitories. I sighed with relief, glad that bloodshed had been avoided. "One obstacle negotiated."

"Where to now?" Ailidh asked, glancing around the reception chamber, trying to take in the grandeur of the vast stone atrium.

I pointed to the paternoster lift chugging at the back of the room, where the walls of the reception chamber joined onto the outer wall of the main tower itself. The platforms were just large enough to take three people and it was by far the fastest way to ascend to the top of the tower. "Your platform awaits, Nexus. I must speak with the Council before we confront Karryghan."

"You can't be serious." Ailidh baulked at the edge of the lift shaft. It was obvious that she had never seen a chain lift before. I smiled, knowing how unnerving it was to try and take a paternoster for the first time. The platforms never stopped, dragged around on an eternal, continuous loop by aetheric engines at the top and bottom of the tower.

Keri laughed and slipped her arm through Ailidh's at the elbow. "Come now, Ailidh, where is your sense of adventure?"

Ailidh yelped as Keri pulled her onto the next paternoster link and I had to suppress a giggle of delight as I jumped after them, the three of us compressed into the tiny compartment that vertically ascended the tower at a rate just faster than walking pace. Ailidh shivered in horror as the lift climbed floor after floor, the light in the paternoster platform getting completely extinguished briefly every time we passed between levels. When the number of floors we had passed told me that we had arrived at the level of the Council Chamber, I grabbed Ailidh and Keri by the elbow and dragged us out of the paternoster onto secure ground once again. Ailidh shuddered and reproached me with a wagging finger. "That was horrible. Let's never do that again."

I kissed her on the cheek in apology, placed my hand on her waist and directed her to the inner sanctum of the Grand Masters, which was on the floor below the Arch Mage's apartments at the apex of the tower. We took our place in the centre of the circle of nine chairs, one for Arch Mage and eight more for the Grand Masters of each School of the Art. I removed the amulet I had taken from the lobby of the tower and attuned myself with it psychically. When I heard the metal of the amulet sing, I sent a message to the Grand Masters of the Art residing in the tower. I did not have to worry about prematurely alerting the Arch Mage, as the amulet's output was not channelled to him. Karryghan was literally as far above problems occurring in the reception chamber as it was possible to be in the Tower of the Aether, both physically and figuratively, due to his rank.

Grand Masters, this is Wizard Gormlaith of Monagealy. I apologise for disturbing you at this late hour, but I need to speak with you as a matter of the utmost urgency. It cannot wait until morning. Please join me in the Council Chamber at your earliest convenience. I would prefer to speak with you all at once, rather than explain myself several times, as time is very much of the essence. I cannot wait long.

We were joined first by my former master, Malvina of Ballinlara, who greeted me with her habitual openness and vulgarity. "Well fuck me forwards and back again!

Gormlaith, where in the hells have you been for the last four years?"

"I will explain everything, as soon as everyone is here." I reassured her, with a hug of delight. We had always enjoyed each other's company and respect, and Malvina could be relied upon to make judgments honestly, based solely on information and evidence, rather than feeling and bias. I knew that she would likely be a powerful ally in the discussion to come.

Next to arrive in the chamber and take her seat was Sorcha of Monagealy, the Grand Master of Illusion. She had always been favourably disposed to me, since we shared the place of our birth, and if truth be known, I had held a crush for her since my fourteenth birthday. With her exceptional skill in glamour charms, Sorcha was perhaps, after Queen Reilynn, the second most beautiful woman in the Western Triad.

The chamber began to fill quickly after that: Aonghas of Birlone, Grand Master of Abjuration; Treasa of Siskine, Grand Master of Transmutation; Ruairidh of Clongarvan, Grand Master of Planewalking; Aisling of Belhaven, Grand Master of Enchantment; Faoiltiarna of Clongarvan, Grand Master of Invocation; and lastly Cinaed of Bray, Grand Master of Conjuration and the oldest wizard on the council, barring Karryghan. Cinaed broke step on entering the chamber when he saw Keri, but noting that the rest of the Grand Masters were already in their seats, continued across the floor and took his place as well. It was no surprise that as soon as he was settled, Cinaed broke the silence first.

"Wizard Gormlaith, as much as I resent being awoken at this ungodly hour, I was persuaded by the rest of the council to join you here. However, if I had known the company you keep, I would have stood in bed." Cinaed said, openly hostile. He pointed at Keri with the index and little fingers of his left hand and asked, "Why, pray tell, Wizard Gormlaith, is *she* fucking here?"

A ripple of confusion and discontent murmured around the room. Clearly Cinaed was the only member of the council who knew Keri by sight. I was certain that the rest of them knew her by reputation, so I signalled to Keri with my eyes the permission to let her answer for herself.

"For the benefit of the members of the council who might not recognise my face, let me provide a name: Keri of Moonchion." Keri snickered with amusement as a wave of alarm washed over me from the psyches of the assembled Grand Masters. "Yes, *that* Keri of Moonchion – and yes, Grand Master Cinaed, if I put my mind to it I could turn you all into puddles on the floor before you had the chance to lift a collective finger. Luckily for you, that is not why I am here tonight."

"Then why *are* you here? Why should I be here, breathing the same air as a heretic?" Cinaed asked, his aged, wrinkled fingers twitching in agitation on the shaft of his wizard staff.

"Because I need your help, Grand Masters," I interjected. "The Arch Mage has committed grave crimes against Cothraine in the search of forbidden power, and he must be stopped, tonight. Karryghan has been searching for a planar nexus for at least the last decade. He initiated the coup that decimated the royal family to aid his search. Four years ago, I uncovered the links between the coup and the Nexus when I was studying the prophecies of the Seer Nevanthi. When I confronted him about it, instead of killing me, he polymorphed me and exiled me from the Guild. It was only thanks to the intervention of Keri that I was freed, just a few weeks ago."

Aonghas of Birlone scoffed loudly. "Poppycock! Fantasy of the highest order!"

"No, it's true! I was there when Keri freed Gormlaith." Ailidh interjected. "And Karryghan had my father kidnapped and killed to discover more about the Nexus."

"Careful, girl," Treasa of Siskine warned. "You cannot just slander the Arch Mage without evidence. Who are you, anyway? And who was your father?"

"I am Ailidh of Croycullen and my father was Eoghan of Ballinlara." Ailidh announced proudly, causing several of the masters to gasp in shock. The colour drained from Sorcha's face and she placed a hand over her mouth. Even though she was not one to normally share gossip, Malvina had told me during my apprenticeship that Sorcha and Eoghan had been lovers before their Master's trials. Malvina had been Eoghan's student at the time.

"To think that I lost sleep to this garbage, I am going back to bed." Aonghas rolled his eyes and made to stand.

"No, Aonghas, wait." Malvina said, her mouth hanging wide open in wonder. "I didn't recognise her at first. It's true. She's Eoghan's daughter. I saw her when I scried Eoghan's workshop in Croycullen. Karryghan did order his abduction and torture. And it was all linked to finding the Nexus."

"But why would he go to the effort?" Aisling of Belhaven asked. "What is so special about this Nexus?"

"Karryghan wants to use it to travel to the plane of the Mystic and attempt to become the new god of magic so that he can cheat death." I explained, to a chorus of mocking laughter from several of the Grand Masters.

"Listen to yourself, Gormlaith." Ruairidh of Clongarvan said, shaking his head sadly. "I have visited many of the planes myself, what you describe is impossible."

"Not if you have access to a Nexus." Faoiltiarna of Clongarvan objected. "I have studied planar conjunctions and if there is any time such a thing would be possible, it is now. And Karryghan is getting *old*. He fears death and the Judgment that awaits him when he leaves the material plane. I would not put it past the scheming bastard."

"You have never liked the Arch Mage, Faoiltiarna. I would expect you to be biased against him." Cinaed retorted.

"And if you had a slit, you would be begging for him to fill it." Faoiltiarna retorted, dismissing Cinaed's objection brutally with a wave of her hand for emphasis.

Keri's laughter filled the potentially deadly silence that followed Faolitiarna's putdown. "It has been over two centuries since I was last in a playground. I had forgotten how amusing they could be."

"Enough," Sorcha interrupted. "This bickering is futile. Speak plain, Gormlaith. Why are you here? Why are we here?"

"If Karryghan were to gain control of the Nexus, the consequences are unthinkable. Who knows what damage he would wreak as the new god of magic? He must be eliminated, tonight."

"Tonight? Why the urgency, Gormlaith?" Treasa said, sounding bemused. "If he has spent so long trying to find this Nexus and failed, I think it unlikely that it will simply drop into his lap."

"Karryghan is not the only being interested in the Nexus. When the planes align at the solstice, every ambitious planewalker in the cosmos will seek out its power, and turn

Dachaigh into a charnel house battling for it. And their number will include the prime evils. The Succubus has already attempted to claim the Nexus, and would have, had it not been for my brother's sacrifice." I explained, my voice cracking with grief as I thought of Cathal.

"What d'you mean, 'attempted to claim it'? You've found the Nexus?" Malvina said, leaning forward in her chair.

I put my arm around Ailidh's shoulder. "Ailidh is the Nexus."

"For the love of the gods, I have had just about enough of this." Aonghas sighed, stirring restlessly.

"Be silent, Aonghas!" Malvina snapped, a frown creasing her smooth face as she concentrated, piecing together what she knew to deduce the truth. "That... makes sense. She is clearly no blood relation of Eoghan's. Eoghan discovered you by accident. Eoghan abandoned the Art to adopt you, to protect you."

"Ruairidh? Is it true? Could she be the Nexus? What can you sense from her?" Aisling asked.

The Grand Master Planewalker closed his eyes and reached out a hand to link his psyche with Ailidh across the floor of the chamber. After a few seconds his liquid brown eyes flew open and widened in shock. "There is a convergence inside her. It gathers energy while we speak."

"So it is true. Ailidh is the Nexus." Sorcha stood and walked over to her, looking deep into her eyes. "If she is the object of the Arch Mage's search, the very thing he must be denied control of, why have you brought her here?"

"Ailidh will not master the power within her before the conjunction and will be unable to defend herself, unless it is unlocked. I have divined that the full potential of the Nexus will only be released once Ailidh has confronted Karryghan, and herein is the danger. We must act before the solstice, and we have to use Karryghan to activate the Nexus without allowing him to assume control of it. I need your help. We need your help. We cannot allow the Nexus to fall into his hands or the possession of a prime evil. We have to act, and quickly." I implored the council, meeting each of their gazes in turn. My heart sank when almost half of them avoided my eyes.

Aonghas stood and gave us all a dismissive wave. "You do what you like. I want no part of this."

A chorus of dissent arose from the rest of the Grand Masters, but Aonghas ignored it all, walking out, seemingly deaf to the protests.

Malvina was especially scathing in her assessment of the Grand Master of Abjuration. "You fucking old coward! You're only interested in protecting your own crinkly, saggy arse!"

Cinaed also stood. "I say we put it to a simple majority vote. I will not take direct action against the Arch Mage. I will not sanction murder in these halls."

Malvina scoffed. "It's not murder, but pre-emptive justice! Think of how many innocents will die if there's a battle for the Nexus in the middle of Clongarvan. Think of how many petty grievances Karryghan would settle if he were to become the Mystic reborn. I say we eliminate him and give the Nexus the ability to defend herself."

"I agree," said Faoiltiarna with a nod. "To do nothing is too great a risk."

"I concur, also." Sorcha walked over to stand with Malvina and Faoiltiarna. "What do you say, Ruairidh?"

"I am sorry Gormlaith, but I agree with Cinaed." Ruairidh stepped across the floor to stand next to the Grand Master of Conjuration, an apprehensive shiver running down his back. "If we were to contend with the Arch Mage and lose..."

"I also will not stand against the Arch Mage." Treasa said, taking her place next to her similarly dissenting peers. "I will not participate in the taking of a life in such a premeditated manner. Sorry Malvina, but it is not justified, even as a pre-emptive action to save innocents."

Sorcha rubbed her face, clearly frustrated at the impasse. "Three votes each. That leaves you, Aisling. You have the deciding vote."

Aisling stood between the two camps, glancing from one to the other indecisively. After a moment, her shoulders slumped and she said, "I abstain."

There was uproar from both trios of Grand Masters, begging Aisling to join their side, but the Grand Master of Enchantment simply shook her head and quietened them with a raised palm. "I cannot do it, I cannot take sides. I will not help you fight the Arch Mage, but neither will I prevent you. The Council should remain neutral in this matter."

"Bollocks, Aisling, you just don't want to risk your pretty little tits." Malvina scoffed.
"I am not ashamed to be afraid of death, Malvina." Aisling retorted.
"I'll be sure to remind you of that when the Executioner comes knocking upon the door of the Tower of the Aether the day after the solstice." Malvina snarled.
"Stop, both of you." Sorcha said, rolling her eyes. "The council has spoken. We will neither aid nor interfere in your quest. I will, however, personally wish you luck."
Keri sniggered softly, tapping the floor seven times in rapid succession with her staff, musing cynically under her breath. "If you want something done, do it yourself."
"Be silent, heretic!" Cinaed snapped at her. "And be thankful that we do not have you burned at the stake for your crimes."
"It would be amusing to watch you try, Grand Master." Keri laughed as she crossed the chamber to the staircase leading up to the Arch Mage's apartment. She waited on the first stone stair, watching the Grand Masters with an arrogant smirk on her face, tapping her staff on the limestone gently once every few seconds, marking time.
"I will be honest, masters. I had hoped for more." I said, feeling downcast and somewhat deflated by the anti-climax of the vote.
Treasa put her hand on my shoulder sympathetically. "You ask too much from us, Wizard Gormlaith. You know only too well the consequences of defying the Arch Mage."
"That I do, Grand Master. That I am willing to risk it all again, what do you think that says about the threat he poses, not just to us, but the planes themselves? And what do you think it says about your reticence to act?" I replied bitterly.
"At least when I face the Dark Rider's Judgment, I will be able to say that I did not set out to murder a man in cold blood." Treasa said and left the council chamber without another word.
I drew Ailidh closer to me for moral support with an arm around her shoulders and told her, "Come, Ailidh. Our destiny awaits us."
"Gormlaith, please wait a moment. Karryghan has an apprentice, Dervla. She too lives in the apartment above." Faoiltiarna warned me, placing a hand on my elbow. "Do

not underestimate her. She is young, but she has formidable power and is a talented duellist in elemental spells. Dervla favours fire spells, so counter her with ice. Her one weakness is lack of focus. Wear her down or distract her. Do not try to compete with her on strength alone."

"Thank you, Grand Master."

"May the Lady smile upon you tonight and may the Mystic forever empower your spells, Wizard Gormlaith. He will if he knows what's good for him." Malvina observed dryly.

Ailidh and I joined Keri on the stairs and we began our ascent slowly. Keri conjured the vial of venom into her free hand. I took a closer look at the glowing green liquid and said, "I know you lied to the queen. That poison is not from an ettercap or a spider. What is it?"

"Tanar'ri venom, I gathered it from the Succubus herself." Keri eyes glittered with malice. "If just one drop enters his blood the Arch Mage will be exceedingly happy for a time, and then he will feel nothing. I will need a little time to prepare my dart swarm. You must keep him occupied."

"The apprentice complicates things." I said with a grimace. I had only expected to be facing Karryghan. I did not rate my chances of fighting the Arch Mage and his apprentice simultaneously.

Ailidh drew the longsword she had inherited from my brother from her belt. *Dìcheall*'s aetherium blade emitted a faint violet light, not just from its ice enchantment, but also from the power it had absorbed from the Succubus when Cathal had slain her material avatar. "Let me distract Karryghan, Gormlaith. You can help me once you have dealt with the apprentice."

"It is a fair tactic." Keri concurred. "Once Karryghan realises Ailidh carries the Nexus, he will not have eyes for anyone else."

"We will need to be quick, Keri. I do not know how long the Arch Mage might need to activate and absorb its power."

The door to Karryghan's apartment opened of its own accord when we were five steps shy of the top of the staircase. Karryghan's voice called out and echoed down the staircase. "I have been expecting you, Gormlaith of Monagealy. I have been watching you since you left the

Royal Marina. Come, and introduce me to these friends of yours."

I stopped at the threshold and glanced around Karryghan's chambers apprehensively. The last time I had entered this room I had left it wearing fur. I saw Dervla, the apprentice Faoiltiarna had warned me about standing to the side of the door. When she made to step behind us, I blocked her path with my staff. "No. You can lead the way, apprentice."

"As you wish, Wizard Gormlaith," Dervla smiled indulgently, walking five steps ahead of us as I entered the chamber, Keri and Ailidh at my sides.

The Arch Mage stood next to one of his many bookcases near the middle of the room, staff in hand and dressed in his elaborate robes of office, his bald head adorned by a jewelled aetherium circlet. "I am impressed, Gormlaith of Monagealy. However did you manage to break the curse?"

I stopped walking when we were still ten yards short of Karryghan, not wanting to get too close. Dervla stepped aside to Karryghan's left, about halfway between us. I kept an eye on her warily, subtly channelling aetheric energy into my staff to blast her with an ice bolt at the first sign of hostility. "I had help, from a friend." I gestured to Keri, who stood a yard behind me on my left.

Karryghan regarded the Wild Mage curiously, as if she was an exhibit standing upon an unmarked plinth in a museum. "Fascinating, I do not know you. And I thought I had met every Master Wizard in the Western Triad."

"My name is Keri of Moonchion, perhaps you have heard of me?"

A look of shock and terror gripped Karryghan's face and he uttered a Word of Power, throwing Keri into the wall with a sudden blast of force, rendering her instantly unconscious. The vial of tanar'ri venom slipped from her hand, but somehow she had retained a grip on her staff. I aimed the head my own stave at Dervla, who simultaneously matched my pose, both of us ready to strike.

"A curious choice of ally, Wizard Gormlaith," Karryghan said, turning his attention to Ailidh. "You I recognise, however. You are Eoghan's adopted daughter. What are you doing here, I wonder?"

Ailidh lifted her sword, pointing the tip at the base of the Arch Mage's throat. "I am here to avenge my father."

"No, no, no." Karryghan chuckled condescendingly. "It cannot be so simple a thing as that. Wait, I sense... no, it cannot be! Gormlaith, you fool! I spent so long trying to find the Nexus, only for you to bring it directly to the middle of the spider's web!"

The goose's head at the top of Dervla's staff began to hiss and I knew she was about to unleash a spell.

"Put out the cat, Dervla," Karryghan lowered his staff and pointed it at Ailidh. "I have a more valuable prize to claim."

The room exploded with elemental energy as spells erupted simultaneously from our three staffs. Ailidh screamed as an arc of lightning struck her in the chest, knocking her backwards several yards to the floor, sprawling on all fours. I did not have time to worry about my adopted sister, as I was fighting for my life in a duel with the Arch Mage's apprentice. Faoiltiarna's warning was accurate. Dervla had a profound connection to the elemental plane of fire, stronger than my affinity with its elemental opposite, ice. Dervla gripped her staff tightly with both hands, trying to overwhelm me quickly. Instead of trying to fight her on even terms, I heeded Faoiltiarna's advice and channelled a steady stream of frost from the feline head of my staff to form a protective shield that would let me avoid injury, rather than trying to bludgeon past Dervla's attack and directly best her in a battle of power. Dervla widened her stance and stood stone still, pushing all of her energy into the tongue of flame lancing out of the mouth of her staff's goose figurehead. I kept my head down and stepped forward, letting go of my staff with one hand, aiming the tip of my staff at Dervla's as I drew Cathal's ever-sharp stiletto from my belt. I rolled my wrist, letting the blade catch the light. I sensed Dervla's focus waver as I closed the distance between us, her fire spitting harder against the cone of frost shielding me. I saw her gaze flicker between the end of her staff and the blade of my knife, and I could feel a building sense of panic contaminate her aura as she realised that her elemental attacks were not getting through my defence. As I closed to within eight feet of her, Dervla redoubled her efforts to break my shield of ice, but by then it was too late. "No!"

As the figureheads of our staffs touched, my cat clamped its jaws around the neck of Dervla's goose, cutting off the flow of fire. I took one last, lunging step forward and thrust the entire length of my stiletto's blade forward to stab between Dervla's breasts, deep into her heart. All of the strength sapped from her limbs and she fell to the floor without a sound, very, very dead. I left the stiletto embedded in her chest and lifted my staff back up into a two-handed grip, looking around the room to find out what had happened to my companions. Keri still lay insensate on the stone tiles, though for just a fraction of a second I thought I saw her fingers twitch briefly on the fore grip of her staff. I heard Ailidh scream again and my eyes found the source of the sound. My sister had gotten up from her knees and her leather jerkin smoked where Karryghan had struck her with lightning. He was backing her towards the rear of the chamber with arc after arc of bright white bolts of elemental energy, making Ailidh shriek every time she was hit. Karryghan was being careful not to kill or injure her, instead gradually feeding the Nexus within her the energy it needed to become fully empowered. Only after the Nexus was active and energised would he kill Ailidh to claim it. Not knowing how long we had left, I shouted to my sister, letting her know help was on the way. "Ailidh, hang on! I am coming!"

Karryghan's concentration broke as he looked over his shoulder, distracted by my voice and suddenly he found himself on the defensive as Ailidh charged him, *Dìcheall* endowing her with supernatural speed. Ailidh appeared to sparkle with power, her eyes glowing with radiant energy. Karryghan backed away with astounding agility for such an old man, parrying her rapid blows with his staff. I was channelling energy into my staff, ready to unleash a force bolt at the Arch Mage when Keri called out from behind me. "Gormlaith, get down!"

I ducked and dropped to the floor as an emerald flock of venomous darts swarmed over my head across the chamber towards Karryghan. He yelled in panic when he saw his doom approach and tried to shoot them down with a narrow crimson light lancing from the top of his staff. The beam slashed through the air and carved a swathe through the flock of darts, burning a glowing scar into the wall behind me. No longer needing to defend herself from Karryghan's magical attacks, Ailidh took advantage of the wizard's distraction and pounced forward, slashing Karryghan across the belly, opening his robe and the sagging skin beneath. The Arch Mage cried out in pain, just as he was struck by the remaining darts. He fell down onto his back, instantly paralysed, his arms and legs twitching involuntarily.

"Yes, we did it!" Ailidh crowed.

I propped myself up on my elbows and turned around to look at Keri. "You were faking."

Keri walked over to me and lent me her hand, pulling me to my feet. "I needed a moment to create the darts. I may have many talents, but simultaneous enchantment and elemental spellcasting is not one of them."

"Is the Arch Mage dead?" I asked Ailidh, who was standing over his body, looking down into Karryghan's face.

"I don't think so. His eyes are still moving."

"Right now the venom will be giving him the most intense erotic climax of his life." Keri chuckled. "We should give him time to enjoy it before sending him to meet the Dark Rider."

My laughter died on my lips when I saw that a green mist had started to leak out of Karryghan's body and was beginning to thicken and coalesce into a form I had hoped I would never again see in my life. "Ailidh, get away from him, now!"

As the mist formed around her, Ailidh collapsed to the floor, moaning, "Oh, gods!"

Keri grabbed my arm and stopped me from running over to her as Ailidh's body shook with convulsions, short arcs of aetheric lightning sparking out of her fingertips, mouth and eyes. "No, Gormlaith. No. Stay back."

I gasped in horror as the mist solidified and changed colour, stepping forward over Ailidh's trembling form and stretching its wings. The avatar was smaller than the one Cathal had slain in the forest, but it was unmistakeably Keri's dread mistress, the Succubus.

KERI, MY SWEETLING. AS EVER, YOU NEVER DISAPPOINT ME. HOW CLEVER OF YOU TO USE MY VENOM TO INCAPACITATE KARRYGHAN AND GIVE ME A NEW PLANAR ANCHOR. I WILL HAVE TWO PRIZES TO TAKE BACK TO THE HELLS.

"Keri, how could you?" I wept, devastated to have not foreseen her betrayal.

Keri said nothing and stepped forward to greet the Succubus. "I live to serve you, dread mistress."
Ailidh groaned and sat up, looking bewildered but otherwise seemingly unharmed by her brush with the paralytic mist.

AT LAST, THE NEXUS HAS FORMED. ITS POWER IS READY TO BE CLAIMED. COME TO ME, NEXUS, MEET YOUR DESTINY.

"No, dread mistress," Keri told the Succubus. My jaw dropped open, my despair put temporarily on hold. Keri gripped her staff with both hands, pointing it at the Queen of the Daevae. The stone tiles beneath the Succubus's clawed feet liquefied and flowed up her legs, holding the demon in place. A dozen purple ropes of force leapt from the walls to bind the Succubus's wings, arms and wrists. "The Nexus has already been claimed. It is Ailidh's, not yours."
The daeva looked down at her mortal servant, shock written across her unspeakably beautiful face.

WHAT?

Keri helped Ailidh to her feet and ushered her around the Succubus's avatar, steering her well clear of the demon's arms and hands, pushing her towards me. Ailidh staggered a few steps backwards, away from the prime daeva, stunned. Keri turned back to her demonic patron. "You can still have two prizes, dread mistress. But you may not have the Nexus."

NO, I WILL HAVE HER! RELEASE ME NOW!

This time it was not Keri who replied. "No. You'll not have me. My power is my own and will stay my own. Go back to your own plane, demon, and stay there. Next time you threaten me I'll not be nearly so merciful."

Ailidh raised her arms and threw her right hand through an arcing spiral, her fingertips leaving a glowing trail through the air. The chamber flooded with a blinding white light, forcing me to close my eyes. I sensed aetheric lightning sparking and crackling through the whole chamber. I stumbled and fell to the floor as I was buffeted by a swirling wind as strong as a summer hurricane. I clung to my staff and pressed my weight into the square lime flagstones, trying to remain in place until the storm had passed. When the light was dim enough for me to open my eyes once again Keri, Karryghan and the Succubus were nowhere to be seen.

39 - Keri

"Well, that was brilliant." I said dryly, as the blinding light faded and I came back to my senses. I blinked and tried to take in my surroundings. I lay on the floor of a huge chamber made entirely of bone. The air smelled of blood, sweat and lust. Before me was a giant throne made from the tessellated skeletons of ten thousand corpses. The Succubus sat upon it, looking down at my prostrate form with an aura of amusement. My robe and staff were nowhere in sight, but despite my nakedness, I made no attempt to cover myself. The chamber was warm and humid and I had no secrets or shame to hide from my mistress. The moment of reckoning was at hand for all the sins and depravities I had committed in her name and in my own selfishness. I clambered to my feet and stood before her, unbowed and defiant.

"Is that all you have to say for yourself?" The Succubus asked, her tail twitching threateningly as she leaned forward in the throne, still towering over me. My heart raced with desire at the sound of her voice. It was as deep and as sensual as an ocean of silk. I yearned to bury myself in her flesh and suckle the ecstatic venom from her breasts until my soul withered and disintegrated. I thrilled at the sensation of her touch as the talons on her right hand grazed my face, hard enough to scratch but not cut the skin. "You betrayed me."

"Yes." There was no point in denying it. I was in the heart of her Demesne and my soul was as laid bare to her as my body.

"You *betrayed* me." The Succubus reiterated, her aura crackling with fury and something else... admiration? "To defy a prime evil is to forfeit your soul."

"Yes."

"You knew this." The daeva's glorious eyes sparkled, the wrath in her aura making way for something I would never have anticipated in an eternity: respect. "And yet you still defied my will."

"Yes." I admitted, proud that I would not debase myself by begging for mercy, knowing my life was over and accepting

my fate. I raised my chin, smirking ironically in a final act of rebellion, looking up into the sublimely gorgeous face of my executioner while I waited for the coup de grace to come. "And that," The Queen of Daevae paused and cackled in delight, "that is why I love you."
She wrapped her tail around me, plucking me from the floor as if I were no heavier than a child's doll. I went limp as her stinger drove upwards between my thighs and deep into my belly. Her arms enveloped me and her lips and tongue explored my face and neck as she pumped me full of her venom.

I gave out a soft cry of utter rapture and died.

When my eyes opened once more, I found myself lying on a huge four-poster bed. The columns of its frame were made exclusively from spinal cords twisted together to form rope-like chords and the mattress had been upholstered with tanned leather made from flayed human skins. As I stepped onto the floor I suddenly became aware that I had been transformed. I laughed giddily in wonder at my new form, a mirror image of my dread mistress, albeit smaller. I stood nine feet tall on legs would have appeared more fitting on the rear end of a horse, except for the three talons on my hooves. The curves of my femininity rivalled those of the Succubus herself and I spread my wings experimentally, gauging their span to be over one score feet in breadth. I thrashed my tail, running the barbed tip through the long, slender fingers of my steel-clawed hands. I shivered in anticipation, wondering what the extents of my new powers were. I could still feel my mortal affinity for aetheric energy and instinctively knew that my skill to manipulate it was undiminished, but also that it was accompanied by something else, something ravenous and primal.
"Ah, you are awake at last." The Succubus said, admiring her handiwork with her amber, libidinous eyes. She kissed me long and hard on the lips, her palms exploring the curves of my body, the delectable sensations of her caresses setting my ardour for her aflame once more. She took my hand in hers and led me to one of the arch-shaped portals in the wall of her bedchamber. "Come, my sweetling, I have a gift for you."

She led me down one of the ivory-ribbed arteries that linked together the halls of her fortress. I knew from legend that the Succubus's domain had once been the body of a Celestial that had been entrapped by the Succubus herself and transported to the Second Circle of the Hells, but I had never imagined that I would ever see it for myself. Pleasure tingled through my new body when I realised that this place would now be my home. It had been decades since I had been able to claim such a luxury. "What is it, dread mistress?"

"You will see." The Succubus said with a smile of utterly devastating beauty. "You will be pleased, I think."

As we walked along the artery corridors and through half a dozen other chambers, we passed dozens of the tanar'ri, minor succubi and incubi, all of whom bowed to us reverentially. I recognised some of them as being lust daevae I had bound during my time on the material plane. They showed me the greatest deference of all, interlinking their fingers into a mesh and showing me their open palms as they placed their hands on their forehead in supplication. I made a mental note of where they carried out their duties and resolved to visit them after my mistress had finished her business with me. The Succubus sensed my intentions and kissed me on the cheek. "Do not be gentle with them, beloved."

Eventually we arrived back at my mistress's throne room, only this time we were not alone. Secured to an ivory crucifix was Karryghan the Schemer. Stripped naked of his clothes and his accoutrements of power, the Arch Mage moaned in agony, his wrinkled belly split open by Ailidh's blade. Karryghan had been tied helpless to the cross of bone around both wrists and at the ankles. My mistress had taken a dozen feet of his intestines to use as ropes, binding him using his own flesh. Blood oozed over his waist and down his legs in a constant stream. The volume of scarlet ichor pooling at his feet indicated that he ought to have died hours ago, but that my mistress's infernal power kept him alive.

"Do you like it, my love?" The Succubus asked, standing behind me, with her hands on my shoulders, bowing her head to kiss the side of my neck, her razor sharp teeth grazing my skin tantalisingly. "What do you think of my gift?"

"Thank you, dread mistress." I replied, an insatiable appetite rising in my belly for blood, sex, magic and divine essence. I sensed that I was going to enjoy my damnation. "Prove yourself to me once again, Ceridwyn of the Crimson." The Succubus said, commanding me by my True Name, which even I had not known until this moment. "He and his powers are yours, my servant. *Devour him.*"

My mistress left without another word. I laughed as venom started to drip in anticipation and excitement from the barbed sting at the end of my tail. I licked my lips, spread my wings and stepped forward towards the former Arch Mage of Cothraine. Karryghan began to scream in abject, mortal terror. Unable to contain my hunger any longer, I raised my clawed hands and lunged for his throat.

40 – Ailidh

The swirling air of the Arch Mage's chambers crackled with aetheric lightning as I offered my hand and forearm to Gormlaith, who lay on the floor at my feet. She grabbed my forearm gratefully as I hauled her to her feet and my adoptive sister steadied herself using her staff, its feline figurehead looking equally as puzzled as she did. "Ailidh, what did you just do?"
"Gormlaith, I can see it all." I replied, not answering her question directly. I saw her standing before me, but it was a mere detail compared to the vision I had of the entire cosmos, layer upon layer, plane upon plane, that now dominated my sight. I clutched my head in both hands, overwhelmed by the immensity of my new perception. "It's so beautiful, you wouldn't believe it."
"Ailidh, listen to me. What happened to the Arch Mage, to Keri and the Succubus?"
"They're gone, back to the realm where they belong, the Second Circle of the Hells." I replied, still distracted by the wonder of the infinite planes flickering in and out of my vision. I giggled, "I would not want to be in Karryghan's shoes right now."
Gormlaith stroked her face and torso, checking for injuries. Having reassured herself that she was unharmed, she placed a hand on my shoulder. "Are you hurt?"
"No, I have never felt better." I replied, slightly breathlessly, as I let the power of the Nexus surge through all of my cells. I was hyperaware of every single sight, sound, smell and vibration that was within ten score feet of me. I turned to the door linking the Arch Mage's chambers to the central staircase seconds before it opened, feeling the urgent footsteps running up the tower walls.
Grand Master Malvina barged into the chamber, skidding to a halt when she saw Dervla's crumpled body on the floor and the residual aetheric static crackling from one wall to another. "Fuck a duck!"
I pulled apart my fingertips before my face, drawing a defensive vermillion curtain of annihilation between myself, Gormlaith and Malvina. As Malvina began to reach out to

the shimmering wall of energy that separated us I interjected, "I wouldn't touch that if I were you. Not if you want to keep all of your fingers, anyway."

Malvina stepped back three paces, her eyes wide in alarm. "Where's the Arch Mage?"

"He's been dealt with." I replied, giving her only the details I thought she needed to know. "Karryghan's tenure is as head of the Guild of the Art is over."

"Good! And good riddance, too! It'll be a relief to have some sense of normalcy back within the tower once more." Malvina grinned. "I can't wait to see the look on the faces of those snivelling lickspittles on the council who said it'd be impossible to get rid of him."

"Anyone with strong ties to Karryghan might be advised to retire from their position and pursue a quiet life in the countryside," Gormlaith said, her sapphire blue eyes flickering angrily. "Queen Reilynn will not be well-disposed to keeping Karryghan's allies in positions of power and influence. Frankly, I will be surprised if the Wizard's Guild in Clongarvan survives beyond the end of the day."

"I'll give word to the council and remain here in the tower with the mages willing to swear fealty to the queen and the Crown." Malvina bowed, raising the figurehead of her staff to her brow in salute. "I hope we'll speak again soon, Wizard Gormlaith."

I cut an arch through the air with my fingers, opening a portal from the Arch Mage's chambers to the throne room in Clongarvan's Royal Palace. Without a word I took Gormlaith's hand in mine and we stepped through the shimmering membrane halfway across the city in a single stride.

"Fuck me, what is this witchcraft?" King Sjur cursed, as Gormlaith and I appeared to step out of thin air just a couple of yards in front of him and Queen Reilynn. Braden rushed forward to embrace me, delighted to see that I had survived the battle at the Tower of the Aether, but stopped short when he sensed the aetheric power coursing through me. "Ailidh, what has happened to you?"

"Only what was meant to happen." I kissed him once on both cheeks and embraced him hard. "We are victorious, Braden. Our losses have been avenged."

Braden held me at arm's length, turning his head to Gormlaith in disbelief. His jaw dropped open with an unspoken question, which Gormlaith answered, a bittersweet smile written over her features. "The Arch Mage is gone and the Tower of the Aether swears its allegiance to the Crown once more."

Queen Reilynn slipped her arm through her husband's elbow, weeping with joy. "Nothing can ever bring back my slain kin, but this is the best news I have been given in five years. Thank you, all of you."

"Your majesty, now that the head has been cut from the dragon, it should not be difficult to reassume control of the city, and from there, the kingdom as a whole." Braden said.

"No-one would dare stand against you now, your majesty." Gormlaith concurred. "You have always had the love of the people and now you have both the divine and legal right to the throne."

"That may be true, Wizard Gormlaith, but with Karryghan having claimed the regency of Cothraine and me being already officially recognised as the Queen of Fossfjall, I cannot be the queen of two realms at once, not until the unification treaty is formalised." Reilynn said, leaning upon her husband for moral, rather than physical support. "My future lies in Fossfjall, so that means I must leave Cothraine in the hands of people I can trust until my firstborn son is able to take the throne."

"People like whom, your majesty?" Gormlaith asked, though I could tell from her aura that she dreaded the answer.

"I ought to be insulted that you even have to ask." Queen Reilynn replied, smiling. "You are rather young for an Arch Mage, but given the disgraceful abuse of your predecessor's position against the Royal family I think I will be forgiven for making a political appointment to the office, given that the only alternative I offer to the Guild will be razing the tower to the ground with all of its wizards inside it."

Reilynn took the rapier from her sword belt and placed the blade gently once upon each of Gormlaith's shoulders in turn. "Gormlaith of Monagealy, I hereby appoint you to the office of Arch Mage of the Guild of the Art of Cothraine. May your tenure be long and wise."

Open-mouthed in shock, Gormlaith took to her knee and kissed the back of Reilynn's hand twice. "Thank you, your majesty! I will try to prove myself worthy of this honour."
"That will not be difficult, provided you show the same kind of courage and integrity in office that you did when challenging Karryghan after the coup, and when you helped the rangers prepare their campaign to retake Clongarvan." Reilynn said, grasping Gormlaith's forearm and encouraging her back to her feet.
I wrapped my arms around my surrogate sister, hugging her tightly to congratulate her. "Arch Mage Gormlaith, not bad for a cat..."
Gormlaith's shoulders quivered with laughter and tears as she clung to me hard. "If only Cathal was here to see it."
Reilynn ignored our emotional outbursts, instead calculating the best role for Braden. "Duke Ranger seems an insufficient reward for your service, Lord Commander Braden. I can hardly appoint you to an office that is already yours by right. No, there is only one way I can recognise and honour your devotion to the Crown and your country. Since I cannot be in two places at once, you shall be my proxy here in Cothraine. Until my firstborn comes of age you shall be the Ranger Regent, ruling in my name and providing the country with the stability and fairness it has been crying out for since the usurper's coup."
Braden's mouth dropped open in surprise, making the queen laugh in delight at his humility. She raised hand guard of the thin foil of her rapier to her face, ready to formally assign Braden to act as Head of State in her name. "Close your mouth, Lord Commander, lest I be tempted to dub you the Royal Flycatcher instead."
I waited until Queen Reilynn was finished and handed *Dìcheall* and my sword belt over to the newly-appointed Regent. "You should have this now, Braden. Where I am going, I will not need it."
"Where are you going, Ailidh?" Braden asked, as a whirlwind of aetheric energies began to surround my body.
"Home... I'm going home." I said with tears of joy and regret in my eyes. I blinked and I was gone.

41 – The Dark Rider

"Welcome, Ailidh." I greeted the latest incarnation of the planar nexus with a deep bow of respect. I stood on the plain of golden grass before my eternal stronghold, the Silver Citadel. "I knew you would come to me eventually. You always do."

The Nexus blinked her pale blue eyes and tried to take in the details of her surroundings. "Where am I?"

"This is the first plane of Heaven, Nexus," I said, taking her hand in mine and ushering her to the entrance of my fortress. "There is nothing for you to fear here."

"Am I dead?"

"No, Nexus. Here, like me, you are immortal." I walked her beneath the jagged spikes of the citadel's aetherium portcullis into the private pocket plane I maintained inside first tier of the heavens. "Your place in the Menagerie of Eternity awaits you."

"The Menagerie of Eternity, what is that?"

"It is your true home, Nexus, a realm outside of time and space where every Nexus from the past, present and the future coexist in all of their myriad forms. Within you will find an infinite number of nexuses to share your stories and experiences with, which is just as well. After all, eternity is such a long time, especially towards the end." I told Ailidh with a sardonic smile. I stopped before the portal adjoining the Menagerie of Eternity to the great hall of the citadel's keep. "Alas, I can go no further. I must say farewell to you here."

Ailidh regarded the giant door with an overwhelming sense of apprehension. "Why? What's on the other side?"

"The Menagerie. I cannot exist there, as my presence is required here to stabilise this plane." I said, opening the portal with a psychic command. The doorway shimmered as the portal stabilised, a rippling membrane of pure aetheric energy that crackled audibly, the sound echoing around the great hall.

"So you don't know what is it like in there?" Ailidh asked hesitantly.

"Nothing in the Menagerie can hurt you, Ailidh. There is literally no safer place in all of the cosmos. At any rate, you cannot stay here. You would eventually become a target for daevae and planewalkers, and not even I have the power to repel them all indefinitely. The Menagerie is beyond their reach, beyond even my influence."

"Will I ever be able to leave?"

"This is all part of the cosmic cycle. The planes cannot exist without the Nexus, and the Nexus cannot exist without the planes. But your time on the material plane has passed, Ailidh. You have performed your duty and ensured the stability of the planes for another ten millennia. But the next time you leave the Menagerie, Nexus, you will not be Ailidh."

Ailidh stared into the coruscant portal, which rippled like the surface of a lake in the sunlight of high summer. "I never wanted to be special. I just wanted a normal life: a home, a husband, a family. I never asked to be part of this. Why did this have to happen to me?"

I placed my hands on her shoulders and gave them a tender squeeze of respect, reassurance, love and consolation. "Everything that occurs happens as it was intended to. But that does not matter now, Ailidh. All you have ever wanted and more lies on the other side of this door. It is yours for the taking."

"You're asking me to take a leap of faith."

"Yes, I am."

Tears trailed down Ailidh's cheeks as she closed her eyes, took a deep breath and raised her chin courageously. My face and eyes were hidden and unknowable, shrouded by the eternal shadow of my executor's hood. The Nexus directed one final glance at where she thought her gaze might meet mine before favouring me with a wry half-smile of defiance. Ailidh blew the air out from her cheeks and took a single confident step across the glimmering quicksilver threshold.

Epilogue – Ceridwyn of the Crimson

Time is as slippery as an eel when you are immortal. The harder you try to hold onto it, the more easily it seems to escape through the gaps between your fingers.

I have walked this land for two hundred and fifty thousand seasons. I have watched kingdoms rise and fall. I have known the desire of goddesses and demons. I have felt the fear and adoration of mortals. I have been loved and despised in equal measure. I have seen everything the material plane has to offer: Beaches covered in gemstones the size of your fist; Islands burning from coast to coast with volcanic fire; Herds of cattle the size of cities roaming the grasslands of a savannah larger than a country; Raptors soaring across the sky with wing spans broader than barns; Cities with white marble towers as tall as mountains; Battlefields littered with corpses piled as high as my neck. I have given and received every kindness and every cruelty men or women can visit upon each other. And I have stolen a trillion souls for my dread mistress over the millennia. But my time on the material plane is coming to an end soon. I only have one task to perform before taking my place as the ruler of the Second Hell. There are no more sights for me to see. No new lands to explore. No unknown pleasures I can experience anew. Only one task remains before I fulfil my destiny, one written for me eons before my birth. It is a fine summer's day on the coast at Bray, near a vineyard I have visited more than a thousand times before. The white marble gravel is warm underneath the soles of my thin leather sandals and the harsh blue sunlight of noon warms the thick, curled tresses of my waist-length, crimson hair. A gown of jade silk clings to the curves of my body, a pale shadow of my true, infernal femininity. My stave, fashioned from tall, blackened and twisted rods of red, green and blue aetherium, supports my sure footing on the recently resurfaced road. I carry the air of neither a maiden nor a matron: not so young as to appear inexperienced, but neither so old as to be appear infirm. In the past I have frequently worn vulnerability as a mask to entice my prey, but today I sensed that I would be better served by presenting a mature, confident persona. My intuition was justified when I encountered the wreckage of a trade caravan that had been ransacked underneath an embankment that was known to be a popular ambush site for local brigands. I followed the intoxicating scent of fresh blood away from the road to a youth no more than a score of years old, who had taken refuge in the shade of a vine tree at the side of the road. A short steel quarrel from a crossbow had struck him just above the waist, in the fleshy gap between his hip and ribcage. A painful, debilitating wound to be sure, but not a life threatening one.

"Miss!" he pleaded weakly as I approached him, feigning caution. He kept one hand pressed against his wound and beckoned me towards him desperately with bloodied fingers. "Please, miss! Help me. I'm dying."

I looked around furtively, as if checking for signs of danger. I already knew from the aura of the place that the bandits had long since abandoned the scene. I rushed over to his side with my back bent, to present a smaller silhouette to any outlaws that the young man thought might still be lurking on the escarpment above. I feigned terror when I knelt at his side, my hands flitting uncertainly between his side and his face, seemingly not knowing whether I should touch him.

"Thank you, thank you." The youth panted in gratitude, looking up into my eyes with an imploring gaze akin to that of a lovelorn puppy. "I thought I might die here. Miss, I don't want to die alone."

"Save your strength." I instructed him, making a show of looking at his wound. My wild aetheric affinity smelled the latent arcane power locked deep inside his soul. Yes, he was the one I had been sent for. It strained my powers of self-control not to lick my lips. I touched the fletched end of the quarrel uncertainly, making him cry out in pain. I

snatched back my hand in alarm, taking care to enunciate my words using a modern vernacular. "You've been shot."
"Bandits," He explained breathlessly. "They've killed everyone, stolen everything."
"Shush, calm now. It's over." I stroked his forehead tenderly and looked down reassuringly into his wide, cyan blue eyes, which stared at me with equal measures of agony, panic and hope. I was so well-accomplished at it by now that lying came more easily to me than breathing. "You're safe with me."
"I need a healer. D'you know of one that's nearby?" he said, trying and failing to master his pain and fear. I could see from the way he gazed at me, his pupils flickering uncertainly from my face to the curves of my breasts and hips that he was unsure whether I was a guardian angel sent to save him or whether I was a wishful apparition, a sensual fantasy manifest from his deepest, most repressed desires.
"What's your name?" I asked him, stroking his cheek and neck, partly to console, partly to reassure and partly to seduce.
"Cathal, my name's Cathal."
I felt a stab of regret briefly in my heart, as I recalled the distant and almost forgotten memory of the most honourable man I had ever known. Looking at the youth again, I found to my disappointment that any resemblance, physical or otherwise, was slight at best. I gave the boy a lingering kiss on his soft, trembling lips and said, "Don't worry, Cathal. I'll take care of you."

Printed in Great Britain
by Amazon